'*High Jinx* introduces us to an unforgettable heroine who links the wholesome tomboys of the past with the girl-power pop-tarts of the present.' Julie Burchill

'Girls will think it's a blast.' Adèle Geras, *Guardian*

'A thoroughly modern take on the boarding school stories of the past . . . plenty of laugh-out-loud moments make this novel a great read.' *Sunday Express*

'There's nothing like a little inside knowledge to give a debut a lick of literary veracity, and the five years that Sara Lawrence spent at Roedean have enabled her to add a fresh coat of paint to the boarding school novel. The familiar tenets of cloistered teen life are all here – friendship, feuds and overdue homework – but Lawrence's fast and furious delivery brings the dated genre bang up-to-date . . . Enjoyably raucous.' *Daily Mail*

'Although the book contains strong language and heroines who consume cocktails of vodka and ecstasy tablets, chain smoke and can tell a Chloe T-shirt at 20 paces, it is also comfortingly old-fashioned, as retro in its moralising (don't look down on the working class; you mustn't be on your own with a boy you don't know) as a pair of Fiorucci jeans . . . I love the humour in the writing . . . But most of all I loved that this book is about young women who are – beneath Girls Aloud outfits – just children, and jolly nice ones at that.' Liz Jones, *Mail on Sunday*

'Part *Skins* and part Malory Towers, Sara Lawrence's debut is a modern take on the classic boarding school caper . . . Lawrence's tone is breezy, funny and stuffed to the gills with cool-girls' brand names. It's a joy to read about teenagers having a laugh rather than dealing with abuse or illness.' *London Paper*

Jinxed

Sara Lawrence attended Roedean School, which was founded by her great great aunts. Following her MA in American Literature at Leeds University she became a journalist, working as a staff writer on *The Times* and the *Daily Mail*. *Jinxed* is the sequel to Sara's first novel, *High Jinx*, also published by Faber.

Jinxed

SARA LAWRENCE

faber and faber

First published in 2009
by Faber and Faber Limited
Bloomsbury House, 74–77 Great Russell Street,
London WC1B 3DA

Typeset by Faber and Faber Ltd
Printed in England by CPI BookMarque, Croydon

A CIP record for this book
is available from the British Library

ISBN 978-0-571-23715-9

2 4 6 8 10 9 7 5 3 1

For Charlotte Ross-Parkinson, who was there at the start, read every chapter as it was written and didn't complain once about marathon 'Jinx talks'; for Binny Wookey, who remains endlessly interested – and is beyond generous with her amazing dinner parties; and for Niki Robinson, who not only opened a restaurant but gave me the Russians and a hell of a lot of laughs besides.

Jinxed

'*For Christ's sake, Jinx!* Will you *please* not refer to your grandmother as "that rancid old slag"?'

Caroline Slater, normally a paragon of maternal virtue, stood up and threw the *Sunday Times* travel section she'd been reading wistfully at the groaning pile of newsprint covering the black marble-topped breakfast bar. She then stalked out of the kitchen in the direction of her beloved greenhouses, pausing only to slam the back door behind her.

Jinx sighed. She hadn't meant to upset her mum but, like most of the Slaters, she was suffering from a severe case of cabin fever following an excessively boozy Christmas. What's more, she had to think about packing and getting herself ready to go back to Stagmount – the exclusive girls' boarding school perched atop Brighton's cliff face where she was in the lower sixth – for the start of the spring term. But worst of all, as far as she was concerned anyway, for the first time since she was fourteen years old and allowed out to party with her friends, she had a grand total of zero options for New Year's Eve.

3

Jinx wouldn't even allow herself to think about Liberty, her best friend and partner in crime since they'd met on their very first day at Stagmount. She had no idea where Lib was or how she was doing after the nightmare ending to last term, but she knew for sure that the last thing she fancied was lunch with her mad old gran.

'What have you done now?' asked George.

Jinx's older brother, whose name was usually prefixed with 'gorgeous' by the various girls who tied up the Slater family phone lines day and night wondering if he was 'up to' anything, had just sauntered into the room. He threw a dark-chocolate-coated brazil nut into the air and caught it between his even white teeth.

'Mum's chucking things around the stables in a right old mood and you look like you've been ridden hard and put away wet.'

'I only said I couldn't see why I was being forced to go for lunch when you and Gaymian are allowed to stay here, no bloody questions asked,' Jinx sniffed, stubbing her cigarette out in the overflowing ashtray in front of her. She proceeded to top up her thick black coffee with brandy from the silver hip flask she'd removed from her dad's drawer of 'special things' earlier that morning. 'It's not fucking fair, that's all.'

A sudden hint of a smile threatened to ruin her determinedly grumpy face. 'And *what* was that expression you just used? Jesus, George, you get worse and worse. Where do you even *hear* that kind of shit?'

There was a long pause. '*Frasier*, if you must know,' he

4

said eventually, before grinning widely at his sister. 'I *was* going to pass it off as one of my own but I guess it's too good.'

Jinx, who was back in the groove of her black sulk, shrugged, grunted what was clearly a 'couldn't care less' response and tipped the rest of her supercharged coffee down her throat.

'Come on, little sis.' George shoved Jinx along the bench, sat down next to her and put a comforting arm around her shoulder. 'You've got a face longer than Pansy this morning. What's up?'

It was impossible to stay mad when George was at his most understanding like this. Jinx lit another cigarette and resigned herself to the brotherly pep talk that was surely coming.

'Since you're obviously very taken with the horse theme today,' she said, kind of sarcastically, turning to face him for the first time since he'd come into the room, 'why don't we go for a ride? I haven't actually left the house for five days and I bet the ponies are gagging to get out too.'

George nodded, pleased he was going to get Jinx to himself for a couple of hours. He hated seeing his usually effervescent sister so down in the dumps. A gallop in the fresh air would do her the world of good, and then he planned to have a serious talk with her.

'I saw Pansy practically doing cartwheels around the field when Mum let them out first thing,' he said, standing up and hoisting Jinx to her feet at the same time, 'and Gaymian didn't get home until five o'clock this morning so he won't be up for hours yet. It's you and me, kid. Let's go.'

Pelting down a very muddy track in one of the forest enclosures not far from home, Jinx stood up in her stirrups, folded herself forwards towards Pansy's pricked ears and loosened her reins. The game old hunter belonged to her other brother, Damian (affectionately nicknamed Gaymian by his siblings on account of his sexual preferences). They were soon galloping so fast that Jinx's eyes were streaming and the trees and bushes blurred into one big streak of green.

Feeling the horse beginning to slow underneath her, Jinx sat back in the saddle and peered over her shoulder to look for George. She laughed out loud as she spotted him way behind. His stirrups were so short his knees practically touched his ears and he was bouncing up and down like a huge, demented jockey. She pulled Pansy back into a gentle canter before they slowed to a jerky, high-stepping trot and then an ambling walk.

Jinx drew in great lungfuls of the fresh forest air and stretched her arms high above her head. Flexing her neck from side to side, she realised she hadn't felt this physically or mentally sharp since the day she'd arrived home from Stagmount at the end of term. She'd managed to hold it together until the last day, but winced as she acknowledged the fact that she'd spent most of the Christmas holidays in a haze of tears. She had stubbornly refused to return any of her friends' phone calls and had generally stomped about the place like a bear with a sore head, complaining bitterly about every family activity she'd not been able to get out of.

After about five minutes George pulled up alongside his sister and motioned for her to stop as he fumbled in the top pocket of his jacket for his cigarettes and lighter. He was breathing almost as heavily as Martin's beautiful chestnut thoroughbred, Dillon, who evidently hadn't had much exercise over the last couple of months.

'Jesus,' said Jinx, 'I knew Dad had been busy tying up all his work stuff before Christmas, but I didn't realise it had been *that* bad.' She laughed as she accepted a Marlboro Light from her still-too-breathless-to-speak brother. 'I bet you wish you hadn't insisted on having him today now.' She leaned over to pat Dillon's neck. 'I can't remember the last time I beat you in a race.'

She wiped her grimy, sweaty hand on her clean jeans and smiled with something approaching genuine happiness for the first time since Liberty had been flown away from Stagmount in the Harrods helicopter by her furious father.

'I was going easy on you,' said George with a sideways smirk, delighted to see his sister looking and acting more like her usual self. 'I thought letting you win would cheer you up. I wouldn't have bloody done it if I'd known you'd be this smug, though.'

'Shut up, G,' Jinx said, laughing so hard she had to clutch the front of her saddle for support. 'I won that fair and square and you *know* it. But if you're still not sure' – she gathered up her reins, narrowed her eyes and made as if to belt off across the huge green they were approaching – 'why don't we go again?'

George grabbed her left arm and shook his head. 'I was just kidding,' he said hastily. 'You are the champion. El Champione! All hail, Jinx Slater, fastest woman in Hampshire!'

'Thank you,' she replied, making a mock bow to the left, the right and then in front of her. 'I'm honoured to accept this award. I'd like to thank Pansy, this gorgeous horse right here between my legs, my brother Gaymian – without whose sterling work this horse would be as unfit as my dad's – and last and *definitely* least my brother George, for being so crap at riding he can't even coax a gallop out of a seventeen-hand Irish thoroughbred.'

'So,' said George casually after they'd meandered along in companionable silence the entire way across the open green and were now approaching the home straight, 'still no word from Lib then?'

Jinx scowled. She'd refused to discuss the possible whereabouts of her best friend since she'd told Caroline the whole story in the car on the way home from school, and the Slaters – knowing how upset she was – hadn't pushed her. They preferred to let her talk about Liberty when she felt up to it, but Jinx had been so grumpy, miserable and downright rude a lot of the time over Christmas that George had decided to take matters into his own hands.

'Come on, Jinx,' he continued, refusing to take accept this uncharacteristic moody silence for an answer. 'I know you haven't wanted to talk about it, but I hate seeing you like this. To be honest, you're being an absolute pain in the ass. It's not *our* fault Liberty's gone and we all miss her too. Christmas just wasn't the same without you two goons shrieking, shoving and laughing all over the place. Mum and Dad are really worried about you. It's not fair.'

Jinx's eyes filled with tears. She stared determinedly in front of her, torn between shouting at George to mind his own business before storming off in the most almighty huff and admitting that he was right. The first option was certainly easier, given her current mood, but she loved her family and she was aware that her behaviour was getting worse. Sod it, she thought, resigning herself to a spot of bridge building. It's easier to phone your mother than not phone, yes?

'You're right, G,' she sniffed. 'I'm absolutely gutted about Lib. And I know I've been awful to you guys.'

George said nothing, but he nodded encouragingly at her.

'It's like' – Jinx squirmed in her seat, for she had a real aversion to deep and meaningfuls – 'when you *know* you're being a bitch even as you're doing it. You don't want to be behaving that way and you wish you could snap out of it, but your bad mood has been going on for so long it's become almost a default setting. Do you know what I mean?'

'I'm a guy, Jinx, remember?' George said this with a small self-satisfied shrug of his shoulders. If he could have patted himself on the back at the same time he would have done so. 'We don't do that kind of shit.'

'Shut *up*, G,' Jinx shouted, spinning round in her seat and giving him the finger. 'That's the biggest bunch of bollocks I've ever heard. What about your total hissy fit last time we went skiing? You locked yourself in the bathroom for *hours* because Mum said you looked stupid in those awful skinny jeans you bought. I would say like a little girl, only I don't want to fuel your misogynistic fire. I've seen you strop out of various rooms more times than I can even remember. And what about Gaymian? Are you seriously trying to tell me that my moods are worse than his?'

'Well,' George said thoughtfully, 'I suppose you're right. Gaym *is* the exception that proves the rule.'

'Don't make me laugh,' Jinx snapped straight back. 'Anyway, I thought we were supposed to be talking about me here. Do you want me to continue baring my soul or not?'

'Of course I do. I'm just pleased,' George said, looking at his watch and then winking slyly at his sister, 'that it's only taken you – ooo – about three minutes of chat with your second-biggest brother to revert to the self-obsessed narcissist we all know and love.'

He ducked as Jinx swung her riding crop at his head. The sudden movement surprised Dillon, who'd been moseying along in a very relaxed fashion with his nose practically touching the ground, and the horse jumped about a metre in the air without any warning whatsoever. Jinx winced and shut her eyes. When she opened them a second later a very disgruntled-looking George was sitting in a puddle, completely soaked through, with muddy streaks all over his face and neck. Dillon, meanwhile, had obviously decided he needed to get home as fast as equinely possible. Since he was quickly becoming a chestnut blur in the distance, he'd also evidently discovered a turn of speed that he'd been hiding earlier.

'Shit, George!' Trying desperately trying to hold back what she was sure would be an uncontrollable case of the giggles if she let them out, Jinx jumped off Pansy's back and held out a hand to help George up. 'I am so sorry. I seriously didn't mean for that to happen.'

George shook his head and grabbed hold of Jinx's hand as if he was going to let himself be helped out of his puddle.

'Argh, you bastard!' Jinx screamed when he yanked her towards him and she lost her footing. She toppled forward, then skidded on her knees in the deep mud until she was lying on her front, adjacent to her brother. 'I can't bloody believe,' she said, lifting her head and mumbling through a mouthful of dirt, 'I fell for that!'

'Yeah, literally!' George sprang to his feet and grabbed hold of Pansy, who was standing like a mule, staring half-heartedly after Dillon. 'Well, sis, it looks like one of us will be walking back. And since it was you who started this little incident' – George swung himself athletically on to Pansy's back, gathered the reins together and flicked his sister the V – 'it's sure as hell not going to be me. Bye!'

Jinx sat in her puddle and glared angrily after her brother, whose maniacal bursts of laughter were carried back to her on the wind as he galloped home. Torn between crying and laughing, she chewed her lip and used her sleeve to try to wipe the worst of the mud off her face as she decided which emotion was going to win.

With a sigh, she stood up and ran her hands through her hair, wincing as her fingers became stuck in a particularly filthy clump. She peeled off her sodden jumper, tied it round her waist and began the long trudge back, the occasional giggle escaping her mouth every time she thought of George's extreme surprise at his impromptu fall to earth.

By the time she passed the pond at the end of their road and turned left towards Slater Towers, Jinx felt surprisingly chipper.

Walking down the long drive towards the stables and the back of the house, she decided that when Liberty found a way to contact her she would, and that in the meantime she had to stop agonising about it. She also decided that if she did find herself agonising about it, which was pretty much inevitable given the circumstances, she wouldn't take it out on her family but would instead remove herself to her bedroom until the violent urges passed.

Jinx was washing the mud off the bottom of her filthy jeans and ancient trainers using the hosepipe just outside the tackroom and feeling pretty pleased with her new mature outlook on life when Caroline Slater flew round the corner in her tan Ugg slippers.

'Jinx,' she yelled breathlessly, skidding to a halt in front of her surprised daughter. Caroline *never* wore her Uggs outside and regularly threatened pain of death to anyone – namely Jinx – who might borrow them and think of doing the same. 'I thought I heard the gate slam. Thank God you're back!'

'What's wrong, Mum?' Jinx asked, quickly turning off the tap and shaking the water from her jeans. 'Is everything OK? You've got your Uggs on!'

Caroline looked down at her feet in dazed surprise. She'd left the kitchen at such a stretch she hadn't noticed what she was wearing. 'Never mind that,' she said, grabbing Jinx's hand excitedly. 'I've been pacing about for the last hour, just dying for you to get back. When George eventually appeared and told me you were walking home I nearly combusted!'

'Why, Mum?' Jinx was none the wiser and her feet were beginning to freeze. 'What is it?'

'Liberty phoned,' Caroline cried, gripping both of Jinx's hands. 'She's in Washington, DC!'

'What?' An expression of sheer, unadulterated delight was slowly spreading across Jinx's shocked face. 'When? How *is* she? And what the hell is she doing there? Did she leave a number? Oh, God!' Jinx hugged her mum and started jumping up and down, taking the protesting Caroline with her. 'I'm so *pleased*!'

Caroline drew back and put her hands on her daughter's shoulders. Her eyes filled with tears as she spoke: 'Oh, Jinx, I can't tell you how pleased I am. We've all been so worried about you – and her! For the first time ever, I've not known what to say to make you feel better about things.' She linked arms with a by now equally tearful Jinx as they headed towards the kitchen. 'Come on, darling. Let's go inside and have a cup of tea and I'll tell you everything I know.'

Settled into the comfy sofa by the back door, Jinx crossed her legs underneath her, gripped her oversized blue ceramic mug with both hands, blew on her scalding-hot tea and stared at her mother in amazement.

'So,' she said eventually, 'you're telling me that Amir is so furious with Liberty he has *disowned* her and sent her to the States to live with her mum! In Washington! I almost can't believe it.'

Amir Latiffe, Liberty's very strict Muslim father, had arrived at Stagmount towards the end of last term in such a towering rage over his eldest daughter's perceived indiscretions that – amidst declarations of how she had blackened the good name of Latiffe for ever – he had flown her back to Saudi Arabia, resolutely insisting that she would never set foot on British soil, and Stagmount's soil in particular, again. Jinx had been in bits about it ever since, unable to shake the nagging feeling that she was in some way to blame.

'Yes,' sighed Caroline happily. 'I think it's the best thing that could have happened. That man is far too unpredictable. He made life incredibly stressful for Liberty. She never knew what kind of mood he'd be in, or what threats he might make next. I think she lived on a knife edge with him.'

'Yeah, but . . .' Jinx could hardly get a word in edgeways before she was interrupted again.

'Come on, Jinx!' Caroline fixed her daughter with a narrow-eyed stare. 'I hope you're not going to start defending him, because I shan't be able to listen to it. Your dad and I were absolutely appalled by what he did. I know you and Martin sometimes have rows, but really, that was something else and I don't think I'll ever forget it.'

'I know, Mum.' Jinx seized a window of opportunity as Caroline drew an indignant breath. 'Christ, I was there, remember? Of course I wasn't going to speak up for him. What I *was* going to say is that it seems odd he would want her to go to America. Still, Lib will be delighted to have been sent to live with her mother. But I bet you she feels sad about her dad – even though he was often a complete and utter bastard to her, I think she does love him. God, I can't *wait* to speak to her.'

'Well,' Caroline said, standing up and brushing the dog hairs off the back of her skirt, 'her mum's whisking her off on some kind of retreat holiday in California for a week or so over New Year. It sounds like a real new age place, with no phones or Internet access, but Liberty said as soon as she gets home she'll call you. And of course she'll be back at Stagmount for the start of term.'

'Mum,' Jinx said, suddenly leaning forward and hugging Caroline around the waist, 'I love you so much. I'm sorry I've been so terrible to live with all over the holiday. I'll make it up to you, I promise. What time are we due at Granny's? I'd better jump in the shower.'

'Luckily for *you*,' Caroline laughed, 'Granny phoned

15

just after Lib. Her back's playing up again, so Dad's gone to take her to her acupuncture man. God knows when he'll get home, but lunch is off. I thought the four of us could have something here – or we could go the pub. It's up to you kids. And talking of kids, I'm going to go and get Damian up. If he stays in bed much longer he won't sleep tonight.'

Jinx privately doubted Caroline's chances of getting Damian out of his pit. It would probably be easier and far less stressful to raise the dead, but in keeping with her brand-new extreme good mood she smiled so hard her cheeks hurt until her mum clattered out of the kitchen.

— * —

Jinx was lying on the sofa nose to nose with Flash, the Slaters' much-loved boxer dog (he had his own chair at family meals so he wouldn't feel left out), and having a good think about recent developments when Damian stumbled into the room through the swing door, followed by a hysterically laughing George.

'Yo, D,' Jinx yelled when she saw him. At the same time Flash jumped up, emitting a flurry of belated, half-hearted barks, nearly tipping her off the sofa. 'Have you heard about Lib?'

Damian groaned and collapsed on to the adjacent armchair, sitting on one of the stable cats, who'd been enjoying a snooze in the winter sunlight. 'I hate fucking cats,' he muttered as it yowled and scrambled through the cat flap, all the hairs on its back standing up in protest. 'They've got no respect at all.'

George picked up Jinx's legs and unceremoniously swung them off the sofa before settling himself down at the recently vacated end.

'Bloody hell,' she moaned, instantly forgetting her recent decision to be nothing but sweetness and light as far as her family was concerned. 'I was really comfortable here until you pair of oafs minced in.'

'Shut up, Jinx,' said George. 'The three of us need to have a little chat.'

'What about?' Jinx said, giggling as she poked the still-groaning Damian in the side with a ruler she'd found down the back of the sofa. 'Look at the state of him. What *did* he get up to last night? Hmmm?'

Damian opened one bloodshot eye and fixed it on his sister. 'If you,' he whispered in the hoarsest of voices, 'do that again, so help me God you'll wish you hadn't.'

'Just shut the hell up, both of you!' George stood up, grabbed the ruler off Jinx, opened the back door and threw it into the vegetable patch. Flash, thinking this was the start of a brilliant new game, flew towards the door, but he wasn't quick enough for George, who'd already slammed it shut. 'We need to make a decision about New Year's Eve.'

'It's fucking amateur night,' grumbled Damian, tucking the bottom of his navy-blue tracksuit trousers into his grey rugby socks without opening his eyes, 'everyone knows that. And I'm never drinking again anyway, so you can count me out.'

'Right . . . then I guess it's just me and Jinx who will be RSVP-ing yes' – George winked slyly at his sister –

'to Tarquin Stone-Hall's super glamorous party.'

Damian sat bolt upright, looking more alive than he had all morning. 'Tarquin's invited us to his party? Well,' he said skittishly, 'since it's *him* I guess I can make an exception to my usual no going out on New Year's Eve rule.'

'You're such a terrible snob, Gaym,' Jinx snorted, secretly made up that she'd be spending the evening with her brothers at Tarquin's gorgeous country pile – his parties were legendary but she'd never been allowed to go to one before. And since all of her schoolfriends were out of action – Liberty was probably hanging out with a bunch of hippies in California by now, Chastity had gone skiing in Austria with her mother and her mother's new fiancé, Ian, and Liv and Charlie were going to the party of some friend of theirs in London – this was the best, not to say only, invitation she'd so far received.

'Oh, Jinx,' smirked George, 'don't be so naïve. I don't think it's Tarquin's *ancestry* our dear brother is interested in. I think he's more taken with his *ass*.'

'Well,' said Jinx, her eyes bright with delicious antici-pation, 'I can't say I've ever heard you use the words "super glamorous" to describe any event. Are you sure you're not taking a leaf out of Gaymian's big gay book?'

'Shut up!' George blushed. 'I only said "super glam-orous" because that's the *theme* of the bloody party. It's printed on the invitation. Alongside,' he went on, squinting as he held what looked like a cardboard cutout of a cocktail glass up to the light, 'such gems as "champagne on arrival, Viagra on departure", "dress to impress" and "leave your inhibitions at the door".'

'Oh, my GOD!' screamed Damian, jumping out of his chair and dancing up and down so excitedly that he set Flash off on another flurry of useless barks. 'Isn't the first one the *gayest* thing you've ever heard? I knew it!'

Damian bent down and tried – somewhat half-heartedly – to brush the clinging black cat hairs off the back of his tracksuit bottoms before flouncing out of the room in an extraordinarily high mood considering the pale wreck of a boy he'd been when he'd stumbled in earlier.

Jinx rolled her eyes to the ceiling, jerked her head after her brother and raised an enquiring eyebrow.

George nodded. 'Yep,' he said, laughing. 'The party's in two days' time. So right about now he'll have all the clothes out of his cupboard and on the floor. Deciding?'

'What to wear!' Jinx finished for him.

The pair clutched each other and laughed so hard they fell off the sofa. Flash finally walked out in disgust at these incredibly juvenile antics, but Jinx and George were giggling too much to even notice.

– ✳ –

Jinx sat up and looked vaguely around the place in which she'd found herself lying on a chaise longue covered with a pale silk embroidery. She drew in a massive toke from the bong that was hovering in front of her, belatedly realising that it wasn't simply hanging in the air but was being proffered by a tall, giggling man wear-

19

ing a red trilby. She tried to focus. She was very stoned, very drunk and very tired – or should she make that wired? She couldn't *remember* taking any class As but that certainly didn't mean she hadn't. And even though her current viewpoint was decidedly impressionistic, she realised that she was in an extraordinary room.

She counted about twelve people of indeterminate age and sex lounging in various states of inebriation on hugely overstuffed velvet floor cushions, a couple of four-seater sofas in a rich burgundy fabric flecked with gold thread and two slim boys entwined in an embrace in a brown leather armchair. Jinx was relieved to discover, on closer inspection, that neither was Damian. She loved him but she certainly didn't want to watch her brother making out. Yuck!

The ceiling seemed miles away and the antique coffee table was covered with glasses and ashtrays. Jinx shuddered as she clocked a huge stag's head mounted on the wall above the fireplace, framed on either side by two very gloomy-looking oil portraits of fat men dressed all in black. The remnants of a fire were dying in the grate and the stag's horns had a straggly piece of red tinsel looped from one to the other and back round. One man stood in the corner, wearing what appeared to be a suit made of metal. He was stock still and the rest of the party seemed to be completely ignoring him.

Jinx decided that if she lay here much longer she'd never get up. Memories of earlier in the evening were flooding back into her mind and she giggled helplessly as she recalled Damian's futile flirting with Tarquin. Tarq was gorgeous – if you liked very thin men with aristocratic noses and lots of shaggy black hair – but he'd taken so much acid in his first two years at university he'd obviously royally screwed his brain. He'd merely smiled and gurned throughout all of Damian's overtures until her brother had flounced out of the ballroom in disgust – and after, it must be said, one of the very handsome waiters.

Jinx sat up and steadied herself on the side of her chaise. As her eyes clicked into proper focus mode she realised that the pale yellow silk fabric she'd been reclining on was absolutely filthy and spotted with grease, mud and God knows what stains. There was a thick layer of dust along the edge of the Oriental rug at her feet and the table was branded with circular glass marks. Jinx was glad her mother was safely tucked up in bed at home: Caroline Slater would have a blue fit if her living room looked like this.

As she made her way towards the door, stepping carefully over outstretched limbs and passed-out bodies, Jinx paused in front of the man in the corner.

'Hey, dude,' she said, tapping his arm in a friendly way, 'is everything OK?'

She waited for an answer, but whoever was inside the thing was clearly in a vicious bad mood and refusing to talk to anyone.

'Right,' she huffed, cross that he'd ignored her when she'd made such an effort to include him, 'have it your own way. I was just trying to be nice. Fuck you!'

Jinx stuck her middle finger in front of his visor and

staggered towards the door. She was about to sway through it when George flew round the corner, hotly pursued by a naked girl with long blonde hair who was astride a chestnut-brown pony. Jinx drew back and stared in awe after the three of them as they clattered down the corridor. She was sure she'd recognised the girl . . . and a horse in the house? Maybe she would like to live here!

Standing in the wide doorframe, Jinx suddenly felt rather short. She looked down at her feet and groaned. 'Sod it,' she muttered, miserably contemplating her dirty bare toes. 'I've lost Mum's favourite shoes.'

Clutching her head in her hands, she vaguely recalled that she'd been chatting to a couple of girls on the grand marble steps at the front of the house for a good hour or two at some point earlier. She also recalled – more sharply this time – that she had neglected to mention the borrowing of the purple suede platforms to their rightful owner, who had, incidentally, managed to keep them clean and safe since the freaking sixties or something. Shit. She *had* to find the fuckers.

Jinx purposefully turned left and made her way in the direction of what she was sure was the front entrance. Five minutes later she was delighted to find herself standing at the foot of a stunning Jacobean staircase that wound its way through four floors to the top of the house and was lined with yet more gloomy portraits of ancient fat people, some of whom were astride noticeably thinner horses. Brilliant – the front door was right in front of her.

She suddenly noticed the man in the metal suit standing to the side of one of the dark wooden steps, which were impressively shiny considering the layers of filth that seemed to cover the rest of the place.

'Oi, you!' she yelled, pointing an accusatory finger at him. 'Are you following me?' She was incensed when he ignored her again and stomped up the first few steps to confront him. 'Hey! I'm talking to you! It's *beyond* rude of you to ignore me when I've not done anything apart from try and be *nice*! And how the hell did you get?'

Jinx was in full flow when a gaggle of older girls, enjoying a good old bitch about some poor soul, stopped to look at the commotion halfway up the stairs and started pointing and laughing in her direction.

'Christ,' Jinx muttered under her breath, thinking she recognised one of them as Not So Lovely Lydia. Albeit fully clothed and horseless, she was still one of George's more terrifying exes.

'Is that you, Jinx Slater?' asked the most impeccably groomed, blondest one – definitely, Jinx sadly realised, Lydia.

'Um,' she managed to squeeze out before Lydia interrupted her.

'Girls,' Lydia practically screamed, '*this* is Gorgeous George's little sister. Can you believe it?'

Her acolytes giggled and shook their heads. Jinx wanted the ground to open up and swallow her whole, shoes or no bloody shoes.

'Jinx,' Lydia said, raising a perfectly shaped eyebrow and gesturing at Jinx's filthy feet, 'are you aware that you've got no shoes on, there's a humungous rip in the back of your dress and you are standing on your own shouting obscenities at a suit of armour?'

'Um,' Jinx said again, the shock of this unexpected and highly undesirable encounter temporarily removing most of her powers of speech, 'well, yes actually, I *am* aware!'

Anything else Jinx might have had to say on the subject was lost when the girls turned as one and began screaming with ear-splitting delight as a tall, bronzed, surf god type made a very belated entrance, clutching carrier bags filled to bursting with bottles of vodka, beers and mixers.

In her fury at Lydia's bitchy comments, Jinx momentarily forgot her current shoeless state and aimed a vicious kick at the suit of armour. As her right foot connected with the suit's iron leg, she felt an unimaginable pain in her big toe. She screamed a hell of a lot louder than the girls in the hall combined, stumbled, skidded and fell backwards down the very shiny stairs.

She closed her eyes and waited for the inevitable thud, hoping she'd knock herself out and therefore not have to endure the look on Lydia's smug face.

She felt a thud all right, but it wasn't the kind she'd been expecting. Whatever she'd landed on was pretty soft . . . but sort of hard at the same time. She decided she wouldn't open her eyes just yet but enjoy this unfamiliar swooning sensation for a little bit longer. It was while making a confused mental note to explore other falling-down-staircase possibilities that she realised the arms circling her waist were not her own. She kept her eyes tightly closed as she registered that they were strong, muscular arms, they were warm and they definitely belonged to a man. She surreptitiously sniffed the air and was rewarded with the incredibly sexy combination of smoke, beer, surf wax and chewing gum.

'Jinx,' Lydia was yelling into Jinx's ear, completely destroying her delicious reverie. 'Jinx! Wake up!'

Jinx decided to play dead for a bit longer.

'She's taking the piss. Look at the state of her.' Lydia's voice echoed into Jinx's head from further away than it had been a second ago. 'She's absolutely trashed. She was shouting at that suit of armour a second ago like a proper mentalist. She's only seventeen or something – it's a fucking disgrace.'

'Shut up, Lyd,' said a deep voice that Jinx was sure she recognised. 'You're being a total cow. Here's a newsflash for you – George isn't interested. So why don't you piss off and leave his sister out of it?'

Jinx suddenly knew exactly who was holding her in his gorgeous arms. She'd never have thought it possible to feel this truly appalled and wildly excited all at the same time. Thinking of her dirty feet, ripped dress and no doubt ruinous make-up, she was afraid she might actually vomit. She was so embarrassed at being caught – literally – like this she screwed her eyes as tightly closed as they could go and resolved to keep them shut until she had the first opportunity to leg it. She drunkenly congratulated herself on this awesome plan, not realising that her train of thought was quite so obvious to the other party.

'Hey,' George's best friend Jamie said softly in what seemed to Jinx an impossibly sexy voice.

Gosh, she thought dreamily, how one word can spark a zillion thoughts! She cautiously opened an eye and gave Jamie a quick once-over. She was so stunned by what she saw that she rapidly shut it again and felt a hot flush begin to spread across her face. Damn it! She hadn't seen him since George and Gaymian had taken her, Chastity, Liberty and – Jinx almost had a total gross-out just thinking about the bitch's *name* – fucking Stella Fox to his party last term. Trust her to – oh, my God, she thought, nearly hyperventilating at her most recent unedifying memory – land on top of him from a great height looking her absolute freaking worst.

Jamie, George's pal from school and now the richest art student in Brighton, was a lovely boy. He had a huge trust fund, which he was charmingly embarrassed about, and had used some of it to buy his incredible seafront apartment, about ten minutes west of Stagmount. He'd always felt slightly shady about his vast wealth, so rented rooms out for practically nothing to his mates, most of whom were amazing surfers. He was constantly throwing parties for the rest of his scruffy student chums and Jinx knew him to be an extremely genial host. Since she considered tightness to be her worst personality trait, the closest thing she could imagine to spiritual halitosis, its opposite was always positively ambrosial to her.

Nor did it hurt that he was totally hot. Jamie was six

foot four with brownish-blond hair, complete with golden highlights courtesy of the hours, days and weeks he spent surfing in Brighton and Cornwall, unruly strands of which framed his strong jaw. All the salt and sea air had left him with a permanent honey-coloured tan, and his blue eyes were shot with flecks of green. He looked like the lovechild of David Beckham and Matthew McConaughey wearing just one of P. Diddy's gold chains. Even his clothes were so damned sexy. He was wearing Diesel jeans with a pale green faded T-shirt and navy and silver Onitsuka Tigers trainers in the cool, understated way that was made for beach boys like him.

The last time Jinx had seen Jamie she was so preoccupied with Stella's evil plans for Liberty that she'd hardly given him much thought, though with hindsight she did recall a distinctly hot and bothered feeling when he'd met them at the door. She prayed its repeat wasn't spreading across her chest in the manner of a livid rash at this very moment.

Jinx really liked him; she always had. Since the beginning of last summer holidays in fact, she'd begun to feel a bit hot under the collar every time she saw him. And, to be honest, she had to admit it hadn't taken long for that same feeling to come over her when she just *thought* about him.

'Hey,' Jamie said again, slightly louder this time, '*are* you OK, Jinx? You've been lying there, not saying anything, with your eyes closed for ages. Talk to me, Slater!'

'Oh, my God,' Jinx spluttered, realising she must have been daydreaming in his arms for, like, ten minutes already. She opened her eyes wide in horror. 'I'm totally fine, Jamie. Sorry! You can put me down.'

Practically wishing she was dead and suffering from the most extreme case of embarrassment she'd ever experienced, Jinx struggled in his arms. Ooo, she thought with a shiver, he really was the fittest guy she'd ever seen.

'Easy, tiger,' Jamie laughed, and gently placed Jinx on her feet. 'You'd better start watching your step. I might not be so handily placed the next time you decide to take a flying leap.'

'Um . . .' Jinx stood in front of him, but since she couldn't bring herself to look into his eyes she found herself staring determinedly at the top of his right ear as she tried to speak. 'I —'

She didn't manage to finish her sentence because Jamie tenderly cupped her face with one hand, licked the forefinger of the other and used it to wipe a smudge of dirt from her cheek.

'There you go,' he said, standing back and appraising his handiwork with a wide smile. 'Now you look like the million-dollar babe we all know and love again.'

Jinx felt as if she'd been struck by lightning – and also struck dumb in the process. She very much doubted she was capable of saying another word, even if she'd wanted to.

Jamie put an arm around her shoulder, pulled her in close and gestured at her feet. 'Something tells me,' he said, before turning to wink at her, 'that someone needs to find her shoes.'

'Yes,' Jinx agreed, finally finding her nerve and twinkling up at him from where she was squidged deliciously into the crook of his armpit, 'I do.'

She was mustering the courage to ask him to help her when a woman started screaming and shouting outside. Assorted amazed-sounding cries soon joined the original lone voice. Jinx had no time to organise her thoughts before Jamie grabbed her hand and pulled her outside.

Massed around the turning circle at the top of the drive outside the house was a throng of partygoers. In the middle of them was a woman Jinx recognised – mostly from the local pub, where the Stone-Hall family liked to have rows as drunkenly, publicly and loudly as possible – as Tarquin's mother. Mrs Stone-Hall was very tall and looked incredibly glamorous in a purple silk sheath dress, the bottom of which grazed the ground, affording onlookers the occasional glimpse of her sparkling gold peep-toe sandals. Her long black hair was swept up in a chignon and she was flailing her arms and screaming obscenities at someone they couldn't see. Maternal she was not.

'Bloody hell,' whispered Jamie, lighting up a Marlboro Red and leaning back as if he was at the theatre and trying to get a better view of the stage, 'that woman is an absolute nutter.'

'Do you know her?' asked Jinx, who was deeply enjoying both the spectacle in front of her and the feel of Jamie's hot breath on her cheek as he talked into her ear. 'And who *is* she shouting at?'

'I've met her a few times,' Jamie said, leaning in even closer as he clutched Jinx's shoulder and stood on tiptoes, trying to peer over the crowd. 'She always used to turn up at school pissed as a newt and once had the most almighty slanging match with the headmaster about Tarq in the middle of the car park on the last day of term. She's funny, but totally deranged. I can't see anything from here – let's go and have a closer look.'

Jinx was suffused with delight when she realised that Jamie was still holding her hand, but at that moment George dashed through the front door, closely followed by Damian, and grabbed her other hand.

'We're going,' he said breathlessly, trying to drag her away. 'Get your stuff NOW.'

'George!' Jinx said, knowing that if Jamie hadn't been standing next to her she would have stamped her foot. 'Let go of me! I'm staying.'

'Hey, man.' Much to Jinx's disappointment, Jamie had released her hand when her brothers turned up and now turned to look at his best friend with amusement. 'What's up?'

'That fucking Lydia's been following me all night,' George said quietly, 'so I told her I'd meet her in the green bathroom on the top floor at two o'clock. I was running the hot tap so I could write PISS OFF I'M NOT INTERESTED in the steam on the mirror when I heard her clattering down the corridor ten minutes early. So I legged it before I had a chance to write anything.' George paused and shook his head. 'The thing is,' he continued sorrowfully, 'I think I might have left the

30

tap on.'

'OK,' hissed Jinx, 'so you're a moron. But I still don't understand why we have to leave.'

'*That's* why,' George said, pointing at Mrs Stone-Hall and grabbing Jinx's hand again. 'I don't think she was overly impressed to find her claw-footed Victorian bath languishing on a bed of three smashed ceilings in her kitchen, do you?'

'The only thing *I* don't understand,' said Jamie, laughing in disbelief at George's story and pointing through a gap in the crowds that afforded them an excellent view of Tarquin's mother punching him in the face with an expression of pure, abject fury on her own, 'is why she's blaming the whole thing on Tarq.'

'I was hiding behind a curtain when she ran up the stairs,' George said, wincing at the intensity of the beating in front of them and looking decidedly shamefaced. 'Tarq had been popping pills in his bedroom next door and was presumably making his way back to the party when he bumped into his mum. Since he was the only person up there, she presumed it was him who'd done it. And he was so off his face he presumed he'd done it too and admitted it. That's when she dragged him outside, kicking and screaming the whole way.'

'Bloody hell, George,' Damian said after a long whistle, 'you've really got no shame at all, have you? Why you couldn't just *tell* Lydia you weren't interested straight to her vacant face I'll never understand. But I think you're right, we should scoot. It's never a good thing to hang around at the scene of a crime, especially when you're

31

the perpetrator. Although just think: if I'd had my wicked way with him, poor old Tarq would have been totally in the clear with a – ahem – rock-hard alibi!'

'If you don't want me to vomit you'd better quit the sex talk, Gaym. And fucking hell, George,' Jinx muttered, looking wistfully at Jamie from underneath the eyelashes she'd liberally plastered with ultra-thick black lengthening mascara seven hours earlier, 'this party was just hotting up. I can't believe we've got to cut it short. You are such a cretin.'

'Do you want to come back with us?' George asked, ignoring his sister and turning back to Jamie.

Jinx crossed her fingers and held her breath.

'I'd love to, bud, but I've only just got here,' Jamie said, still laughing at George's antics. 'I've spent most of the night driving around the New Forest with no bloody phone reception and no bloody idea where this mausoleum was. I'd better go and rescue Tarq – and don't worry, G-man, your secret is safe with me.'

Jamie shook Damian's hand, clasped George in a manly hug and tousled Jinx's hair as he said goodbye and prepared to wade into the fray.

As the sketchy trio slipped past the crowd towards the winding drive that would take them on the road to home, Damian stopped and pointed in horror at a pair of beautiful shoes discarded by the fountain. 'Jinx!' he hissed, giving his sister a fright, 'please tell me those aren't Mum's Biba shoes perched precariously on the edge of that fountain!'

'Thank God!' Jinx – who, in all the excitement, had

totally forgotten her earlier mission – darted into the mêlée, emerging a few seconds later triumphantly swinging the purple platforms by their long suede ankle ties. 'Gaym, you're a legend.'

Jinx daydreamed her way through the last few days of the Christmas holiday, constantly replaying the scene with Jamie in her head – and imagining a fair few more besides. She finally stepped off cloud nine and started throwing things haphazardly into her trunk for the beginning of term about five minutes before her very impatient dad was ready and waiting to drive her back to school.

– ✳ –

'Jesus Christ!' said Martin Slater, swerving to avoid an ill-placed bollard and just managing to keep both his cool and his racing-green E-class Mercedes on the road as he rounded the sharp corner of Stagmount's long drive. 'Who the hell are *they*?'

'God, Dad, not you too,' Jinx said, giggling as she looked up from the text message she'd just received from Chastity, who was also en route back to school, and spotted what had caused their near miss. 'Men are so bloody predictable.'

Sashaying along the drive towards Tanner House, where all the lower sixth lived, a few metres in front of the car, were three visions of identical blonde loveliness. Jinx could hardly blame her dad for staring – indeed,

33

she had passed many happy hours in assembly and chapel doing exactly that herself. It would have been nigh on impossible for man, woman or beast to ignore these three.

'Those,' said Jinx with a knowing smirk, 'are Stagmount's very own and very infamous Russian triplets: Olga, Masha and Irina. You must have seen them before, Dad – they've been here as long as I have. Don't you remember George falling practically flat on his face when he saw them at speech day last year?'

'No, I don't,' Martin said as he parked the car. 'All I remember from speech day last year was its interminable length. I must have dozed through most of it – or tried to anyway. So who are they? Are they in your year? I must say they certainly look a lot . . .' Martin faltered before continuing, '*older* than you and your friends.'

Jinx flipped the rear-view mirror over to her side in order to spy on the sisters without having to turn around.

It was impossible to tell them apart unless they were standing in front of you and you had been watching them covertly for three and a half years, as Jinx and her friends had, monitoring every difference. Despite this unceasing surveillance, Jinx still had no idea which was which from this distance, but they were all so beautiful and perfect she supposed it didn't actually matter.

What Jinx and the others didn't know was that the triplets could be easily, instantly identified by the different-coloured large stone set in the centre of the gold ring each wore on the third finger of her right hand. These had been given to them by their oligarch father before they left Moscow for Stagmount three and a half years earlier. Olga's was a blue diamond, Masha's a green one and Irina's pink. Despite sharing literally everything else, the triplets never swapped these over.

Five feet nine inches tall and perfect size tens, all three had expertly highlighted honey-blonde hair that fell to just above their elbows in graceful waves. They were wearing pale blue skinny Ksubi jeans tucked into tie-up black Ugg boots. The girl in the middle had a black silk Prada bomber jacket and the one on the left a beige Stella McCartney trench coat over a charcoal grey polo neck, while the one on the right was swathed in an oversized Nicole Farhi cashmere throw in berry red.

Jinx considered their undulating progress of perfection in silence for a few seconds before turning back to a decidedly dazed Martin. If she didn't know better she'd have sworn she heard a groan escape her dad's lips as the girls drew alongside the car and, with exact synchronicity, waved cheerily at Jinx before walking through Tanner House's front door.

'Curiouser and curiouser,' muttered Jinx, who was also watching them go in. 'They were in the upper sixth last term, so I wonder what they're doing in Tanner. Maybe they've been moved down – which wouldn't surprise me, given what I know about their so-called work. I suppose they could be dropping something off, but that doesn't seem likely. They're lovely girls, but I've never once seen any of them run a single errand. We

35

always say that people are too afraid to ask them to do normal things because they're so beautiful.'

'Well,' said Martin, flinging the driver's door open and dashing round to the boot with what looked to Jinx like unseemly haste to get into Tanner House before the girls disappeared, 'since we're finally here let's get you in and sorted.'

'Jinx Slater!' Brian Morris, Jinx's housemaster and a very good egg, stood alone in the small reception area. There was no sign of the Russians anywhere. Clutching a clipboard to his chest, Mr M also appeared a bit stunned as he threw an arm around Jinx's shoulders before clasping Martin's hand in a firm handshake. 'Has anyone ever told you you're like a bad penny? Always turning up! How are you both? Good hols, I trust?'

'Lovely, Sir,' said Jinx, conveniently forgetting that she'd spent most of her time at home mooching about in the most almighty strop. 'And isn't it fanTASTIC news about Liberty! She spoke to Mum a few days ago. Do you know when she's coming?'

'Yes, it is, and yes, I do,' said Mr Morris, winking at his favourite pupil. Jinx had saved him from being fired – and probably worse – when the dreaded Stella Fox falsely accused him of sexual harassment at the end of last term, thus earning herself a special place in his heart for ever. 'We've been told to expect her first thing in the morning, definitely in time for assembly. She's flying to Heathrow from LAX and coming directly here from the airport. I imagine she's in the air right now, so don't worry – you won't have too long to wait.'

'Wow,' sighed Jinx, 'I can't wait to see her. We haven't not spoken for this long since we first met and I've really missed the bitch!'

'Jinx!' barked Martin. 'Watch your language. I'm sorry, Brian, she's obviously forgotten she's not at home now.'

He turned to Mr Morris, who was trying to hide his laughter behind the clipboard he was holding back to front, on which Jinx's eagle eye immediately spotted the Tanner House register. The two men embarked on a boring chat about Southampton's football team, which both supported passionately, and Jinx used the opportunity to quickly scan the register.

'Fuck!' she yelled as she read 'Olga, Masha and Irina Prozorov' at the bottom of the first page, blithely oblivious to the furious glare Martin immediately directed at her. 'I knew it! Why have the triplets been moved down, Sir?'

'Well, Jinx,' said Mr Morris, hastily turning his clipboard the right way round so that the list faced his chest, 'we – the school and their parents, that is – decided that the girls could do with an extra year at Stagmount before sitting their A levels and that it was in their best interests to recommence the lower sixth.'

'Basically then,' said Jinx, nodding knowingly, 'they screwed up their mocks and, since the school doesn't want to lose its place at the top of the league tables, they've been forced down. Brilliant,' she continued cheerfully, 'I've always thought they looked wicked fun and now we get the chance to find out for sure. Come on, Dad,' she said, waving at Mr Morris and hoisting her favourite brown leather Simultane handbag with a white leather Pegasus stitched on the front on to her shoulder, 'we can't stand about chatting all day. Let's get the trunk into my room before we say our fond farewells. Catch you later, Sir!'

Martin sighed as he recalled sitting in his car at the front of the house for at least an hour as he waited for Jinx to finish packing, but didn't say anything about it. He also decided not to mention the fact that he'd had to turn back for home as soon as they'd got on the motorway because Jinx had forgotten her beloved gold and cream Nike Hi-Tops. He had point blank refused to turn back again when she realised she'd also forgotten the giant jar of Marmite Caroline always bought her at the start of term, chucking a £10 note from his emergency stash at her and telling her to bloody well buy another one. Since she'd be making a definite profit out of it, Jinx had been very happy with this arrangement and the rest of the journey had been spent mostly harmoniously listening to the top forty on Radio One. Still, at least he'd be able to play his favourite Crosby, Stills and Nash CDs all the way home, he thought cheerfully as he hefted Jinx's monster trunk along the corridor to her ground-floor bedroom.

Having extracted another £20 from her dad's pocket without him noticing when he'd hugged her goodbye, Jinx was sitting happily on her bed and contemplating her room. Contrary to the school rule which stated that all rooms must be cleaned of every personal item at the end of every term, she'd left up the posters, photos and notes which adorned every inch of available wall, cupboard and window-frame space. Groups and organisations occasionally rented the school in the holidays for conferences and things, and Jinx assumed the rule existed in case the people who came to stay didn't want airbrushed pictures of Justin Timberlake or Brad Pitt staring down at them all night. Boring bastards, she thought, smirking round the place with satisfaction. It had taken her ages to get it exactly the way she wanted and she was fucked if she was going to be made to do it all again.

Hmmm, she mused, lying back on her bed and crossing her arms beneath her head, she must get hold of a picture of Jamie. She wished she'd thought about it before leaving but made a mental note to steal one from George's room the first time she went home for the weekend.

Jinx got off the bed and opened her cupboard door. She peeled one of the myriad photos that adorned the inside of it from its blue-tacked fixing and lay back down, holding it in front of her. A black and white Polaroid, taken by Caroline, who obsessively documented every single thing that ever happened to any member of the Slater family – including snapping dead pets in their shallow graves while the rest of the family sobbed at a respectful distance – it showed Jinx and Liberty on the day they'd met. That was three and a half years ago, but seemed like twenty. They both looked so small and afraid, tiny first years on the first day at school. Jinx loved that picture, and she loved Liberty even more. God, she was relieved they'd gotten away pretty much unscathed by last term's upset.

'Chas!' Jinx screamed, dropping the photo on to her bedside table and jumping up as Chastity Maxwell pushed open the door and stood there looking impossibly glamorous in a Prada coat with skin tight navy-blue Sass and Bide jeans tucked into the ubiquitous Ugg boots. She was clutching a bottle of red wine and sporting a gorgeous skiing tan. 'How the hell are you? I've missed you!'

Jinx flung herself towards her second-best friend without waiting for an answer and they squealed with delight as they jumped up and down on the spot, deliriously happy to see each other after a month apart.

Punctuated by the occasional ear-splitting shriek, their conversation went on at high speed for a good ten minutes without pause for breath, until they both laughed and collapsed exhausted on to Jinx's bed, belatedly realising that in their excitement they had taken in hardly a word of what the other was saying.

'So,' Chastity said breathlessly, yanking off her boots and bundling her long blonde hair into a messy ponytail on the top of her head, 'Lib's back tomorrow?'

'Yep,' said Jinx, grinning widely and bunching a pillow behind her back against the wall. 'I can't tell you how awful it was until she phoned.' She paused, then admitted, 'Well, how awful *I* was, if you want the truth. I couldn't deal with it at all and the poor family got the

40

brunt of it. We're all the best of friends now of course, but I did behave seriously badly. I feel quite shady about it to be honest!'

'Come off it, Jinx,' Chastity said, reaching across her for another pillow. 'We *all* do it. Christ, I'm sure they've done it themselves. Look what a bitch I was to Mum and Ian all last term. And he's such a nice bloke! He couldn't have been any nicer when we were skiing and I really, really like him now. I wouldn't worry about it any more if I was you, Jinx.'

Chastity was expertly uncorking the bottle of very expensive Pinot Noir the newly lovely Ian had given her as a going-back-to-school present when Jinx slapped her forehead and squealed again.

'Oh, my god,' she screamed, 'in all the excitement I forgot to tell you! I can't believe it!'

'What?' Chastity demanded as Jinx jumped up and down. '*What* haven't you told me? Come on. You can't leave me in suspense like this!'

'Only that the triplets are joining us in the lower sixth this term,' Jinx said triumphantly, very pleased to be the imparter of such great gossip. 'They're moving back into Tanner and everything.'

'Really?' asked Chastity, emitting a long, low whistle. 'Olga, Irina and Masha are in *our* year now?'

'Yep,' Jinx said, opening her window, leaning out and lighting a cigarette. 'They fucked up their mocks, so they're being moved down. Mrs B's obviously in a panic about her league tables.'

'Wicked,' replied Chastity. 'I've always been *fascinated*

by them. How cool!'

'Didn't you do ballet or something with one of them in the second year?' Jinx asked, carefully stubbing out her cigarette and placing it on the windowsill with an eye to smoking the rest later.

'Yes!' Chas slapped her own forehead, wincing as she misjudged it, leaving a red mark right in the middle of her eyebrows. 'I did! I can't believe I'd forgotten all about it. Irina was in my tap-dancing class. She was lovely – always smiling and very funny actually – but I was always too mesmerised by her beauty to ever dare speak to her.'

Chastity frowned and took a sip of her wine. 'Although,' she continued, 'we were never sure if it was Irina or one of her sisters. Some weeks she was amazing – so good the teacher would practically wet herself – and then other times she slouched and stomped and no one could understand it. We all thought it was hilarious of course, but the teacher would almost be crying with disappointment. Then the next week she'd be back to brilliant.'

'Imagine,' said Jinx admiringly, 'if you had identical triplets – or even a twin – the mind-blowing stunts you could pull! Wouldn't you be pranking people all the time? I know I *totally* would. I wonder what the others are like – do you know anything about them?'

Liv and Charlie, who had been best friends since they'd stolen the gardener's tractor two and a half years ago and tried to do handbrake turns in it on the grass tennis court, yelled, 'What others?' in unison as they pushed and shoved their way into the room and into each other before diving on top of Jinx and Chastity, screaming hellos and happy new years and spilling lots of red wine all over Jinx's clean sheets in the process.

'Fucking hell!' said Jinx, righting herself and staring up at Liv, whose shoulder-length brown hair had been cropped to within an inch of its life and dyed so black it looked blue. 'Your hair looks *amazing*. When did you do that?'

'Well,' said Liv, self-consciously running a hand over her new ultra-short and ultra-fashionable do, 'I've had the same old, same old hair since I was born practically, so I thought, you know, new year, new term, new barnet. I did it last week in London. My mum's still not speaking to me, but I love it!'

'Jinx is right,' agreed Chastity, 'you look freaking fantastic. So much older too . . . Hey! Maybe I should get mine done.'

The others fell silent as they contemplated Chastity. With her long blonde hair and jangling Tiffany bracelets, her appearance was strictly fluffy, but once riled she was famous for throwing the most almighty strops. As they looked at her, her friends were all wondering how to tell her that having her golden mane chopped off would surely be the worst personal style decision she could make.

'But Chas,' Jinx exclaimed in a sudden fit of inspiration, remembering that Chastity adored her mother above all else, especially since her media-mogul father had fallen – missing, presumed dead – off the side of his

43

yacht in the South of France when she was very young, 'what would your mum say?'

'Jinx is right, Chas,' Charlie swiftly jumped in. 'Don't you always say your mum loves your hair like that?'

'That's true,' Chastity said, fondly patting the huge ponytail on top of her head. 'She'd be gutted. I guess I'm stuck with it for the time being.'

Liv and Jinx shared a secret relieved look. Chastity's features were simply too strong to cope with a crop like that, although none of them fancied telling her. Far better, for a peaceful start to the term, to let her think she'd made the decision on her own.

'Right,' said Jinx determinedly, standing up and surveying the filthy sheets she'd only put on her damn bed twenty minutes previously, 'I can't take this any more. Look what you bastards have done to my bed!'

'Sorry, Jin,' Charlie apologised, trying to brush off the worst of the wine but leaving an even worse stain in its place. 'Why don't we sit in the common room? I'll go and grab a few drinks first, then meet you in there.'

Grumbling good-naturedly about the mess they'd made of her room, Jinx linked arms with Chastity on one side and Liv on the other and forced them to skip down her corridor towards their favourite common room. It was complete with squashy sofas, giant bean-bags and – best of all, as far as the girls were concerned – a huge plasma screen TV fully equipped with Sky Plus, DVD and CD players.

'Ooo,' Jinx said with a sly grin when Jamie and New Year's Eve popped unbidden into her mind as they approached the door, 'there's something *else* I've got to tell you lot too. Remind me when Liberty gets back.'

Completely ignoring her friends' protestations that it would actually *kill* them to wait a second longer for her gossip, Jinx pushed open the common-room door.

— ✳ —

The sight that greeted them was unlike any other Jinx had witnessed. They all stood in the doorway, speechless with shock and admiration. The Russian triplets were sitting near the window, around a card table that had appeared from somewhere. It wasn't the bottles of vodka so casually laid out on the green baize in front of them, or the gold-tipped black cigarettes smoldering so insouciantly in the ashtray, or even the huge piles of £10 and £20 notes in the middle of the poker game they'd obviously been enjoying for some time that shocked the three in the doorway.

No, it was the presence of a very tall, moody-looking, raven-haired man sitting there so cosily with the triplets, as if it was his God-given right to be in the strictly female-only lower sixth-form common room that threw our girls into a spin. Shit! The triplets obviously were as indifferent to school rules as people claimed. The man, who must have been at least thirty-five, looked towards the door, gave the girls standing there a very obvious once-over and nonchalantly raised a hand in greeting.

The triplets looked up from their card hands at his movement, simultaneously waved, smiled and

45

chirruped, 'Hi, girls,' before turning back to the game, identical expressions of fierce concentration etched on each remarkable face.

Fanny Ho, a boyish Chinese girl who had smuggled her girlfriend Maureen Mo from Hong Kong to Stagmount the previous term, keeping her hidden in her bedroom until she'd finally cracked under the pressure of harbouring an illegal immigrant and admitted all to a very sympathetic Jinx, breezed out of the adjoining bathroom and sat herself happily down at the poker table.

Fanny had also been in the year above, but had had to stay down in the lower sixth last term due to a nasty bout of glandular fever that had left her totally poleaxed for six months. None of them had realised it before, but she was clearly great pals with the triplets. Jinx was surprised. She really liked Fanny and thought her escapade last term was one of the funniest things she'd ever heard. She was only sorry she'd been sworn to secrecy, but she'd promised never to tell anyone and she fully intended to keep that promise until the day she died.

What surprised her about Fanny's friendship with these girls was that, nice and all as she was, Fanny was a seriously excellent student. She was an amazing tennis player, a superb musician and a notorious maths geek who raced to the library first thing every morning to read the trickiest business pages of the *FT* before breakfast. The triplets, on the other hand, were notorious for never going to lessons if they could help it and avoided the sports fields like the plague. What's more, they had been chucked out of the choir – despite its being compulsory for all lower school girls to attend rehearsals alongside the orchestra once a week – when a large cache of Russian vodka and foreign cigarettes had been discovered behind some loose bricks at the back of the choir stalls.

'Jinx!' Fanny said when she spotted her loitering in the doorway, jumping up and smiling. 'It's great to see you! How are you? Good hols?'

'Great thanks, Fan.' Jinx smiled at her. 'And Liberty's coming back tomorrow too, so all is right with the world.' Jinx paused and coughed delicately, unsure of how to broach the topic in front of all these people who had no idea about Maureen's existence. 'How is your, um, friend Maureen doing?'

Fanny laughed, her eyes sparkling. 'Oh, she's fine, but we're not really, you know, such *good* friends any more.'

'Right.' Jinx threw her a conspiratorial wink. 'Well, if you speak to her, tell her I said hello.'

'If I do I will,' Fanny replied with a smirk and a shrug of her shoulders, which indicated to Jinx that Maureen and Fanny's relationship was pretty much dead in the water, before gesturing round the table. 'Hey – do you girls know the triplets?'

The three of them were approaching the card table as Charlie, clutching two carrier bags filled with lurid multicoloured alcopops, ran into the room, then skidded to a halt behind them. She took one look at the group by the window, pointed at the man in black and hissed loudly and incredibly obviously to everyone else,

'Who the hell is *that*?'

The triplets and Fanny dissolved into conspiratorial laughter and it was left to the man to stand up and extend a courteous hand to a shocked Charlie. 'My name is Igor,' he said self-importantly and in heavily accented English, 'and I am the bodyguard of the Prozorov triplets. I will be staying at Stagmount and watching over the ladies until they complete their studies.'

'Really?' asked Charlie, her face turning pink as he pumped her hand up and down with what looked like excessive force. She was dying to ask a few more questions, like what exactly the girls needed a bodyguard *for*, but didn't quite dare to in the face of his decidedly off-putting blank stare. 'Well, I'm Charlie. It's, um, lovely to meet you.'

'This is Jinx, Liv and Chastity,' Fanny said, pointing at each of the girls in turn as she introduced them to the triplets, 'and this is Olga, Masha and Irina.'

'Oh, Fanny,' said the girl who had been introduced as Olga with a giggle, 'how long have we been at school together? I'm not Olga, I'm Masha!'

'And I,' said the one they thought was Irina, 'am Olga.'

The three of them dissolved into laughter at the four stricken faces in front of them.

'Don't worry,' said Masha, showing a flash of such bright white teeth as she smiled the girls thought they might be blinded. 'We don't care what you call us. We're used to it. We like it!'

'We always see you girls around school,' said Irina,

48

'and we always think you look like the most fun from your year. Where is your friend,' she asked, pointing at Jinx, 'the pretty, dark-haired girl? You two are always laughing and joking together and we always say you two are naughty sisters just like us.'

Jinx, who was privately thinking that Fanny and Maureen had nothing on *these* girls when it came to pranking everyone into thinking they were the same person, was delighted that the stunning triplets so obviously wanted to make friends with them all. If nothing else, it looked like the vodka would be pretty much free-flowing for the rest of the school year.

'That's Liberty,' Jinx said with a smile, having quickly decided it would be just too much effort to explain the reasons for her late arrival back at school. 'She's flying in from the States. She'll be here first thing tomorrow – she'll be so excited that you three are in our year. She always talks about your amazing clothes!'

'How kind,' said Masha, glowing warmly at Jinx and throwing a delighted smile at her sisters. 'We always try to look our best and we love it when people notice our clothes.'

'Come and have a vodka with us,' urged Olga, banging her glass on the table in invitation. 'We are nearly finished with our game anyway.'

'Don't mind Igor,' added Irina, noticing the concerned looks Jinx and the others were directing at him. 'Except for when we need a fifth at cards or something, we treat him as if he is invisible. He likes it,' she continued, when the girls looked at each other in shock at such blatant rudeness right in front of the poor man. 'He has to be alert for danger at all times.'

The triplets raised their hands in front of their faces at the exact same time and in the exact same way as they gave the exact same sarcastic 'ooo, *scared*' impression.

Jinx looked at Chastity, Liv looked at Charlie, then – no further overtures required – the four of them settled happily into the nearest sofa. No one saw the expression of suppressed rage that passed briefly across Igor's face.

When Mr Morris tried to pop his head round the door a couple of hours later to enquire about the high noise levels coming from the common room he found his path blocked by an intractable Igor. Despite becoming quite angry, the housemaster could not persuade him to stand aside, thus giving the girls a few precious minutes to stow the vodka bottles in the games cupboard, open the windows and spray a load of Irina's über-expensive, limited-edition Solange Azagury-Partridge's Stoned perfume around the room to mask the smell of the black cigarettes. Mr Morris probably wouldn't have cared anyway. He was renowned for his easygoing attitude towards the girls in his care, regarding them as young adults and treating them accordingly – he let them smoke in the garage outside reception so long as they cleaned up the butts on a regular basis and keep alcohol in moderation in their rooms. All the girls loved him but Igor clearly didn't know – or give a shit about – any of that.

Although she was pretty trashed by now, Jinx nudged Chastity, pointed at Igor and gave her the thumbs-up sign. 'S'brilliant,' she slurred as they made their way to bed after many a prolonged farewell to the triplets, Fanny and each other, 'we can do whatever we want so long as he's around.'

Mr Morris frowned as he switched off the common-room lights and made his way to his small flat at the side of the main house. Tomorrow morning, after the first assembly of term, he planned to have a very serious word with Stagmount's much-beloved headmistress, Mrs Bennett, on the subject of the triplet's blatant disregard for school rules and Igor's obduracy in the face of them.

'I was told – actually, make that *promised*,' Mr Morris muttered crossly to Myrtle, 'that he had been briefed.' The ancient, rake-thin whippet he'd inherited from Jinx's former housemistress, Mrs Gunn, when she resigned suddenly at the end of last term peered up at him with a look of love etched on her long, mournful face but remained silent.

Mrs Bennett was gripping the edge of the eagle-shaped maple lectern on the dais in front of her and vastly enjoying the sound of her sonorous voice as it echoed pleasingly around the cavernous, wood-panelled assembly hall. Stagmount's entire student body and staff were gathered there to hear her first-day-of-term speech.

'So, in summation, I am going to announce the head girl of each year.'

'Oh, God,' whispered Jinx, nudging Chastity and

pointing at the dreaded Daisy Finnegan, who'd positively revelled in her role as chief lower sixth pen pusher and sucker up throughout last term, 'I just *know* she's going to be it again. Look at her – I can't bear it!'

Although the pair of them had terrible headaches and only faint recollections of the last portion of their vodka binge in the common room, they had woken up at seven o'clock and lain around giggling raucously at absolutely nothing while they waited to give Liberty a heroine's welcome back to Stagmount. In her honour, they had killed – or rather toasted – a few fatted croissants and brewed a cafetiere of Jamaican ground coffee beans they found at the back of a store cupboard. Unfortunately, as Mr Morris told them when he and Myrtle emerged yawning at ten to eight, Liberty's plane had been delayed, so she wouldn't be back at school until at least morning breaktime.

The upshot was that they were even more exhausted this morning than usual at the start of the spring term, and were both in the grip of extreme hangover hysteria, an unusual condition which mostly afflicts people in pairs. Sufferers cannot stop crying with laughter at everything their opposite number says, find even the unfunniest actions of normal (i.e. sober) people deeply suspicious and therefore side-splittingly hilarious and – most surprisingly, given the damage surely sustained by the brain during the previous evening's excesses – discover themselves to be possessed of a gift for riffing, banter and chitchat of the wittiest variety that continues unceasing until one or both manage to fall asleep. On waking, most sufferers sadly find themselves once again in possession of a 'normal' hangover: headache, upset stomach, generally wishing they were dead, etc., ad infinitum. But Jinx and Chastity still had a good few hours of glee ahead of them yet.

'Look,' hissed Chastity in Jinx's ear as the two of them leaned over to the left to peer at where Daisy was sitting, a few rows in front and to the side of them, 'she's pretending to be all casual about it, but check out how white her knuckles have gone clenching the front of that pew.'

'Puke indeed,' giggled Jinx, deliberately mishearing and flicking a deeply satisfying V sign at Daisy when she turned round to glare self-importantly in the general direction of the muffled noise they were making. 'I'd like to blow chunks all over her. And maybe,' she continued with a most undignified snort, 'I'll do just that when we get out of here. My tummy feels like it needs a good old clean-out.'

'To be fair,' Chastity whispered back, 'you could probably easily do it if you just got a whiff of her death breath. In fact, you could probably do it right here right now just *thinking* about it.'

Jinx wrinkled her nose in disgust but had no chance to respond, for Mrs Bennett chose that very second to loudly announce, 'And our penultimate head girl, for the lower sixth form and for the second term in a row, is Daisy Finnegan.'

Daisy stood up and smirked around the room as her appointment was acknowledged by the sound of some

53

very forced and feeble clapping. In fact, if you want to know what the sound of one hand clapping is like, then what greeted this news wasn't far off.

Daisy smoothed a lock of lank ginger hair from where it had escaped the straggly ponytail she usually wore high on her head before sitting back down, the infuriatingly smug expression still plastered across her greasy face.

'Who is *that*,' Irina asked Jinx, leaning over to whisper in her ear from the row behind. 'We've never seen her before. Is she in our year?'

'Yep,' muttered Jinx, who had no idea which one of the sisters was addressing her. She was keeping a beady eye on the teachers, lined up in diagonal rows either side of Mrs Bennett, who were beginning to crane their necks and shoot pointed glances in their general direction. 'Worst luck she is. We'll fill you in later.'

'*Quod denique.*' Mrs Bennett permitted herself a small titter at the vast sea of faces staring blankly back at her – she just loved to throw Latin words and phrases into ordinary conversation. 'Or, for those of you who haven't been paying quite as much attention to your homework as you should, and finally –'

'Get on with it, for fuck's sake!' whispered Liv to Charlie, who tittered nervously as she noticed Miss Strimmer and Miss Golly, Stagmount's much-hated sports teachers, turning the twin laser beams of their furious eyes towards her.

'I would like to welcome two new members of staff to our Stagmount family,' finished Mrs Bennett, to an immediate chorus of ooos and ahs from the intrigued girls.

These sounds of delight, it must be pointed out, were solely based on the slim-to-none rank outside chance that one of the new teachers would be a fanciable man.

'Replacing Mrs Dickinson in the French department,' Mrs Bennett said, to a chorus of loud cheers and whoops from the girls that reflected how happy they were that the Dick, as she was universally known, could torment them no longer with her hateful pop quizzes, 'is Mr Benjamin Christie. Can you stand up please, Mr Christie, and give the girls a wave so they know who you are?'

A small, shy figure sitting at the very back of the staff rows to Mrs Bennett's right half stood, half crouched and raised a hand to his forehead before sitting straight back down again.

'Now, come *on*, Mr Christie.' Mrs Bennett, who was big on personal presentation and maintaining at least an aura of self-confidence at all times, was beginning to rather regret having left this appointment to the bursar while she was away on holiday over Christmas. 'Do stand up properly. I don't imagine most of them have any idea what you look like!'

Mr Christie stood up and waved timidly around the room. About five foot seven, with mouse-coloured hair and thick tortoiseshell glasses, he was wearing a brown cord jacket with worn leather patches on the elbows over a cream shirt and faded blue trousers. The expression of pure, unadulterated terror on his face told all those watching him that he found standing in front of this crowd absolutely excruciatingly. The more enterprising and evil-minded girls among them immediately wondered how he would cope in a classroom.

'Poor bugger,' whispered Chastity dismissively to Jinx. 'Do you think he has any clue how his life is about to take an inevitable turn for the worse?'

'God knows,' said Jinx. 'And where's the other one? To be honest, I didn't notice any new faces up there this morning. Although it's not like that poor bastard's particularly memorable and –'

Mrs Bennett coughed. She was finding it hard to summon up any feeling of confidence in Mr Christie's ability to do anything, let alone teach some of this lot. She loved her girls, but she also knew exactly what many of them were capable of if not kept in line by a very firm – metaphorical, naturally, for Mrs B was nothing if not an incredibly civilised woman – hand. She would be prepared to bet a million pounds that this one had come cheap. God above, she thought with a jolt of realisation, this was probably his first job. She would need to have a serious, once-and-for-all chat with the bloody bursar. Obviously it was his job to keep an eye on finances, but at this rate his enthusiasm for saving money would wreck the school if she wasn't careful. His attitude towards the well-being of Stagmount was becoming positively cavalier!

'And last but not least,' Mrs Bennett said, sending a silent prayer heavenwards that this was indeed the case, 'I would like to introduce Mr Dirk Hanson, Stagmount's first ever football and cricket teacher. Where are you, Mr Hanson?'

Mrs B didn't need to look around for long. Within seconds an impressively stacked man of thirty or so was racing from the back of the hall to the front, a streak of lime green in a heavily branded Adidas tracksuit with white stripes down each leg. The girls were too busy staring in wonder at him to say anything, and Mrs Bennett stood stock still behind her lectern, staring just as hard.

At the very last moment before he reached the stage, just when it looked as if he was going to crash into it, Mr Dirk Hanson threw himself into the air and executed a perfect backflip. He jack-knifed in mid-air before landing on his hands next to a very shocked headmistress. He flick-flacked himself into a normal standing position and, as he did so, every single person in the room got an eyeful of the exact outline of his cock and balls through the thin fabric of his trousers.

'Fucking hell,' guffawed Jinx, whose jaw was nearly on the floor. 'Did you see that? I think he did it on purpose. He is hilarious!'

'Don't you mean did I see *those*?' replied Chastity, laughing just as hard. 'He looks like a total prick, but imagine the *fun* we're going to have with him.'

'Where do we sign up?' agreed Liv. 'I don't think spring term has ever looked this promising before.'

'Hello, girls,' drawled Mr Hanson, smoothing his gelled hair back into place, smug in his belief that he was cutting something of a dash up there on stage in front of all these little ladies, his tracksuit perfectly complementing his St Tropez tanned face and torso. 'I'd prefer to be called Coach – if, of course, that is agreeable to you, Mrs Bennett.' Then, without waiting for an answer, he flashed the headmistress his most blinding smile. 'Coach D. Hanson.'

Although Mrs Bennett was seething inside, she regained her outer poise remarkably quickly. 'Well, if that's what you are used to then that is what the girls must call you. Coach D. Hanson, everybody,' she said, sounding for all the world as if she was introducing a new act at a cabaret night. 'I'm sure you will find lists of his various training sessions on the sports board. That's it. Here's to a great term. School dismissed!'

The entire school filed out of the room in Mrs Bennett's wake but at a much slower pace, and with about a trillion decibels more noise as they avidly discussed the newcomers. Most of the speculation admittedly revolved around the football coach, but many of the girls had lived in fear of the Dick's detention list, so the fact that such an obvious wimp was taking her place did not go unnoticed either.

'I have never,' said Olga to her sisters as they traipsed towards the door, followed by a dark-suited Igor, 'seen anything like him in my life.'

'I know,' said Masha with a giggle, waving as they passed a few girls from the upper sixth before they caught up with their new classmates. 'It is most odd, but I have suddenly acquired a strong desire to learn to play cricket and football.'

'Me too,' smirked Charlie. 'It's funny that. Come on, dudettes. Let's hit the notice boards before they get swamped!'

— ✳ —

Stagmount's corridor, which had the dubious claim to fame of being the longest in any building in England, was filled to bursting point with girls of all shapes, sizes, ages and hairstyles clustered around the sports area of the notice boards. Seeing the glamorous group from the lower sixth make their approach, a gaggle of younger girls instantly melted away from the team lists and training schedules they had been busily rifling through and stood respectfully aside.

The girls giggled as they noticed that some wag had already crossed out the coach's name at the top of the list and written 'DIRK DIGGLER' in thick black marker pen in its place. The three pay phones opposite all had long lines of junior girls waiting impatiently to speak to their parents and beg them to sign the permission slips needed for any extra lessons in the lower school.

For social anthropologists interested in the many and varied dominance hierarchies of teenage girls, this corridor could provide most of the answers they were looking for. In general girls who didn't like their own year group ignored them, while mixing between the years just wasn't done. In the corridor, however, you never knew who you were going to come across next.

To the casual observer, the mud-stained brown carpet

and newly painted pale lemon walls marked nothing more unusual than a walkway to maths. To the girls, though, the corridor was the site on which feuds and promises were hung, drawn and quartered before being squeezed dry of every last shred of gossip. It was used by all years at all times and was thus an emotional hotbed of jealousies, hatreds, admiration and crushes.

Crushes were always, *always* directed from younger girls to older ones. Queen bees of all ages and their cliques reigned supreme and side by side, but were careful never to tread on the toes of anyone older than them. Protocol simply insisted upon it.

A first year, for example, would rather walk on hot coals than have to pass a big group of sixth formers, who would be far too wrapped up in their own concerns to even notice the junior's passing. The junior, conversely, would think of 'the encounter' – as it invariably became in her mind – for weeks. So it was that Jinx and the rest paid no attention to the younger girls, who had all removed themselves to a respectful distance as the lower sixth made a beeline for the training lists.

Jinx and the rest – although maybe not the triplets, come to think about it – had been in awe of the sixth formers when they'd been in the lower school and it was simply part of the natural order that the lower years should now be in awe of them. This unquestioning adoration was helped by the fact that, as soon as they reached the sixth form, girls were exempted from wearing the school's dreary uniform. The more fashionable of them had even earned a slavish following among a group of third years who actually kept notes on who wore what when. The Russians, Liberty and Chastity all featured in this list, but the rest of them wore their Juicy tracksuits and Ugg boots too often to be counted. Needless to say, and hilarious as they would have found it, none of them had any idea of the list's existence.

True to form, the lower sixth hardly even registered the younger girls' existence as they shrieked and laughed and clutched each other while reminiscing about their new football teacher's antics that morning in assembly. He'd only been at the school for about five minutes but was already approaching mythical status.

'Bloody hell,' snorted Liv with sarcastically exaggerated disbelief as she eyed the A4 pages lining the cork board. 'Look at this. Not one of Coach D. Hanson's junior training sessions has a single space left in it.'

'God,' Jinx replied, looking over the same lists with a knowing smirk. 'It's amazing what a quick flash can do for Stagmountians' sporting ambitions.'

'All the little ones will be growing crushes on that terrible man as fast as you can say "prick",' agreed Chastity, not noticing the large number of red faces this remark caused among the girls still waiting for them to finish with the board.

'We are signing, aren't we?' asked Irina, confused.

'Of *course* we're signing, um, love,' Jinx said, having privately decided last night that she was never going to refer to the triplets by name again. She patted the one she thought was Masha on the shoulder. 'None of us is going to miss getting down and dirky for anything.

Ooo,' she said suddenly to Chastity, who was writing her name at the top of the sixth-form list with a flourish, 'make sure you put Lib down too. She'll kill us if we forget her!'

All signed up and still sniggering at the memory of Coach D. Hanson's acrobatics show, the girls linked arms and trailed off in the direction of classroom 4B, where they had to meet their tutor, the eccentric Mrs Carpenter, to get their timetables for the term.

'Hey,' Liv said as they pushed open the door, 'do you think he'd been practising all night? We should call him Coach V. Handsome from now on. He obviously fancies himself enough.'

Roaring with laughter, the girls settled into their usual seats. Chastity and Jinx sat next to each other in the very centre of the back row, leaving the seat on Jinx's right-hand side free for Liberty to claim when she got back. Liv sat next to Chastity and Charlie sat on the other side of Liberty, closest to the big picture window that looked out over the playing fields and towards the sea. The five of them had shared every back row opportunity they could for the last three and a half years and had no intention of changing anything just because they were in the sixth form.

Fiona Cooper, a geeky-looking girl who had been in Friedan House with Chastity before their entire year moved to Tanner House at the beginning of the Christmas term, was sitting on top of Liberty's empty desk, swinging her legs and catching up on holiday gossip with the others when Mrs C wafted into the room in an overpowering cloud of Bulgari perfume. She was clutching a mug of ultra-strong coffee and dressed in one of her customary all-black and very stylish outfits, accessorised with various items of chunky silver jewellery. She beamed around the room as she swung herself into her ergonomic chair and shuffled a bunch of papers on her desk.

'Well, girls,' she said, leaning forward conspiratorially and smiling around the room – a sure sign to her class that she remained as gloriously indiscreet as ever – 'I'm sure I hardly need to ask what you thought of *that* little display.'

'Oh, don't worry, Mrs C,' Liv called out. 'We're all signed up and ready to learn the offside rule, or whatever it's called. We'll keep you posted, for sure.'

'Excellent work, Olivia,' replied Mrs C, using the exact same tone of voice she would have employed if Liv had just turned in a perfectly written composition or scored straight As in a series of tests. She was clearly in one of her extremely good moods. 'Please make sure that you do. Now then,' she said, before taking a great gulp of coffee and looking round the room again, more purposefully this time, 'am I right in understanding that we have three new friends joining us this term?'

Irina, Olga and Masha waved prettily at Mrs C from where they were sitting in a huddle underneath the window. She stood up to welcome them before suddenly spotting Igor, who was being his usual intractable self and sitting silently in the middle of the empty row behind them.

'Oh,' she murmured, patting her hair and sitting back

down rather suddenly. 'Hello.'

The barest ghost of a smile seemed to flicker about Igor's mouth before disappearing entirely.

'I don't believe it,' hissed Jinx at Chastity. 'Look at her! She fancies him! What the bloody hell is going on round here? Is there something in the water, do you reckon?'

'This,' replied Chastity, an expression of sheer delight etched across her face, 'is going to be a very interesting term indeed. What with one thing and another, I reckon we're in for a bit of a roller-coaster ride.'

– ✳ –

Jinx, Chastity, Liv and Charlie sat clustered around the end of one of the long tables in the lower school dining room, where the whole school rushed at half past ten every morning to gorge themselves on hot drinks and biscuits to ward off hunger pangs in the notoriously tricky hours between break and lunch. Heads bent close together and brows furrowed with concentration, they were poring over the timetables Mrs Carpenter had handed out in a rush at the end of tutor group meeting and stuffing themselves with biscuits from a loaded plate in the middle of their space.

Jinx was on her fifth cup of tea and ninth ginger nut – although none of them was counting – when Liv screamed, jumped on to her chair and started doing a war dance.

'Fucking hell, Liv,' grumbled Chastity, who had sloshed a load of tea over the front of her Smythson diary, which was covered in the softest leather in the palest pink. 'I *wish* you wouldn't make these sudden movements.'

'I don't believe it!' Liv yelled, completely ignoring Chastity and waving her timetable above her head, making such a spectacle of herself that the attention of every single person in the crowded dining room was absolutely riveted on her. 'I just don't believe it!'

'What?' said Jinx, giggling at both Chastity's extremely cross expression and Liv's mad dancing. 'What don't you believe?'

'Have none of you retards,' said Liv, clambering down and giving the finger to one of the assistant housemistresses who had been foolish enough to glare and shake her head at Liv while she'd been dancing on her chair, 'spotted the glimmering sign of freedom we've *all* been given this term?'

'O M fucking G,' screamed Charlie, excitedly banging a fist on the table as she enunciated each syllable and offering up her other hand to Liv for the obligatory high five they always shared when they had good news. 'I've just spotted it. I can't believe it either!'

'Shit,' said Jinx, jabbing her finger at the timetable in front of her after avidly looking around at all the others. 'We've all got Tuesday afternoons totally free!'

'Lib too?' Charlie asked anxiously from the opposite side of the table, craning her neck as she tried to read the two sheets spread out in front of Jinx upside down and smirking happily when she saw it was true. 'Shit! We really are going to have the best term ever.'

'Yep,' Jinx crowed, 'we've *all* got it. From twelve o'clock every single week until the end of term. First one's tomorrow. What are we going to do —'

Jinx couldn't finish her question because someone had come up silently behind her and covered her eyes with their hands in the 'guess who?' gesture the girls used whenever they managed to sneak up on each other unawares.

Jinx inhaled. Breathing in the familiar smell of Acqua di Parma perfume mingled with top notes of tobacco, Juicy Fruit, leather and denim, she felt like crying with happiness as she turned round and enveloped a gorgeously olive-tanned Liberty in the most almighty bear hug.

'You little witch,' Jinx said, smiling widely as she released her best friend before quickly appraising her with a one-second once-over, 'are those Miu Miu shoes?'

'Yep,' replied Liberty, a definite smug twinkle in her eye as she pointed the toe of one stunning raw-silk shoe in beautiful burnt orange with a golden wedge heel in front of her and waved her foot about. 'They're well nice, innit! And what are we going to do about what?'

She collapsed on to the empty seat next to where Jinx had been sitting, grabbed Jinx's hand and squeezed it really hard.

'I can't tell you how happy I am to be here,' she said, not-so-surreptitiously wiping a tear from the corner of her eye with her free hand. 'I've missed you guys so much and I couldn't stand not knowing whether I'd be back this term or not.'

'Tell me about it,' Jinx agreed, shaking her head in relief at the sight of Liberty sitting next to her like this, pulling her close in another massive hug and speaking softly into her ear. 'I couldn't believe it when Mum told me I'd missed you on the phone. I refused to go anywhere for days in case you managed to call, so I couldn't believe it when that was the one bloody time.'

'I know,' said Liberty. 'Your mum said you'd been really upset. I was worried about you, Jin. Did you have good hols?'

'No,' Jinx replied with a shake of her head. 'I was a total wreck for most of the time. The last week wasn't too bad, but I want to hear about you – I've been *dying* to know. What happened when you left here? What's going on with your dad? How is it living with your mum and what the hell were you doing spending New Year's Eve in a hippie commune?'

'Bloody hell,' whistled Chastity. 'That's a lot of questions.'

'Christ, Jinx,' said Liv, laughing, 'we've only got ten minutes before the end of break! Why don't we talk about all of that later and fill Lib in on what she's missed so far this term?'

'OK, OK,' Jinx agreed before waving Liberty's timetable dramatically in front of her face. 'First things first. Check this out, Lib.'

Liberty studied the sheet, a slow smile of realisation spreading over her face.

'Have you seen it?' yelled Chastity, bouncing up and

67

down in her seat, so excited she couldn't contain herself a single second longer. 'We've all got them! All of us have got the same free periods every Tuesday from twelve o'clock onwards!'

At this outburst all five girls jumped on to their chairs, linked hands across the table and danced up and down, screaming the whole time with exuberant and very loud over-excitement.

Mrs Frick, an assistant housemistress at Steinem House and the earlier recipient of Liv's middle finger, shook her head in disgust at this childish display but decided against going over to remonstrate with them. She didn't fancy being ridiculed in front of her young charges, most of whom were staring admiringly at the lower sixth, clearly highly impressed by such frankly devilish behaviour.

'Miss, Miss,' said Katie Green, an unattractively chubby new girl in the second year with big vacant eyes and a permanently wistful expression on her rather stupid-looking face, as she tugged on Mrs Frick's sleeve. 'Did you look after any of those girls in Steinem?'

'No, Katie,' snapped Mrs Frick. 'Thankfully I did not. And I am not "Miss". My name is Mrs Frick.'

'Sorry, Miss,' replied Katie, gazing longingly after the lower sixth as they danced and skipped their way through the wide swing doors of the lower school dining room to get to their favourite double art lesson. 'I didn't know. At my old school we called all the teachers Miss.'

'Well,' said Mrs Frick crisply, furious with herself for

not daring to say anything to Liv, 'at Stagmount we don't.'

— * —

'Come on then, Lib,' Jinx said as the two of them lay snuggled together under the duvet of her single bed at ten o'clock that evening after they'd chilled out in the common room with the others since supper, talking about nothing much and watching MTV. 'You've got to tell me. What the hell happened with your dad when you left here?'

'Well,' said Liberty, giving a small, sad giggle, 'I watched a hell of a lot of episodes of *The Antiques Road Show*.'

'Whaaat?' squealed Jinx. 'Trust you, Liberty Latiffe, to get through the possible loss of your personal and political freedoms by watching a load of grinners wittering on about their shitty old bits of furniture.'

'What's a grinner?' asked Liberty, sitting up and reaching for the bottle of Evian she always took out the fridge just before bedtime. 'Is that what the contestants are called?'

'No, it's a general term for an old person,' Jinx replied, grinning with delight. 'It's great, isn't it? George came up with it on Christmas Day when Granny came round. He said old people always seem to be grinning, so he calls them grinners. I love it.'

'I love it too,' Liberty said, giggling happily this time as she tucked herself back under the covers before wrapping a warm arm around Jinx. 'And I love *you* even more. Honestly, Jinx, I don't know what I would have done with myself if Dad had stuck to his original plan. I seriously don't think I could have stood to live in Riyadh for the rest of my life. It's a fucking hellhole and I hated every second of it.'

'Oh, sweetheart. So where did *The Antiques* freaking *Road Show* come into it then?' asked Jinx, determined to get the full story before they went to sleep. 'Damn it, Watson, I want details!'

'Watson?' said Liberty, scratching her head, obviously confused by this unexpected reference. 'What do you mean?'

'You know,' sighed Jinx, exasperated, 'Sherlock Holmes's sidekick. Anyway, don't stop. I've waited *months* – well, OK, it was only one, but it certainly seems like more than that – to hear this story!'

'OK, OK. Give me a bloody chance,' Liberty said, stretching her arms above her head as if about to engage in a serious sporting activity.

'Sorry, darling. You're right,' said Jinx instantly, snuggling down further under the duvet in preparation for a big bout of listening. 'Hit me with it and I promise not to interrupt again.'

'OK. So when we flew out of here in that fucking helicopter,' Liberty carried on in the small voice she always used when she was sad, 'he turned to me and said that we were flying straight home to Riyadh and that he would never be speaking to me again.'

'What about your passport?' Jinx asked, forgetting her earlier promise to keep quiet in her bid to get the whole gory story in one swoop. 'How could you have gotten there without it?'

'He can do anything he wants.' Liberty sniffed disdainfully. 'He probably asked one of his fucking mates in the government to sort it out for him. Anyway, the point is he flew me straight back there and didn't say one word to me throughout the entire flight, the car journey the other end and for the first two weeks of the holidays.'

'Oh, my *God*,' said Jinx, shocked even though she knew of old the type of emotional blackmail and bullying Amir Latiffe was capable of. 'I can't believe it, you poor angel.'

'My bitch of a stepmother totally ignored me too,' Liberty continued, 'not that I gave two shits about her. Although, to be fair, having me around again was probably her worst freaking nightmare as well. The only person I had any human contact with was Maia, one of the cleaners. She gave me lots of hugs and snuck me in the odd packet of fags when she could. She even managed to get me a couple of Western magazines from God knows where. If Dad had found out she'd have lost her job for sure, so I'll be eternally grateful to her. In fact, the night before I left for Mum's I gave her $200 – it was all I had on me but she seemed well pleased with it.'

'Shit!' Jinx said, gripping Liberty even tighter. 'I can't even begin to imagine how terrified you must have been, stuck all on your own out there with no one to talk to and no idea what was going to happen next.'

'Yeah, it wasn't pleasant,' replied Liberty in the

world's biggest understatement, 'not at all. Anyway, I'd kind of resigned myself to the fact that I'd be trapped in Riyadh for the foreseeable future, but what I couldn't resign myself to was the fact that I had no way of contacting you – or anyone, even Mum. He took my mobile as soon as we got to the airport, disconnected my computer and all the phones near my rooms. He's also got one of those machines that record every call ever made, so he'd have known if I'd used one of his. I was *desperate* to talk to you, but I didn't want to piss him off any more than he was already, so I decided the best thing to do was sit tight and wait his mood out.'

'I can't even begin to imagine it,' Jinx said, wiping a furious tear from the path it was wending down her cheek. 'I mean, I obviously knew how cross he was and I had a fair idea he'd be making your life a misery as punishment, but I had no clue just how bad it was for you.'

'It was completely horrendous,' agreed Liberty, privately thinking that right now there was no place on earth she would rather be than lying in this small single bed with her best friend in the world at her beloved boarding school, 'and that's when I became addicted to that bloody antiques programme.'

'Jeepers,' whistled Jinx, nudging her. 'Things *must* have been bad.'

'It was the only thing I could find on TV that reminded me of home,' Liberty said, laughing. 'I watched it for hours every day, crying my eyes out. It seemed so funny and stupid and inconsequential, but I loved it. All those gormless punters incapable of mustering up any greater enthusiasm than a slight pucker of the lips or the faintest glimmer of a frown at the news that their terrible painting or sideboard or whatever piece they'd lugged miles from home was worth thousands more than they paid for it made me feel safe somehow.'

'Well,' said Jinx, privately thinking that Liberty must have been on the brink of a major mental meltdown and also wondering where she had learned the word 'inconsequential', 'I'm just glad it offered you some comfort. So what happened to make your dad change his mind?'

'It was terrible right up until the day before I called and spoke to your mum,' continued Liberty, 'then everything went kind of mad.'

'What happened?' Jinx prompted again gently. 'What made him change his mind and send you to your mum's?'

'You know,' mused Liberty thoughtfully, 'I've asked myself that question so often and I still don't really have a clue. The only thing that makes any sense at all is maybe my stepmother was so pissed off at having me mooching around the place all depressed that she insisted he send me away. I don't know. All I *do* know for sure is that one evening Dad bursts into my room and very tersely tells me to pack my stuff up as I'm going to live with Mum. Tomorrow. And in freaking Washington, DC, of all places.'

'Bloody hell!' said Jinx, who was properly shocked by

73

all of this. 'I'm surprised you're so normal still, Lib. I'd have gone stark raving mad by this point!'

'Yes, well,' Liberty replied, 'since I wanted to get the hell out of there as fast as possible in case he changed his mind or something, going mad wasn't really an option.'

'I suppose not,' murmured Jinx, thinking that Liberty had kind of changed. Not in any really obvious ways, but she seemed a hell of a lot more mature and sure of herself than she had been last term. And, especially given the fact she'd obviously spent most of the holidays crying and watching crappy TV, Jinx couldn't help but notice that her vocabulary had definitely improved. She'd used loads of words she never normally did since she'd arrived back.

'So the next thing I know is I'm on a plane out of there,' Liberty continued, 'and I still hadn't spoken to anyone about anything so I didn't know for sure what to expect, but Mum was waiting at the airport to meet me.'

'Phew,' whistled Jinx, 'I bet you were glad as hell to see her.'

'I was,' Liberty agreed. 'The whole thing was pretty emotional, as you can imagine. She'd had no idea what had been going on. She just got a phone call that morning telling her what flight I'd be on and to make sure she was there to pick me up. Which she was. So then she drove me back to her place in Georgetown, where she's living with her new husband, Chris. He's a politician and quite quiet, but he's a really nice guy and obviously 'madly in love with Mum.'

'What's it like out there?' asked Jinx, thinking that this was one of the maddest stories she'd ever heard. 'Have they got a nice place?'

'Yeah, it's beautiful,' Liberty said, smiling in the dark as she thought about it. 'A gorgeous colonial town house near the university. I'll dig out some photographs for you tomorrow – you'll totally love it.'

'So then you went off to California for New Year?' asked Jinx. 'What was that all about? Mum said the two of you had gone to some sort of hippie commune.'

'Well,' Liberty said, laughing, 'it was more like a spa, but there were loads of weird beards there. Mobiles were banned – not that I had mine anyway, since Dad never gave it back – and there was no Internet. They had poetry readings and jazz nights and it's supposed to be the most "relaxed" place in the world. It was cool, you know, hanging out with Mum, catching up on everything and generally sorting out my head, but I'm so pleased to finally be back here. For most of the hols I honestly thought I'd never see you again.'

'So are you going to live with your mum permanently now?' Jinx asked, still reeling somewhat from all this crazy information and trying to take everything in. 'I can't even *tell* you how happy I am it's all worked out like this. Honestly, Lib, I don't know what I would have done with myself or how I would have coped if you'd been made to stay in Saudi.'

'Tell me about it,' said Liberty. 'I've been having the exact same thoughts – but in reverse, obviously. Anyway, that's pretty much the long and short of it. Did you ever hear anything about what happened to Stella?'

'No,' Jinx said shortly, 'and I don't care either. I never want to see that bitch again in my life. She nearly ruined yours and I'll never forgive her for it. The less we talk about her the better as far as I'm concerned.'

'You're right,' Liberty agreed solemnly. 'I can't believe I fell for all that shit and I can't *believe* what she did to me. You'll be pleased to know I've made a solemn vow to myself that I'll never be sucked in like that again.'

'I know you won't,' said Jinx, yawning widely and switching off the lamp on her bedside table, 'and don't worry – neither will I. It was like torture not being able to pick up the phone and speak to you whenever I wanted, and I never want that to happen again.'

'No,' Liberty agreed, before poking Jinx in the ribs and grinning at her. 'And all I want us to do this term is hang out, relax and have *fun*. I've had enough excitement to last me a lifetime.'

'Me too,' replied Jinx, followed swiftly by a monster yawn, 'and don't worry – nothing ever happens in the spring term.'

'You're exhausted,' said Liberty, 'and so am I. Let's hit the hay and talk more in the morning.'

'You're right,' Jinx agreed. 'I am tired. Those triplets had us hitting it hard last night. You must be knackered too, what with all your travelling of late. Goodnight, darling. Sleep tight.'

'You too,' whispered Liberty, 'you too.'

Settled and happy, Jinx and Liberty both fell asleep

thinking that everything was finally back as it should be.

– ✳ –

'Paul!' Chastity screamed, leaning precariously out of the taxi window that she, Jinx and Liberty had taken from Stagmount to Brighton's seafront. She waved manically at her boyfriend of sixth months. 'Over here!'

'Fucking hell,' Liberty muttered in an undertone to Jinx as Chastity threw open the cab's back door and propelled herself into a stream of heavy, fast-moving traffic with no thought for either her personal safety or the taxi driver's mental stability and launched herself on to Paul, who was standing at the entrance to the pier holding a bunch of roses. 'Did you see that? Nice to know she's still bloody crazy.'

The three of them had dashed out of their English lesson with Dr Brown about the Romantic Poets, the last of the day for them every Tuesday now, and quickly decided to make the absolute most of their first free weekday afternoon ever.

Liv and Charlie had insisted they must attend to some mysterious business in town but had promised to join the others for dinner later. It didn't take long for Jinx, Liberty and Chastity to decide to get stoned on the beach, visit the Sea Life Centre – great with a few reefers inside you – and then generally mince about the small funky shops in Brighton's Lanes before they went for a curry. It was, without a doubt, going to be a perfect day.

'Thanks, Jinx,' Paul said, using the inside of his parka

jacket to shield his face from the strong wind blowing straight off the sea as he relit the rather damp spliff the four of them were sharing as they sat on the beach under the shelter of a stone breaker. 'This is strong stuff!'

'I know,' Jinx said, sighing happily and digging a hole in the pebbles in front of her using her heels. 'It's great, isn't it?'

'Sure is,' replied Chastity, inhaling deeply before passing the joint to Liberty. 'I'm pretty stoned already. Are we going to the aquarium? Or should we go shopping instead?'

'It's too cold for shopping,' exclaimed Jinx, sitting up straight. 'Come on, guys. We haven't been to the aquarium for *ages* – you promised!'

'Yeah,' Liberty said with a smile, knowing how much Jinx loved it, 'we did promise. Come on, you two. You know how she loves the sharks. We can go shopping later.'

'And have dinner?' said Paul, looking anxiously round at the girls. 'Please promise me you're not going to make me starve all day.'

'Paul,' Chastity said, hugging him tightly and smiling round at the others, 'have you *met* us? We live to eat, remember? Of course we're going to feed you!'

'Yep,' agreed Jinx, 'and I would also like to remind you of the rather excellent selection of cakes, sweets and crisps that the Sea Life café serves to its discerning clientele.'

'Come on then,' said Liberty, picking up her tan Mulberry Bayswater handbag and wrapping her stunning green, pink, gold and purple striped Missoni scarf tightly around her neck before she hauled Jinx to her feet. 'If we don't go soon this one will spontaneously combust.'

'Shit!' Jinx exclaimed suddenly as two guys wearing thick black wetsuits and carrying surf boards under their arms dashed past them before launching themselves into the darkly raging sea and paddling furiously. 'What with all the excitement since we got back to school I *still* haven't told you bitches about my New Year's Eve!'

'I knew there was something I was supposed to remind you about,' said Chastity, pulling Paul back down on to the stones and another ready-rolled spliff out of her pocket. 'Spill!'

By the time Jinx had finished telling her friends every detail about Jamie and her unscheduled flying leap down Tarquin's grand staircase into his arms, all three of them were staring at her, mouths agape. Even Paul had been hanging on to her every word.

'So this Jamie then,' he said, looking – if this was possible – even more pleased by Jinx's revelations than the girls did, 'he surfs, does he?'

'Yep,' said Jinx proudly with a toss of her head, delighted at the unprecedented opportunities for showing off this story was giving her. 'He's practically a pro.'

'And he's in a band as well?' Liberty asked wistfully. 'A proper band?'

'Yes,' Jinx said, not *quite* so sure of herself this time, but still feeling smug as hell. Anyway, she was *sure* George had said something about the two of them being in a band at university. 'He plays guitar.'

'Wow,' said Chastity, who was grinning delightedly. 'Well, we all thought he was great when we met him last term and we can't wait to get to know him properly!'

'Totally,' Paul agreed. 'Much as I love hanging out with you girls, it would be nice to have at least one other guy here too. He sounds great. When can we all get together?'

'He is great,' Jinx agreed, feeling slightly panicked at the realisation that her friends seemed to think the two of them were a done deal though they were clearly anything but, 'and I really, *really* fancy him, but he's my brother's friend. I can't just go round inviting him to things . . . can I?'

'Of course you can,' said Chastity, making a massive snorting noise. 'If you don't ever see him how the hell are you supposed to get him to ask you out?'

'She's right,' Liberty instantly agreed. 'You've got to get him to come out with all of us one night.'

'I can't!' squealed Jinx. 'I'm too embarrassed. What the hell would I *say*?'

'Oh, for fuck's sake, Jinx,' Chastity said crossly. 'Stop being such a wimp. How do you think I would ever have got it together with Paul if I hadn't sent him that note?'

'Wasn't it an anonymous letter, Chas?' asked Liberty, giggling and digging Jinx in the ribs at the same time. 'Correct me if I'm *wrong*, but I seem to recall it was Paul who asked *you* out and you confessed to the letter a month or so later.'

'Whatever,' snapped Chastity, glaring at Paul to let him know that should he even be thinking of saying a word to prove her wrong he would regret it. 'My point is that if she doesn't say anything then he'll totally forget her and probably start going out with someone else. Jamie *is* gorgeous after all.'

'Thanks a fucking bunch,' Jinx muttered, throwing a pebble towards the sea with great force and taking a deep toke on the last of their spliff. 'I feel really, you know, buoyed up and confident about the whole thing now. Some friends you lot are.'

'Come on, Jinx,' Liberty wheedled. 'We're only trying to help. You are the best, prettiest, cleverest, most charming and funny friend I've ever had and if he doesn't jump at the chance to hang out with you then the guy's obviously a total retard and not worth any of your bother, OK?'

'Thanks, angel,' said Jinx, putting an arm around Liberty's shoulders and squeezing her tight. 'You're right – I know you are. I just feel really, like, totally *squeamish* about calling him up out of the blue. But you guys are right. I'm going to do it.'

'Thank fuck for that,' said Chastity, standing up determinedly and hauling Paul to his feet at the same time. 'Finally she comes to her senses! It's about to start blowing a serious gale out here and I for one would prefer to be inside when it does so. Are we going to the Sea Life Centre now or are we not?'

Pleasantly stoned, the four of them linked arms and

headed back towards the pier and the aquarium's entrance. Their heads were bowed and Jinx, who was on the outside of the row closest to the sea, cupped her right hand over her ear and wished she was wearing a hat as they walked directly into the fierce wind that had picked up massively even during the forty or so minutes they'd spent sitting chatting in the shelter of the breaker.

'Bloody hell,' Liberty said, rubbing her gloved hands together as they stood in front of a brightly lit tank filled with multicoloured fish and a backdrop of stunning coral. 'I want to go back to California. My hands are still absolutely frozen.'

'Come on, guys,' Jinx said, eyeing the arrows on the floor in front of them. 'Can't we go straight through to the sharks?'

'No!' Chastity replied. 'We're going to do it in order first and then you can do whatever you like. Christ, it's like being with an unruly child.'

They all laughed. Only once in the first year had they made the mistake of visiting the aquarium on a weekend. The place had been absolutely overrun with screaming, red-faced brats and their harassed, wrecked-looking parents. Jinx and Liberty had, in all honesty for once, been planning to spend that Saturday afternoon finishing off their summer art projects when a particularly hateful child, his entire outfit plucked straight from the pages of the Boden catalogue, made a grab for Jinx's extra-large tube of burnt sienna. He had smiled beatifically, staring them straight in the eye, before callously, cruelly holding the fat tube above his head and laughing as he squeezed it all over their easels, covering the sheets of paper they'd tacked carefully in place with Jackson Pollock-style streaks of shit-brown paint and completely ruining their beautifully rendered starfishes.

His mother had smiled the dazed smile of the permanently post-natally depressed as she grabbed little Lucifer's hand and led him away. Jinx and Liberty had been too shocked to speak at the time. Their explanations fell on deaf ears when they got back to school and they were given Ds in art. None of them had been back during bank, public or school holidays since and would no more consider going outside of term hours than they would reading *The Economist* if given a choice between that and the new *Heat*.

The Brighton Sea Life Centre had been a huge draw for Stagmountians since it opened in 1872. Designed by the celebrated pier architect Eugenius Birch, it was an instant, fashionable success and within a few years was extended to include a roof terrace garden and music conservatory. Stagmount's teachers had, interestingly, always remained cheeringly blind to any possible high jinx that a visit to the aquarium might engender. On the contrary, for more than a century they had positively shoved the girls out of the door and down to the seafront, never seeming to stop and think that an afternoon spent gazing at a sea lion or an octopus could possibly be a ruse to cover up other, less desirous activities. To the girls these days, the Sea Life Centre represented the gateway to the rest of the town and the many and varied pleasures that Brighton had to offer; to the staff it was a living museum and therefore wholly above reproach.

Jinx and Liberty sat on a bench set at the back of a dark alcove in the empty building, staring into a black tank in front of them. The light from inside the tank, caused only by the purple-tinged fluorescent jelly fish it contained, was illuminating the girls with a ghostly pallor as they shared a packet of cheese and onion crisps and a Diet Coke, purchased from the stoners' paradise vending machines strategically positioned exactly halfway round the course as shown on the floor plan.

'Shit, Lib,' said Jinx with a stoned giggle and through a crunchy mouthful of crisps that seemed determined to stay anywhere but inside her mouth,' this is like a lava lamp but a zillion times better.'

'You're totally grossing me out,' Liberty said, also giggling as she brushed tiny bits of crisp from the sleeve of her charcoal-grey cashmere zip-up and reached for the Coke. 'Try not speaking with your mouth full next time, Slater. Where have the lovers got to?'

'I don't know,' said Jinx with a smirk as they both craned their necks, trying to spy out Chastity and Paul from whichever nook or cranny they were no doubt vigorously exploring, 'but I bet they're perfectly happy wherever they are.'

'I bet. Now then, Missy,' Liberty said, turning to Jinx and giving her the full benefit of her big, black-rimmed, liquid eyes as she gazed at her friend's face,

84

'what's all this about Jamie then? How come you didn't say anything before? I think the whole thing is totally brilliant and I'm just dying to hear all the details – spill, Slater!'

'OK, OK,' Jinx said, ducking as she pretended to shield her face from an invisible bank of imaginary paparazzi photographers. 'Let me have a drink and I'll talk.'

Liberty passed the remains of the can to Jinx, who grimaced as she swallowed and felt the remaining few flat and warm millilitres of backwash running down her throat.

'I didn't say anything *before*,' she said, 'because they wasn't really a "before", was there? You arrived yesterday and we kind of did all your stuff last night, so I guess this is our first opportunity.'

'You're right,' agreed Liberty. 'It's been pretty freaking hectic already and I for one am looking forward to a far more relaxed term than the last one. I'm so pleased about our free Tuesdays too. Even though here we are and all, I still can't quite believe it.'

'Me too,' Jinx said, sighing happily as she aimed the empty can towards the bin to their left, 'and don't worry. The only thing I'm in the market for this term is fun, and lots of it. And it's most definitely the more the merrier as far as I'm concerned!'

'You BITCH!' screamed Liberty when Jinx finished her speech and pinched the underside of Liberty's upper arm through her cardigan. 'What the hell did you do *that* for?'

'Sorry,' Jinx said with a shrug and a wink. 'I thought

you said you needed help believing in our timetable. I was just helping out. And I can't stand it any more – please can we go through to the shark pool? *Please?*'

Strolling through the gloomy tunnels lit by the lights of the various tanks and pools, following the white painted arrows leading visitors ever towards the exit, Jinx's attention was caught by a brightly lit tank containing a whirling spectacle of beautiful brightly coloured species from Australia's Great Barrier Reef. She dragged Liberty over to have a closer look.

'Look at that one!' she said, pointing at the information board at the side. 'It's called the Dogfaced Puffer. Remind you of anyone?'

'Mrs Gunn!' Liberty cried without pausing for thought. 'Look at the jowls on it!'

The puffy-faced fish swimming at the back of the tank bore such an uncanny resemblance to the pair's vile former housemistress, Mrs Gunn, that the girls had to hang on to each other to stop collapsing in a hailstorm of giggles.

'What about him?' Jinx asked, pointing at an incredibly grumpy-looking specimen. 'What's his name?'

'"The Dusky Flathead,"' intoned Liberty, using a faux-serious newsreader's voice as she studied the notes, '"is a well-camouflaged bottom dwelling predator that feeds on smaller fish."'

'My God,' Jinx cried, 'it's Stella in fish form – same personality traits and everything. I knew I didn't like the look of it!'

'Eww,' said Liberty with a shudder, pointing towards

the back of the tank, where the ugliest fish they'd seen yet was crouched underneath a rock, shooting baleful looks all round the tank, 'what the hell is that?'

'It's called the Weeping Toad Fish,' Jinx said with a smirk, 'and I give you exactly ten seconds to liken it to someone we know.'

'Daisy Finnegan,' Liberty screamed, 'it's got to be!'

'Got it in one, sister,' replied Jinx, offering the palm of one hand for Liberty to high-five, 'got it in one.'

Standing in front of the 'Touch but Don't Move' pool, Jinx and Liberty were egging each other on to see who could stick their finger deeper inside a black frilled sea anemone. They still had no idea where Chastity and Paul were but their attention was instantly diverted from their friends' whereabouts when a couple of baby sharks, each about thirty centimetres long, were brought in by one of the keepers and sloshed into an empty salt-water pool alongside the one they'd been casually leaning over.

After expertly eyeing up the attendant, a long-haired boy of about eighteen who was deeply in thrall to Guns N' Roses on his iPod at that moment, absolutely unaware of any visitors to his section as he played lead guitar on stage with his heroes in his head, Jinx nudged Liberty and nodded meaningfully at the sharks.

Liberty's eyes grew wide as she looked and she started digging around in the bottom of her massively over-stuffed Mulberry Bayswater handbag, trying to locate the digital camera she took everywhere with her. Jinx and Liberty loved nothing more than compromising photographs of themselves and each other in the midst of their various escapades and would go to great lengths to get what they always – and only half jokingly – referred to as 'the perfect shot'. A real live shark would be one of their finest coups yet, a definite contender for the prized slot in the middle of the shelf above Caroline Slater's Aga.

Clutching their bags, they stealthily crept across to the shallow shark tank, one eye on the totally transfixed heavy metal fan, who was so deep into his fantastical daydream he probably wouldn't notice if a troupe of leprechauns wandered in and started line-dancing.

Liberty readied herself with the camera as Jinx leaned forward and took aim, her hands hovering a few centimetres above the long back of one of the leathery-looking sharks. She turned to Liberty and winked to signal that she should get the camera ready to roll. Then she lowered her hands and felt them close around the shark's surprisingly sandpapery skin. She gripped it tight and prepared to yank it out of the water and hold it next to her face for a second while Liberty recorded the event for posterity.

As Jinx twisted her body round to face the camera a lump of weed fell from where she had casually left it in the unzipped inner pocket of her own oversized bag. It fell straight into the water. Struck dumb at the horror of losing most of her stash in one fell swoop like this, Jinx watched it drift below the surface as if in slow motion. Thanks to this hesitation, she was way too slow in releasing her shark and attempting to fish the green lump out of the water. She'd barely started her rescue mission before the second shark awoke from its apparent stupor, swam lazily towards the skunk, eyed it reflectively and then swallowed it whole.

'Fuck!' hissed Jinx, staring aghast at Liberty, 'That's pretty much all the weed I stole from George before I came back to school. What are we going to do for the next couple of weeks?'

Whatever suggestions Liberty might have been about to make were lost to the sharks as a scantily clad Chastity, clutching her shirt close to her chest and carrying her coat and jumper in the other hand came dashing round the corner and headed straight for the exit without so much as a by your leave. Jinx and Liberty barely had time to look at each other before Paul skidded round the same corner. One leg in and one leg out of his jeans, he was obviously also in a terrible rush and hardly looked at his friends as he flew past them.

'What the –' said Jinx to Liberty as they gazed openmouthed after their friends.

The arrival of a clearly highly agitated and rather portly security guard not so much hot on their heels as rather a cool distance behind, reduced her to silence again.

'Where'd they go?' he yelled, red in the face and shaking his fist. 'I'll get 'em this time, mark my words! What if any kiddies had walked past, eh? I won't stand for it! Bloody disgusting it is!'

'Oh, my God,' whispered Liberty, ushering Jinx as fast

after the three-man race as was possible without being unseemly. 'Quick, let's go and see what happens.'

— * —

'I can't believe it,' said Jinx, laughing so hard she had to put down her fork. 'I just *wish* you'd been arrested – imagine having to call Mr Morris to pick you up from the clink!'

A fresh wave of laughter coursed around the square table the four of them were sat at in the window of the Lal Quilla, one of their favourite restaurants along Brighton's seafront. Liv and Charlie had never turned up, claiming 'unfinished business', and had said they'd see the others back at Tanner. Since they'd sat down half an hour ago, Chastity's face had alternated between the colour of the pink carnations in the white vase in the middle of the table to deeper than the rich red cloth which covered it. It was currently a pretty steady fire-engine red.

'*You* can't believe it?' Chastity remarked incredulously. 'Trust me, *I'm* the one that can't bloody believe it.'

'And me,' said Paul, with feeling.

'Yes, well,' Chastity continued, tying her hair in an even tighter ponytail, as if to cleanse her mind of the nasty thoughts that were obviously tormenting her, 'it wasn't you, Paul, who was tapped on the back by a fucking security guard while you were happily giving your boyfriend a blowjob by the crocodile pool, was it?'

'No, you're right, Chas,' muttered Paul, 'but it was me

90

he shouted "fucking paedophile" at when I still had my pants around my ankles and just when those two old ladies were walking through.'

'Whatever,' Chastity sniped, tossing her ponytail behind her head and determinedly picking up her knife and fork as she flashed furious blue eyes at him. 'I've never been so embarrassed in my life.'

Paul smiled indulgently at his girlfriend and reached for her hand under the table. As he smiled into her eyes, stroked her hand and whispered that he loved her, Jinx and Liberty clutched each other and made such loud gagging noises that the waiters swooped on them, desperate to find out what was wrong with their meal.

Panic over and waiters reassured, they didn't speak to each other for the next ten minutes as each one shovelled in as much delicious Indian food as possible. They'd had the munchies so bad when they arrived that they'd gone even crazier with their ordering than usual, and these girls weren't known for holding back. So far they had ploughed their way through assorted poppadoms, chutneys and pickles, chicken korma, pilau rice, garlic naan breads, sag paneer, sag aloo and tandoori king prawns. They were currently finishing off a 'reserve' course of lamb tikka, loving every mouthful and wondering whether ice-cream sundaes would be a step too far.

'Great day, guys,' said Jinx as they finished signing their credit card receipts and started looking round for their coats, 'the best. And special thanks to Chas and Paul for providing the entertainment.'

'I know,' Liberty said slyly, 'dinner *and* a show – who'd have thought we'd be this lucky!'

'Shut up, you stoner cretins,' squealed Chastity, shoving Jinx in the back and propelling her at great speed through the door and out on to the street. 'It's high time you two got boyfriends of your own and stopped laughing at mine.'

'Stoner cretin?' said a deep and sexy voice in Jinx's ear as her inevitable flight across the street was broken and stopped by a pair of strong arms that encircled her waist from behind. 'Surely that girl can't be talking about you, Jinx Slater?'

Jinx could not believe her ears. She couldn't, simply couldn't, countenance the fact that the best thing that had happened to her in her life to date was happening – and without any warning whatsoever, just like the last time in fact – again.

'Jamie?' she whispered, feeling like swooning all over the place but managing to hold it together as she turned round, making a conscious effort to do so as deliberately and sexily as she could. 'You are the absolute last person I expected to see! What the hell are you doing here?'

Jinx focused her attention on Jamie and was delighted to see he was looking as hot as ever in faded, low-slung Evisu jeans, a navy-blue T-shirt emblazoned with a dragon picked out in silver and gold threads and the same Onitsuka Tiger trainers he'd been wearing on New Year's Eve.

She pulled herself together and, feeling doubly pleased that she'd made an effort with her make-up and worn her nicest grey skinny Sass & Bide jeans with her leopard-print slip-on shoes and favourite black polo neck, shot him a wide smile. Studying his gorgeous face, she realised he was amused about something or other. Oh, God! He must think she was an absolute crazy. Why, oh why, couldn't she just bump into him in a nightclub or a bar or when she was doing something normal?

Using the tiniest corner of her eye to check him out, Jinx realised he was desperately trying not to laugh. She decided she'd better pull herself together and so gave him what she considered her most mature questioning glance. Not that she wanted to rush their encounter in the slightest – she'd have been happy to stand and stare at him all day – but she felt it was important to keep up at least the pretence of conversational momentum.

'I live here; remember?' he said in response to Jinx's quizzical look, his grin so cheeky and inviting it almost stopped her heart right there in its tracks. He gestured along the street in the direction of Stagmount. 'That's my block. You've been to a couple of my house parties, right?'

'Right,' she murmured, 'right. Of course I have. That one last term was great, by the way.'

'Hey, mate!' Paul jumped in, saving Jinx from whatever terrible banality might occur to her next and offering his hand to Jamie. 'I'm Paul, Chastity's boyfriend and general friend to this lot of reprobates. I picked Chas up from your place last term – it looked like it was kicking off in there.'

'Hi, Paul,' Jamie said with a friendly grin, clasping Paul's hand in his and patting him on the shoulder before turning his gaze on a beaming Chastity. 'Of course I remember you – and I've met you a few times, haven't I, Chastity?'

'You sure have,' Chastity replied, slightly too skittishly for Jinx's liking – she had one bloody boyfriend already, for Christ's sake! – 'and it's lovely to see you again. You should come out with us next time, shouldn't he, Paul?'

Ignoring the furious looks Jinx was shooting at Chastity and a frantically nodding Paul, Liberty couldn't stop herself from jumping in feet first as well.

'Jamie,' she said, giving him a bigger hug than Jinx thought appropriate in the circumstances, 'it's *great* to see you! Chastity's totally right, we should definitely arrange a big night out.'

'That,' said Jamie, turning to Jinx and wrapping a warm arm casually around her shoulders, 'sounds like a great idea. I'll organise it with this stoner cretin I've got here, shall I?'

'Perfect,' snapped Liberty, beaming at him and winking at Jinx. 'Make sure that you do.'

'Liberty!' Jinx hissed in her ear. 'Bloody cool it, will you? I don't want him thinking I'm some kind of stalking psycho.'

'So,' continued Liberty breezily, completely ignoring Jinx, 'were you off home when Jinx threw herself at you?'

'*Liberty!*' Jinx hissed again, but to no avail.

'I was out checking on my car actually,' Jamie replied,

94

hooking his thumbs into the belt hooks at the front of his jeans and rocking slightly as he stood there in what was – according to Jinx anyway – an almost *maddeningly* sexy fashion. 'My housemate Daz borrowed it yesterday and I haven't checked it out yet. I thought I should see if it still had four wheels, an engine, windows – you know, the usual stuff.'

'Tell me about it,' agreed Paul, shooting an amused glance at Chastity, who was learning to drive and kept insisting he take her out and about so she could practice. 'I've been worried about mine lately.'

'Hey,' Jamie said, jangling the bunch of keys in his pocket, 'were you guys on your way back to Stagmount?'

'Yep,' said Jinx, staring up at him through her lowered lashes. 'We were just about to find a cab.'

'Well, in that case,' Jamie said, ostensibly speaking to the group but with all his attention focused on Jinx, who was holding her breath and had suddenly gone very still, 'why don't I drive you? I should take it for a quick spin anyway and check that Daz hasn't done any lasting damage.'

'Thanks,' Jinx said delightedly, 'we'd love it, wouldn't we, girls?'

'That's really kind of you, mate,' said Paul, who always made a point of delivering Chastity and her friends direct to their door before heading home himself, 'and it means I can get straight off from here.'

While Paul and Chastity snogged each other's faces practically *off* on the pavement, not giving a damn for the sensibilities of anyone who might be walking past, and made totally unnecessary baby noises as they said their goodbyes, Jamie strode off down the road to pick up his motor.

Liberty let out a low whistle as she and Jinx clutched each other and stared appraisingly after his exceedingly pleasant rear view.

'Bloody hell, Jinx,' she said, digging her blushing best friend in the ribs and cackling madly, 'that boy is *hot*! No wonder your face is currently changing colour even faster than Chastity's was earlier.'

'He is hot, isn't he,' Jinx replied dreamily, 'and don't you think he's just so, like, goddamned *nice* as well?'

'Of course,' Liberty assured her. 'I always think it's super-sexy when boys make a real effort to be nice to a girl's pals too.'

Jinx blushed as she thought about it. Liberty was totally right – the way Jamie had taken such an interest in her friends was beyond sexy. The fact that he obviously wanted to make a good impression on *them* made her feel like he was really interested in *her*.

'And he was great with Paul,' Liberty said, nudging Jinx and jolting her out of her reverie. 'I really like him.'

'Jinx the minx!' yelled Chastity, running over to join the two of them after Paul had jumped on his bus and blown her a kiss from the open door. 'I am seriously impressed. He's gorgeous and obviously mad about you.'

'Do you really think?' asked Jinx, blushing again and beginning to wonder if her cheeks would ever return to their normal pale peachy colour. 'Isn't he just being friendly cos of George and stuff?'

'Shut up, Slater,' Liberty and Chastity yelled in unison.

'Your problem,' Chastity continued, pointing at Jinx with a very fierce expression on her face, 'is that you don't take yourself seriously enough. If you want him you can get him, of course you can, but you've got to make a bloody effort. Put – ha! – your back into it, girl.'

Whatever Jinx might have had to say about this was lost to the increasingly fierce wind blowing off the sea as Jamie pulled up alongside them in a mud-splattered old black BMW estate, George Michael's *Faith* blaring out the speakers.

'I fucking love this song,' said Liberty, yanking open the passenger side front door and shoving Jinx on to the tan leather seat before slamming it shut and jumping in the back, pulling Chastity after her. 'Nice car, dude!'

The four of them accompanied George at top volume all the way along the seafront. Jamie's car smelt pleasantly of dogs and salt, no doubt from all the time he spent hanging ten; the boot was stuffed to the brim with wetsuits and a huge breast-shaped pot of surf wax lay by Jinx's feet. She picked it up and giggled as she read the top. It was called Mrs Palmer's Mighty Mound and claimed to have smaller, harder nipples to guarantee satisfaction. Jinx shivered deliciously but imperceptibly. Jamie had swept a great pile of CDs, yellowing newspapers and magazines on to the floor to give the girls space to sit down and the general ambience was very relaxed.

The song ended just as Stagmount came into view, looming above the cliffs. Even though myriad lights were twinkling through the gloomy sky, it had a very austere look. In summer, the stone seems to absorb the sun and visitors professed astonishment at the huge Gothic building's warm beauty, but in winter they invariably likened it to a prison. Today was so wet and miserable it was very much the latter. The weather made such a difference that the bursar – always with one beady eye on the endless, expensive repairs the building required – had decreed that prospective parents should be shown round only during the sunnier months.

'I've always wanted to come up here,' Jamie said with a sideways smile at Jinx and using his rear-view mirror to wink at the girls in the back at the same time, 'but I never quite got round to it. I thought I'd be lynched for sure if I got caught. Infiltrating Stagmount is in most of my pals' top ten fantasy events.'

'You're not alone,' said Chastity with a giggle, leaning forwards and resting her arms on the back of Jinx's headrest. 'Paul's friends all say the same thing. And the headmistress once told me that during the Second World War, when they had to hand the place over to the army, there was a sign up in all the dorms that said, "If you need a mistress in the night ring this bell." According to her, that bell had never seen so much action in its life.'

'Did she say that?' asked Jamie, surprised. 'That's not quite the language I imagined the headmistress of England's most exclusive school for girls would use. I guess she's keen to move with the times, huh?'

'Well,' said Chastity, 'she probably didn't use those *exact* words, but you know what I mean.'

'Chas just loves to paraphrase,' said Jinx, emitting a most unladylike snort and immediately wishing she hadn't, given the present company she was currently trying to impress. 'She never lets the truth ruin a good story.'

'So,' Jamie said, turning to Jinx and resting a hand lightly on her thigh as they waited at the traffic lights by the marina, 'if I find myself in need of a mistress in the night what bell do I press?'

Jinx squirmed in her seat as he locked eyes with her. She was stunned by the intensity of the shockwaves of pure, unadulterated lust that immediately began coursing through her body and, once again, found herself frozen to the back of her seat, bereft of speech. This whole losing-the-ability-to-talk thing was becoming pretty freaking tiresome pretty freaking rapidly. She made a quick mental note to get a bloody handle on herself ASAP.

'You ring Jinx of course,' said Liberty, realising Jinx wasn't about to say anything of any note any time soon and jumping in to help her out. 'She loves nothing more than a good old chinwag in the middle of the night.'

Jinx, Chastity and Liberty all laughed. Jinx loved her sleep and was notoriously fierce with anyone who dared to phone at what she considered an unreasonable hour. She always intended to put her phone on silent before she went to bed, but rarely managed to get round to it as she usually fell asleep as soon as her head hit the pillow. At that moment, though, she decided it would never be switched to silent again. She also knew that in the unlikely event she was ever woken up by Jamie, she'd be the exact opposite of cross about it. Rude maybe, she thought with a delicious shudder, but certainly not cross.

What did make her cross was when the lights went green and Jamie had to take his hand off her leg to change gear. She sank back in her seat and surreptitiously studied his profile as he drove. God, he was a good driver – fast, but totally in control. There was something incredibly sexy about being tightly buckled in next to a great-looking guy who took his corners fast but never made you feel unsafe. And his tunes were pretty fantastic too. Out of ten, Jinx decided, a small smirk spreading across her face, she would give him eleven.

When Jamie pulled an expert handbrake turn and swerved into the space next to Mr Morris's outside Tanner House Liberty barely had time to say goodbye to him before Chastity grabbed her by the hand and pulled her out the car quick smart. Yelling something decidedly shady and improbable over her shoulder about homework, she dragged her through the front door and straight into Jinx's bedroom, where the two of them would sit on the bed giggling while they waited for Jinx's return and the most almighty post-mortem.

'So,' said Jinx brightly, picking up her handbag and turning to Jamie, 'thanks *so* much for the lift. I really appreciate it and so do those ungrateful bitches.'

Jamie laughed and turned off the engine. 'Allow me,' he said, jumping out of the car and strolling round to her side before opening the door with a flourish.

'Thanks,' said Jinx, yet another – Christ, this was becoming bloody relentless – massive blush staining her cheeks. She was convinced it was an unsightly purple colour but it was, in fact, a very pleasant pale strawberry. 'You *are* kind!'

He didn't step aside to let her pass, so she stood rather awkwardly in front of him and wondered if he was going to kiss her. She was too focused on the highly distracting combination of praying the answer to her silent question was yes and admiring the gorgeous stubble that graced his strong, tanned jaw with flecks of gold below his generous, widely smiling mouth to notice that her fingers were crossed so tightly they were beginning to hurt.

Jamie threw an arm around her shoulders and drew her in close to him in a hug that was anything but friendly as far as Jinx was concerned. She leaned her head briefly against his chest and breathed in that wondrous smell. It brought back such intense memories of New Year's Eve and all her subsequent daydreams about him that she felt her knees might actually give way at any second. Jinx clenched them together – she was determined to get a grip and not start gibbering like an idiot at him again. No way. From now on Jinx Slater was going to be in control.

'Hey,' he said, his voice decidedly lower than it had

been in the car, 'I'm really glad you ran into me, Slater. And your friends are great. We'll definitely arrange that night out.'

He let go of her, leaned forward and dropped the tiniest, lightest and most sexy kiss Jinx had ever had right on her lips.

The lust that Jinx had experienced in the car was instantly bested by the most animal feeling she had ever had. It was so unlike anything she'd known before that, when she was telling Liberty about it later on, she swore she'd actually seen stars. Now she had no time to say anything before Jamie bent forward and did it again. Jinx found it hard to believe that such feather-light kisses on the lips – so light she might have sworn they never even *happened* were it not for the white-hot laser beams of lust that shot through her body – could physically affect her in the same way as if she'd been punched hard in the stomach. When he tugged gently on the curly strands of hair sticking out of her short ponytail, she really felt winded. It threw her into such a spin that she had no time to react before Jamie flung open his door, settled himself back behind the wheel, started the engine and reversed out of the space.

Jinx stood on the curved stone path outside Tanner House's front door and watched Jamie razz it off down the drive towards Brighton with his flat, throbbing, unidentifiable music once again pumping out of the half-open windows. Her stomach was churning in the most disturbing way and – if she'd been able to use her brain at all – she would have understood the true meaning of 'dazed' for the first time in her life. Fuck, he was *amazing*.

And *fuck*! What with all the excitement she realised she'd forgotten to give him her phone number. Well, fuck it, she decided, unaccountably finding it impossibly hard to think unless her thoughts involved a particular expletive of a carnal nature, if he wanted to speak to her it would be pretty freaking easy for him to get hold of her. The ball was most definitely in his court and, Jinx mused happily, that was no bad thing.

She floated through the door on cloud nine. Completely unaware of the few girls lounging about reading magazines in the reception area, she was also unwittingly observed by a grinning Mr Morris – accompanied by his ever-present canine companion, skinny Myrtle, as per – who was on his way outside to lock up for the night. He had, of course, seen it all before in his ten years in charge of the lower sixth and Tanner House. Sighing nostalgically as he recalled his own first girlfriend and how passionately he'd loved her, he hoped Jinx would make the most of it. In his experience, more often than not these teenage romances ended in tears. But on the other hand, he reflected happily, they sure as hell were fun while they lasted.

Apart from a big row involving some juniors who'd been caught trying to drill a hole through the wall of the sports hall shower room in order to spy on Coach Dirk Hanson while he lathered himself right next door to them after a hard morning's training, the next couple of weeks Stagmount served up were pretty standard spring-term fare.

Daisy Finnegan had been as annoying as hell and as ever. She'd taken to stomping about the place in her stupid Garfield slippers, cleverly accessorised with a greasy ginger ponytail and death breath, constantly trying to enforce the pettiest, most boring rules – to no great avail, it has to be said. The girls called any encounter with Daisy 'being fingered' and delighted in winding her up as much as possible. However, Jinx, who was normally the ringleader in these situations, was so busy thinking about Jamie that she barely responded when Daisy told her off for smoking in front of the first years, and merely nodded dreamily when she was 'fingered' for forgetting to supervise an entire week of second-year preps and told she'd have to do two weeks next term to make up for it.

The triplets were as friendly as ever when the girls saw them in class, but they kept mostly to themselves in the evenings now and rarely ventured into the common room for the nightly televisual diet of soaps, MTV and *America's Next Top Model* that the rest of them followed so rigidly throughout term time. It seemed – shock horror – that Mrs Bennett's little chat with the sisters at the beginning of term about Stagmount's values and what they were going to do with their lives after school might actually have done the trick in getting them to at least try and pass a few A levels before they left.

Igor still tramped his customary five steps behind the

triplets, as inscrutable as ever. The girls had become so used to his shadow-like presence that they hardly noticed him any more, although they *did* notice Mrs Carpenter continually trying to catch his eye in their tutor group sessions. They found it especially hilarious when she turned up one morning wearing a shocking-pink pashmina over her customary all-black outfit in an obvious bid to get his attention. She also hadn't exhibited any of her usual 'bipolar' mood swings to the dark side. In fact, she'd been nothing but sweetness and light since the first day of term. The girls weren't complaining – indeed, they were very grateful to Igor, for when Mrs C got into one of her sudden evil-incarnate moods no one wanted to be within range. They were convinced she was madly in love, and Mimi Tate and Chloe Thompson were running a book on how long it would take the odd couple to get it on.

Furthermore, it had rained cats and dogs on the day the lower sixth were supposed to have had their first football session with Coach Very Handsome. That one had been cancelled due to the inclement weather and since it had started snowing heavily at the weekend the girls of the lower sixth had still not been able to witness Dirk – as most of the school now referred to him – in action.

Chastity and Liberty had not stopped talking to Jinx, and anyone else within earshot, about how amazing Jamie was. Charlie – who had mysteriously sprained her wrist the other day, only minutes after she recovered from a badly twisted ankle, but seemed strangely reluctant to give the others any details – and Liv were also pestering her daily that they be allowed to meet him too. Jinx was playing it cool, but inside she was both delighted and smug as hell that the guy she was obsessing about had been such a huge hit with her friends. And although she hadn't quite descended from cloud nine just yet, she *was* beginning to wonder if Jamie would ever call to arrange the night out they'd all talked about when he'd dropped them back at school the evening after the aquarium visit.

'Jinx is not with it at all,' Liberty complained to Chastity one night as the two of them trudged back to Tanner House from the old reference library, heads lowered against a driving wind that seemed determined to blow them off their feet. 'I can totally see why, though.'

'Me too,' sighed Chastity in agreement. 'That guy is hot. Like total! I just wish he'd crack on with it and bloody well ask her out. Then she might return to the land of the living.'

Jinx was blissfully unaware of any of these conversations taking place as she lay on her bed for hours at a time, staring at the ceiling. Her eyes were usually open but she saw nothing in front of her as thoughts of Jamie played in a constant loop in her mind and Smiths records played non-stop in her CD player.

She'd never experienced an all-consuming crush like this one before and it hit her hard. Her eyes practically rolled round in the back of her head as she replayed the car-park scene over and over in her mind, occasionally adding in a few new scenes of her own just for fun. In fact, she so often found those tiny kisses and that lightest tug on her hair accosting her mind at unexpected moments that the whole business was beginning to get just a bit impractical. How the hell was she supposed to conjugate French verbs for Mr Christie – who was an absolute wimp, as predicted, although an absolute angel from heaven compared to his predecessor, the Dick – or talk intelligently about the importance of the growth of a poet's mind with special reference to Wordsworth's *The Prelude* if she never knew when to expect the return of the memory of the most physical experience she'd ever had and the inevitable blanking of whatever it was she happened to be doing at the time?

Of course, it must be said that when she was in her room alone at night she positively encouraged these same thoughts, coaxing them out of the box in her head where she attempted to stash them during the day. She practically swooned as she lay in bed, reliving every moment in glorious Technicolor. Liv had slipped her a few buds of skunk weed on the sly to replace the stash that had met its untimely end in the shark pool and Jinx had taken to stuffing a towel up against the small crack between her door and the floor, flinging her window wide open and lighting up. She would smoke furiously, listening to records and thinking filthy, delicious thoughts. She often came round from her various daydreams to take a sip of the glass of wine she kept constantly by her bed these days and found herself actually squirming with the sheer intensity of all that was going on in her mind.

Jinx was now sitting in the library, supposedly poring over the English essay she was writing – 'Is *The Winter's Tale* a tragic comedy or a comic tragedy?' Funnily enough, she couldn't quite manage to work herself into a sweat about it even though it was due in, like, yesterday. Distractedly, she chewed her pen. Although pretty much every girl in the school had begun praying for snow as soon as the weather reports suggested it might happen, she was rapidly getting well bored of snowball fights, slushy pavements, wet clothes and being cold. No matter how many scarves she twisted round her neck, she'd been freezing for days and had resolutely decided that you can *definitely* have too much of a good thing. She had also discovered a hole in the bottom of her favourite old Ugg boots that the cobbler in town had sworn blind he was unable to mend, despite the sign above his door which read 'Miracle worker. NO job too challenging!' It was too wet and cold to spend much time outside, she'd wasted pretty much her whole free afternoon yesterday trying to get her bloody Uggs fixed and she was beginning to feel ever so slightly ratty and claustrophobic. The teachers banged on relentlessly about their big exams next term and the girls had been set such a correspondingly huge amount of homework that, since their trip to the aquarium, none of them had managed to escape into Brighton either.

So, most of the school was mincing about in the corridor on Wednesday after lunch. The girls were mostly hanging around in small groups, flicking each other dirty looks and generally looking bored and cross, when the ear-splittingly loud peals of the fire alarm sounded, jump-starting everyone into instant action.

Joyous at the thought of anything remotely exciting happening – even a fire; hey, *especially* a fire – the whole school rushed outside as one, squealing and elbowing their way through the double-height double doors that were made of the strongest oak, had come from a castle in France and were reputedly at least three hundred years old. Once outside, they quickly started milling about in the courtyard in front of the main entrance, shrieking at the tops of their voices in the mistaken belief that they could compete with the din the alarms were making. They pushed and shoved each other into very ramshackle lines and generally behaved absolutely contrary to the strict health and safety rules and codes of conduct the school had in place for such an event.

'Olivia Taylor,' said Daisy Finnegan, closing in on Jinx's little group with a determinedly self-important look etched on to her ugly face, 'no one would ever guess you were in the lower sixth, carrying on like that and making a spectacle of yourself.'

'What the –' Liv looked round in shock from where she had Charlie in a headlock and was attempting to throw her over her shoulder into the flowerbed in front of Mrs Bennett's big office window. 'Oh, it's you.'

Turning back round when she saw who was addressing her, Liv completely ignored Daisy, who was still bleating inanely about something or other. What had started out as a definite play fight between Liv and Charlie was rapidly becoming a real-life brawl, each trying to prove she was stronger than the other.

'Oi!' Jinx yelled when she realised what Daisy was talking about, grabbing Liv's arm and yanking her away from Charlie. 'What the fuck's going on? Cut it out!'

'Yeah,' agreed Liberty, who had wrapped her Missoni scarf so many times around her neck it looked like she didn't have one. She pulled on her black leather Chanel gloves as she gave the pair of them a disbelieving look. 'It's, like, totally not cool to be rolling around in the fucking shrubbery in front of the whole school.'

'Thank you, Liberty,' sniffed Daisy, in the mistaken belief that Liberty had intervened to help her out. 'It's nice to see that at least some of us at Stagmount have manners.'

'Fuck off, Daisy,' Liberty replied immediately. 'Why don't you go and pick on some of the lower school? *We're* not interested.'

Katie Green, who had been loitering nearby throughout the skirmish, was thrilled to witness her favourite senior school girls in such exciting action at such close quarters. So she was less than impressed when Daisy – trying to save what little face she had left – turned on her and, in no uncertain terms, told her to hurry up and join her form for the mandatory roll call that took place following a fire alarm. Katie was even more flustered when she heard the others giggling at Daisy's no-nonsense tone.

She was too dimwitted and self-obsessed to realise that the girls she was so enamoured of were not laughing at *her* but at Daisy. She suddenly felt a deep hatred for the head girl of the lower sixth, who had dared embarrass her like this in front of her heroines. She didn't care how much older than herself Daisy was; she, Katie Green, resolved there and then to make Daisy Finnegan pay.

Finally, and certainly not quickly enough for Mrs Bennett's liking, the entire school was split into the six houses the girls lived in. Despite having always studied together, the sixth form had been divided into four alphabetical groups among the four main-school houses for their first three years at Stagmount and this was only the second term they'd all spent sleeping under the same roof in Tanner House.

Each of the junior-school houses was named after a famous feminist. Jinx, Liberty and the dreaded Daisy had lived in Wollstonecraft under Mrs Gunn's oppressive totalitarian regime – somewhat paradoxically, they'd always remarked, given the great Mary's arguments against the subjugation of women. Then there were Pankhurst, where Chastity had been kept in line by her housemistress Hammerhead, of whom she was actually still very fond; Steinem, where all the sporty red-stocking girls – so named because of their bright red hockey socks – plus Liv and Charlie had lived, and which had won practically every single house match in the history of the school; and Friedan, where Fiona had lived, and which was considered 'creative' – not that *she* was.

At the start of their final year, the upper sixth moved en masse yet again, this time into Sea House. Built in the early seventies, it was a low white building enjoying uninterrupted views across the pitches to the ocean beyond, hence the name. It was under the very relaxed charge of Dr Brown, Stagmount's most senior English teacher, and the oldest girls kept very much to themselves there. The closer they got to university, the official thinking went, the more independence they should be entrusted with. This explains how the upper sixth – and their parents, who were still forking out vast fees – were conned into cooking all their food on site for themselves and keeping their own rooms clean. What more than compensated for this, however, was the fact that they were allowed to keep their cars at school and – best of all, according to the girls, most of whom spent hours in the lower school dreaming of what awaited them in their final year – were subject to a very basic curfew that required them to be at Stagmount only during their timetabled lessons.

After taking what seemed – to their headmistress, anyway – a further age to arrange themselves in lines depending on form within their houses, the entire Stagmount student body finally stood in the main school quad in front of Mrs Bennett.

Frequently checking her watch, Mrs B looked around for the bursar, who never seemed to be there when she needed him. After making a superhuman effort to drown out the clanging bells she was sure were going to leave her with a bad case of tinnitus, she dimly registered that this had been very much the case of late where the bloody man was concerned. As she stood at the top of the steps that led towards the drive and the front door, she pulled the jacket of her Jaeger suit tighter around her, impatiently tapped her foot and made a mental note to have it out with him at the earliest opportunity.

'Girls!' she yelled, waving her arms above her head, trying hard but failing dismally to divert her school's attention away from the ear-splitting cacophony and towards her. 'GIRLS!'

'Look,' sniggered Charlie to Liv, their earlier brawl in the herbaceous border totally forgotten. 'Poor old Mrs B's having worse than shit luck today.'

'I know,' Liv replied, snapping her gum impressively loudly as she used the toe of one of her tan leather Frye boots to gouge a hole in the wet grass beneath her feet, 'but freaking freezing as it is, I for one am delighted to be outside, whatever the cause. We've been cooped up like rats in a science experiment for almost two weeks – no outings into Brighton, no games, no fresh bloody air even! No nothing!'

'And,' Charlie said, fixing Liv with a meaningful look, '*we* need to get out and bloody practise!'

'Well really, girls. I am *very* disappointed in all of you.' Mrs Bennett's voice floated vaguely over the girls in front of her, but hardly anyone was paying attention anyway.

'Whatever,' Jinx remarked cheerily with a sideways wink at Liberty, 'I'm sure she'll get over it.'

'Yeah,' Liberty snapped back, 'eventually.'

Katie Green was standing mutely behind them, in the next line across, but the two lower sixth formers had no idea they were being closely watched.

'Girls!' Daisy Finnegan tapped them simultaneously on the shoulder in a bid to make them be quiet, behaving and sounding exactly like one of the freaking teachers. 'You are setting *such* a bad example to the lower school!'

'Piss off, Daisy,' said Jinx, nudging Liberty in the ribs and giggling. 'You can hardly talk!'

'Yes,' Liberty said, right on cue, 'your very personal approach to personal hygiene is much more dangerous to susceptible young minds than anything we might do. What if everyone in the third year suddenly stopped taking baths?'

'Yeah, or stopped shaving their –'

Whichever part of Daisy's anatomy Jinx might have insulted next was lost to the wind as most girls rushed forwards out of their lines, the momentum of the stampede irresistibly dragging these three along with them. They found themselves propelled to just in front of an apoplectic Mrs Bennett, where they joined the crowd in craning their necks to gawp at a very bedraggled figure rushing piteously along the drive towards the quad from the direction of the sports hall.

'Look! It's Dirk!' yelled Liv across the crowd to Jinx, jumping up and down and waving her arms above her head to attract the attention of her friend, whose curly blonde hair she'd spotted bobbing about in the midst of a particularly excitable group a few scrums along. 'Watch him go! Run, Dirk, RUN!'

What with all the excitement, it took everyone a

moment or two to notice that the fire alarm had come to an abrupt stop, leaving an eerie, echoing silence in its wake. The girls were filled with expectation, while Mrs Bennett seethed in almost palpable fury.

Dirk seemed unaware of the tension as he advanced, ever more slowly, towards the stone steps where Mrs Bennett was standing. He shuddered to a stop and collapsed right in front of her feet. It was only then that the girls saw the livid red stain that was rapidly spreading over his white expanse of his Aertex-covered back.

Mrs Bennett's grim face turned a chalky grey colour as she leaned forward and surveyed the crumpled figure lying before her. The girls had been stunned into a shocked silence. The only noise for a couple of awe-filled seconds was that of the rain beating down against the wax proofing of the jackets worn by a sensible few. Two things then happened simultaneously. Dirk raised his head, moaning piteously, and, as he did so, a celery stick fell from his collar to the ground, where it bounced half-heartedly before coming to rest on the drive near his outstretched, trainer-clad foot.

As a few surprised guffaws escaped the girls, the bursar dashed through the door and skidded to a halt beside Mrs Bennett, whose jaw was so low by this point that they could see all the way to her tonsils. Puce in the face and sweating profusely, even in the cold rain, the bursar stared wildly around as if in a daze before dashing down the steps and dragging Dirk to a sitting position using the collar of his shirt for leverage.

Everyone was too busy staring at what was taking

place on the front steps to notice the inscrutable Igor slipping through a side door that led to the basement below Steinem House. He looked around surreptitiously, smoothed his hair down and nonchalantly strolled to the back of what had been the Tanner House line but now resembled the crush in front of the main stage at Glastonbury.

Everyone, that is, except Katie Green, whose solid bulk had allowed her to resist being swept forwards alongside her classmates in the stampede. She watched with interest as Igor checked his mobile phone and smiled slightly before assuming his typical bodyguard stance of slightly parted straight legs finished off with a direct stare and sharply folded arms. She *knew* it was of note, but she just wasn't sure why. Never mind, she thought to herself smugly as she stored the information away, it would come in useful one day. The mental dossier she was building up on the likes and dislikes, movements and alliances, clothing, general ambience and overheard conversations of the lower sixth was becoming so huge there was barely room for a single other thought inside that brain of hers. One thing was certain anyway – somehow she was going to make the lower sixth be friends with her.

Katie's vaguely moronic musings were interrupted when the school matron-in-chief, Sister Minton – fondly nicknamed Mister Sinton by the girls since time immemorial in honour of the bristly moustache that grew unchecked between her prominent nose and surprisingly full lips – bustled on to the scene. Her starched blue uniform with its prim white edges creaked stiffly as she walked, and the school fell silent as one.

'Good God, man,' she said, her words resounding in the silence as she inspected Dirk, reached out a finger to his shirt, licked it and shook her head, a derisory smile playing about her lips, 'do pull yourself together. It's tomato juice . . .' She paused and ran her tongue around the inside of her mouth. 'Albeit mixed with a lot of vodka, I'd say!'

'But I . . .' Dirk looked round with a dazed expression on his silly tanned face, suddenly realising the intensely, excruciatingly, unbelievably embarrassing fact of where he was and what he was doing. 'I thought–'

'Yes,' cut in Mrs Bennett in icy tones, 'I would very much like to know what you thought. And,' she finished on a high note, 'exactly what the bloody hell is going on here!'

'I was in the gym, having a shower,' Dirk mumbled, 'when I heard voices coming through the air vent. At first I thought,' he continued more loudly, his confidence growing as he progressed, 'it was nothing more than people working out. But then I realised the voices were foreign and I felt sure I could smell smoke, so I decided to investigate.' He looked around in disbelief, as if he could hardly trust the words that were about to come out of his own mouth. 'I mean, smoking? In the *gym*?'

'And?' Mrs Bennett needed only to slightly raise her right eyebrow as she said this in her coldest voice to rapidly drag Dirk's attention back to the much more pressing matter at hand.

The school had never been as quiet it was now. Muffling coughs, stopping sneezes, leaving the gum in their mouths unchewed, the girls knew instinctively that as soon as Mrs Bennett remembered their presence here on the frontline they'd be sent back to their various houses post-haste and never know what had caused Dirk to be doused in Bloody Marys, which he obviously believed to be his own blood. And since that would be total misery, they were all very much united in their telepathically arranged silence.

'Well,' the coach bristled self-righteously, 'I don't know about *you*, Mrs Bennett, but I will not tolerate the use of tobacco, and certainly not in the sports hall! Anyway,' he carried on swiftly with an audible gulp when he registered black look he saw pass across his boss's terrifying face, 'I threw on my clothes and jogged across to catch the law-breakers in the act – whoever was there was *definitely* smoking. Unfortunately,' he said, with a sad downwards glance at the feet that so rarely let him down, 'I skidded on the new flooring as I was running over and my trainer squeaked really loudly.'

Jinx had to suppress a snort of laughter at this point and Liberty clutched her hand in sympathy. Dirk really did cut the stupidest, most pathetic figure they'd ever seen, slumped on the floor before the headmistress's feet with that stupid celery stick lying next to him like a discarded relay baton in the special vegetable race.

'Yes,' he continued, blissfully unaware of the very quiet hilarity this was causing among the watching girls, 'that was definitely what gave me away.'

'Mr Hanson!' Mrs Bennett's words cracked as if she'd fired them out of machine gun, once again waking Dirk to the reality of exactly who he was dealing with here.

'Well, yes, anyway,' he mumbled, 'the next thing I hear is a noise like gunshot and I'm covered in blood.' At that point he caught sight of Mister Sinton's raised eyebrow – Christ, the old broads at this school really were something else entirely – and decided it was definitely in his best interests to qualify this statement. 'OK, tomato juice or whatever it was. So, thinking I'm under siege and my life is in danger, I run out of there as fast as possible, trying to reach the cover of the main entrance, only to find all of you out here waiting for me, like a welcoming party at the end of a marathon. What's *that* all about?'

Having decided not to bother answering her new football coach's question for fear of losing her temper entirely, Mrs Bennett belatedly realised that every word of this bizarre exchange on the front steps had been heard. 'Girls, you've been outside in the wet and the cold for quite long enough. Before you go, I want to see every single member of the school in the theatre tomorrow morning before breakfast. Seven thirty a.m. and not a second later. What happened here today was an absolute disgrace and had there been a real fire . . .' Mrs Bennett shuddered in an uncharacteristically theatrical fashion. 'Well, I don't like to think what the consequences might have been. But I am going to get to the bottom of all of this, mark my words.'

Not particularly cowed by these veiled threats of dire

retribution, the girls shuffled off much, much more slowly than they'd arrived and with only about a third of the volume. However, as soon as the lower sixth had passed the corner of Friedan House, which made up the last end and side of the very-scuffed-up-and-far-less-verdant-after-its-trampling quad, and turned the corner to Tanner, and were thus away from Mrs Bennett's all-seeing eyes, if not her ears, the volume rocketed right back up. Hot topic number one, obviously, was who the hell had seen fit to throw a fully loaded Bloody Mary at Dirk's head from the mezzanine balcony of the gym that looked over the indoor tennis courts!

From where she was dawdling near the end of her house line, patiently waiting for all the older girls to scramble through the double doors first, Katie Green's ears pricked up like a loyal dog's when she heard the unmistakable sounds of the lower sixth's shouts of raucous laughter. She noticed Mrs Bennett roll her eyes in exasperation at the exact same time. She also noticed the headmistress dismiss Dirk with a wave of her hand and turn to harangue the bursar about his tardy arrival on the scene, his tardiness *generally*, his downright infuriating unavailability and above all the lack of support she felt she was receiving from him this term. Mrs Bennett sure did give great lecture and he grew ever more puce in the face as she thrilled to her theme.

Finally, Katie witnessed Daisy Finnegan rush to Mrs Bennett's side from where she had been loitering in the middle of the quad, a disgustingly sycophantic look plastered across her spotty face as she offered her assistance in this, as she put it, 'terrible time of crisis'. Katie smirked as she spied Daisy being dismissed as summarily as Stagmount's football coach had been a few seconds earlier, then made her way through the doors and turned left in the direction of her own house, chewing the inside of her lip in a thoughtful manner.

− * −

Desperate to get dry and warm, Jinx, Liberty and Chastity crashed through the front door of Tanner House into the foyer, thinking only of hot showers and their tropically heated common room. They were startled to see Olga, Irina and Masha lounging on the overstuffed bright pink sofa wearing their matching 2BFree very cool roll-top tracksuits and flicking through three copies of the same issue of *Marie Claire*. Their long blonde hair was drawn into three very neat identical ponytails and their matching 'barely there' make-up was pristine. There was no way on earth these three had been at the mandatory post-alarm roll call in the freezing cold quad like the fairly ratty-looking others had.

'Hi, girls,' said Irina. Sitting in the middle, she was holding a watermelon-flavoured Juicy Tube in one hand and a small jewel-encrusted hand mirror in the other, an alarming-looking double-page, black-and-white fashion shoot in the magazine open across her loosely bent thighs. 'Did we miss anything?'

The triplets dissolved prettily into laughter at this and the others were so impressed by their complete mastery of such an extreme level of nonchalance that they had to join in.

'No,' Chastity said through a decidedly porcine snort, 'you didn't miss a thing.'

'What are you talking about?' yelled Liberty, furiously unwinding her extra-long scarf and throwing it dramatically to the floor. 'What about the fire alarm and Dirk and the Bloody Mary? They missed *loads* of things!'

'I know,' replied Chastity, who had fallen prey to a fresh fit of hysterics at Liberty's outraged reaction and was gripping the side of the coffee table in front of her for support, her long blonde hair covering half of her profile, like a lopsided coquettish curtain. 'I was being sarcastic, for Christ's sake.'

'Hey,' said Jinx, looking around in surprise, 'where's Igor? I'm sure I haven't seen you three without him once this term.'

'Oh,' Olga responded swiftly, tugging the smooth end of the ponytail that was hanging over her left shoulder as she did so, 'we, er, told him he could go for a walk and we'd be fine in here for an hour or so. So tell us, what happened at roll call?'

'God, he really *is* under the thumb, isn't he?' said Jinx after a giggle that drowned out the last question − to Olga's evident annoyance, given the small frown that passed briefly across her ravishing high-cheekboned, heart-shaped face before disappearing entirely, unnoticed by any of the girls standing in front of the triplets in the straggly manner of a slightly trampy mass job interview at a scuzzy bar. 'Do you think it pisses him off?'

'Does what piss him off?' Olga asked, looking up

innocently at Jinx through lowered lashes. The tortoise-shell–rimmed rectangular reading glasses she was wearing lent her the air of a very sexy secretary enjoying some downtime after a day at work and Jinx hesitated before replying.

'You know . . .' Jinx squirmed and wished she hadn't said anything, but she'd started so she'd finish. 'Having to do what – well, what you lot say all the time. When he's, um, you know, like . . . a grown man and everything.'

'No!' the triplets yelled simultaneously, clutching each other as if this was the funniest thing they'd ever heard. 'We're in charge and he knows it!'

At that moment an icy wind blew through the room as someone flung open the front door with great force and stood there for a second before slamming it shut. This caused such a fierce gust that the roaring fire Mr Morris always lit in the grate under the mantelpiece about an hour before the girls came back for the evening flickered, hissed and seemed to be on the brink of going out.

'Bloody hell!' said Chastity crossly, complete with a correspondingly angry shiver. 'This is like being in a bad horror film. For Christ's sake, whoever's out there, either come in or go out, but whatever you do – and *I* certainly don't give a shit either way – JUST SHUT THAT FUCKING DOOR!'

'Ladies,' Igor said with a pained glance at Chastity before shooting a sinister glare around the room that seemed to linger especially malignantly on the triplets, 'good evening.'

123

'Good evening,' the girls chorused, barely hiding their laughter at Chastity's bad timing – and the previous conversation between Jinx and Olga that they were sure Igor must have overheard before he shut the door.

'So,' Irina said, her super-glossy pale pink smile full of mischief, 'we were just explaining to these girls how we let you go out for a walk, Igor.'

'Did you enjoy it?' Masha enquired, fake solicitous in the face of Igor's unreadable blank glare. 'Was it nice to be out in the fresh air . . . all alone?'

'I never shirk my duty,' Igor replied after a long pause. He appeared to teeter on the brink of saying more, but the stern mask slipped back on to his face and he stood silently at the back of the room, arms folded and eyes narrowed.

The triplets shared a quick, conspiratorial look and stood up as one, laying the magazines on the coffee table in a line in front of them with perfect, unthinking symmetry, before waving goodbye to the others and ushering Igor in the direction of their corridor on the third floor.

'Well,' said Jinx, collapsing with a very satisfied sigh on to the end of the recently vacated sofa and picking up one of the discarded magazines, 'that was weird to say the least.'

'Yeah,' Chastity agreed, unzipping the sides of her long boots, kicking them off and settling in at the opposite end. 'I've never seen Igor express any emotion whatsoever, but just now he seemed really out of sorts.'

'The triplets are so bloody rude to him, though,' Liberty said as she jumped over the coffee table and landed sprawled in the middle space between her friends. 'I'm not surprised he seemed pissed off – I bloody would be if someone I worked for spoke to me like that!'

'*I* can't believe they just couldn't be bothered to go to roll call,' sniffed Daisy Finnegan, her grease-covered and currently bright-red-on-account-of-the-cold nose pointed as high as she could manage without affecting her breathing. She had come in just behind the others and witnessed the whole exchange. 'They really don't seem to care about Stagmount at all.'

'Shut up, Daisy,' mumbled Jinx, flinging her head back against the cushions and closing her eyes, as if too weary to carry on.

The three memorably unsanitary years she'd spent cooped up at close quarters with Daisy Finnegan, suck-up artiste extraordinaire, in Wollstonecraft House had given her not only the strong feeling that she'd be sincerely, utterly delighted if she never had to see or speak to her again, but also a very healthy disregard for anything – however true – that might pop out of her mouth.

'Newsflash to Fingers,' Jinx said, rolling her eyes heavenwards and letting out a long, bored sigh, 'nothing's changed and no one gives a shit. Still.'

Daisy's eyes bulged with fury but she didn't say anything as she stamped her foot, flicked her greasy ponytail in disgust and stomped off in the direction of the corridor she shared – unfortunately for them – with Jinx and Liberty.

Chastity, who had been texting Paul on her mobile phone, so engrossed in whatever message her flying fingers were tapping out that she'd completely missed Jinx and Daisy's exchange, suddenly screamed in rage and threw her phone against the opposite wall.

Jinx and Liberty didn't say anything as the handset crashed to the floor, reduced to a mangled mess, tiny parts flying everywhere, but turned to stare at Chastity open-mouthed.

'Fucking Paul!' she yelled, throwing the magazine she'd picked up earlier in quick succession after her phone. 'Sometimes I really *hate* him.'

Jinx and Liberty remained silent, their eyes wide with shock. They had never once heard Chastity say anything bad about Paul. Quite the reverse in fact! They often joked about how totally vomit-making they found her usual sickly sweet conversations. And if they unfortunately happened to find themselves in the same room as the loved-up pair when they hadn't seen each other for, ooo, about ten minutes they always made as fast an exit as possible to avoid the gross-out slurping sounds and despicable baby talk.

'What's he done then?' asked a somewhat nervous-sounding Jinx eventually. 'Is everything OK?'

'No, it's fucking NOT!' yelled Chastity, banging her fist on the table for emphasis. Not, to be honest, that she much needed it. 'That's it. I've fucking had enough.'

'Whoa there, Chas,' said Liberty, grabbing Chastity's hand for fear she might break a few bones if she carried on in the same mentalist vein. 'Stop freaking out and just tell us what's going on.'

'He's totally changed recently,' Chastity said, hanging her head sadly. 'I don't know what's got into him. We've hardly had any rows at all in the whole seven months we've been going out and now all he does is make stupid sexist remarks that really piss me off. He only stops patronising me when he wants a shag.'

'So what did he say just now then?' asked Jinx curiously.

She barely managed to inject the necessary tone of concern into her voice. This was freaking interesting – she'd *never* seen Chastity lose it like this and as far as she could see Paul was a really decent guy. Well, he'd only ever been sweetness and light when *she* was present, that was for sure.

'He said ages ago that he was looking after his parents' house for a couple of weeks starting on Saturday,' sniffed Chastity, 'and he hasn't mentioned it for a while so I thought I'd text him and see what was going on.'

'And?' Liberty prompted gently, a consoling hand placed just so on Chastity's knee so that she could examine the flawless French manicure she'd spent an hour and a half doing in the art room that morning without being observed.

'He said he still was, so I suggested we have a huge house party there next weekend. I thought we could all go – you could invite Jamie, Jinx, and maybe your brothers – and a few of Paul's friends from college.' Chastity stopped speaking and another look of fury passed across her animated face.

'Sounds great,' Jinx said, smiling at the mention of Jamie as she instantly forgot about Chastity's woes.

'Well, it's not going to fucking happen, so you can take that smile off your face for a start,' raged Chastity, furious at the lack of support she was getting.

'Shit,' muttered an instantly deflated Jinx. 'I'm *sorry*. Do carry on.'

'He replied: "Great idea – let's have you, me and one other girl."' Chastity's condemnatory voice rose to a shrieking pitch as she finished her sentence.

'Bloody hell!' said Jinx, stifling a snort of amused laughter. 'You need to relax, Chas. George says things like that all the time. I'm sure Paul's only joking. And anyway' – here a definite snort did slip out – 'if he isn't – I'll do it!'

'Yes,' agreed Liberty, a huge smirk plastered across her stunning face, 'you're a total babe, Chas. I'd do it too! In fact, where exactly is this party taking place? I must stick it my diary!'

'Shut up!' snapped Chastity. 'I haven't finished yet. That's not even the worst of it.'

'Come on then, Chas,' Jinx said, already bored with what she saw as Chastity's total inability to laugh at herself. 'What *else* has he done?'

'He told me to invite the triplets too.' Chastity looked pleased with this incontrovertible evidence of her boyfriend's badness. 'What do you think about that then?'

'In that case wild horses couldn't keep me away,' Jinx replied, winking at Liberty. 'They are total *foxes*!'

'Mmm,' Liberty agreed, 'me too. Imagine it . . . them three, us three . . . in fact, I reckon we should get rid of Paul. He'd only be in the way.'

'You two are fucking impossible,' yelled Chastity, jumping up and grabbing her bag. 'I'm going to bed. Thanks for being so understanding.'

'Come on, Chas,' chorused Jinx and Liberty in stereo. 'We were only joking!'

Chastity said nothing in response as she picked up her boots and shoved the *Marie Claire* under her arm, but as she stalked off down the corridor the pair on the sofa distinctly heard a very dismissive 'What a pair of total *bitches*' float through the half-open door towards them.

They looked at each other, as if to say something about this, but before either of them could comment on Chastity's evident all-consuming wrath they had clutched one another and burst into the most furious fit of hysterical giggles they'd suffered all term. As they rolled about all over the place with extreme glee, Jinx reflected that, far from making them *dull*, all work and no play was driving the lower sixth into a frenzy of unusual stormy moods and extreme bad temper. It was obvious that they'd been cooped up inside for far too long and Jinx sincerely hoped that Chas and Paul would make up fast, as a massive house party would be just the place for them all to let off steam and chill the hell out.

Having been rudely awoken a whole hour and a half before their usual time and then forced to struggle down the drive to attend Mrs Bennett's punishment roll call, at which the entire school sulkily endured a telling-off on the grandest scale, none of the lower sixth were in a particularly good mood by the time they made it to breakfast.

Most unusually, there had been no giggling whatsoever on the trudge back to Tanner and the collective bad mood showed no sign of changing for the better any time soon. The triplets were the only ones who looked as sprightly as ever. Giggling and joking a few metres behind the rest, they'd disappeared upstairs as soon as they got back – no doubt to apply the truckload of make-up their studiedly 'natural' look required – and hadn't been seen since.

'So,' said Mimi Tate through a mouthful of toast, spraying crumbs all over the breakfast table she was sharing with an uncharacteristically quiet Jinx, Liberty, Liv and Charlie, 'did any of you guys hear the bursar and Mrs B having the most God-almighty row after the alarm stopped going off yesterday?'

'No,' Liv replied, looking interested in what someone was saying to her for the first time since she'd opened her eyes that morning. 'What was it about?'

'No idea,' Mimi said, thoughtfully spreading a corner of brown toast with more Marmite and reaching for her mug of tea, 'but man, she was going for it!'

'Who was going for what?' Chloe Thompson asked, chucking her stuffed to bursting book bag on the floor and squeezing herself on to the end of the bench next to her best friend, who immediately looked boot-faced at this unprecedented invasion of her personal space, to which she was extremely attached.

Anywhere they went as a group, Mimi always got the best seat. It was a knack she had – even at really packed-out house parties with no beds, sofas or even any freaking floor space to be seen, she always skipped downstairs the next day as fresh, glowing and well rested as if she'd spent the night in the presidential suite at the Dorchester, having found a spare double complete with fresh sheets and bottle of Evian on the bedside table with no apparent effort at all.

'Bloody hell, Chloe,' said Mimi indignantly, staring at her with a pointedly evil glare, 'you could at least *ask* if I mind before you use your fat ass to shove me practically off the end of this bench.'

'Shit,' muttered Liberty in an undertone to Jinx at the exact same time as Charlie rolled her eyes at Liv. 'Why is everyone in such a freaking bad mood all of a sudden?'

'Fuck off, Mimi,' snapped Chloe, not at all pleased by this description of her ass – which, incidentally, was pretty peachy and not fat in the slightest – and flashing her eyes dangerously. 'Who died and made *you* queen of the fucking world?'

'Come on, guys,' Jinx said, snapping her fingers to distract the pair at the end from the huge fight that was obviously brewing between them. 'It's not worth it.'

'Yeah,' added Liberty, 'you two are normally as tight

as me and Jinx – let's not ruin the day before it's hardly even started with a stupid row about nothing.'

'Sorry,' Chloe muttered. Staring into her Bran Flakes, she didn't look up.

'Yeah,' Mimi replied quietly, taking an unprecedented interest in the square of toast she was slathering with butter, 'me too.'

'So, Mims,' Liv interjected, keen to put an end to all this bitching, 'tell us more about Mrs B sounding off to the bursar. What was she saying?'

'Screaming more like,' said Mimi with a laugh. 'I've never heard anything like it from any of the teachers, and especially not her. I would have stopped to listen to more of it, but Jo came out of the office and I didn't feel I could just stand there like a lemon.'

'I heard them too,' Chloe said, sitting up straight. 'It must have been just after you did. I was walking down the corridor on my way back from clarinet practice and I could hear the yelling all the way from the music school.'

'When I went by she was banging on about him being unavailable all the time,' Mimi said, nudging Chloe with a giggle, 'and how he was supposed to be her number two.'

The more puerile the joke, the funnier the girls always found it, and none of them could stop themselves from sniggering madly at this one. Their earlier hissy fits had been totally forgotten.

'The fire alarm was a total shambles, though,' Charlie said, having recovered the ability to speak faster than the others, 'and we all know how hot she is on stuff like that. I haven't seen her that pissed off for ages.'

'And what about bloody Dirk?' Liv asked, still sounding completely amazed at the weird antics of the football coach none of them had met properly yet. 'What the hell was *that* all about?'

'Well, *I* think it had something to do with those Russians.' Daisy Finnegan's smugly self-satisfied voice cut over the top of them, rudely interrupting the conversation she had been shamelessly eavesdropping on from the next table across. 'Why weren't they at the fire alarm?' She paused, as if what she was about to say was very profound indeed and should therefore be listened to most carefully. 'And who drinks vodka apart from them? *I* think it was them who threw the drink over Coach Hanson and then set off the fire alarm to give themselves time to escape the scene. My dad told me that their dad makes Roman Abramovich look like a pauper.'

'Daisy,' Jinx said, turning round in her seat and fixing her old nemesis with the worst death stare she could summon up at such short notice, 'I can't help but wonder just how many times this week you're planning to force me to get rid of you. You certainly seem to be enjoying the sensation anyway. Now, for the last and final time, will you just FUCK OFF!'

'Go on, Daisy,' Liberty added, knowing how the slightest thing could set any of them off just now and wanting to diffuse the situation before it got any worse. 'Leave us alone.'

'There's a good girl,' said Liv, with a sly wink at Mimi and Chloe, as Daisy picked up her bag, shot Jinx a very black look and stalked out of the kitchen, slamming the door behind her. 'Easy does it.'

'She drives me fucking crazy,' Jinx snapped, pushing her plate away from her and glaring round at the others, as if daring them to say she'd gone too far. To be honest, she had a sneaking suspicion that she *had*. It wasn't like Daisy had been rude to her or anything, or even said anything particularly annoying, but the bad mood currently sweeping the lower sixth was catching and snapping at Daisy had become something of a natural reflex for Jinx.

'Yes,' Liv replied thoughtfully, clearly not listening to a word Jinx was saying, 'and I hate to say it – sorry, Jinx – but I think she's probably *right* about the fact that it was the triplets who drenched Dirk in vodka-based cocktails.'

'Me too,' Charlie agreed firmly. 'They *weren't* at roll call with the rest of us, we all saw them when we came in so we know they were back here way before we were and you've got to admit it's exactly the kind of thing they wouldn't give a toss about.'

'It's pretty funny whichever way you look at it,' Liberty interjected, surprisingly sensibly. 'I mean, who cares if it was them or not? It's no skin off any of our noses.'

'I know,' Jinx moaned, putting her head in her hands. 'Look at us, all fighting and snapping and bitching and basically having no fun at all. I'm bloody bored of non-stop homework and teachers talking about exams all the time like it's the end of the world. This crappy weather is driving me crazy too.'

She didn't mention it, but Jinx was also beginning to think that she would never hear from Jamie again either. It was, she thought, bloody unfair that just when she decided to admit to all her friends – and herself – that she really liked him he should disappear off the scene without so much as a by your leave. Embarrassing too, she reflected unhappily.

'We need a massive night out,' Chloe said, her big green eyes shining under the fringe of her sleek brown bob for the first time since she'd joined them at the table. 'We'll all go bloody stir-crazy otherwise.'

'I've got it!' Liberty cut in, banging her mug on the table. 'What about Paul's house party? That's supposed to be next week, right, Jinx?'

'Chastity's Paul?' Liv asked, interested. 'I really like him. Sounds ace.'

'Hold on,' said Jinx, shaking her head at Liberty. 'Were you even *there* last night? They had a massive fight, remember? About his bloody house party – and from the sounds of it, I wouldn't get your hopes up too high, kids.'

At that moment Chastity flounced into the room. Although she looked gorgeous in her skinny grey Top Shop Baxter jeans teamed with a black cashmere polo neck, lots of chunky silver jewellery and dark brown Ugg boots folded down halfway to her ankles, the thing that really made her look stunning was the beaming smile plastered across her face.

'Hiya,' she trilled, greeting them in her happiest singsong voice, perching herself precariously on the opposite end of the table closest to Mimi and Chloe and leaning over to grab a piece of toast from the rack in the centre. 'How is everyone?'

'Well,' Jinx said with a disbelieving snort at Chastity's new-found sunny disposition, 'at least one of us is in a better mood this morning. I take it you've made up with Paul?'

'Yes,' Chastity sighed dreamily. Smiling happily around the table, she was clearly totally smitten once more. 'We're back on.'

Jinx was pleased to see her pal on the up, but she couldn't help thinking that it was bloody unfair that Chastity could behave so badly, screaming and yelling blue murder, and still have Paul running after her, when she, Jinx, behaved like the coolest girl on the planet, all sweetness and light, jokes and gags, and yet remained resolutely ignored by her major crush. The way she was looking at it now, she had to admit it was possible that Jamie had not even registered her exist-ence at all. She chewed unhappily at her thumbnail as the horrid realisation began to stick in her brain: he probably thought of her as nothing more than George's annoying little sister.

'Don't bite,' Liberty said suddenly, interrupting Jinx's unhappy reverie as she slapped her friend's hand away from her mouth with what Jinx considered unnecessary force for the time of day. 'Come on. You know how cross you'll be later when you have to file them *all* down to match!'

'OK,' Jinx said moodily, sitting on her hands. 'I won't. And don't slap me again – I can't stand it.'

Liv, sensing another storm brewing at their usually happy breakfast table, stood up and clapped her hands together.

'Right,' she said in the brisk sergeant-major voice she always used to rally her troops for the brilliant scams and schemes she so often came up with, 'since Chas and Paul have made up we need to start Operation House Party.'

'You're on,' Mimi responded immediately. 'We need something to look forward to or we'll all go stark raving mad.'

'Actually,' Chastity cut in, looking slightly flustered again, 'Paul's parents are coming back early, so we definitely can't do it there.'

'OK,' Liv said, ever practical and keen not to let the good mood slip away, 'we'll have a night out instead.'

'Yep,' agreed Jinx. 'It doesn't matter *what* we do, so long as we've got something to bloody well look forward to.'

'What about that Sugar Club on the seafront?' Charlie asked. 'Liv and I went there with my brother last term – the music was awesome and we danced all night. We've all got our fake IDs, right?'

Everyone nodded. Fake IDs had been an essential part of their lives since they were about fourteen. Liv had an old driving licence that belonged to her sister Liz, who was twenty-one; Liz had given Charlie one of her friend's old hall of residence entry cards; Jinx had a University of Bristol student card that one of George's many blonde girlfriends had left behind after a dirty weekend in the New Forest; Liberty had the brunette version – stolen to order by George after she'd banged on about how unfair it was that Jinx had one and she didn't; and Chastity's mother's fiancé had created her an amazingly good copy of his British Library card – it was amazing how unobservant people were – on his Mac and slipped it to her on Christmas Day. He'd even laminated it – he was *so* back in the good books.

All rifts and unhappy thoughts forgotten in their delight at the prospect of some actual fun in the immediate future, the lower sixth pushed their dirty plates to one side, conveniently forgot to hear the bell announcing the start of the daily chapel service, pulled their chairs forward and gathered in close around the table for a serious discussion about the weekend headed by Liv and Charlie.

Mr Morris poked his head through the crack in the door about ten minutes later and was delighted to see the girls getting on so well, laughing and joking without a care in the world as they wrote lists of names in their notebooks. He had been in charge of Tanner House for the last ten years and had been expecting fireworks of some kind or other by this stage in the term. He knew of old that by the time the girls reached the spring term of the lower sixth their newfound freedoms and the novelty of them all being in the same year at last had worn off enough for them to start looking elsewhere for entertainment. This, combined with the usually dreary weather and the increased pressure from the academic staff, given the serious mock-A-level exams they were due to take at the end of the summer term, usually caused bad tempers, stormy fights and lots of tears. Since he'd hardly had to administer any hugs or Kleenex at all yet this term, Mr Morris smiled happily to himself and pulled the door closed quietly behind him. He whistled for Myrtle and set off on a walk round the squelchy grounds, delighted that he finally had a group of girls who basically got on with each other and their lessons with hardly a word of complaint.

Marching up the steep, narrow and winding stairs clearly marked DOWN that led to the top floor above the main entrance, the tower of which housed Stagmount's excellent, world-renowned modern languages department, anyone who had seen them earlier would have been shocked at the transformation for the better in the moods of the lower sixth.

There was no reason for them not to take the staircase marked UP other than force of habit. They certainly weren't doing it to piss off the new French teacher, Mr Christie, who was proving very bland indeed. The girls didn't care too much — they were pretty happy to relax and try to actually learn something for once. His predecessor, Mrs Susan Dickinson — the Dick — had been an absolute witch, causing misery far and wide throughout the school with her interminable pop quizzes, sarcastic attitude and liberal use of the detention system. The pupils in her class had spent most of their lessons defensively fielding awkward questions, too petrified of not knowing the answers to really take a whole lot else in.

They'd started huffing up the DOWN and vice versa purposefully to piss off the Dick; it had been one of only a handful of very small victories in their continuous war with her. She was now safely removed to a small cottage deep in the South Downs and although her retirement had come very suddenly, everyone – including teachers, cleaners and ground staff – was so pleased to see the back of her that there'd been no speculation whatsoever about her reasons for upping and leaving so quickly.

No one had connected the move in any way with Mrs Gunn, Jinx's vile former housemistress, doing exactly the same thing at the same time. Only Jinx knew the truth, for it was she who had caught the Dick and Gunn sucking face, and probably a lot of other things she didn't much care to think about – thank God it had been pretty dark in there – in the bike sheds at the end of last term. She had, rather cleverly she thought with a tiny smile, pretended to record the sick event on her mobile phone and used the threat of revealing the imaginary footage to blackmail them both into resigning pretty much straight away. She giggled to herself as she imagined the unspeakable couple snuggling up in bed together every night and getting up to unspeakably filthy activities in their vegetable patch, happy as Larry she was sure. Total gross-out!

Sitting slumped in their seats, the French class was watching Mr Christie write examples of the subjunctive verb on the blackboard behind his desk. With expressions ranging from mild lack of interest – geeky Lulu Cooper – to absolutely catatonic – Liberty – it was clear they all needed a good old run around in the fresh air. Thankfully, although the day was as cold and dreary as any they'd had recently and the sky was as dark and gloomy as ever, the downpour during yesterday's roll call was the last any of them had seen of what had begun to seem incessant rain and it looked as if football was on for the first time this term. And boy did they need it.

As they raced down to the pitch on a total high at being out of that boring bloody French lesson, hair blowing in their faces thanks to the wind coming straight off the sea, the lower sixth were amused when they clocked a line of blushing third years coming up the hill towards them in the direction of the changing rooms. Constantly looking over their shoulders to where Dirk was sorting the red and blue bibs into two piles, the younger ones giggled and waved, clearly even more smitten with the idiot than ever. The man himself, still incongruously tanned for the time of year, was sporting yet another brightly coloured Adidas tracksuit with matching trainers.

The triplets, who had never once been seen to participate in any sporting activity apart from ballet and tap dance, as well as a very occasional game of tennis, during the entire time they'd been at the school, were leading the pack down to the large pitch closest to the sea. In the summer term it doubled as an athletics track and was surrounded by a high verge, complete with lots of benches for parents who didn't wish to sit on rugs during the traditional summer sports day picnic. But with the darkly churning sea furiously smacking into the cliffs beneath them, it looked bleak as hell today.

Wearing the pink and white football shirts with matching socks that they'd purchased in town especially for this occasion – to the great hilarity of the rest of the lower sixth – Olga, Irina and Masha provided light relief as they ran elegantly towards their destination. Their long, blonde, perfect ponytails streamed out behind them like three sheets of golden silk and their long, slim legs had taken on a charming pinkish tint thanks to the cold air. Jinx found herself looking at them and wondering if they *ever* found themselves in embarrassing situations or looking less than their best. The sigh she let out as she inwardly admitted to herself that both of these eventualities were highly unlikely was lost to the wind as the girls came to a stop in front of Dirk.

Grinning like a maniac way more at the triplets than anyone else, the coach fiddled with the gelled spikes of hair he spent hours every morning training to stand up from his head like his Premiership footballer idol, Cristiano Ronaldo. He was congratulating himself as he reflected that moving to Stagmount from the mixed comprehensive in Southampton where he'd previously taught was the best move he'd ever made. Yes, he thought with a smirk, these girls really were something else and – best of all, as far as he was concerned – there were no spotty boys around, taking the attention away from him.

Unnoticed by anyone down on the pitch, Katie Green stood outside the swimming-pool changing rooms that the girls used before and after their football lessons and stared down at her heroines. An expression of wistful longing masked the jealous fury that was running rampant through her veins as she considered Daisy Finnegan's proximity to Jinx, Liberty, Chastity, Liv and Charlie – the girls she thought about as she tossed and turned in bed every night. Daisy didn't even *like* them. So how was it fair that she got to spend all day and night with them when Katie couldn't?

They don't even know I exist, Katie thought, and resolved to do something to change this. She was convinced that if only the lower sixth knew who she was they would love her. She hadn't thought of anything to make them notice her yet, but as soon as she came up with a suitable plan she resolved to put it into action. Her crush was definitely becoming unmanageable – these members of the lower sixth who had barely registered her existence were literally all she thought about. However, Katie's current thoughts were interrupted when Betsy Johnson, one of the most popular girls in her year, sprinted out of the door and towards the main school, obviously late for something or other. Betsy shot Katie a look of such pitying disdain as she passed her that the other flushed a dull red before turning to trudge to the shower block.

Meanwhile, down on the pitch the lower sixth, busily warming up for their first football lesson by sprinting round the edge of the vast field, were unaware of any scrutiny.

'Gather round, girls,' Dirk Hanson shouted, marvelling at the amazing stroke of luck that meant it was actually his *job* to tell these long-limbed lovelies what to do while watching them cavort about in very few clothes, 'and I shall explain the basics.'

'My God,' muttered Chastity to Liberty and Jinx, who were standing on either side of her, after listening to Dirk's self-loving pep talk for a few minutes and watching his theatrical demonstrations almost disbelievingly. 'I don't think I've ever met a more conceited prick in my life. What a laugh!'

'I know,' said Jinx through a delighted fit of giggles, 'and look at the triplets staring at him as if they've never seen anything like it. This is going to be hilarious.'

From her office Mrs Bennett was also watching the lower sixth larking around in the fresh air for the first time this term. The uptight expression she'd sported for the past few days softened slightly when she took a break from her furious pacing up and down and paused by the huge picture window that looked straight down over the pitches to the rough sea beyond.

Her smile quickly became a frown, however, as she watched Coach Hanson pull Xanthe Miller from the pitch, where she had been a very creditable centre forward, and throw himself into the game in an orgy of

144

one-upmanship and showing off. He pranced all over the place, demonstrating his fancy footwork and doing endless keepy-uppies with the spare ball he kept on the sideline in between sending down long shots that the girls had no chance of dealing with. This was not what Stagmount was all about, oh no. She was beginning to think that the hiring of a football coach was nothing more than a useless gimmick which would afford the girls no more sense of themselves as sentient human beings able to do anything they wanted than a return to the archaic cookery lessons she'd struck off the syllabus pretty much as soon as she arrived.

The headmistress sighed as she moved away from the window, bent down to straighten one of the bronze-sculpted racehorses that adorned her coffee table, sighed again, pushed her black-rimmed Prada spectacles to the bridge of her nose and sat down on the rather drab swing chair she had insisted – much to the not-so-silent chagrin of the interior designer appointed by the board of governors to 'jazz the place up a bit' – upon having for when she was working at her computer. She didn't turn to look at the screen, but rather stared thoughtfully at the portrait of Jennifer Tanner, the eldest of the three sisters who had founded the school as a feminist experiment in 1865 and who looked down at interviewees and miscreants alike from the opposing wall.

Mrs Bennett had been in an unusually bad temper since the absolute shambles the girls had made of the roll call after the fire alarm. The fact that the bursar hadn't appeared on the scene until the last possible moment was also preying on her mind. She couldn't put her finger on exactly what it was that was bothering her but she was sure that something, somewhere wasn't right. She racked her brain for the appropriate word to describe how she was feeling and sighed again – more heavily this time – as she realised the one that would do the job most truthfully was uneasy. She had always placed great store by her instincts and she didn't intend to stop now.

Suddenly feeling a lot happier, Mrs Bennett sat up straight and raised an eyebrow at the portrait opposite her as if laying down a challenge. She was going to get to the bottom of whatever the bursar was up to and that was a fact. She rang the bell that signalled to Jo, her secretary, to put down the *Closer*, *Now*, *Grazia* or *Heat* magazine she was currently poring over and press the connecting buzzer in response. She then ordered a cafetiere of freshly ground coffee and a blueberry muffin over the intercom, kicked off her shoes and settled back in her chair to have a good old-fashioned think about things.

Slumped in the old reference library, trying her very hardest to concentrate on the complicated French translation that was due in Mr Christie's pigeonhole first thing next morning, Jinx smiled as she applied a truckload of Carmex to her already over-balmed lips and sat back to think about the lower sixth's football lesson that morning. God, but Dirk was an idiot. He'd been staring so intently at the triplets' long, slender legs he'd completely missed Chastity's amazing goal from the other side of the field and – the bloody fool – the rest of the girls pulling their shirts over their heads and running around the goal with their tits practically out in response. Stupid prick!

Jinx examined her nails and picked at a couple of chips in the bright pink Jessica varnish she'd applied in a very slapdash fashion in front of the telly the night before – the bloody stuff was called 'flirty', she thought morosely, not that *she'd* been doing much of that lately, except in her head. She rummaged around in the depths of her handbag for the small mirror she always took out with her, emblazoned with the legend 'Don't treat me any differently than you would the queen' on one side and 'I'm bored, please send drugs' on the other. Holding it up in front of her face, she leaned back slightly to study her eyebrows as best she could in the dim February afternoon light that was struggling to stream through the latticed library windows.

'Oi,' hissed Liv, looking up from where she was sitting directly opposite Jinx on the narrow library study benches. 'Have you finished that French prep?'

Jinx shook her head and frowned. The last thing she needed was a bloody *minder* watching her every move from across the way. Especially Liv, for God's sake!

'Well, crack on, love,' Liv said, running an exasperated hand through her very short hair. 'I want to have a look at it when you're done. I'll swap you my English essay.'

Jinx sighed, pushed all thoughts of Jamie and why he

hadn't called her to one side and turned her attention back to the boring translation. Why did nothing interesting ever happen to the deathly dull characters in these ridiculous stories? Who gave a toss about Madame Dupont and her boring bloody son going on yet another silly outing to the fucking market, which seemed to be staffed entirely by tossers, morons and retards? It was, she supposed, no wonder they both looked more than a tad on the porky side, what with all the quiche lorraines, tart tatins and whole sides of pig they regularly carted home with them. Whatever, Liv's offer was enticing enough to set her straight back to work. Only a fool would attempt two preps instead of one, and even as bored rigid as she was right now, Jinx was certainly nobody's fool.

The pair of them had been hard at it, heads firmly down, for a good forty-five minutes by the time Jo bustled over, shaking her own Titian-red head at the sheer injustice of having had practically no time alone to put her feet up and enjoy a good old read about Britney, Paris and Nicole's latest goings-on.

'Jinx Slater,' Jo said, tapping the back of Jinx's chair to get her attention, 'I've been all over the school looking for you.' She paused and looked confused. 'I didn't expect to find you in *here*. Are you working?'

Jinx looked round indignantly. 'I *do* occasionally, you know,' she said. 'Especially this bloody term – we don't seem to do anything else these days.'

'Too true,' muttered Liv, a brief but unmistakable expression of disgust passing across her innocent-looking face before she sighed and returned her attention to the large pile of books in front of her.

'Well, anyway,' said Jo, handing one of her black and red lined memorandum notes to Jinx, 'someone phoned for you. I would have left it in your pigeonhole as usual, but he said it was extremely urgent that you call him back as soon as possible.'

Jinx raised her eyebrows. She had no idea who would call her at school like this; everyone she knew had her mobile number. She never went anywhere without it and very rarely received calls on the school line.

'Funny name . . . for an uncle,' Jo said, directing a knowing smirk at Jinx before bustling off self-importantly in the direction of her desk and Lazy Lohan's latest hook-up.

Jinx unfolded the paper. When she saw what it contained she couldn't stop herself from emitting a loud shout of laughter, causing several people in the library to turn round and give her evil looks for daring to breach the peace during important revision time like this.

'FOR: Jinx Slater,' it read in Jo's curly, black and very posh handwriting. 'FROM: your uncle Jamie Trouser-Snake. RE: he urgently needs to know if you are available to accompany him to special-needs line-dancing on Saturday afternoon. Please phone him ASAP.'

Jinx smiled delightedly. Her heart was pounding at what felt like a hundred beats a minute, her face was transfused with a peachy glow and she experienced a physical clench of excitement that gripped her stomach and refused to let go as she transferred the number scrawled at the bottom of the sheet into her phone. She tapped the digits as happily into the little keyboard as if she were banging out a truly amazing house remix on a set of silver decks at the closing night of Space in Ibiza.

'Bloody hell,' giggled Liv after leaning across the desk – flashing the top of her bright pink lacy French knickers at the whole room in the process – and reading the note herself. 'Well, Slater . . . I'm impressed! You've done the perve, now it's time to do the swerve!'

'What?' hissed Jinx, jumping up and shoving her books haphazardly into her 'I Love Me' white canvas book bag with a big glittery purple heart on the side. She chucked her lip gloss, pencil case, phone and the half-eaten king-sized Mars bar she'd been thoughtfully nibbling on as she wrote into her handbag without much more ceremony.

'I'll tell you in the garage,' Liv replied with a surprisingly lewd wink, given her general countenance of beyond-reproach innocence. Grabbing Jinx's hand, she dragged her as fast as possible towards the door and freedom. 'Come on!'

– * –

Liv and Jinx were sitting on orange plastic stacking crates next to the groundsman's tractor in the semi-darkness of the garage behind the tuck shop, drawing deep tokes from a strong skunk spliff. Liv, who really was an extraordinarily *handy* kind of person to have around the place, had produced it from her pencil case with a flourish as soon as they'd crawled under the slightly open sliding garage door and settled down comfortably.

'So what's all this perve and swerve business then?' Jinx asked with a small stoned-sounding giggle, clutching the note tight against her thigh, where it lay in the pocket of her grey skinny jeans.

'First you perve, then you swerve.' Liv looked at Jinx, inhaled and creased up before continuing. 'It's standard love talk, Jinx. My sister and her friends say it all the time. Basically, when you, like, really fancy someone and you've got a major crush on them and you're thinking about them all the time – that's called perving, when you *perve* over them.'

Jinx nodded approvingly. She totally got it. She also, come to think of it, still had a small crush on Liv's sister, who'd been four years above them at school and had left three years ago. Liz had appeared impossibly glamorous and exotic to all of Liv's friends and now that she was one of only a handful of students to get on to Manchester University's amazing drama course, her cool-rating had gone through the roof.

'And *then*,' continued Liv, 'when you decide to do something about it, seal the deal, cross the line, make a move or whatever you want to call it, that's when you *swerve* someone. And the action of swerve is swerving. Get it?'

'Like total,' Jinx said, plucking the spliff from Liv's outstretched fingers and smiling with delight – all the girls loved to pick up new words and phrases like this and then do them to death among each other. 'I love it. In fact, I can't wait to tell George – he gets off on stuff like this. He'll definitely love it too.'

'So, to return to the matter at hand,' said Liv, snatching the spliff abruptly back, inhaling, exhaling and blowing a lot of impressive smoke rings as she did so, 'it's bleeding obvious that Jamie is, like, totally digging the Jinx-meister's action. When are you going to call him?'

'I don't know,' Jinx squeaked, suddenly terrified at the thought of having to hold an at least reasonably intelligent conversation over the phone with the object of her heart's – and a few other things besides, if she was honest – desires. 'He said "ASAP", so maybe . . . um . . . tonight? And what the hell am I going to *say* to him?'

'You've got to plan it,' said Liv firmly, using her most no-nonsense tone and fixing Jinx with a stern look. 'And you've got to work out what you want to do on Saturday before you speak to him too – that way you'll be able to make things go your way without any effort at all. Hey! You need to relax!'

'Fuck!' Jinx started as if she'd been shot when the garage door began to creak open. Someone was obviously hauling on it from the other side and she hastily stubbed out the rest of the spliff before shoving it deep into one of her extra-tight pockets. Suddenly she felt a decidedly warm spot pressing against her thigh. Damn! She obviously hadn't been thorough enough in her stubbing out. She winced at the thought of the inevitable burn mark on her brand-new most favourite pair of jeans ever, but there was no time to do anything else about it.

Jinx and Liv sat stock-still and stared at the garage door like deer caught in the headlights. It was halfway open before they breathed two massive sighs of relief and started breathing normally again.

'Bloody hell!' hissed a somewhat breathless Jinx as she realised the intruders were none other than Liberty and Chastity. 'You two gave us such a freaking fright. I thought I was going to get expelled for sure this time! What the hell are you doing sneaking up on us like that?'

'Don't get your knickers in a twist,' said Chastity, marching to where they were seated and leaving Liberty to yank the door back down into its customary almost-closed position. 'We were sitting by the art room window, saw you two running down here all helter-skelter and decided to come and share the love. No one *else* saw, so there's no need to have a major freak-out about it.' She paused and sniffed the air hopefully. 'You *did* come in here to smoke a joint, didn't you?'

'Of course we did,' Liv said, motioning to Jinx to get the spliff back out of her pocket. 'Have you *met* us? There's no other reason on earth that we'd be hiding out in here on such a dank and dreary afternoon.'

'So what's new?' Liberty asked, looking expectantly at Jinx and Liv. 'What's with all the running around like crazies in the rain stuff?'

'I have perved. And now,' said Jinx with a delighted giggle, 'I am going to swerve.'

Liv offered her hand to Jinx and the pair of them

high-fived before collapsing into hysterical floods of laughter.

'What?' asked Chastity, who was fastidiously checking her crate for dirt and dust before she sat down on it, legs crossed demurely at the ankles as if she were at the Royal Opera House, waiting to see a Christmas performance of *The Nutcracker* with her very rich dowager aunt.

'Yeah, what are you two on?' Liberty said, reaching for the joint, lighting up and inhaling deeply. 'Apart from this, obviously!'

'She's only gone and had a phone message from Sir Jamie himself,' Liv burst out, unable to withhold this exciting information a second longer. 'He wants her to call him and said something about going out on Saturday.'

'Yeah,' said Jinx with another decidedly porcine snort of laughter, 'he's taking me to a special-needs line-dancing class.'

'I don't get it,' Liberty said, looking confused. 'Why would he want to take you to that? And you'd better make sure you don't laugh like that when you're speaking to *him*, Jinx, or there's no way in hell you'll be going on a second date, that's for freaking sure!'

'OK, OK,' Jinx mumbled, reflecting that she really must learn to be more ladylike in her enthusiasms. 'Point taken. Anyway, it's true. Jamie phoned Jo, saying he was my uncle Trouser-Snake, and could I phone him to discuss our plans for Saturday. Well, I take it that was what he meant. It was pretty funny. Look.' Jinx paused, rummaged in her pocket for the note – which, she was dismayed to see, now had a big brown burn mark – and passed it over. 'Check it out.'

There was a brief silence as Chastity and Liberty bent their blonde and brown heads together over the note and digested its contents. They looked up at the exact same time a few seconds later, matching expressions of thrilled excitement on their expectant faces, waiting to see Jinx's reaction at their having read it. They were not to be disappointed.

One of Jinx's form teachers at prep school had once written a most accurate and excellent description of Jinx on her end-of-term report card. The woman, who had liked Jinx a lot but recognised a potentially loose cannon when she saw one, had compared her to a Golden Retriever puppy. And furthermore, she had elaborated, the kind of puppy that needed a *lot* of training and discipline if it was not to piss on the floor with excitement every time someone walked into the kitchen or chase its tail in circles until it fell over at the prospect of a walk.

Well, that might have been a little harsh – and Caroline and Martin Slater had loved it so much they'd framed it and hung it on the wall of the downstairs loo – but the general gist was that Jinx was the kind of girl who could work herself into such a state of excitement she was in imminent danger of actual spontaneous combustion. Sometimes the smallest things could set off a bout of such hysterical giggles that she would have to leave the room and sit quietly for five minutes on her own, taking deep breaths, wiping her eyes and regaining her self-control. With big things like this, she would be practically climbing the walls and dancing on the ceiling. And sometimes, of course, she could be calm and collected and show no more reaction than anyone else. The thing is, she just wasn't predictable. And her friends loved her for it, because most of her moods were of the excited, happy variety. It was a right laugh to be around Jinx on a high, that was for sure.

'SO?' yelled Jinx, leaping off her crate and jumping up and down in a state of extremely agitated high spirits, 'WHAT DO YOU THINK?'

'I think it's fucking ace,' said Chastity, grabbing one of Jinx's hands and squeezing it hard, 'and you can invite him to the Sugar Club on Saturday!'

'Me too, and Chas is right,' Liberty agreed, before narrowing her eyes at Jinx and staring at her thoughtfully, 'although what the hell are you going to *wear*?'

'Never mind that now,' Liv cut in – she found Liberty's obsession with fashion somewhat draining to say the least, not that she ever looked too badly turned out herself. 'We've got to work out what she's going to say on the bloody phone first!'

What with all this perving and swerving, wardrobe issues and phone call concerns, Jinx barely knew whether she was coming or going. She sat with her knees pulled up tightly to her chest, linked her arms around them and leaned forward towards her pals, an expression of such rapt attention on her glowing face that any teacher who saw it would assume, rightly, that she was giving nothing less than 110 per cent to the task at hand.

They sat there and for two full hours non-stop dissected the note – not that it was particularly nuanced, but whatever! – what Jinx could possibly wear on Saturday and what, exactly, she should say on the phone that evening. Eventually, every possible permutation of everything covered, the girls – who had also run out of weed by this time – decided it was far too cold to be skulking about like tramps in the dark. The four of them linked arms and hot-footed it across the pitches back to Tanner House in search of their three current main interests: central heating, crumpets loaded with butter and jam, and the newest season of *America's Next Top Model*.

Katie Green sat by the window of her small cubicle room in Steinem House and stared avidly out past the drive in front of her house towards the tuck-shop area. She had been sitting like that – in the dark, with her face pressed up against the cold glass of the resolutely not double-glazed window and her hands hugging her chunky knees tight to her flat chest – for at least three hours without moving. She had seen Jinx and Liv dash down the steps and let themselves into the garage from the window of the sanatorium, where she had been busy unsuccessfully begging Mister Sinton for a note to let her off games. At the sight of them, Katie had suddenly – and to the great confusion of Mister S, who'd been waiting patiently for the inevitable waterworks — lost all interest in her losing battle, made her excuses and dashed back to Steinem, hoping she wouldn't miss them leaving in the short time it took her to get from the san to her room. She was not disappointed.

Only a few minutes after sighting two of her big five fascinatingly engaged in some extracurricular and no doubt illegal activity, Katie felt she'd practically won the jackpot when she spotted Liberty and Chastity making their way towards the garage and disappearing inside. About an hour later, her excellent vantage point afforded yet more interest as Charlie — she could hardly believe her luck at spotting all her heroines in one sitting like this — nearly fell out of a taxi that stopped abruptly by the main gates, threw some money in the direction of the driver, swayed and then began to stagger up the drive.

At first Katie thought the older girl must be drunk. It was only when she noticed Charlie dragging her right leg behind her that she realised the sixth former was sporting a terrible limp. Katie watched, thoughtfully, as Charlie struggled towards the entrance, keeping close to the small hedge that ran the whole way along the drive. Katie's reverie was destroyed a few seconds later by someone banging on her door as they passed, giggling and then running away. She glowered as she got up to put the light on and thought about how much she really, really hated being at this bloody school.

Jinx sat on Liberty's bed, rather incredulously watching her best friend pull item after item of sheer fabulousness from her wardrobe. Liberty, her wild hair bunched on top of her head in a gorgeously messy bun, scrutinised each garment before throwing it towards the 'possible' pile to her left or the 'definitely no' pile to her right. Even when Jinx occasionally dared to take her life in her hands and voice the opinion that things were going in the wrong direction, Liberty totally ignored her and the right-hand pile continued to grow considerably larger than the left.

Jinx was messing around with a large pot of Mac gold glitter, blending it into the back of her hand, when Liberty spun round. 'I've got it!' she squealed. 'I knew there was something I'd forgotten.'

'What?' Jinx asked, barely bothering to conceal her yawn of absolute, total boredom. She loved clothes but really, this was ridiculous. How long had they been shut up in here? Christ, she needed to make the bloody phone call first. She hadn't even seen *EastEnders*. *And* she still had to copy Liv's English essay before tomorrow morning. This evening was fast becoming a bloody farce. But since Liberty would be well upset if Jinx said anything, she resolved to try her best to stick it out and at least pretend to be interested.

'Look at *this*,' said Liberty, ripping a photograph off the wall by her bed and pressing it into Jinx's hand. 'I *love* you in this dress!'

Jinx studied the photo, taken last summer half-term by Caroline before the whole family went off to a television

159

awards ceremony in London, where Martin had picked up a gold gong for his work as creative director of a top London advertising agency. She smiled as she realised that yes, even if she did say so herself, she looked pretty damn hot in her multicoloured silk Simultane shift. Her face fell as she realised she'd also drunkenly shoved it to the back of her crowded wardrobe when they got home late that night and had promptly forgotten its existence. Until now, anyway.

'But it's not here, Lib,' Jinx wailed, now absolutely set on wearing this or nothing – and she didn't think *nothing* would make her first date with the divine Jamie go down quite the way she hoped. 'It's at home!'

'Don't worry about it,' replied Liberty. 'Why don't we go back to yours on Friday and pick it up? Your mum phoned a couple of days ago and asked if she was ever going to see us again – we could kill two birds with one stone. I'd love to see them all anyway.'

'OK,' Jinx said, sitting up and looking enthused for the first time since Liberty had announced her position as head stylist for Saturday's event. She decided to act on it immediately. 'That sounds great. Let's do it! We'll get on a train straight after art and be home by dinner. Mum will be thrilled, I can pick up my dress and George can drive us back here on Saturday afternoon just in time for bright lights, date city!'

'Excellent!' Liberty shoved all the clothes littering the bed on to the floor and flung herself down next to Jinx. 'We can take all our washing back too.'

'Yeah,' agreed Jinx, 'and have a massive dinner and see

the dogs. In fact, the more I think about it the more I can't wait – I feel like I haven't been home in a freaking *age.*'

Sitting cross-legged and alone on her bed a few minutes later, having been propelled at high speed out of the next-door room by its owner-occupier, one Liberty Latiffe, Jinx opened a can of Diet Coke and took a few reflective sips as she gazed at her mobile phone, which was lying on top of the pile of largely unopened textbooks on her bedside table. This was fucking ridiculous. Wasn't she supposed to be, like, a way cool dudette? Well, she sure as hell wasn't behaving like one. No, she was acting like the biggest wuss in the whole freaking world. Jinx mentally punched herself in the face and reached for her phone. She was making this bloody call and she was making it *now.*

'Hello?' Jamie's voice answered after the third ring and Jinx felt her heart leap with excitement at the sound of it.

'Hi, Jamie,' she said, thinking that – thank God – she sounded remarkably cool, calm and collected in spite of what was currently happening to the inside of her stomach. 'It's Jinx.'

'Ah, naughty Jinx Slater finally gets off her butt and calls me back,' Jamie said in a very low and sexy voice that seemed positively brimming with innuendo to a totally love-struck Jinx. 'Hel-*lo*. I hoped it would be you. Don't move!'

Jinx sat uncertainly on her bed, holding the phone to her ear as all went silent at the other end. She couldn't stop the frankly ludicrous thought passing through her mind that there was a sniper sitting on the roof waiting to shoot her, so she didn't move a muscle. After an uncomfortably long pause during which a reddening and slightly sweaty Jinx wished she'd taken off her jumper earlier, she heard heavy, rushing footsteps thudding across the line until a heavy-breathing Jamie picked it up with a clatter and said, 'So, where were we, Slater?'

'Um,' Jinx replied uneasily, just a touch unnerved by the whole business, 'you were . . .'

'Yes, that's it. I was about to ask you out,' Jamie said firmly, immediately bringing Jinx's spinning mind right back to the matter at hand.

'So?' he said, a huge smile lending his voice a very warm, teasing tone, 'can I tempt you? Saturday?'

'*Gosh* – a date!' Jinx snapped right back, all unease totally brushed under the nasty navy-blue carpet of her single room. 'I'd love to, thanks very much.'

'Sweetheart, that's great. I hoped you'd say yes.' Jamie paused enough to allow a throaty chuckle to drift down the airwaves and hit a beaming Jinx's delighted ear before continuing, 'So here's the deal. I'm having a party at my place on Saturday.'

Jinx nodded as she thought that this wasn't quite the tête-à-tête she had envisioned, but smiled at the realisation that it sounded like a hell of a lot of fun and much less scary than having to deal with him *à deux*. Shit, though, what about the solemn promise the lower sixth had made to each other to go out and have a total blast on Saturday night?

'Um, the thing *is*,' Jinx said after a quick-fire think, ripping tiny slivers of paper off the sides of the note Jo had given to her in the library earlier, 'I've kind of got –'

'Don't worry about it,' Jamie's voice cut Jinx's off in the middle of her sentence. 'You can bring whoever you like. In fact, I'd say the more the merrier.'

'OK,' said Jinx, not really noticing the presumption in his tone as she thrilled inside at having her major crush on the phone like this and being able to invite all her friends to his house party, which would be infinitely cooler than a night in a seafront nightclub. 'I'll tell Liberty and Chastity and everyone. They'll definitely be up for it.'

'Great. Come round at about seven and bring a few bottles. And Jinx . . .' The lingering pause seemed positively pregnant with promise to Jinx, until Jamie added decisively, 'I'm really looking forward to seeing you.'

'Me too,' she replied, blushing a deep red and distractedly screwing the note into a tiny ball with her free hand.

She was going to crack a gag about trying to keep hold of her shoes this time and hadn't even managed to ask if George would be there on Saturday night when she realised that the silence from the other end of the line meant he'd put the phone down. Well, she thought to herself, exhaling deeply and banging on the wall that she and Liberty shared, that went better than expected.

Jinx might have known there'd be no need for her to attract Liberty's attention. She'd barely banged once before her door was flung open and Liberty and Chastity burst in and leapt on top of her on her bed. They'd obviously been sitting in the corridor outside, ears firmly attached to the door, just waiting for the conversation going on inside to end so they could go over every aspect of it in endless detail.

The three of them were so over-excited they didn't notice Liv running down the corridor towards a very bedraggled Charlie, an expression of extreme concern on her face. The pair went into a huddle in the alcove by the common room. Not long after this, Liv started laughing uncontrollably at whatever it was Charlie was telling her. Their tortuous ascent up the adjacent stairs to the first-floor bedrooms a few minutes later – the pain in her leg obviously intense, Charlie was leaning heavily on Liv's arm – also went completely unnoticed by their friends. Jinx et al. were now making so much noise in Jinx's room they'd already woken Lulu Cooper up from where she was trying to have an early night in her room two corridors along and three floors up.

Having spent two solid hours giggling and shrieking at everyone's horoscopes in all the trash magazines they'd bought at Brighton station for Friday's train home to Hampshire, Jinx was now sitting on her bed opening endless dreary bank statements and chucking them into the bin underneath her bedside table barely examined. She had no idea why – when she never had any bloody money anyway, and even when she did she never had it long enough to actually necessitate paying it in at the freaking bank – they sent so many of the damn things.

She hardly had to strain her ears over and above The La's 'There She Goes', which was playing on her digital radio, to hear Liberty having an extremely animated conversation with her parents downstairs. God, she thought, as she breathed in great lungfuls of the crisp country air that was breezing through the open window at the head of her bed and looked around at her pink and white striped bedroom that had remained res-olutely unchanged since she was twelve, it was good to be home. It was also great, she grinned massively at the thought of this, to have Liberty back where she belonged and clutched to the collective bosom of the adoring Slater family. Caroline and Martin, both sport-ing suspiciously bright eyes, had leapt on her as if she was their own daughter when the taxi the girls had hailed at the station dropped them off at the front door.

Lying back against her perfectly squashy pillows, Jinx fondled Flash's ears with contentment and a very real sense that all was right with the world. Although Caro-line often waxed long and lyrical about how unhygienic – never mind the bloody hairs! – it was to allow the dogs on to their beds, the rest of the Slaters paid her scant attention and Jinx was especially enjoying the long and emotional homecoming love-in that she and Flash were sharing right now.

As early as *she'd* thought polite – which wasn't very, but no one really noticed – Jinx had left her parents and Liberty in the kitchen and sloped off upstairs, mumbling something under her breath about needing to sort her washing out. Instead, she'd hot-footed it straight into George's empty room and immediately located three gorgeous pictures of Jamie plastered to the whiteboard above his sink. Jinx had painstakingly unstuck them from their blue-tack fixings, moved a few other pictures around to conceal the obvious spaces left behind by their removal and strolled happily along the corridor to her own bedroom at the back of the house.

She held her ill-gotten gains in front of her, looking at first one and then another as if she were about to play her best hand during a game of poker at a super-casino. Grimacing fiercely when she heard Caroline yelling up the stairs at her about dinner, she carefully placed the purloined photos between two empty pages in the big leather-bound desk diary she kept on top of her chest of drawers and then followed Flash, and the smell of her favourite garlic and rosemary roasted potatoes, down the wide main staircase, along the painting-filled hallway, past the dresser that held a riotous bunch of flowers in a blue glass vase, through the red dining room and into the kitchen, where the Slaters always ate when there were only a few of them in residence.

Caroline was pulling a huge and wonderful-smelling leg of roast lamb from the Aga when Jinx slipped into her seat and reached for the open bottle of Pinot Noir in front of her. She gave Liberty – who was listening to Martin tell a story about his latest video campaign and laughing in all the right places – a discreet thumbs-up to indicate she'd located the dress and turned her attention to her mother as Caroline started heaping leeks and carrots swimming in her glorious homemade cheese sauce on to Jinx's plate.

They chomped happily and giggled at Martin's ridiculous jokes until the harmonious atmosphere was abruptly shattered when Caroline casually mentioned that she'd spoken to Martin's sister Perdita on the phone that day. Jinx nearly choked on a rogue piece of potato and Martin flushed red at the very reminder that Perdita the Terrible still stalked the earth, no doubt causing misery and destruction wherever she went.

'She said,' Caroline continued determinedly, resolutely ignoring her husband's and her daughter's horrified reaction, 'that since Jinx has clearly turned into such a lovely young lady she was thinking of sending Cassie to Stagmount next year.'

Jinx really did start choking at this point and, since Martin and Caroline were too busy facing up to each other to notice that their only daughter might actually be dying right in front of them, it was left to a smirking Liberty to attempt to give her the Heimlich manoeuvre.

'Fuck!' gasped Jinx when she'd recovered the power of speech and wrestled herself away from Liberty's surprisingly strong grip. 'I hope you told her there was *no way* that little bitch would fit in. Or *get* in for that matter – she's practically retarded!'

'Oh, don't be ridiculous, Jinx,' Caroline said, defiantly helping herself to more lamb and heaping redcurrant jelly on to the side of her plate. 'Cassie will be absolutely fine at Stagmount. And she's doing very well at school, so there should be no problem with the entrance exams.'

'For Christ's sake, Mum! They've got names like a bunch of fucking dogs,' Jinx moaned, earning herself an approving look from Martin – who'd clearly forgotten his previous tough new zero-tolerance policy where swearing was concerned – in the process. 'I keep expecting them to have a son and call it Lassie. And then they'll need a Pongo. And a Greyfriars fucking Bobby. Oh, God, I can't stand it!'

'You *like* Perdita,' snapped Caroline, who was fast losing patience with her family's easy ability to slip into total histrionics. She really couldn't see why everyone didn't just get along with each other. 'You told me so last summer. And anyway, where she sends her daughter to school is none of your business.'

'It bloody well *is* when I'm the one who'll have to see her every sodding day,' muttered Jinx sulkily, putting her knife and fork together and pushing her half-full plate away from her. 'And you're right, I *did* like Perdita. Until I realised she'd given birth to the spawn of the devil anyway.'

Liberty, who had zero idea what was going on, nudged Jinx's leg under the table and raised her eyebrows enquiringly.

'Don't worry, Liberty,' said Caroline, whose eagle eye missed practically nothing. 'Jinx and Martin are being ridiculous. Perdita is Martin's sister and Cassie is her daughter. We haven't seen them for a while, which is why you won't have met them yet.'

'In fact, we haven't seen them' – Martin paused and looked Liberty directly in the eye, as if to give her a sense of the momentousness of what he was about to say – 'since Cassie tried to shoot her father during one of Caroline's big family barbecues about four years ago.'

'Yes,' Jinx said, quickly picking up the tale to capitalise on Liberty's expression of wide-eyed shock, 'and then the little ho bag turned the gun on me when I dared to suggest she put the fucking thing down and chill the hell out.'

'But –' Liberty's question about where the hell the retarded cousin had managed to get hold of a gun from was cut off in its infancy by Caroline.

'It wasn't a gun,' she snapped. 'Don't be so bloody dramatic, the pair of you. It was an air rifle,' she said, turning to look imploringly at Liberty. 'And Cassie did find the damn thing in George's room, so we can't consider ourselves entirely blameless.'

'I suppose that's *one* way of looking at it,' Jinx said disgustedly, while picking her teeth with her thumbnail, safe in the knowledge that this habit drove her mother wild with fury. 'I can't believe I'm going to be a bloody laughing stock in my last year thanks to *that*.'

'Well,' Caroline replied briskly, 'it might be earlier than that. If Perdita can get Cassie in she's going to try and move her at the start of next term. And,' she continued, shooting an 'I very dare you' look at Jinx, 'I don't want to hear another word on the subject. If Cassie *does* go to Stagmount you will make damn sure she has a nice time there or I'll want to know the reasons why. And that's the end of this discussion. Can I interest anyone in ice cream?'

Despite the raised eyebrows and knowing winks that flew between Martin, Jinx and Liberty after this pronouncement, the rest of the evening passed without incident. The four of them drank two more bottles of Wolf Blass Yellow Label, finished the tub of Ben & Jerry's Phish Food ice cream, followed swiftly by a large bar of Green & Black's Maya Gold chocolate, and watched *Notes on a Scandal* on Sky Box Office. All in all, the Slaters went to bed that night having had a lovely evening.

Jinx stretched, yawned, pushed up her 'Princess Sleeping' pink satin eye mask and rolled over to look at her radio alarm clock when she woke the next morning. It was only half past nine. Bloody hell, she thought, lying back against her pillows with a weary-sounding sigh, going back to school always screwed her body clock. Even if she wanted to stay in bed until lunchtime at the weekends she was so programmed to get up early that she never managed it. And since it always took her about two weeks to get back into her holiday rhythm she only really slept as much as she wanted to for about seven weeks of the year. Although Jinx was a big believer in fresh air and always slept with her window open, she relished snuggling deeper into the warmth of her goose-down duvet as the radio played her current favourite Amy Winehouse song. Liberty had taken to sleeping in the guest room adjacent to Jinx's at the beginning of last year, both of them having agreed that a night alone in a deliciously comfortable double bed was a small price to pay when they chatted late into the night at school all the time.

Jinx groaned as she heard the unmistakable sounds of Caroline giving the dogs their breakfast in one of the utility rooms directly beneath her bedroom. She *adored* Flash and couldn't stand it when stupid people said that dogs don't have the same depth of emotion as humans. As far as she was concerned, horses and dogs definitely had their own distinct personalities and one look into their eyes was enough to tell you they also experienced feelings on the grand scale.

However, it was one thing to love your dog like a brother, but completely another to have to get out of bed on a freezing-cold February morning to let him in the door before he scratched all the paint off. Even Gaymian didn't do *that*! Jinx resigned herself to the fact of getting up and gave herself five minutes tops. And sure enough there he was – barking, whining, scratching and yelping. She knew of old that he wouldn't give up until she opened the door. The Slater dogs would all eventually come when they were called, lay off the postman most mornings and could usually be trusted not to piss in the house so long as they weren't left alone for too long, but none of them was what you could describe as particularly well trained.

Whatever, she thought, as she lay back against her pillows and stroked the soft black and white folds of Flash's squashy nose, at least he wasn't boring. She'd hate to have a dull dog. She imagined it to be the canine equivalent of having a really unpopular child. Just as bad, she suspected, as having a kid who was never invited to parties and didn't have any friends would be a dog that hid behind doors when people arrived at the house or refused to run after a ball on the beach.

'Hey!' Liberty, sporting a pair of George's old boxer shorts incongruously but sexily matched with a pale peach silk camisole edged with white lace, peered round the slightly open door. 'I thought I heard you letting the beast in. He's never going to learn, is he?'

'Could you resist this?' Jinx asked, sounding for all the world like the slightly demented but very loving mother of a lunatic child, as Liberty shoved Flash over and crawled into bed next to her.

'Shall we smoke a joint?' Liberty asked languidly, reaching over to pat Flash's brindled bottom as she ignored Jinx's question.

'That's what I love about you, Lib,' said Jinx, reaching for the silver Body Shop tin emblazoned with a big green marijuana leaf that had been filled with Hemp moisturising products when she'd received it last Christmas from her grandmother, but was now far more appropriately full of king-sized Rizlas, filters, cigarette ends and a massive lump of Moroccan Black hash found behind a photo frame in Gaymian's room, 'your reliability. In an uncertain world you represent the voice of continuity.'

'What,' Liberty yelled indignantly, sure she was being mocked but not quite certain how, '*are* you talking about?'

'Never mind,' mumbled Jinx as she set about constructing a massive joint. 'And hey, Mum said George would be back from Bristol by lunchtime. He sent me a text yesterday saying he was really pleased we were all going to Jamie's too. He can have something to eat, put a wash on and then ship us all straight back to Brighton.'

'Hmmm,' Liberty agreed half-heartedly, before sitting up straight as the beautiful dress hanging on the back of Jinx's wardrobe door caught her attention. 'Are we going to get changed here then? There's no point in us going back to school and out again, or we'll have to come up with some lie about what we're doing and where we're going.'

'Yeah.' Jinx nodded. 'You're right. We'll hang out here all day until it's time to sort ourselves out ready to leave. Then we'll get changed and head straight off to Jamie's.'

The girls flung on dressing gowns thoughtfully stolen from the Sanctuary spa in London by Jinx at the end of her last – highly successful until she had gleefully shown off her spoils in front of the packed commuter train home – mother/daughter bonding day and sauntered off to Gaymian's room. The small flat roof easily accessed via the big picture window behind his desk was not only an absolute suntrap but also hidden from the rest of the house, unless someone peered right out of Caroline and Martin's bathroom window. These two factors had combined to make it easily the Slater kids' number one favourite place to turn on in the morning.

'You know, Lib,' Jinx said, as she leaned against the red-brick wall, pulled her dressing gown tighter around her body and turned her face to the dazzlingly bright winter morning sun, 'it's really funny to think that the last time I sat here I was completely miserable, wondering if you were OK and if I was ever going to see you again. And now – well, everything's fucking great!'

'I know,' Liberty replied, resting her head momentarily against Jinx's arm. 'Everything *is* fucking great. And I'm so excited for you tonight with Jamie. I'd love it if you two got together. He's so cool and such a dude. Great clothes too!'

'And he's got loads of nice friends,' replied an extremely over-excited Jinx, punching Liberty on the arm so hard she squealed. 'We can go on double dates!'

Unfortunately, Liberty's rather high-pitched squeal caught the attention of Martin Slater, who was currently taking great care with the flossing of his immaculate white teeth in his en suite bathroom. He put his floss aside, rinsed his mouth with a handful of water from the tap and pulled the blind up in order to open the window. He peered out towards the field where the neighbouring farmer's cows were enjoying a late, just-delivered breakfast of sweet-smelling hay and was gratified to see nothing remotely out of the ordinary going on there. He had long held suspicions about just how trustworthy the farmer was and had often woken up sweating from terrifying nightmares in which a pack of gypsies had taken the place over.

Caroline, of course, regularly and loudly told him not to be so bloody stupid, but something similar had happened to a business associate and he hadn't slept easy since. He turned his head awkwardly to peer over to the other side, but didn't expect to see anything much of note occurring over by the stables and the back of the house. His deep displeasure at seeing his daughter and her best friend smoking what was undoubtedly – now he caught a whiff of it on the morning breeze – a very strong joint caused him to jolt involuntarily. He screamed in pain as his neck caught in a very uncomfortable twisted position and froze tight.

Cursing at full volume as he pelted along the corridor with his neck stuck out at a forty-five-degree angle from its usual position and wearing only his blue and white striped pyjama bottoms, Martin burst into Gaymian's room, intent on giving the miscreants a piece of his mind at the very least. Didn't they have some bloody *work* to do? Sometimes he really wondered whether paying those exorbitant school fees term after term was bloody worth it. He was pulled up short by the gales of laughter he heard as soon as he entered the room.

The girls' extreme mirth was evidently largely to do with having been caught in the act by him just now. They'd obviously turned round to witness the neck-freezing episode when he'd yelped involuntarily with the pain. In *his* day, he thought furiously, kids had some bloody respect. If *his* father had caught him smoking a

175

reefer at their age – in his own bloody house, for God's sake – he'd have had his bottom tanned, his allowance stopped and his car taken away indefinitely. At the very *least*! Either way, he certainly wouldn't have sat there and *laughed* – practically in the poor man's face.

God, sometimes he couldn't help but think that his kids were getting seriously out of hand. He really must readdress the thorny issue of parental respect. As it was, Martin felt suitably deflated by the current lack of any and therefore disinclined to make a scene. Since he also wasn't sure his neck was currently up to handling a major freak-out, he consoled himself with standing by the window, leaning awkwardly over in order that the stoners could see and hear him, and saying loudly, 'At least try and lay off in the bloody *morning*. For Christ's sake, girls, at your age you should be out seizing the day, not sitting around here watching your precious youth fly by through a stoned glaze! And if your mother catches you there'll be hell to pay.'

Feeling that his parental duties had been more than fulfilled by this, he turned round self-righteously and prepared to finish his morning ablutions. He was not impressed at all when he reached Gaymian's door to hear yet more gales of manic, unstoppable laughter overtake the by now helpless pair. Looking back, he saw the girls collapse against each other on the small roof in a pile of shuddering hysteria and Jinx start to wipe her frantically streaming eyes and nose on the bottom of Liberty's dressing gown, which he realised with a shud-der, now he studied it more intently, closely resembled the one that had been missing from its rightful hook on the back of his dressing-room door for the last few weeks.

After spending the morning screaming and shouting with irrepressible laughter every time they saw, heard or even thought about Martin and the doobie incident, Jinx and Liberty gorged themselves on one of Caroline's glorious chicken, halloumi cheese, asparagus, sun-dried tomato and avocado salads at lunchtime and then went upstairs to Jinx's room. They planned to go through Jinx's wardrobe and their make-up for this evening's activities, so had loaded themselves up with a six-pack of Diet Cokes pilfered from Martin's special 'mixers' fridge, a packet of dark-chocolate digestive biscuits from the larder and Chastity's latest compilation CD – she made these regularly during evenings when she was supposed to be revising, handing them out to her best mates the next morning in tutor group. This one had her writing scrawled over the front in green marker pen. Chastity, never known for her modesty, had called it 'just another mix – epic as usual' and they couldn't wait to get it blasting out.

Lying on the white sheepskin rug that covered 90 per cent of Jinx's bedroom floor, Jinx and Liberty were sharing another spliff. They'd thought about taking it outside, but it was so cold and they felt it would be mean to raise Martin's blood pressure any further. When Jinx suggested swiping a few of her mum's strong-smelling Diptyque candles from their various locations around the house to mask the whiff of weed, it had seemed like the most civilised thing in the world for the two of them to take to Jinx's bedroom after loudly and loftily proclaiming that they would be working on their revision and therefore must not be disturbed for at least the next two hours.

'I feel like I'm in a boutique hotel,' Liberty said, sighing ecstatically as she rolled around on the ridiculously comfortable rug. 'I can't tell you how much I've missed *this*. I love coming here.'

'I know,' Jinx replied, her current satisfaction levels also at an all-time high. 'I love school, but I can't imagine how people must have coped in, like, the seventies, when boarders were only allowed home at half-term.'

'Talking of the seventies,' Liberty added, directing an obvious smirk over to the uncovered legs on show in the space between the top of Jinx's socks and the hem of her tracksuit bottoms, 'are you planning to shave your legs or is this a considered look? Do you think Jamie digs the whole boho thing? Because, just so you know, it's not quite the same this time round . . .'

'Fuck you, Latiffe!' Jinx screamed, throwing the biscuit she'd been nibbling at Liberty but missing and hitting the wall instead. 'How very dare you! Of *course* I'm going to shave my fucking legs. I'm waiting for *you* to finally finish hogging that bloody spliff and then I'm going to run myself a long hot tub and wallow in it . . . oh, for an hour at least. And before you start with the beseeching looks, *I'm* in Mum and Dad's bathroom today, so you can piss off to the green one!'

'*Touché*,' said Liberty with a laugh, waving her hand in

the flame of the rose-scented candle in an attempt to intensify its delicious smell. 'I like the green one best anyway. Hey, Jinx . . .' Liberty paused and rolled over on to her front, eyeing her pal before continuing. 'Have you thought about what you're going to tell George about Jamie? Are you even going to bother saying anything, or what?'

'Hmmm,' murmured Jinx, who had actually been thinking about this very issue on and off for the last few weeks, and more intensively during the last couple of days, but had yet to mention anything about it to her friends. 'George knows we get on, obviously. But I haven't decided whether I should tell him how *much* I like Jamie. I've been trying to think about what's best, but to be honest we've been so freaking busy lately I haven't come up with anything. What do you think I should do?'

'I don't know,' Liberty said, drawing her words out in a manner which indicated she was currently engaging in very deep thoughts indeed. 'Maybe . . . *nothing*. Yes,' she continued, sitting up as she warmed to her theme, 'what's the point of saying anything when you don't quite know what you're saying yet – if you see what *I'm* saying, of course?'

Jinx, who saw exactly what Liberty meant and liked the thought of saying nothing a great deal more than she liked to think about George's reaction to the news that she was in love with his best friend, nodded happily. She took a last deep toke on their spliff before putting the still-smouldering end into a Coke can, where it hissed and sizzled fiercely for a few seconds before going out.

- * -

Lying in water so hot the mirrors wouldn't de-steam for hours after she'd pulled the plug, her face and body bright red from the heat, Jinx reached over to replace the pot of intensive Frizz-Ease conditioning mask on the shelf at the side of the roll-top bath and ran the hot tap. She dumped half a bottle of Kiehl's Original Musk into the running water and smiled as the glorious scent punched all others out of its way as soon as it hit and mingled with the damp bathroom air. Discovered by Kiehl's in a mysterious vat labelled 'Love Oil' in their apothecary in the fifties, it had been discovered by Jinx in the Brighton branch of Space NK on one of her many shopping trips there last year. Truly, though, gimmick or not, its heavy scent was redolent of romance. It smelt like the most brilliantly passionate love affair but also, somehow, of the bittersweet nostalgia that follows its end. Not that Jinx had ever experienced much of either, but whatever, here's hoping!

She took a deep breath and pushed her head back and under the water. She held her breath as long as she could before rising, Venus-like, from the water and using both hands to smooth her wet hair away from her face. She examined her rather stubbly calves, reached for Martin's new razor – God, he went properly psychopathically *mad* when he eventually cottoned on to the fact that his wife and daughter did this all the time – and propped a foot between the taps, ready to make her legs shiny and beautiful even in the dead of winter.

Some women, she thought with a shudder, claim that shaving one's legs is anti-feministic. Well, as far as Jinx – who considered herself an excellent feminist – was concerned, she'd rather cover herself up in one of her grandmother's disgusting khaki tent dresses than lie on a beach without having dealt with her bikini line, legs and armpits. It wasn't a sexist thing either, as she also couldn't stand to see men covered in unsightly moustaches, beards or – eeew – chest rugs. Christ, hair removal was common bloody courtesy as far as she was concerned. And making it into something it was so blatantly *not*, that was the real crime against feminism: a fucking own goal from a moron insider. Didn't these ridiculous people have more important things to think about – like, you know, equal-pay issues, fighting with the so-called 'pro' lifers and changing the appalling rape laws? Anyway, she reflected a few seconds later, running an admiring hand up and down her own gleaming shins, if nothing else one's pins always felt so lovely and smooth afterwards.

Jinx and Liberty both jumped as if shot when their full-body moisturising session in Jinx's bedroom was rudely interrupted by a sudden fierce banging against the locked door. George had only been home for five minutes but the noise levels were already verging towards ASBO territory.

'You'll have the sodding neighbours round in a minute if you carry on like that,' Jinx yelled. 'We're busy – we'll be down in a second. Fuck off and raid the fridge or something!'

'All right, all right,' George said, his booming voice not at all muffled by the heavy oak door. 'Keep your hair on, sis – we don't *have* any bloody neighbours. We're at the top of a long drive and surrounded by farmland, remember? See you two downstairs.'

'I definitely,' said Liberty with a worried glance at the door, 'think you should keep all the Jamie stuff to yourself. I don't think George would be pissed off about it in the slightest, but can you imagine the bloody *jokes*?'

'I know,' replied Jinx firmly, pulling on her old favourite black velvet Miss Sixty tracksuit bottoms over her now glistening legs. 'You're right. It would be awful. I'd be constantly looking over my shoulder, worried about what he was saying and to whom. He's never quite worked out what's appropriate and what's not.' There was a thoughtful pause as she slipped a hot pink Kenzo T-shirt she'd filched from Caroline's dressing room over her head. 'Or maybe he *has* and just doesn't care who he winds up. Either way, I'm not saying a freaking word.'

Tripping down the stairs half an hour later in a cloud of L'Artisan Parfumeur's Fou d'Absinthe – Jinx thought her current favourite perfume the scent equivalent of wearing full body armour – and Bulgari's Au The Vert – Liberty's far more subtle choice – shaved, body-oiled and moisturised, nails painted and fake-tanned up to the max, the girls felt very pleased with their pre-party preparations indeed.

They pulled up short when, through the banisters and the half-open door beyond, they spied a small blonde girl lounging on the overstuffed white sofa in the huge drawing room the Slaters hardly ever used. Decorated predominantly in varying shade of white and cream, it contained Caroline's beloved baby grand piano, hundreds of family photographs in all kinds of frames and shelves groaning under the weight of myriad poetry books. It was very much Caroline's room and the family normally only hung out in there to drink champagne and open their presents on Christmas Day.

'Oh, fuck,' moaned Jinx to Liberty as the girl stood up. 'I'm sure that's Lydia. She was such a bitch to me on New Year's Eve – God, I hope she's not coming to Jamie's party too.'

'I bet you she *is*,' Liberty replied, equally morosely, for she'd heard all about Not So Lovely Lydia's New Year's Eve antics from a still-irate Jinx at the beginning of term. 'Otherwise he wouldn't have brought her back here, would he?'

'Finally!' George, clutching a bottle of Laurent-Perrier Rosé and four champagne flutes – which looked too cosy by half as far as Jinx was concerned – pushed through the swing door from the kitchen and stood looking up at them from the hall with a very cheeky grin. 'I thought you might have died up there. Come and have a drink.'

Thinking what an absolute bona fide fool he was,

Jinx grimaced at him as Lydia stood up – very elegantly, considering the ridiculously high heels on her pointy black shoes and the fearsomely tight black pencil skirt she was sporting underneath a ruffled cream silk shirt – and moved over to the marble fireplace, affording her an excellent view of the two halfway down the stairs. Jinx knew that she and Liberty were being appraised as Lydia leaned against the marble mantelpiece with her back to the grate, slowly lit a cigarette and, as she exhaled, pushed her chest out and sucked her tummy – which was pretty flat anyway – in.

'Jinx,' she said eventually, in an incredibly fake nice voice as if the New Year's Eve incident had never happened, 'how lovely to see you. And this must be the famous Liberty.'

'Hmm,' Jinx grunted rudely, barely looking at Lydia – she still couldn't quite *believe* the woman was in her house like this – before she turned straight back to a grinning George, who was clearly oblivious to any tension whatsoever. 'We need to ask you something – can we have a word upstairs please?'

'Sure thing,' said George expansively. 'Let me dump the champers down here and I'll be straight up. What do you want? Have you run out of weed again?'

Jinx didn't bother to reply but pulled a disgusted face, grabbed Liberty's hand and stomped back upstairs, where the two of them hovered round the corner from the bathroom long enough to hear Lydia's tinkling laugh ring out loud, proud and evidently very pleased with itself, from the drawing room.

'Christ!' hissed Jinx. 'That's high-pitched enough to break the fucking glass on every frame in the room. Mum would go *mad* if she knew he was letting that slut smoke in there too. What's he thinking of, inviting her to Jamie's tonight? Last time he saw her he couldn't get away fast enough. What a fucking idiot.'

'What's up, sis?' George said, running up the stairs two at a time before sweeping Jinx off her feet and spinning her round in a huge bear hug. 'Excited about tonight?'

'Put me down!' squealed a not-at-all-amused Jinx, thumping him on the back in protest at the same time. 'And what the hell are you doing bringing *her*? I thought you hated that bitch!'

'Ah,' George said suavely, before turning round to administer the same greeting to a grinning Liberty and thereby buying himself a few seconds to think of an explanation that would satisfy his irate sister. 'Yes. Well. Things have – er – *changed* on that front.'

'I'd say,' retorted Jinx, staring mutinously at him and silently daring him not to come up with a better explanation than that. 'Come on – let's have it. How did the Wicked Witch of the West con you this time?'

George stood in front of them, looking thoughtful – *how best to put this to my kid sister?* – but was saved from answering by his mother, a great number of shopping bags dangling from her arms, shoving open the front door with a clatter. As she walked in, Caroline caught sight of the three standing up there at the top of the stairs and smiled, before sniffing the air and turning round to see the drawing-room door open.

'Jinx!' Caroline said, suddenly furious. 'Have you been smoking in my music room? It's really not fair,' she continued, on a roll now, shaking her fist menacingly up the stairs. 'You know I can't bear the smell of smoke when I'm practising. And what on earth will the vicar think when he comes round later to go through Sunday's hymns?'

Jinx's outraged protestations never got the opportunity of an airing as Lydia chose that moment to creep round the open door into the hall, slinking against the wall like one of the dogs when they knew they'd done something wrong. She had at least, the others realized as they watched her adopt a prize fawning position in front of a very confused Caroline, managed to jettison the offending fag somewhere en route.

'Lydia,' Caroline said, with about as much enthusiasm as if she'd been greeted by a massive pile of dog mess on the hall carpet, and much to Jinx and Liberty's amusement, 'how . . . nice to see you.'

'Hello, Mrs Slater,' replied Lydia, in such an obsequious tone the others were left in no doubt whatsoever that, if she could have curtsied without looking like even more of a prize pillock than she already did, she would have done so. 'It's lovely to see *you*. And,' she continued breathlessly, looking up at a decidedly unimpressed Caroline from underneath her long black eyelashes, which were currently batting up and down at an astounding rate, 'I'm really sorry, but I have to tell you it was me smoking in your beautiful piano room, not Jinx. I *am* sorry – I really had no idea you were so anti!'

'Well,' Caroline replied briskly, gathering her bags around her ready to take them upstairs, 'no harm done. You're welcome to smoke in the kitchen – George,' she said, directing a meaningful look up the stairs at her son, who immediately started down them in response, 'will find you an ashtray.'

Jinx grinned at Liberty as George made a big show of ushering Lydia through to the kitchen, promising her champagne and as many cigarettes as she could fit into her mouth at any one time. Caroline raised her eyebrows as she drew level with the girls and grabbed Jinx in a massive hug.

'Sorry, darling,' Caroline said extra-solicitously – with no idea of the vast amount of gurning and winking going on between the two girls behind her back – 'it was really mean of me to blame you. I might have known it had something to do with that bloody girl. I still haven't forgiven her for dying my new white bath towels bright pink instead of her hair. The last I heard she and George weren't speaking at all after they broke up. When did she come back on the scene?'

'I don't know, Mum,' Jinx said breezily, not at all displeased at having her mother wrongfully blame her like this, convinced she'd benefit from it later. 'George is an idiot, obviously. Where's Dad?'

'He went next door to talk to the farmer about the cows. In fact, you don't want to pop round and get him back, do you, darling? I can't face going round there after last time.'

'He's probably drinking homemade nettle wine and talking about hobgoblins by now,' muttered Jinx, thinking that the trek across two big fields to rescue her father from the pair of weirdo psychic horse whisperers who lived 'next door' to the Slaters and who just *loved* to chat – for hours, non-stop – was the last thing she felt like doing right now. She brightened considerably, however, as the obvious solution presented itself. 'Can't *George* go, Mum? Lydia would probably love to get outside and have a mini-ramble. She's so sporty!'

Caroline, cottoning on very quickly, thought this a simply marvellous idea and disappeared rapidly downstairs to put Jinx's evil plan into action. Their rival thus easily dispatched of, Jinx and Liberty sniggered at each other for a while before settling down to the serious business of emptying their make-up bags on to the floor, rooting about for long-lost eyeshadows and forgotten glosses while phoning Liv, Charlie and Chastity for last-minute fashion consultations. They also decided – in order to take the 'edge off' the car journey with Lydia and the grinning fool, naturally – to smoke one more spliff.

Pulling up outside the imposing white building where Jamie's penthouse apartment occupied the whole top floor, Jinx reflected that it was a very good thing George had been given such an amazing new car stereo for Christmas. As it was, she and Liberty had spent the whole two-hour journey sitting in the back and singing along to the *Dance Anthems* album they'd lifted from Gaymian's room, while furiously texting their friends and each other about what a total loser George's girlfriend was.

Completely unable to hear anything Lydia might have said to them, they pointedly ignored her anyway, reasoning, as they so often did when presented with any situation out of the ordinary, that it was worth it for the practice if nothing else.

Checking her face for the final time in her hand mirror, Jinx was delighted with the incontrovertible evidence that her mascara had for once stayed put on her eyelashes and her nose still looked as pleasantly shine-free as it had in the bathroom mirror just before they'd left home.

Liberty nudged Jinx hard in the ribs, winked and pointed up to Jamie's windows and the surrounding decked balcony, just visible from the road as George backed expertly into a space right in front of the building. All in darkness save for a few multicoloured pulsing disco lights that illuminated, off and on, a couple leaning over the balcony railings sharing what looked like a joint, there was most definitely a carnival atmosphere up there. When George cut the engine and turned round to smile extremely smugly at his passengers in the back for getting them here not only in one piece but practically to the door like this, they could all hear the dull yet wildly exciting throb of some seriously hardcore house music pumping through the night air.

Liberty snatched Jinx's mirror out of her hand and, using the glow from the streetlights outside, pouted at herself for a few seconds from various angles. A pleased smile showed she was extremely happy with the stunning reflection pouting right back at her. She slipped on the crushed-silk Miu Miu heels in burnt orange she'd kicked into the foot well as soon as they'd set off, opened the back door, stood up and smoothed down the front of her black Stella McCartney bubble dress. She'd straightened her long hair so that her choppy fringe swept seductively over one eye and she looked gorgeous. Good enough, as George had rather inappropriately said after doing a double take when he saw her walk down the stairs at home earlier, to eat.

In the silk Simultane shift dress, worn over skinny black jeans teamed with her most favourite shoes ever – glittery gold Top Shop platforms with a chunky golden heel – and a short black-and-white houndstooth French Connection swing jacket, Jinx looked pretty damn hot to trot as well.

The two of them stood on the street and looked each other over approvingly before doing a noisy high five and squealing with excitement, much to Lydia's disapproval. Jinx caught sight of Lydia's I'm-too-cool-for-school disdainful look and flicked a quick V sign at her back. This caused Liberty to snort with laughter and Lydia to spin round again and fix them with a blacker look than one would have thought such a small, silly girl capable of producing on a dark night like this.

And if that look was bad, thought Jinx and Liberty at

the same time but unbeknownst to each other, then the one she fixed upon the objects of an impromptu wolf whistle from George a few seconds later was something else entirely. This was positively malevolent, evil enough to send a real-life shiver down both their spines and make them immediately crane their necks in that direction too.

'Fucking hell, Jinx,' hissed Liberty, nudging her friend really quite hard in the ribs in her joy at being the first to realise what had caused the commotion. 'I can't believe it – look at *that*!'

Sashaying down the pavement, looking as if their names were in fact Sheba, Salome and Scheherazade instead of the rather drab Chekhovian originals, were Stagmount's very own identical Russian triplets.

George's was by no means the only jaw that came to rest nearly on the floor as they approached. Passers-by, the drivers and passengers of three cars stuck behind a red traffic light, a motley bunch of students – drinking cans of cider and wearing ostentatiously holey attire, they couldn't have stereotyped themselves better if they'd tried – sitting on the bench at the bus stop, a glamorous old lady in a mink coat with big hair and a slash of scarlet lipstick walking her black pug very slowly down the seafront side of the pavement, a cyclist illegally going the opposite way on the same side and, of course, Jinx, Liberty and Lydia ranged alongside George on the other, were all equally enthralled by the spectacle of the sisters marching along.

Arms linked, striding in unison, flashes of bright

white teeth occasionally glinting in the dark against their glossed lips and lightly tanned faces, the three talked and laughed among themselves. With their hair flying out behind them, they looked as if they were playing the heroines in a Hollywood blockbuster currently on location in a seedy seaside town, filming the short but explosive and impressive trailer for cinema. At first Jinx and Liberty were too stunned by the whole scene, the passers-by and everything, to realise that the triplets were crossing the road at high speed specifically to talk to *them*.

'Liberty! Jinx!' said Olga loudly, beaming at them in the friendliest way and taking each of their left hands warmly in both of hers. 'How funny to see you here. We are going out for dinner – would you like to come with us?'

'Yes,' added Masha, putting an arm round Liberty's shoulder and squeezing her in the most tender, loving way. 'We would love that.'

'That's *so* kind of you, girls,' Liberty replied, loving the fact that the traffic light had gone green but the three cars had remained in their stationary position and none of the other onlookers showed much sign of moving anywhere fast either. 'Normally we would have *loved* to have dinner with you, but we're going to a party in this building and we're already kind of late.'

'Maybe,' said Jinx, raising her eyebrows meaningfully at George, trying to get his attention, 'you guys should come and join us after you've had dinner? You haven't met my brother yet, have you?'

Ignoring the absolute daggers that Lydia's eyes were now shooting into Jinx and Liberty's shapely backs, George managed to get a grip on himself and asserted immediately that the triplets were of course more than welcome to attend the party, that they *must* do so. 'In fact,' he added in an incredibly cheesy tone of voice, 'I will personally be very disappointed if you do not.'

Lydia ignored Jinx's and Liberty's pretend gagging and also the triplets as they laughed prettily at it, said their goodbyes and sauntered off down the road – nearly causing a ten-car pile-up as a lady turning right before the pier took her eyes off the road for a few seconds too many, managing to recover herself and her vehicle only just in time. Lydia also ignored George's conciliatory tone as he offered to take her arm, turned on her heel and started marching determinedly in the direction of Jamie's front door without a backwards glance.

Standing by the door of the bedroom where they were supposed to leave their coats, unable to get in because the current occupants were having very loud sex in there, Jinx and Liberty were banging impatiently on the door at the same time as giggling to each other about how furious Lydia had been when the triplets came on the scene. Feeling highly over-excitable anyway, due to the high-end levels of fabulousness she was sure this night was capable of producing, Jinx was just doing a very mean impression of Lydia stomping off when she turned round and came face to face with her.

Liberty snorted with sudden laughter. She just couldn't help herself. The whole Lydia thing was becoming way too much like hard work. Jinx and her *were* here to have fun, after all, and the expression on Jinx's face *was* a perfect comic mix of horrified guilt at finding the subject of her little one-man show suddenly standing in front of her like this and rage at being caught in the act by the same.

'I bet you think this is really funny, don't you, Jinx?' Lydia's lip trembled, but she folded her arms and raised her chin so that she seemed built entirely of a series of angry, angular points. 'Well, you don't understand it now but you will. You wait until you see someone *you* like slobbering after someone else. Or *three* someone elses! See how you like it. I bet you'll go mad!'

'I won't actually,' said Jinx firmly, eyeing Lydia with more disapproval than ever. Didn't the fucking girl have any self-control, for God's sake! 'And, for the record, Lyds, you're only TWENTY-TWO. I can't fucking stand being patronised by people who are, like, four and a half years older than me and seem to think they've had all these life experiences and whatever and are therefore licensed to preach. The whole thing's so freaking stupid.'

Jinx made a disgusted face, grabbed Liberty's arm and dragged her off to the double doors leading to the decked roof terrace complete with hot tub, huge Indian-style cushions strewn around the floor and a white canopy to shelter revellers from wind and rain.

'*This* is more like it,' she said, breathing a sigh of relief as she turned to Liberty and grinned. 'What a fucking wet blanket that Lydia is. She's the type of girl who makes a point of not having any friends prettier than she is.'

'Yeah . . .' said Liberty, gazing in sheer delight at all the beautiful, interesting-looking people lounging around the candlelit low tables and not really listening to a word Jinx was saying.

'You know,' said Jinx, warming to her theme and quite unaware of Liberty's total lack of interest, 'as far as *I'm* concerned, I *like* having attractive people around. It makes the world seem a happier place somehow and it's aesthetically pleasing if nothing else. It's great to always have someone to perve over, and anyway, you shouldn't discriminate. Why *shouldn't* attractive people be treated well? It's not the triplets' fault they're so freaking good-looking, is it? They're just being friendly, for fuck's sake.'

'Lydia's like a prettier version of Daisy,' said Liberty, half listening.

'You're so right,' Jinx replied, as she looked around casually, hoping to spot Jamie but not wanting anyone to know what she was up to. 'But I mean, Christ – she's only twenty-tossing-two. You'd think she was sixty-four at *least*, the way she was banging on to us about all that "one day you'll understand" bullshit. Please, darling, promise me you'll punch me in the face if you ever hear me talking to any seventeen-year-olds like that when *we're* her age. Anyway,' she said, looking around once more before deciding her best bet for finding Jamie was if they moved about a bit, 'fuck her. DBM. That means don't bore me. No, not *you*, Lib, Lydia of course!' Jinx rolled her eyes quickly so Liberty wouldn't spot her. 'Let's go and get some urgent drinks – I'm dying of thirst over here.'

Throwing their coats behind a mammoth navy sofa, the two of them wended their way through the very well-dressed throng to the makeshift bar two black-uniformed cocktail waiters had set up in the corner of the outside deck. George still hadn't reappeared from wherever he'd scarpered off to as soon as they'd come in, but what with the amazing canapés knocking around and a set of wicked beats coming from the silver decks in front of the glass wall of the living room just inside, this party most definitely had the makings of an out-standing night.

'Where are Liv and Charlie?' Jinx leaned over and yelled in Chastity's ear, trying to make herself heard above the amazing tunes a female DJ – wearing a short, tight pur-ple boob-tube dress over bare shoulders and legs liber-ally dusted with sparkly body powder, strappy silver sandals and a pair of huge angel wings made of white feathers and silver sequins – was spinning on the decks.

As soon as the dirty blonde, slightly louche-looking self-styled angel started playing Prince's 'Kiss', pretty much everyone at the party rammed themselves into the living room at once. Big as it was, since there was not enough space for anyone to throw any shapes to speak of, they were currently all jumping up and down in time to the beat. Bouncing off each other and everyone around them, splashes from held-aloft drinks occasionally landing on their hot skin and momentarily cooling it down, the girls were having the most incredible time.

Jinx had seen Jamie once or twice out of the corner of her eye, but hadn't yet managed to say hello to him. He was wearing now faded, once dark blue Wrangler jeans, a white T-shirt with a picture of KFC's Colonel Saunders on the front in neon pink, kind of like an Andy Warhol print, and Spring Court shoes. The overall effect was way cool and pretty amazing to a completely smitten Jinx. Although the meeting and greeting of all his friends, as far as it appeared to her anyway, was obviously a bloody time-consuming old business and Jinx was beginning to wonder whether she would *ever* get him alone.

George had resurfaced and was studiously avoiding Lydia's eye while chatting up lots of the more arty girls, who were mostly wearing variations on tight black outfits accented with flashes of bright neon colour – shoes, handbags, hairbands or chunky statement pieces of fluorescent jewellery. Lydia, conversely, was in the thick of what looked like an off-duty doting rugby scrum. Lots of well-built boys wearing pink, blue or white open-necked shirts ubiquitously and unimaginatively paired with pale blue jeans and brown loafers were clamouring to fetch her more drinks or invite her to dance. She looked a hell of a lot happier than when they'd arrived, that was for sure.

Although Chastity and Paul had arrived at eight thirty, about half an hour after Jinx's crew, there was still no sign of Liv and Charlie and neither of them – most unusually – was answering her mobile phone. Whatever, it was now half past nine, the party was in full swing and they were all so busy having a total blast they didn't give the missing two more than the occasional, cursory thought and a quick, mental two fingers at their amazing negligence.

After a few more energetic songs, during which Jinx and Liberty both noticed that Chastity kept edging towards them and away from her boyfriend, the foursome stumbled outside to cool down in the chill night air. Sweating quite a lot after all that vigorous aerobic exercise on the dance floor and flushed with the combination of great music and stunning raspberry mojitos, caipirinhas and dirty martinis that the bar guys were dishing out at a rate of knots, they were also imbued with the general sense of excellent well-being that a great party always fosters among those hanging ten in the chill-out area. Finding a few spare striped silk floor cushions scattered around a low table holding tea lights in glass jars, some dirty champagne flutes and a massive bong, the girls flung themselves down and kicked off their shoes while Paul went to the bar on a cocktail mission.

'Fucking hell,' sighed Liberty, taking a huge breath as she leaned on her elbows and flexed her neck back and from side to side before exhaling slowly, 'this party is *fantastic*. Where are Liv and Charlie?'

'Don't forget the triplets!' Jinx said, giggling as she kicked off her golden heels, curled her legs underneath her and reached for the very professional-looking bong lying centre stage on the table in front of them. 'Fuck, guys . . . check out this bad boy!'

'What about the triplets?' Chastity asked, reaching into the black quilted Chanel handbag on a gold chain her mum had given her for Christmas, pulling out a lump of sticky hash and chucking it at Jinx. 'Are they coming tonight too? When did you speak to them?'

'We bumped into them on the street when we got here,' Liberty said, not so subtly eyeing up a beautiful dark-haired boy who had just sat down at the next table and was smiling right back at her. 'They practically created a public affray when they stopped to talk to us, as per.'

'You're damn right,' added Jinx in a joke Rastafarian accent, crumbling the hash into the bowl and taking out her lighter before reverting to her usual voice. 'And a private one too, judging by Lydia's freak-out when George couldn't take his eyes off them. I never liked her anyway. *And* she had the cheek to tell Lib and me we'd understand "one day". The fucking bitch is only bloody twenty-two. Anyway, I think he's well shot of her.'

'Yes,' Chastity said, in much quieter tones than normal, looking over her shoulder to where Paul was coming towards them, carefully balancing a circular silver tray laden with fruit-filled cocktails. 'I guess he is.'

An 'Everybody's Free' remix came on and Chastity cocked her head to one side, frowning thoughtfully at the lyric before she turned back round to face the table. Next to her, Jinx, who thought Chastity was definitely not quite as enthusiastic about the evening as she could have been, was offering her a toke on the massive and fully loaded bong. She held her hair back, leaned forward, inhaled deeply and exhaled a potent cloud of smoke together with an appreciative naughty giggle just as Paul reached them with the tray.

'For God's sake, Chastity,' he said, looking really cross and not bothering to lower his voice in front of the others, 'you know I can't stand it when you get stoned.'

'Stop being such a fucking nob, Paul,' Chastity hissed, her eyes flashing cobalt daggers at him. 'You're really bugging me. I can do whatever the fuck I like.'

Even though they were pretty baked, Liberty and Jinx looked at each other in horror – they had *never* heard Chastity and Paul speak so dismissively to each other as this.

'Mojito, Jinx?' Paul said, avoiding Chastity's eyes and pointedly turning his back on her to face the others. 'Liberty?'

'Um . . . thanks, Paul,' said Jinx quietly, not quite sure where to look, 'that's great.'

Liberty accepted equally meekly and they immediately started downing their cocktails in great long gulps – not least for something to do in the face of such icy froideur coming in waves off their formerly loved-up pals. Chastity stood up without a word, surprisingly steady on her feet given the huge amount of high-grade Nepalese Twist – a real connoisseur's smoke, incidentally

– hash she'd just ingested. She turned on the thin steel heel of her black pointy Prada boots and stalked off in the direction of the relative privacy of the hallway inside. It was obvious to all of them that her intention was for Paul to follow right after her. Without a word and with an extremely pissy look on his face, he did so, leaving behind Jinx and Liberty, who were more than a little drunk, stoned as hell and shocked by the angry scene they'd just witnessed.

'Trouble in paradise,' said Jinx, giggling nervously at Liberty, 'who'd have thought it?'

'*I* would,' Liberty replied mischievously, giggling right back at her. 'They've been bitching and moaning at each other all term. I'm not surprised in the slightest. Oh, look! Here come the triplets.'

'And Jamie,' Jinx moaned, spotting him striding along purposefully behind them. What she really felt like doing right now was putting her head in her hands at this unfortunate conjunction, but she knocked that impulse on its head and smiled widely and, she hoped, alluringly in the direction all four were descending on them from. 'Please God let me not make a fool of myself again,' she whispered, sending her prayer heavenwards.

'Don't worry, Jin,' Liberty said quickly, after catching all but the first word of this plaintive statement on the strengthening breeze coming off the sea. She gave the triplets an admiring once-over, squeezed Jinx's leg in what was supposed to be a gesture of reassurance but only succeeded in wrinkling the silk shift dress even further and smiled encouragingly at her. 'You look stunning.

Anyway,' she continued, undermining the effect of her words somewhat, 'pretty as they are, you're so much more fun. And Jamie likes you, we *know* he does.'

Jinx's attention was fully diverted from the triplets – and indeed every single other person in the entire world – when Jamie dropped down right next to her, threw an arm round her shoulders, pulled her in close and dropped a tiny kiss on the top of her head in greeting.

It took Jinx a couple of seconds to come round from the inevitable swoon this action put her into her. When she did so she found Jamie's face level with her own. He was staring deeply into her eyes, his lips mere millimetres from her own, and the hand he'd snaked round to the nape of her neck was tugging suggestively on some curly blonde tendrils of hair. He was so close she could see each individual freckle on his nose, the different gradations of colour in his green irises and the creased vertical lines along the bottom of his lower lip. He was going to kiss her, she knew he was, and at that moment she both closed her eyes and did actually stop breathing. She felt the hand tighten against her neck, pulling her forwards slightly, and then Jamie's mouth pressed hard against her own. She parted her lips involuntarily and gasped, and pretty much as soon as she felt his tongue enter her mouth he pulled away, squeezed her shoulder and dropped into the seat next to her.

When she'd composed herself enough to look over to the table Jinx was not at all displeased to see Olga, or one of them anyway, racking out some lovely long lines of cocaine on quite a big square mirror she'd fished out of her gold Marc Jacobs tote bag. She was 100 per cent certain each and every one of them had seen everything, but thank God no one seemed to be staring at her. Jinx, hyper aware of Jamie's hand on her thigh, was on the lookout for anything that might return her heart to its normal routine and stop this leaping about in her chest it was doing.

Jinx and Liberty had taken coke once before, in London with Gaymian. Although they'd had a great time it wasn't something they'd ever think of buying for themselves. They spent their money mostly on booze, weed and the occasional disco biscuit. When they went to indie nights in the local pubs they'd get pissed and stoned, and when they went clubbing – or sometimes, to be honest, just for the fun of it on a boring Sunday afternoon – they took Es. Although coke wasn't really on their radar, they were sure as hell pleased to see it laid out before them like this tonight. The whole evening seemed somehow *much* more suited to a few civilised lines than great piles of weed ingested through the huge bong, which would only leave them exhausted and messy later on.

'So, Jinx, what's up?' said Jamie, hugging her close to his chest and tracing the line of her jaw with his forefinger.

Even though this position was actually quite uncomfortable and her neck was beginning to ache from being twisted unnaturally to the side, this action sent Jinx into practically the biggest spin she'd ever been in her whole life after the earlier kiss.

'Mmm,' she murmured, closing her eyes for a second, savouring the sensation and surreptitiously trying to stretch her neck by rolling her head round without appearing insane, 'what a freaking great party. Thanks so much for . . . Ooomfh!'

Jinx shot up in surprise after finding herself suddenly launched from Jamie's supportive arm into an undignified sprawl on her side of the cushion with no warning whatsoever. How did that happen? She looked round in confusion before frowning as the reason swam into focus in front of her. Her gaze fell on her brother and stuck there. She might have known George would bloody well have something to do with it. There he was, the grinning idiot, practically shoving Liberty off her seat as he squeezed himself on to the corner of it, smarming over the triplets at the same time as patting Jamie vigorously on the back, congratulating his best friend for holding yet another brilliant bash.

'Drinks, girls?' George said, winking at Jinx. He was obviously beside himself with excitement at his good fortune that the girls he was *really* talking to had actually turned up and mistakenly assumed his sister would share his enthusiasm.

'Yes, thanks,' Jinx snapped straight back, knowing what he was up to and deciding to play him at his own game. 'We'd love some, wouldn't we, Liberty?'

'Um,' George replied, looking at the triplets' full glasses, the meticulously laid-out lines of coke on the table in front of them and – most of all – their charming smiles. He mentally cursed his sister in the worst way. *Damn it*. He knew she had him over a barrel. He could hardly not get her what she wanted for fear of looking like a churlish bastard in front of these total honeys, could he? 'Sure thing, sis,' he continued in a level voice, smiling winningly at the identikit stunners opposite him. 'Coming right up.'

'Grab me a Corona, mate,' Jamie shouted after George's retreating back before sitting down again.

This time, he was opposite Jinx and Liberty and adjacent to the triplets, who were sitting at the head of the table, most attractively arranged around each other in a coil of slender denim-clad legs, perfectly highlighted sleek ash-blonde hair and a veritable cloud of Opium perfume.

Drinks order duly noted, Jamie turned his attention back to the incredibly interesting group of young ladies at this table. 'So,' he said, leaning forward and smiling inclusively round the table at them, 'is it true that you Stagmount girls have got a house*master* looking after you up there?'

'Yes,' they all giggled, before Liberty, really quite drunk now, added with a football-chant kind of yell at the end, 'We love Brian!'

'That bloke,' Jamie said, with a huge mock sigh at the sheer unfairness of it all, his grinning profile glowing golden in the candlelight, 'must have one of the best jobs in the world.'

'Do you think,' Jinx asked, taking advantage of George being at the bar to look over at him incredibly flirtatiously, '*you'd* be any good at pastoral care and . . .

suchlike, Jamie? Brian must be nearing retirement age by now – if you really think it's such a great job maybe you should apply.'

'Maybe I should,' he agreed, his eyes fixing Jinx to the spot as they flickered over her with unmistakable interest. 'You girls are permanently over-excited. What you need is some training and discipline.'

'Oh yes, please. Training and discipline are *exactly* what I need,' replied Jinx, looking up at Jamie from underneath her lowered lashes and feeling a delicious shiver run the whole way through her body. 'Are you very, very strict?'

'Yes,' Jamie said, winking at her. 'But I do reward good behaviour.'

The triplets didn't seem to be paying much attention to the whole sordid little dominatrix scene Jinx and Jamie were playing out, although the white bits of Liberty's eyes did seem to be a great deal more prominent than usual. After delicately hoovering up a line each using a silver snorter that formed part of the necklace Masha so rarely left the house without, Irina generously proffered the mirror to Jinx and Liberty. They took it and placed it on the table in front of them, while Liberty dug around in the bottom of her handbag for one of the £50 notes she'd stuffed in there straight from her knicker drawer before they left school to go back to the Slaters the day before.

As Liberty passed the mirror and the note she'd rolled into a thin funnel shape to Jinx, narrowly managing to resist poking her in the ribs for the Jamie chat but raising her eyebrows up and down furiously to indicate she deeply wanted to, George arrived back with a cocktail in each hand and two bottles of Corona with lime sticking out of the two deep pockets at the front of his jeans.

'I think something's going on outside, mate,' he said to Jamie, nodding over to the bar, where the student Jamie had paid to act as chief security man was now in an anxious-looking huddle with the barmen. 'They said something about a fight . . . I'd go and take a look if I was you.'

'My apologies, ladies,' Jamie said, jumping up and making a mock bow, 'but this delightful chat is most definitely to be continued! Don't move!'

'I spat in it, by the way,' George murmured in Jinx's ear just as she was finishing her first long swallow of delicious Sea Breeze and he was moving over to shamelessly steal Jamie's prime seat by the triplets. 'Hope you enjoy it!'

'You fucking asshole,' Jinx hissed back, swallowing the urgent desire she had to give her brother the worst dead arm he'd ever experienced, along with the remains of her drink. Or, better still, she could give him a dead leg – a really good one of those would have him limping for a couple of hours at *least*.

Aside from anything else, she was steaming cross that he'd so effortlessly succeeded in getting rid of Jamie. George had obviously, she thought with a smug smile, mistakenly assumed Jamie fancied the triplets and got him out the way to clear the field for himself. Well, she concluded with another self-satisfied smirk as she pulled the bottoms of her skinny jeans back down over the tops of her shoes, he'd get a surprise and a half when he realised that it *wasn't* the stunning triplets Jamie was interested in but rather his own dear sister.

'Come on, Lib,' said Jinx, standing up and beaming at the triplets – God, it wasn't *their* fault her brother was such a freaking moron and the more she saw of these girls the more she liked them. 'Let's go and find Chastity. We should at least see how she's doing.'

'Bye,' Liberty and Jinx trilled together in response to the triplets' effusive waving and protestations of many more bags of drugs to be had yet. 'And don't worry. We *so* will be back!'

'Where do you think Igor is?' Liberty asked as they wandered over to the crowd that was fast gathering by the balcony railings, looking at something happening on the road down below. 'They give him the slip all the bloody time now.'

'Yeah,' agreed Jinx, not really paying too much attention to the question of Igor's whereabouts since she was now much more interested in finding out what everyone was gazing at over the side. 'He's the worst bodyguard in the world. You'd think their dad would at least get someone who was up to the job, wouldn't you?'

As soon as Jinx had managed to squeeze herself into a small gap between two whooping boys and peer down herself, she turned round with a horrified expression on her face, grabbed Liberty's hand and wordlessly pulled her along the decking and down the main staircase that led to the street.

The sight that greeted them at the open door was so shocking it pulled them both up short for a few seconds. Chastity, her face transformed into a snarling mask of rage, the sheer intensity of which neither Jinx nor Liberty had ever witnessed before, was sitting on Paul's prone, outstretched body, bouncing up and down in fury and screaming obscenities in his ear.

Just as Jinx was gathering air into her lungs to scream at Chastity to let him go and get the hell off him, a police van, complete with flashing blues and a screaming siren, screeched to a handbrake halt at the side of the pavement.

'Oh, fuck!' said Jinx to Liberty, grabbing her best friend's arm in horror as three policemen jumped from the back of the van and surrounded Chastity and Paul. 'Fuck, fuck, FUCK!'

Chastity, stunned into sudden sanity by the lights, noise and close proximity to the boys in blue, raised her ghostly, tear-stained face and stared at the policemen in bewilderment. Paul, his own face an unbecoming shade of green that was becoming more bilious by the second, raised his head and looked round at Chastity. The movement unseated her from the small of his back and she tumbled to the side of what the voyeurs were pretty safe in their unanimous assumption was her *ex* boyfriend. She lay curled in a defeated little heap on the pavement, her Chanel bag to the side of her, prostrate at the feet of the police as if she were begging forgiveness.

Without any warning whatsoever, the frozen tableau in front of Jinx and Liberty began to show signs of movement. Paul creakily raised his head once more, turned and proceeded to deliver a stream of evil-smelling, orange projectile vomit towards Chastity's stomach area, legs and – cue involuntary shudder from Liberty – Prada boots. What had appeared to be taking place in slow-motion rewind now became a hive of frenetic activity.

'What the . . .' said the senior policeman in disgust, covering his mouth and nose in a vain attempt to disguise the smell. 'I've seen some sights in my life,' he continued, very much in the manner of an actor doing warm-up exercises before going on stage, 'let me tell you, but that is the most absolutely disgusting one yet. 'Ere, love!' He bent down to address a by now quietly sobbing Chastity, who was staring at her vomit-covered body in utter disbelief and wondering if she would ever in her life recover from this terrible scene. 'Are you all right?'

'I'm the one who's not all right, for fuck's sake!' said Paul bitterly, standing up and steadying himself on the ornate lamppost next to him when it was touch and go whether his legs would support him. 'Why are you asking *her*? She –'

Whatever slander Paul was about to commit against Chastity's hitherto good name was lost as another stream of evil sick, more orange – if that was possible – than the last lot, careered out of his mouth and on to the pavement next to Chastity. The force of the projection was so great that it seemed to go on for ever, suffering a fearsome amount of splash-back as it hit. Unfortunately, where Chastity had shuffled herself out of the way of the first puddle in order to assess the damage to her person was also right next to where the second stream hit. Jinx and Liberty found they were too disgusted even to turn away as the splashes landed all over Chastity's face, causing her mascara to drip down from her now stuck-together eyelashes and her hair to stick to the side of her head. It was the most filthy fucking shower any of them had ever seen, and that was for sure.

No one watching would ever forget this. In fact, the story was passed on so many thousands of times it became an urban legend. Thousands of faked YouTube videos would claim to be the original, but thankfully Chastity herself never came across any of them and basically lived a full and happy life in blissful ignorance of the whole 'vomit on your girlfriend' phenomenon.

'Oh, dear God,' muttered one of the policemen, a nice chap, a born and bred Brightonian who had a lovely daughter at home about Chastity's age. He crossed himself and turned to his colleagues. 'I've never seen anything like it. This poor lassie – we've got to get her home, lads.'

'Oh, fuck,' said Jinx again, much quieter this time but with even more feeling than the first. She couldn't imagine Mr Morris's, or, even worse, Mrs Bennett's reaction to them being dropped back at school in the middle of night with a full police escort. 'Fuck, fuck, *fuck.*'

'Paul,' Liberty said suddenly, thinking admirably on her feet around the same dilemma and rushing to his side, 'are you OK? Shouldn't you go to *hospital* or something?' She looked pleadingly at the policemen, directing the full benefit of the dual beam of her soft brown eyes into their own, slightly bloodshot versions. 'Can't you take him? I've never seen anyone being sick like that.'

'Yes,' Jinx added firmly, understanding exactly what Liberty was getting at and dashing over to help her. 'I think she's right. What would happen if he died on the street and you hadn't dropped him off at A&E? I'm sure there'd be a terrible fuss. Well . . . the *Argus* would make something of it definitely.'

This cunning mention of the local paper finally got through to the policemen. They moved over to the side of the van, where they stood muttering among themselves for a couple of minutes before marching purposefully back to the girls. The only sounds were the omnipresent squawk of the seagulls and the sea rolling the pebbles back and forth on the beach beyond the road. The partygoers leaning over the side of Jamie's penthouse balcony, who had all been stunned into silence when the vomiting started, were now avidly awaiting the verdict from the police. Chastity had finally cottoned on to the enormity of the problems they would face if the policemen insisted on taking them 'home' and was now also silently willing them to take Paul and leave her alone.

'Right, son,' the burliest cop said, looking with extreme distaste at Paul but offering him his arm nonetheless, 'come on. It'd be best if you got yourself checked over.'

'I'm fine,' Paul said, shaking him off and shooting a seriously filthy look at Chastity. 'I'm severely allergic to fish, that's all. I haven't had a reaction like this since I bit into a crispy fish ball thinking it was a chicken nugget three years ago. In fact,' he said, his green face quickly turning red with fury at the thought of what he might have been subjected to this time, 'I think you should ask this girl here what she had for lunch. Go on!'

'OK, OK, keep your wig on,' said the cop, shaking his head and turning to Chastity. Kids today, hey! 'What did you have for your lunch then, love? And don't worry, I'm only asking to keep the peace between you two. I'm sure – ha ha – whatever it was won't constitute a criminal offence of any kind.'

'I wouldn't be so confident of that if *I* was you,' muttered Jinx in an aside to Liberty, unable to stop herself from cracking the gag despite the severity of the situation.

'I had a tuna mayo sub actually,' Chastity said dreamily, while shooting a triumphant look at an apoplectic Paul, 'and I really, *really* enjoyed it. I guess I forgot to brush my teeth afterwards too.'

'If you really loved me like you said you did,' Paul said dramatically, looking at the lamppost as if it was a tree and he was in fact Heathcliff, 'you would never have eaten fish for lunch knowing you were seeing me later.'

'I forgot,' Chastity replied nonchalantly before leaning in close to Paul and whispering her punch line so the policemen couldn't hear. 'I guess I was too *stoned*.'

'Oh dear,' Liberty whispered to Jinx after seeing the look of pure, unadulterated fury this revelation caused to pass across Paul's normally cheery face, 'I know she's cross but I don't think she should have said that. I've got a bad feeling about this.'

Liberty was proved right as, only a second later, all hell did indeed break loose. Paul leapt at Chastity with such a deranged look in his eye that all the onlookers were convinced he meant grievous bodily harm at *best* and drew in sharp intakes of breath. The burly police-man – who couldn't stop thinking just how like Chastity his own eldest daughter, the light of his life, his absolute pride and joy, was – moved in front of Paul and caught him mid-flight. He bundled him off to one side and treated him to a few stern words about controlling himself, being a man and accepting when things were over. Paul, already incensed by Chastity, became wildly furious at the sound of all this.

'Why don't you phone up STAGMOUNT,' he screamed, delivering his parting shot with the true venom of the recently dumped, 'and ask them where their lower sixth is right now? I bet the teachers up there would just love to know what their *young ladies* are doing messing around in town at this time of night.'

'You bastard,' Chastity hissed at him, her fury now easily matching his own, 'I can't believe you'd stoop that low. Well, Paul, if you want the honest truth you can have it – I've been bored as hell by you for weeks now, *months* probably. I only kept seeing you because I couldn't be bothered with the aggro of finishing it, but now I wish I'd done it sooner. You're pathetic and I NEVER want to see you again. *Best leave it, yeah!*'

With that, Chastity turned on her heel and strode over to Jinx and Liberty, who tried their best to appear supportive and not to squirm away too much from the bits of sick still clinging all over their second-best friend. All three turned defiantly and stared at the policemen, wondering what they'd do with this particular bit of information. Sadly, they didn't have to wait long to find out.

'What *are* you all doing out here?' asked the leanest of the men, removing his hat and scratching his head as if puzzled by the whole affair – which indeed he was. 'Have you been at that party up there?'

'No,' Jinx said firmly, eyeing Paul and making it very obvious that if he dropped them in it again Chastity would be the least of his worries. 'We've just been mucking about on the seafront.'

There was no way in hell Jinx wanted to link the four of them on the pavement with Jamie's party in the penthouse. As if it wasn't bad enough that her brother was inside with the triplets, the whole place was awash with drugs and she didn't fancy Jamie's chances much as the host if these dudes started wanting to have a look around. She had the definite feeling in her bones that at this stage in proceedings it was best all round to claim no connection with anything or anyone other than the group of them here in the street.

Paul didn't say another word, but looked guiltily down at his feet before stumbling off into the night after a final, despairing glance at his most definitely lost love. Chastity, it must be said, was practically gagging at the time as she flicked unidentifiable lumps of sick from her jeans so she didn't even notice him leaving.

At the very moment the policemen were ushering the three girls into the back of the van – having let Paul go, they absolutely insisted on dropping the girls safely back to school, as a 'friendly gesture' no less – Liv and Charlie rounded the corner, Liv leaning heavily on Charlie's arm, as if she'd twisted her ankle or something. They stood stock still a couple of hundred metres down the pavement, clasped their hands over their mouths and seemed poised to yell out some kind of greeting. However, when Jinx, Liberty and Chastity turned as one and glared at them they realised it was in their best interests to keep a low profile and stayed skulking in the shadows of a skanky bed and breakfast place, with what looked like a guitar case propped against the low wall next to them.

The accident-prone pair watched helplessly as their form-mates were driven east along the seafront towards the marina and Stagmount beyond. The three inside the back held on to the security straps for dear life and stared at each other, speechless with horror. At least this time, the unhappy trio thought, grateful for any small mercies at the losing stage of the game, there were none of the lights and sirens that had heralded the police's first appearance.

Katie Green looked at her pale pink plastic Swatch watch. It was just past midnight and she'd been sitting by her window staring out over the pitches, across the marina, at the lights of the funfair on the end of the pier and towards the town for a little over an hour and a half now. She wasn't expecting to see anything of interest tonight, but she'd developed an attachment to this spot since she'd so fortuitously spotted the lower sixth dashing in and out of the garage that day. Since then, this had become the only place she felt able to try and unravel her muddled thoughts and she quite often found herself slipping away from the noisy girls in her year to come and sit here quietly on her own.

Half-heartedly thinking that she really ought to get to bed if she was to have any hope of making it to Sunday service in the morning, Katie leaned forward and drew in one last deep breath of the bitingly crisp sea air. She drew back when she spotted a shadowy figure making its way along the path from the main schoolhouse towards the old cricket pavilion. Hugging the line of bushes, whoever it was clearly didn't want to be discovered and was up to no good. Katie drew her blanket around her shoulders and peered more intently out of the window, dying to know who she was looking at.

At that moment, a shaft of moonlight broke through the layers of cloud, illuminating a slender figure with unnaturally white skin and unusually bright orange hair. Fate once more had chosen to smile on Katie. She nearly passed out cold with excitement when she realised that the furtive figure was none other than

Daisy Finnegan, head girl of the lower sixth and completely unwitting recipient of huge amounts of mental vitriol from this particular second year.

Daisy, who had woken in a cold sweat thinking of next week's chemistry exam only to realise she'd left her homemade revision table of chemical equations in the cricket pavilion, where she'd been conducting a stocktake of the equipment in readiness for next term, was muttering crossly to herself under her breath. She was particularly aggrieved to have forgotten this colour-coded spreadsheet, for it had taken her a whole two days of the Christmas holidays to construct and she liked to have it to hand to glance at whenever she felt panicky about the imminent exams, which was surprisingly often. It was freezing outside and, even though Daisy was an undeniable suck-up, swot and sneak, she was thinking longingly of her bed and wishing she wasn't so conscientious. Jinx and the others were not the only ones feeling the pressure from the teachers. Daisy often wished she could be more effortlessly casual about things, like so many of the others in her year, but the requisite 'chill out' gene just seemed to be missing in her.

While Daisy was staggering along the pitches in the freezing cold in search of her lost revision aid, the three in the police van had recovered their voices and were subjecting the policemen in the front to a barrage of pleading, sob stories and desperate last appeals to be released before they reached the main gates. At the same time, they were all so worried about the repercussions from the school they couldn't help but throw barbed remarks at each other in between their plaintive and increasingly vociferous remarks to the coppers.

Jinx was beyond furious at having had to leave both Jamie and the party in such a freaking undignified manner, avidly watched by absolutely everyone there. She was not sure she'd ever again be able to hold her head high when mincing along the streets of Brighton for fear of being identified. Liberty was wondering how the hell she'd managed to get involved in another massive scrape so soon after last term's débâcle and worrying about what Mrs Bennett would say to her in particular about all of this. And Chastity was like a feral cat, lashing out at Jinx when the latter frequently and viciously saw fit to lay the blame squarely at her door.

'Wild horses couldn't have dragged me away from that party,' Jinx muttered, glaring at Chastity's puke-covered face and thinking for the first time that she bloody well deserved everything that happened earlier, 'but you and three flying pigs managed it perfectly. Jamie will never speak to me again.' Jinx fixed Chastity with a steely glare and began ticking off the rest of her grievances on her fingers: 'Liberty never got that guy's phone number, we never got to have any more of those free drugs, God knows what's happened to George and, for the grand finale, we're probably all going to get expelled for sure. And Liberty and I were signed out for the whole weekend, so as far as the school's concerned we're not even anywhere near Brighton. So, yes, Chastity, thanks for a whole bunch of *nothing*.'

'You bitch,' hissed Chastity, 'you absolute fucking bitch. I don't suppose you give a shit that Paul and I have split up and I'm covered in fucking SICK from head to foot, do you?'

'Shut up, guys,' Liberty said, fortuitously cutting off Jinx's imminent reply in the negative, which would have driven Chastity even more wild and probably resulted in a night in the cells. She was terrified the police would hear and insist on speaking to their headmistress. 'We've got approximately two minutes and we have to *do* something.'

Katie Green was also determined to do something, though she had no idea what. She just knew she couldn't let Daisy Finnegan get away with creeping about in the middle of the night like this. A unique potential for revenge was staring her in the face and she mustn't let it pass by. Surely, she thought, her brain ticking over slowly but steadily, there was something she could do to screw Daisy. A teacher, that was it! That was the answer to all her problems! Somehow she had to alert a member of staff to Daisy's nocturnal wanderings without drawing attention to herself. But *how*?

Katie had no idea but she forced herself to think back to the day of the fire alarm, when Daisy had so, like, uncaringly humiliated her in front of her heroines. This exercise was an attempt to drum up an even greater strength of feeling and hopefully find a solution. It did-n't take long to work, amazingly enough. After only three minutes of reliving the unfortunate scene – during which time Daisy finally reached the shelter of the pavilion's porch – Katie experienced her first-ever 'Eureka' moment. Somehow she had managed to coax a plan out of her addled mind. No, she thought recklessly, clutching her tummy in excitement, it wasn't so much a plan as a bloody *brainwave*. Now all she had to do was put it into action. And this, of course, was the hard bit.

While Katie turned left out of Steinem's inside back door and began creeping silently along the corridor towards the art room, the sanatorium, the old reference library, Pankhurst and ultimately Mrs Bennett's large house beyond, the police van was turning off the coast road and making its way towards Stagmount's main gates. And Liv and Charlie – oh, the bitter injustice of it all – were at this precise moment sitting with George, Jamie and the triplets, snorting down great lines of cocaine, downing icy cocktails, listening to yet more amazing music and generally having a bloody lovely time at the party.

Katie paused for breath a few metres along the wall leading to Mrs Bennett's front steps and the smart, navy-painted door with its big brass knocker smack bang in the middle at the top of them. She knew that no one was around, but at this time of night the school seemed eerily quiet and was an undeniably frightening place to be. The darkness didn't help her nerves much either. The most ordinary objects and buildings took on a spooky, paranormal glow under the dim, greenish glare of the lampposts randomly dotted about the place and Katie took a few deep breaths to steady her nerves before she made her final assault.

Completely unbeknownst to her, the police van containing a by now very subdued Jinx, Liberty and Chastity, who were slumped together in a sorry lump at the back of the van, exhausted and pretty much resigned to whatever sick joke fate intended to throw at them next this evening, was slowing to allow the electric gates to roll to the side.

Daisy meanwhile, having recovered her study aid and felt a couple of drops of rain, decided to come off the pitches and take the main drive back to Tanner House and – oh, happy day – the two duvets she slept under all year round. She was just traversing the quad in front of the main entrance when the police van swung through the main gates and Katie banged fiercely on Mrs Bennett's door before running away and flinging herself behind a handy camellia bush in the flowerbed running alongside the outer wall of Pankhurst House. These events, some admittedly more unfortunate than others, converged at exactly the right moment for a sleep-deprived Mrs Bennett, wrapped in a fog of exhaustion and a floral Cath Kidston dressing gown, to fling open her door in time to see the police van slow to a halt in front of one of the – oh, the bitter irony – many sleeping policemen along the drive and Daisy round the corner from the main school.

Katie had to shove one of her fat fists into her mouth to muffle her scream of appalled shock when she saw

Jinx, Liberty and Chastity clamber wearily out of the sliding back door of the horribly distinctive blue and white van and arrange themselves silently in front of their headmistress. Mrs Bennett was so horrified at the sight of them – not least their law enforcement entourage – it was all she could do to push the lingering thought that she must still be dreaming from her mind. When she saw Daisy Finnegan standing uncertainly to the left of the bedraggled but still a zillion times more glamorous three, their headmistress did an actual double take. For once, Mrs Bennett found it difficult to believe her own eyes!

The burly policeman – who, it must be said, was beginning to wish they'd left the girls to their own devices down on the seafront – removed his hat and coughed. Mrs Bennett cast an experienced eye over the shady as hell girls in front of her, the embarrassed policemen beyond and wisely decided to get to the bottom of this particular mess using the softly, gently approach.

'Right then,' she said in a tone that brooked no arguments from any of them, 'everyone inside. Chop-chop, come on. We can't stand around in the cold like this.'

Jinx, Liberty and Chastity, eyes cast firmly to the ground, began to shuffle up the steps, too shocked even to register that, after three and a half years' often intense speculation as to how it would be inside, this was the first time any of them had ever set foot in Head's House, as Mrs Bennett's abode was known. After removing their hats, the policemen followed them.

Only Daisy hung back. Reluctant to associate herself with this motley crew, she intended calmly and fearlessly to tell Mrs Bennett about her innocent mission and be on her way.

'Don't even think about it, Daisy Finnegan,' snapped Mrs Bennett, crooking an impatient finger and hurrying the malingerer inside. 'I am *especially* surprised at you!'

'But . . .' Daisy's downright foolish attempt to answer Mrs Bennett back was cut off by what appeared to be a relative of the karate chop, but with not such a straight arm and a hissing sound. Daisy recoiled, and as she did so her trusty sheet of chemical equations caught on the wind and whirled up, up, up in the night air before disappearing on a sudden strong gust round to the back of Mrs B's pad.

'Inside, NOW!' the headmistress barked.

A truly terrified Daisy abandoned all thoughts of telling her side of the story, or ever seeing her revision aid again, and hurried up the steps as quickly as she could.

Behind the camellia bush an unfortunately positioned Katie found herself the recipient of a load of wet leaves and dirty water, dumped on her from where they had been pushed along the gutter by rainwater. Blinking furiously, she wiped some thick black grime from her woebegone face and raised her head in time to see the revision timetable fly up into the air as Mrs Bennett's front door slam behind Daisy. By happy accident, the timetable, which had danced for a while in the wind above the decked terrace at the back of the house, chose that moment to shoot across the side of Pankhurst and float to the ground, where it landed right next to Katie's bush. Katie reached for it, cast a curious eye over the meaningless symbols on the front, then instantly lost interest and scrunched it without another thought deep into the back pocket of her baggy brown cords – possibly the most unflattering item of clothing anyone at Stagmount had ever possessed. There was no way in hell she was going back to bed just yet, so she settled into the squelching mud to wait this one out.

Jinx, Liberty, Chastity and Daisy sat very close together on a white and red striped silk sofa in a dramatic drawing room. Huge earthenware pots containing Triffid-sized green plants were bunched variously around, lending the blood-red walls, massive gold-framed mirrors and tiny exquisite paintings the air of having been hung in a jungle. A rug very similar to the Bokhara in her study covered most of the dark and highly shined wood floor, its navy blue, red and dark purple pattern entirely visible through the big chunk of glass that served as the headmistress's coffee table.

They had barely had a chance to sit down and glance round before the burly policeman took the initiative, apologised for waking Mrs Bennett, assured her that the girls had been doing nothing wrong and insisted that he and his fellow officers were merely *chivalrously* dropping them home at the end of an obviously tiring and emotional night. Mrs Bennett pursed her lips at this but thanked the officers for their kind gesture and promised to see that everyone got to bed as soon as possible – she even managed an airy laugh or two, albeit through gritted teeth – before she ushered them out of her house.

The headmistress then swept back into the drawing room and positioned herself on a high-backed, ornately carved wooden chair directly opposite the girls' sofa. She sat there for a few seconds, thoughtfully studying the four overwrought faces in front of her.

Jinx and Liberty looked scared and tired, but basically seemed fine. Daisy, Mrs Bennett couldn't help noting, was dressed most oddly compared to the others. Maybe she was not the model pupil they had all imagined and was actually one of those 'new geek hardcore ravers' she'd read about in the *Sunday Times* style section last weekend. She simply must be making a statement with her school tracksuit, no bra and wellington boots teamed with no make-up to speak of and a flowery blanket over her shoulders. Quite what this statement was, however, the headmistress had no idea. Either way, right now it was obvious to everyone in the room that Daisy really did not want to be there.

Sobbing quietly into her hands, shaking like a leaf and occasionally moaning incoherently through her haze of snot and tears, Daisy was clearly not used to being 'in trouble'. She had no idea about the outwardly cool and calm exterior it was crucial to maintain during these difficult encounters if one was to stand even the slightest chance of being able to talk oneself out of it. But Mrs Bennett didn't notice Jinx edging away from Daisy, the most disgusted look plastered across her face, since she was busy studying Chastity Maxwell.

Chastity looked, frankly, as if she'd been run over and left for dead. Rather than being merely tear-stained, her usually pretty face seemed to have two tyre tracks running down her puffy cheeks. Her eyes had almost disappeared, to be replaced by two red golf balls with red and white slits where the sparkly baby blues used to live. She also, Mrs Bennett belatedly realised with a horrified shudder, appeared to be covered in vomit. Dear God, this job was no way near as glamorous as people so often assumed it was.

Keen to get the girls out of her house and into their beds as quickly as possible, Mrs Bennett made an executive decision to deal with this matter in the morning. Even had they not been delivered to her doorstep in the back of a police van, she knew just from looking at them that the girls were exhausted and way too upset to deal with anything reasonably, rationally and sensibly. And Mrs Bennett was, above all, a reasonable, rational and sensible woman. This is why she was so excellent at her job and so popular with the girls, the staff, the parents and the governors. This is also why she was continually phoned up by newspapers for quotes on everything from education to female adolescence issues and was even beginning to develop quite a following on the Internet.

'Right then,' she said softly, looking at the girls remarkably kindly, given the circs, 'I think the best thing for all of us is to get to bed as quickly as possible. We obviously have a lot to discuss, but I'm sure it will keep for the morning.'

'Mrs Ben –'Taking advantage of the head's new, calm mood, Daisy had decided to try and explain her non-involvement once again. This was a massive mistake.

'Daisy Finnegan,' Mrs Bennett snapped in the iciest voice any of them had ever heard, 'if you don't want me to lose my temper I suggest you do not say another word until the time that I ask you a direct question.'

Daisy nodded sadly, sniffing and trying in vain to halt the fresh flood of tears this announcement had brought to her eyes. If nothing else, the others thought, beginning to feel almost sorry for her for the first time in their lives, she had the bloody sense not to respond verbally.

'So,' Mrs Bennett continued, standing up to indicate that this cosy little session was most definitely at an end, 'I want you to go straight back to Tanner House and get into bed. You're all absolutely exhausted and there is no point keeping you up a minute longer than necessary. I shall telephone Mr Morris now and tell him to expect you. We will meet in the morning and get to the bottom of exactly what's gone on here. I'll see all of you in my office first thing after chapel. And girls,' she said, smiling warmly at Jinx and Liberty and squeezing Chastity's shoulder reassuringly, 'try and make sure you *do* sleep. I don't want any of you doing anything silly like sitting up worrying all night.'

They nodded meekly, then stood up and filed shame-facedly out of Mrs Bennett's drawing room. Once outside, they walked as fast as they could without running, maintaining a determined, grim silence until they rounded the corner past the sports hall and gained cover of the line of rhododendron bushes. As soon as they knew they could no longer be observed, they slowed to a trudge and gaped at each other in horror.

Jinx was the first to break the silence. 'Bloody hell, Daisy,' she said, still not understanding what possible sequence of events could have led her old nemesis from Wollstonecraft House to this pass, 'what on earth have you been up to? I couldn't believe it when I saw you standing next to us out there. Where did you *come* from?'

'I realised I'd left my chemistry revision in the cricket pavilion,' wailed Daisy, still hugely distressed by this extremely unfair case of mistaken identity or whatever it was she was currently embroiled in, 'so I got up and went to get it in case I woke up early and felt like memorising some equations.'

'Serves you fucking right then,' mumbled Liberty meanly, before instantly regretting it when Daisy cast a truly anguished glance in her direction. 'Sorry, Dais . . . sorry. I really am.'

'And then,' Daisy continued, much mollified by the unprecedented apology, 'I was walking back to Tanner when out of nowhere a police van passed me on the drive and when I came round the corner Mrs Bennett opened her door and then you guys got out and then . . . well, you know the rest. What am I going to *do*? What if I get expelled? My parents would kill me!'

'Come on, Dais,' Jinx said, torn between laughing at the ridiculousness of Daisy's increasingly high-pitched explanation and crying at the thought of her own no-doubt imminent expulsion, 'we'll tell her the truth tomorrow and you'll be fine. She'll just probably say you were an idiot for not leaving it until morning and fucking *apologise* to you or something. I really wouldn't sweat it if I was you.'

'Do you really think?' Daisy asked, eyes shining hopefully at Jinx.

'Yeah, I do. It's us' — she looked at Liberty and Chastity — 'who need to be coming up with the best damn story in the world right about NOW.'

'Do you promise you'll tell her I wasn't anything to do with the police and things?' asked Daisy, still not quite able to trust that Jinx and the others wouldn't stitch her up as part of some 'hilarious' gag. 'Really promise?'

Jinx looked over at Daisy and inexplicably felt truly sorry for her. She felt bad about all the times she'd been mean and made up her mind to be as nice as possible to her from now on and hopefully score some karmic points — let's face it, she needed them.

'Of course we will, Dais,' Jinx said firmly. 'Don't worry about it. I can't believe what shit luck you've had!'

'The only thing *I* don't understand,' said Daisy suddenly, looking at Jinx, 'is why Mrs Bennett opened her door when she did.'

The others looked at her blankly. They hadn't thought about this at all.

'What do you mean?' asked Chastity, speaking for the

first time since they'd left the police van. Considering the river of tears she had cried this evening, it was no surprise she sounded like Dracula after a night on the lash.

'Well, think about it logically,' said Daisy, sounding – for once comfortingly – exactly like one of the teachers. 'She'd obviously dashed out of bed in a rush as if she'd heard something outside, but nothing was making a noise. It was too windy for the police van driving past on the tarmac to make enough noise to wake anyone up and I was walking silently past the buildings. I was so shocked to see the van drive past me that I didn't think about it at the time, but I suppose I was vaguely aware of some kind of banging sound.'

'I don't get it,' Chastity said impatiently. 'What are you saying?'

'I'm saying,' said Daisy, looking over her shoulder to where they had come from and shivering dramatically, 'that I think someone knew you lot were going to be driving past at that time and decided to drop you in it by knocking on her door and running away.'

'*What?*' asked Liberty, horrified at the very thought. 'Who would want to do something like that to us?'

'Someone who's got a grudge,' replied Daisy knowingly. 'It could be anyone.'

'Hold on a fucking second,' Chastity cut in exasperatedly. 'I don't think it's right to imply that someone at Stagmount might have a grudge against us. We're actually, like, some of the most popular girls at this freaking school.'

'Exactly,' said Daisy darkly.

It didn't occur to any of them that the person who had brought Mrs Bennett rushing to her front door might be somebody who had a problem with Daisy. The whole thing was just too left-field, too goddamn unlikely, too daring.

It was now nearly two o'clock in the morning but Katie Green was far too agitated to feel it. She had watched as the four lower sixths set off at a smart pace down the drive in the direction of Tanner House. She saw Mrs Bennett watch after them until they rounded the corner, one hand on her chin and the other on her hip, as if she was deeply worried. She noticed none of the girls looked back once, pointedly almost, in the embarrassed manner of people who know they are being watched but can't stand the sensation for whatever reason. She was soaked through, covered in mud and slime, hiding behind a camellia bush on a cliff just to the east of Brighton in the middle of the night in the freezing cold and she didn't feel a thing, because she was too busy trying to force her barely adequate, cretinous brain to make sense of everything that had just happened.

Whatever, Katie knew she had to get herself back to Steinem House and the safety of her room as soon as possible. Mrs Bennett had shut the door behind her half an hour ago. One by one the drawing room, hall and upstairs lights were turned off and Katie wrongly assumed that Mrs B was by now safely asleep. The headmistress was, in fact, lying in bed and staring at the ceiling, worrying about the girls she'd just sent back to Tanner. It was one thing drinking champagne and eating strawberries at Wimbledon and Glyndebourne every year thanks to her position as Stagmount's headmistress, but quite another dealing with sobbing, sick-covered girls in the middle of the night, and she took her *in loco parentis* role very seriously.

Still, she needn't have worried too much. Chastity, Liberty and Jinx were currently inviting a surprised but pleased Daisy Finnegan to Jinx's room for an emergency crisis discussion meeting before chapel at half past eight in the morning. They wouldn't normally bother to attend on a Sunday morning after such a late night, but wisely decided it would do no harm to their cause whatsoever to be observed singing lustily in the pews. And after getting over the terrible initial shock of it all and Mr Morris's 'disappointed' face when he met them at the door, they each went to bed reasonably confident they'd somehow manage to scam their way out of it in the morning. Thank God for Mrs B deciding to postpone things, they unanimously agreed – she really was the most amazingly civilised woman they were ever likely to meet and they were beyond freaking lucky to have her as their headmistress.

Contrary to their expectations and within minutes each and every one of them, despite all the upset and histrionics on the grandest scale, was fast asleep as if they didn't have a care in the world.

Katie stood in the dark of her room and shed her seriously messed-up clothes. She stuffed them into a plastic bag and dumped them underneath a pile of clean towels at the back of her wardrobe, figuring she'd wash them later. Using most of her L'Oréal moisturising face wipes, she cleared the rest of the grime from her face, hands and neck, then got into bed. If she had been a religious girl she might have prayed for guidance at this point, but unfortunately for her Katie was completely lacking in spirituality of any kind. Instead she lay in bed, mindlessly popping Maltesers into her mouth and sucking them until they went soggy, wondering what on earth her heroines had been doing out in town and how come they ended up being brought back to school by the police. Shocked didn't even come close to how she was feeling right now. Shock and awe were more like it – she couldn't help but be deeply, deeply impressed by the radical antics she'd witnessed tonight. What exciting, glamorous lives those girls lived, she thought as she closed her eyes, still sucking away furiously.

Jinx woke up the next morning a few minutes before her alarm clock and stretched happily before tensing rigid as the events of the previous night slowly filtered into her growing awareness of what was going to be a huge headache.

'Fuck,' she muttered crossly to herself, reaching for the two-litre bottle of Evian she always kept on her bedside table and banging weakly on the wall by her bed that adjoined Liberty's room. 'We are in *so* much fucking trouble.'

Jinx lay back against her pillow and held her hand horizontally in front of her face to see how much it was trembling. Oh dear, things really did not look good from this frankly depressing side of last night's amazing party. She felt so low and morbid she couldn't stop the thought passing through her mind that one day she might turn yellow and die just like George Best.

Thinking of the footballer immediately led her to reach for her phone and punch out a quick text message to her second-oldest brother, as she always did in times of hangover crisis. No matter what Jinx might have done, she could rest assured that George would have gone one better. The comforting thought that at least she hadn't been the *worst* behaved always made her feel a lot better about things. George was also a master at getting himself out of trouble and would surely advise his little sister on the very best damage-control methods she needed to put in place right now.

Jinx's door was silently pushed open. In the frame stood a wild-haired Liberty, who, judging from the black lines etched deep into the huge bags beneath her eyes, had neglected to take off her make-up before she got into bed last night. Without a word, Liberty lifted the corner of Jinx's duvet, got into bed and snuggled up against her best friend. They lay there not speaking, just staring at each other in appalled horror, until Jinx's phone made its customary trilling sound to indicate she'd received a text.

'"STOP PRESS! Woteva u do REITERATE that u WEREN'T in the care of the school at the time and there is technically NOTHING they can do to punish u. Peace out, bitches",' she read aloud to Liberty, before adding excitedly, 'He's right of course, Lib. We were signed out for the weekend, so whatever we got up to was Mum and Dad's responsibility and nothing to do with the school. So long as they stand up for us – which they so will – we're going to be totally fine.'

'What about Chastity?' Liberty asked. 'What can she say?'

At that moment Chastity walked into the room. And although she was very pale indeed, she was smiling and looked a zillion times happier than she had by the end of last night. She sat down on the end of Jinx's bed and grinned at the pair of them lying in it, who were looking at her rather warily, as if not sure quite what emotion to expect next.

'Don't worry,' said Chastity. 'I'm fine. I was so *drunk* last night I think I might have overreacted. But,' she continued firmly, 'Paul and I are definitely over. He's been driving me mad for ages now, but I didn't say anything because I kind of felt embarrassed about it after how much I went on about how I liked him. It just changed and I don't really know why, except I know I want to be single like you guys. I'm so bored of constantly missing out on things with you girls because he and I have got some boring bloody couples thing to do.'

'I still can't believe he told the police to phone the

236

school,' Liberty said with a disgusted sniff. 'What a complete asshole.'

'Liberty!' Jinx said sharply.

'What?' asked Liberty. 'I can't!'

'Yeah, but it's not really appropriate to start slagging off her boyfriend when the relationship's barely cold in its grave yet,' said Jinx, nudging Liberty meaningfully and raising her eyebrows in Chastity's direction. 'Is it?'

'Oh, God,' Chastity said airily, waving a hand in front of her, 'don't worry about it. I'm so over him. What I *do* need to bloody worry about is what the hell I'm going to say to get out of this mess. Have we got any ideas?'

Jinx, with no help whatsoever from Liberty, who took this opportunity to have a small cat nap, explained the situation regarding the intricacies of the signing-out system, parental responsibilities versus school control and the fortunate convergence of facts as far as they pertained to herself and Liberty. As Jinx talked, relief flooded Chastity's face, bringing a little bit of much needed colour to her cheeks and a pleased sparkle back to her still-pretty-bloodshot eyes.

'Well, I'm fine too then,' she said, exhaling with relief and practically crossing herself in thanks. 'As far as the school is concerned, I was with Mum and Ian. Since I *was* planning to stay the night with Paul, I signed out yesterday before I left, saying I was off to see them. They won't be up yet, so I'll text Ian and tell him to say as far as he was concerned I was meeting up with you two in town and we were going to go out for dinner before getting a taxi back to his flat. Your parents say the same thing and we're all fine.'

'Brilliant,' said Jinx enthusiastically. 'Mine will so do that. I'll call them in a minute and give them the briefing. And we'll say that on our way to getting a taxi to go back to school you started being sick – food poisoning or something – and the police stopped to help us.'

'We'll say,' Liberty added, surfacing from her snooze as Daisy pushed open the door and stood in front of them in a ratty pink dressing gown and her infuriating Garfield slippers with massive dark circles under her strangely pale eyes, 'we were so worried about you, Chas, we thought it was safer to get you back to school in case you couldn't stop being sick and needed urgent medical attention from Mister Sinton. But that you then miraculously recovered in the van on the way back – they can't disprove a thing.'

The three of them laughed delightedly at the sheer simple genius of this plan and Daisy stared at them aghast. She could hardly believe her eyes – how could they be so flippant and casual about all of this? If it had been *her* in this amount of trouble she couldn't be sure that suicidal thoughts wouldn't be passing through her mind.

'B-b-but,' she stammered, 'won't Mrs B ask you loads of questions?'

'So what?' said Jinx, bored of the whole damn issue. All she wanted was five freaking minutes to herself to think about Jamie and the things he'd said to her before she'd been so rudely taken away from his amazing party. 'We stick to our stories like glue and there's nothing they can do. Our parents won't make a fuss – they knew exactly what we were up to and they won't want the trouble if nothing else. And we *are* seventeen, which is practically an adult, even if we *do* live in a boarding school.'

'Yeah,' agreed Chastity, 'and don't worry, Daisy – we'll spill the truth for you too. Everything's going to be fine.'

'That's really kind,' said Daisy with a blush. She wasn't used to this level of niceness from these girls and she was kind of wishing she hadn't always set herself so dead against them. Maybe it wasn't too late to make friends, she thought wistfully, before deciding this was highly unlikely. But it would be nice to put an end to the cold war she and Jinx had sustained for three and a half years.

'I tell you what,' she said, very touched by the mental picture she currently had of herself wearing angel wings and benevolently handing an olive branch to Jinx, 'I'll help you investigate who banged on Mrs Bennett's door and got her to rush out and catch us all like that. If we all put our heads together I'm sure we'll come up with a plan.'

'Thanks, Daisy,' said Jinx, smiling at her genuinely for maybe the first time in her life. 'That's really nice of you.'

'Yeah,' Liberty agreed, following her and Chastity out of Jinx's room, 'it is. Thanks.'

Left in blissful peace at last, Jinx straightened out her bedding without getting up – one of her special skills was making her bed without actually leaving it – and lay back against her newly fluffed-up pillows. She was desperate to have a quick think about things in the ten minutes remaining to her before she simply had to get in the shower in order not to be late for chapel. Jumbled thoughts of Jamie jostled for space in her mind with the ghastly end to the party and curiosity about what might have happened with George and the triplets, alongside what the hell had caused Daisy Finnegan to suddenly become so nice and what had kept Liv and Charlie away for so long.

Sadly, the snooze button on her phone alarm went off before she'd made much headway. Jinx got out of bed reluctantly, shrugged into her dressing gown and flip-flops, grabbed her Anya Hindmarch wash bag and sauntered off to the showers to think about what she would say to Mrs Bennett in her office later that morning.

Standing shoulder to shoulder with Liberty and Chastity, with Daisy Finnegan at the end of the pew next to Chastity, Jinx was singing 'Onward, Christian Soldiers' with all the might she could muster. She had no idea just how terribly she was out of tune. A devilish headache was rumbling just of out reach of the three Nurofen she'd swallowed with a quick cup of coffee before leaving Tanner House. She prayed it would stay away from her frontal lobes for at least as long as it took her to get back into bed, where she fully intended to spend the rest of the day, listening to soothing music and recuperating from their now scarily imminent chat with Mrs Bennett.

Chastity, meanwhile, was feeling remarkably chipper about things as she sang along perfectly. The thought that she was now free to do exactly as she pleased, like all the others, made her very happy indeed. She so wasn't the kind of girl who needed a boyfriend, and since her relationship with Paul had become little more than a major drag she was just relieved to have got rid of him and not regretful in the slightest. Chastity Maxwell was one way-cool customer.

Liberty was thinking wistfully of the dark-haired boy who had been smiling at her before they'd left the table area. She wondered if she could get Jinx to find out about him from Jamie, of whom she thoroughly approved.

Mrs Bennett was standing at the front, just across from the vicar in his pulpit, singing along word and pitch perfect without any need of the hymnbook. She was covertly observing the four sixth formers in their pew towards the middle of the chapel and marvelling generally at the ability of teenagers to recover from what at the time they think is the worst event in the world. She and Mr Morris had looked over the weekend register books and already realised that, since the girls had all been legitimately signed out of the school, there was precious little they could do in terms of official punishment.

Mrs Bennett was actually quite glad about this. She hated to make a scene unless it was strictly necessary and she knew that these were basically nice, decent, sensible girls who only occasionally found themselves in hot water. Yes, the police van was certainly *unfortunate*, but she was sure they'd have a reasonable explanation. Another excellent thing about Mrs B, from the girls' point of view right now anyway, was that, being so very reasonable herself, she assumed a basic level of reasonability in other people and treated them accordingly. The only thing that really surprised her was Daisy Finnegan's involvement in the affair. As far as she was aware, Jinx's crew had never seen eye to eye with Daisy. Something had obviously changed there too, she thought, and maybe that was a good thing – for both sides.

As the last verse began her eye swept from the lower sixth to the few members of staff in their two pews right at the back of the chapel. The bursar stood at the end, his red mottled face vivid against the white collar of his shirt, the charcoal grey of his suit and the pale pink of his tie. Next to him was Dirk Hanson, wearing a most inappropriate electric-blue tracksuit with a fluorescent yellow stripe down each arm. Since she rarely saw the bursar here during the compulsory twenty-minute weekday services, Mrs Bennett was surprised to see him at this hour-long Sunday version. Across from them on the other side of the aisle were Mrs Carpenter, all in black as per, but accessorised with a surprising canary-yellow hat, with Igor the bodyguard standing next to her – very straight, tall and proprietorial – and Sister Minton almost bursting out of her customary starched navy-blue uniform.

After scanning the cavernous chapel and not seeing the triplets anywhere, Mrs Bennett looked back at Igor and wasn't quick enough to stop a small frown from passing across her face. Even from this distance she thought he looked at her strangely for a moment, as if he'd spotted her frown and knew what she was thinking. It was ever so disconcerting to feel watched all the time. She was Stagmount's headmistress, for goodness' sake, she shouldn't feel policed and monitored in her own school. What the hell was he doing here if the three girls were nowhere to be seen? She had already spoken to the bursar about whether it was really necessary for the triplets to have a bodyguard after Mr Morris had complained at the start of term. Sweating even more profusely than usual and wiping his florid forehead with a wringing-wet handkerchief to little effect, the bursar had basically told her that if she banned Igor the triplets would leave immediately. He had also indicated that this would be disastrous for the school's finances, as they had at least six or seven female cousins whose names were all down on the future-pupil list.

Forty-five minutes later, sweeping out a few paces behind the vicar and the choir in their flowing white robes, Mrs Bennett made a couple of mental notes. She intended to find out why Igor had been at the service and the triplets hadn't. It was about time she pinned the man down for a little chat. Also, as she had never spoken to the triplets' father – so far he had dealt exclusively with the bursar on all school matters – she decided to rectify that situation. Having said goodbye to the vicar, she ordered a pot of coffee and a plate of biscuits and settled down on her office sofa to await the girls.

Traipsing down the corridor after chapel, none of the lower sixth on their way to see Mrs Bennett bothered to untie their navy and green striped ties, as they normally did as soon as they were released from that place. It was, they'd agreed on their way over that morning, no bad thing that school rules insisted upon girls wearing their best uniform for Sunday service. If all their plans failed, at least they looked the part of adorable, slightly contrite but basically responsible, hard-working schoolgirls in their navy blazers, white shirts and sensible shoes. Chastity, who was definitely rocking the 'sorry' look, had even divided her hair into two pigtails. Jinx stifled a giggle, wondering why her friend hadn't gone the whole hog and painted big brown freckles on her cheeks.

Since it was Sunday, Jo's desk outside Mrs B's office door was sitting empty, bereft of its usual chaos of magazines, coffee cups and hundreds of papers, letters and memos. The four of them paused by its unusually clean surface and eyed each other. No one wanted to take the initiative and knock. Jinx, Liberty and Chastity also needed just a couple of seconds to compose themselves and iron out any potential fits of nervous giggles.

With a suddenness that shocked them into standing to attention and practically saluting, the door flew open and Mrs Bennett was in front of them. She ushered them into her office amidst gentle enquiries as to why on earth they hadn't knocked sooner, gesturing for them to sit down and help themselves to coffee and biscuits. All of them – apart from Daisy, who was shaking with pure nerves alone – had too big a hangover to contemplate holding a cup of hot coffee during this ordeal.

Delicately leaning forward on a leather armchair, legs elegantly crossed slightly to the side and at the ankle, Mrs Bennett raised her dainty green and gold bone china coffee cup to her lips and took a sip. As she did so, she observed the girls through the black-rimmed Prada spectacles that had slipped slightly down her patrician nose. The four of them in front of her on the sofa looked somewhat worn around the edges this morning, but a great deal happier than they had appeared last night. Each was perched on the outer rim of the sofa cushions, keen to appear as eager, alert, sensible and responsive to their headmistress as possible.

'You are,' Mrs Bennett said, smiling slightly to soften the blow, 'wallies, dingbats and sillies of the first order.'

The girls giggled slightly, not quite able to believe that anyone anywhere in the whole world still used these kinds of insults and storing them up to tell the others later.

'However,' the headmistress continued in a steelier tone, 'I was not at all amused to be confronted with the four of you and a police escort at my front door last night. And I intend,' she said, looking them in the eye one by one, 'to get to the bottom of exactly what it was you were up to.'

'Well, Mrs Bennett,' said Jinx, deciding to jump straight in and get this ordeal the hell over with, 'we certainly can explain everything to you, and I shall do so right away.'

'I hope you can,' replied Mrs B, fixing her with a gimlet eye, 'because that is most definitely not the kind of image Stagmount either wants or needs.'

'Yes,' muttered Jinx, momentarily thrown and flicking an aghast glance at Liberty next to her, 'of course, Mrs Bennett. So . . . um . . . where was I? Oh yes,' she continued hastily, having recovered her composure, 'the thing *is*, we had all arranged to meet for dinner in town, before heading back to Chastity's mum's place in London on one of the late trains and then come back to school – the regular way, ha ha – this evening.'

'And?' Mrs Bennett said as Jinx paused for a much-needed breath.

'And we had a lovely meal at a pizza place, although Chastity had a seafood pizza, which, you know, is never really a good idea, what with all the calamari rings on it.' Jinx paused again and quickly wondered if calamari was a dangerous enough foodstuff known for poisoning in its own right. She looked at Mrs Bennett's sceptical face and decided not. 'With prawns . . . and mussels. Yes, mussels, lots of them. Oh, and even some cockles and whelks and . . . um . . . those orange seafood sticks you get in supermarkets, sort of shaved over the top of it, under all the cheese, I think. It was very stringy anyway.'

'And?' Mrs Bennett snapped again, baffled by all this talk of filthy pizza toppings and wondering darkly if

Jinx was joking.

'And, well,' Jinx said sadly, with a downward glance intended to convey extreme dismay, 'with all of that sloshing around inside her and maybe a bad mussel or prawn or something, when we were on our way to the station Chastity suddenly started being sick.'

'Yes, Mrs B,' Chastity said, a bit too matily for the headmistress's liking, especially considering the situation they were currently in, 'it was awful. I just couldn't stop. I vomited and I vomited and I *vomited*, and then I vomited some more.'

Mrs Bennett, remembering with a shudder the sick she'd spotted all over Chastity's person late last night, was beginning to look slightly alarmed for her Bokhara rug and tasteful soft furnishings.

'It's true, Mrs Bennett,' agreed Liberty with relish, 'it was – literally – the sickest thing I've ever seen. It was just pouring out of her as if it would never stop. And it was the most bright orange colour, like paint or something. Man, it was gross as hell.'

'Yes, thank you, Liberty,' snapped Mrs Bennett, slightly confused to be addressed as 'man' but deciding it would be simply too exhausting to get into a debate about that now. 'Though that doesn't explain how the Sussex police force came to be involved. If one of you would be so kind, I'd like to get this wrapped up sooner rather than later. Contrary to popular belief, I do not enjoy spending my Sundays dealing with school matters.'

'Well,' said Jinx, once again taking on the role of

spokesperson, much to the others' relief, 'Chastity was being so ill we had to stop walking and sort of stand with her at the side of the pavement on the busy seafront road. People were slowing down their cars as they drove past, it was that much of a spectacle. Anyway, then the police stopped to see what was going on and offered us a lift back to school. We tried,' Jinx said, in her most sincere voice, staring intently into Mrs Bennett's eyes and holding her gaze without blinking, 'to stop them, but they simply insisted upon it. And anyway, with Chas so ill, we thought getting her back here and into bed must be our priority.'

Daisy, meanwhile, was slack-jawed with wonder at the most virtuoso performance she'd ever witnessed being played out on the stage of this sofa she herself was also sitting on. She literally couldn't believe it, so much so that she'd forgotten her own predicament totally. She only remembered it when she heard her own name in the conversation and snapped back to attention.

'And Daisy,' Chastity was now saying earnestly, 'was not involved at all. She just got caught up in the confusion alongside us. But, Mrs Bennett, we absolutely swear on our mothers' lives that she wasn't out in town with us and hasn't done anything wrong.'

'I'm sure it's not right to swear anything on your mother's life, Chastity,' said a somewhat appalled Mrs Bennett, who'd never come across the charming expression before. 'What a horrid, nasty thing to say. Please never let me hear you do so again.'

'Sorry,' mumbled Chastity, suddenly feeling

absolutely horrified with herself, staring at the shiny black patent-leather pair of Marc Jacobs Mary Jane shoes she'd rather incongruously matched with her school uniform and thinking about how much she loved her mum.

'So,' the headmistress continued, flicking a glance at her watch and wondering what she'd have at her favourite restaurant – The Saint on St James's Street in Kemp Town – that lunchtime with her journalist friend who had a fabulous expense account, 'even if you didn't go out of the school grounds, Daisy, what on earth were you doing wandering around in the middle of the night? No girl is supposed to be outside her house after eleven o'clock, you *know* that.'

'W-w-well,' stammered Daisy in response, absolutely unused to being spoken to like this since she was such a big suck normally and never got in trouble, 'I woke up and realised I'd left my chemistry revision guide in the cricket pavilion. I'd been in there, sorting out the bats and balls and whites and things for next term, and the guide must have fallen out of my folder as I shut the door.'

'So you got out of bed and walked over there *in the middle of the night* to retrieve it?' said Mrs Bennett, thinking that Daisy Finnegan really must be a little touched in the head.

'Yes.' Daisy nodded, her face looking paler than ever against her ginger hair and her eyes almost popping out of her head in terror.

'Well,' said Mrs Bennett, deciding to give the whole

thing up as a bad job – while considering the possibility of cutting loose with steak and chips alongside a couple of glasses of great red – 'I really do think it was foolish, if not downright foolhardy behaviour, but I'm sure you've learned your lesson and I won't be taking this any further.'

'Oh yes,' agreed Daisy, tear-pricks of relief causing her eyes to shine suspiciously brightly, 'I have.'

'And as far as the rest of you are concerned,' she continued, fixing the girls with a gimlet eye, 'I've spoken to your parents and – since you were all signed out for the weekend and technically not in the care of the school – I can't punish you as heavily as I would *like* to.'

The girls winced collectively at the positively icy new edge to their headmistress's voice and shuffled back slightly on the sofa.

'In fact,' she went on sternly, thinking of how Caroline Slater had let out a snort of laughter when informed of the situation earlier that morning and how Chastity Maxwell's stepfather, or whoever he was, had whistled appreciatively as if actually impressed by what he seemed to see as her rock and roll antics, 'I was rather surprised at the levels of nonchalance affected by all of your parents regarding this matter.'

The girls smirked – they couldn't help it. This was too good. Of course their parents wouldn't make a scene – this was an excellent story to be told at the next dinner party – and anyway, where the hell's the point in making a fuss about stuff? At least their kids weren't teenage crack whores, in gangs, on (many) drugs or out robbing old ladies. Although if it was possible for Daisy's mouth to fall open any further they doubted it.

'But what about my parents?' she wailed, hot tears spilling rapidly down her cheeks at the thought of how upset and disappointed they'd be with her. 'They must have gone mad! What am I going to *do*!'

'Calm down, Daisy,' snapped Mrs Bennett, who had a horror of hysteria, particularly – ironically – in school-girls. 'Your parents were the only ones who didn't answer the phone, so they are none the wiser about any of this, and I certainly won't be ringing again to tell them about your lost revision aid. But Daisy,' she carried on in more gentle tones, 'I think you need to try and relax a little bit. It really wouldn't have killed you to wait until morning to retrieve it, would it? I don't want any of my girls falling ill through overwork. There's plenty of time for you to do your homework in normal school hours.'

Mrs Bennett turned her attention back to the others, not liking the smirks she'd just witnessed at all. 'So, I've been looking at your timetables and I see you all have Tuesday afternoons free.' She paused slightly before delivering her hammer blow, experience telling her it would give the punishment that much more impact. 'Since the three of you have turned flouting school rules into something of a sport, and since the sports hall needs a spring–clean before next term, Mr Morris and I have decided that you are the perfect ones to help us out in your free time until the end of term, starting this Tuesday coming.'

'But –' Chastity attempted a weak defence, but wasn't surprised when Mrs Bennett started speaking again, cutting her off completely as if she hadn't said a word.

'I want the entire place turned inside out, all of the equipment labelled and catalogued and put neatly in its rightful place. And,' Mrs Bennett said, almost purring with satisfaction at her final thrust, 'the sports staff will be on hand to make sure everything is done their way. Right, that's all.' She stood up and clapped her hands together before throwing open her door and ushering them out. 'I don't want any of you leaving the school boundaries for the rest of the day and I have told Mr Morris you are not to receive any visitors either. I suggest you all take it easy today and think about next week's lessons. I imagine you three have had quite enough excitement recently to last a lifetime.'

'Well,' said Jinx, linking arms with Liberty and scuffing her shoes on the drive as they walked back home to Tanner House, 'that could have been a lot worse.'

'Hmm,' Chastity said with a sniff, tossing her nose in the air as she so often did when she felt something was beneath her. 'I *guess*.'

'Come on, Chas,' Liberty said, upbeat. 'Jinx is right. We got off fucking lightly considering what could have happened last night. So we lose our Tuesdays – big freaking deal. We never had them before and we seemed to survive OK. The worst thing is being confined with the fucking sports staff for hours on end, but I'm sure we'll cope.'

'You know what, Lib?' Jinx asked, smiling at her best friend in astonishment as something clicked in her head. 'I think you've really changed!'

'What do you mean?' Liberty replied indignantly, snatching her arm away from Jinx in mock fury. 'How very dare you?'

'No, no,' giggled Jinx, 'not in a *bad* way. I just mean you seem a lot more, I don't know, like, sensible or something this term. Although not,' she added hastily, spying Liberty's disbelieving expression, 'in a boring way at all. You're still *you*, you just seem to have your head screwed on a bit tighter, that's all. I suppose you're a bit more streetwise.'

'We still need,' interrupted Daisy, who'd been chewing her lip thoughtfully as they walked along and didn't really care to analyse whether or not Liberty's personality had, in fact, changed at all, 'to work out what happened last night. There's a meeting of all the head girls this afternoon and I'm going to ask the other heads of year if they've seen anything or know anything. I'm absolutely determined to get to the bottom of this one. Someone stitched you guys up, and by extension me too, and it's not fair.'

'Thanks, Daisy,' said Chastity as they started up the path that led to Tanner House's front doorway. 'That's really kind of you. If we do find out who did it they're going to get the nastiest shock of their fucking lives. No one makes *me* do chores and gets away with it.'

'I'm totally ruined,' said Jinx, flopping down on to

the sofa as they walked into the reception area. 'I need to have a little lie-down and a think about things.'

'Me too,' agreed Chastity, lying down on the same sofa in the opposite direction and coiling her arms around Jinx's bent knees. 'Wiped out.'

'Broken, destroyed and,' added Liberty with a sigh, lifting up Jinx's legs and squidging herself on to the end of the sofa by Chastity's head, 'wrecked.'

'Right then,' said Daisy, looking a tad uncomfortable at this frank exchange and moving towards the exit, in search of her neat and tidy desk, where all the pens and pencils were lined up in neat rows alongside Post-it notes in every colour, stickers and dictionaries of all kinds. 'Well, I'm going to go and make myself another chemistry crib sheet. I'll see you girls later.'

'Laters, Dais,' the sofa-ridden three chorused, weakly waving her off before collapsing in a heap again.

'So,' muttered Liberty, tickling Jinx's feet after a few minutes' comfortable, companionable silence, 'are we going to, like, lie here all day long or go and watch music videos or *what*?'

'Music videos,' trilled Chastity, 'but can you carry us there, Liberty? And can we get our duvets out of our rooms?'

'Yes!' agreed Jinx. 'And a packet of custard creams from the kitchen!'

Suitably furnished for an afternoon of extreme relaxation, the three of them got into their Juicy tracksuits, fired up the central heating and settled into the common room. It being Sunday lunchtime with only three weeks left of term, the school was deserted. And since anyone who had stayed in had done so to work they had the place to themselves.

After three solid hours of *America's Next Top Model* interspersed with VH1 golden oldie music videos during the adverts, Jinx, Liberty and Chastity had roused themselves to chatting about the previous evening. They were more alert than they'd been all day. This was helped along, no doubt, by the extreme sugar rush that eating at least ten very sweet biscuits in one sitting causes.

'Do you believe that thing people say about the truth always coming out when you're drunk?' Chastity asked, rolling round on her sofa so she could see the others' faces.

'I think it's total bollocks, Chas,' replied Jinx instantly, for this was one of her pet topics and she could sound off for hours about it. 'I think *all* kinds of shit comes out when you're drunk – truth, lies, showing off, whatever – and whatever *does* come out is not from a conscious mind.'

'Yeah,' agreed Liberty, carefully biting the top off yet another biscuit and staring at the television, 'I think the same as Jinx.'

'The thing is, Chas,' Jinx carried on, warming to her theme, 'drunk people don't generally purvey considered opinions, do they? I quite often *lie* when I'm drunk – more so than when I'm sober, anyway. I normally think it's funny at the time.'

'What about during an argument?' queried Chastity,

who was thinking about Paul and feeling bad for the first time about some of the things she'd screamed at him in the street.

'Well,' said Jinx, knowing exactly what Chastity was getting at, 'sometimes – in an argument or whatever – you're so cross you just look for the worst possible, most wounding thing you can say. And when you're drunk and having an argument you don't have the same sense of boundaries that you have when you're sober. You just want to upset the other person as much as possible.'

'Hmm,' nodded Chastity, clearly not yet convinced by this, for although she didn't regret breaking up with Paul in the slightest, she didn't want to make the guy suicidal or anything – what a drag *that* would be.

'And you'll notice,' Jinx carried on, wanting to make Chas feel better about things but also really believing what she was saying, 'it's *always* smug, victim-type people who latch on to drunken bad behaviour and emphasise the drunken part of it. I think it's so they can use the excuse of every bit of drinking being bad and negative, when we know most of it's hunky-dory. It's like one night in fifty that goes bad, which I don't think is too bad a price to pay for fun and games the rest of the time.'

'Fucking killjoys,' added Liberty supportively.

'Exactly, Lib,' said Jinx with a smile. 'They constantly justify why they're always right and everyone else is wrong, and it gets freaking tedious if you ask me. It's the ultimate "I told you so" from boring people who are too afraid of rocking the boat or – God forbid! – losing control to risk ever having any fun in their lives.'

'You're so right,' agreed Chastity, feeling a hell of a lot better about things after this pep talk. 'I don't trust people who don't drink – what have they got to hide?'

'Who doesn't drink?' giggled Olga, pushing open the door and leading a procession entirely made up of her sisters into the common room, thereby causing the others to forget their conversation entirely. 'Are they feeling OK in the head?'

The girls on the sofa laughed delightedly and ushered them over to spill all about the party. Wearing skinny jeans, pumps and soft cashmere jumpers in blue, green and pink to match their diamond rings, the trips looked as stunning as ever and betrayed not a single shred of evidence of a late night.

'My brother's been unusually silent all day long,' said Jinx, winking at the girls. 'Whatever did you lot get up to last night? We've been dying to find out!'

'Forget about *us*,' said Masha, running her fingers through her hair so that her green diamond ring sparkled in the harsh light from the long bulb on the ceiling. 'We want to know what the hell happened to you girls. People came over to us and said you'd been taken away in a police van. We couldn't believe it, but then George said this morning you had texted him about what to say to Mrs Bennett. Is it true?'

'This morning?' Jinx almost screamed with shock. 'You were still with George this *morning*?'

'Why yes,' sighed Irina. 'He picked us up from our hotel and took us to Bill's for breakfast. We really like him and his friends very much.'

'That bastard hasn't even texted me back to see what happened with Mrs Bennett,' Jinx snorted, furious at her brother's apparent total lack of concern for her physical and mental well-being, 'and now I find out he's been squiring you lot all over town. Well, I'm pleased you had a good time with him, but he's going to get a flea in his ear the next time I speak to him.'

'So come on then,' urged Masha, sitting forward eagerly and clasping her hands together in anticipation. 'Tell us what happened last night!'

'Yes,' agreed Olga, draping herself very elegantly over a giant Bart Simpson beanbag Mimi Tate had stolen from her younger brother after Christmas and brought back to school to sit on during her favourite *EastEnders*, 'come on!'

In the face of such pleasing interest in their latest exploits, and from such damned good-looking girls too, Jinx, Liberty and Chastity were more than happy to regale the triplets with highly exaggerated scenes from last night's theatrics. Halfway through their tall tales, Igor mooched into the room, threw a dark look at the triplets and settled himself into an old leather armchair by one of the windows. He stared out to sea and didn't appear to take any interest in the girls' conversation. After a few minutes they forgot he was even there and carried on as normal, shrieking and laughing and generally behaving very boisterously indeed.

If they *had* paid any attention to him they would have seen him absent-mindedly twisting what looked like a replica of the triplets' rings but in white on the middle finger of his right hand and staring thoughtfully out the window.

Judging by the glowing reports, George had been at his most charming, funny and naughty self and had made a massive hit with the triplets. Jinx couldn't help but reflect that at least she'd get amazing presents if one of these birds ended up as her sister-in-law. Not, of course, that George was likely to be able to keep himself in their good books for very much longer. Trouble had a way of following him around and she couldn't imagine this would be any different from the other relationship disasters he had endured.

— * —

At ten o'clock, when they had just finished watching *Wife Swap* and were beginning to say their goodnights and gather up all their stuff ready for bed, Liv and Charlie swept into the room in a cloud of what smelt like real ale.

'Where the hell have you two been?' yelled Chastity, jumping up and dropping the duvet she'd just neatly folded on to the floor in her excitement. 'We've been trying to ring you both all freaking day!'

'You smell like a bloody brewery,' sniffed Jinx admiringly. 'What the hell have you been up to?'

'Um,' giggled Liv, flopping on to the floor in front of Jinx's sofa and dragging an equally-unsteady-on-her-feet Charlie after her, 'we've been, you know, hanging ten in town.'

For some reason this statement caused the pair on the floor to clutch each other and start screaming with laughter. Whatever they'd been doing, they were clearly more than a little soused. The others doubted they'd get much sense out of either of them, but pressed on with their questioning nonetheless.

'Come on,' Chastity insisted. 'What *exactly* have you been doing? And what the hell kept you last night? Although,' she added thoughtfully, 'it's actually pretty good for you two that you weren't there earlier or you'd be cleaning out the fucking sports hall alongside the rest of us.'

'What?' demanded Charlie, the realisation that she and Liv must have missed a whole lot more school chat than they thought slowly filtering into her befuddled mind.

'Yeah,' slurred Liv, resting her head on Charlie's lap and peering up at the others through half-lowered eyes, 'spill!'

All thoughts of bed pushed aside, Jinx, Liberty and Chastity immediately launched into yet more of the luridly embellished tales they'd already spun the triplets. Even though they'd heard it all before, the Russian girls didn't make tracks for bed either. Igor was still in his chair by the window, but none of them paid him any attention. If they had, they would have seen him staring out to sea with an expression of pure longing on his face. He looked the very picture of stoicism as he sat there, occasionally letting out a deep sigh. But no one was interested in him. Instead, they settled down again

for a glorious gossip, bitch fest and lots of comic speculation as to who might have banged on Mrs Bennett's
door.

None of them took Daisy's theory particularly seriously and they pretty much assumed the whole thing
was basically down to sheer bad luck. Jinx was much
more interested in hearing about George from the
triplets anyway. And they in turn quizzed her relentlessly about her feelings for Jamie. She was flattered by
their interest, so pleased they clearly adored her brother
and so keen to talk about Jamie that she answered their
questions for two hours straight without a break.

Liv and Charlie were so shocked to hear about Paul
and Chastity splitting up they made her retell the whole
gory story in exhaustive detail and, what with all the
excitement, everyone forgot to ask them what *they'd*
been up to. They also failed to notice a nasty scratch on
Charlie's elbow.

It was past midnight when they got to bed and each
of them fell asleep within seconds of their heads hitting
their pillows. But while every other person who lived in
Tanner slumbered, Igor remained sitting in his chair in
the dark common room. He got up to open the window and, as he did so, a tear glinted on his cheek. It was
illuminated by the quarter-moon which cut almost as
stark a figure as Igor tonight, so bleakly did it seem set
against the night sky.

Miss Strimmer and Miss Golly eyed a defiant-looking

Jinx, Liberty and Chastity with inappropriate amounts of glee as the three lower sixth stood in front of them. It was Tuesday, the bell signalling the end of the lunch period had just rung throughout the school and the girls had turned up at the sports hall to begin the first of their afternoon punishment cleaning sessions.

Lunch had been a particularly filthy effort on the part of the terrible catering company Stagmount used. Called Finch & Jack, it had been nicknamed Pinch & Slack by the girls since pretty much the first day the company had taken over the contract. Slimy chicken with hairs still visible on the undercooked, puckered skin, overcooked cabbage swimming in gross, greasy margarine and potatoes with black bits in them did not help make the girls feel good in any way about what their afternoon held. Oh no, quite the reverse.

All three were in moods as filthy as their lunch had been when Dirk Hanson flew through the doors and came to a halt in between the two female sports staff, slinging a matey arm around each's neck. The girls nearly vomited at this point. The sight of someone *willingly* touching these total tools was almost more than they could bear.

Strimmer wore a short navy netball skirt every single day, winter or summer, and the girls were used to the faintly horrific sight of her mottled tree-trunk thighs glowing red with exertion as she ran around, shouting rather more abuse than praise at the girls. Where Strimmer was quite short and rather fat, Golly was tall and thin, and all the sporty girls loved them. The pair regularly held cringe-making little tea parties for their favourites in their office in the sports hall. Watching a bunch of schoolgirl sycophants hanging on to their every moronic word was almost enough to make you want to die on the spot, it really was.

So much for Mrs Bennett's clique bashing – they ran the absolute worst one in terms of exclusivity. No one sane would want to be in it, obviously, but that was rather beside the point. Strumpet and Gosh – as they were known – were the only two people who looked unhappy at the end of term. Neither had ever married, or was ever likely to, and it was hard to imagine them living any kind of normal life outside the school. Since they both spent every waking hour lording it over the girls, organising interminable house tournaments of every conceivable kind and refereeing – or fixing, more like – matches against rival schools, it was impossible to imagine them going to the pub or to the local garden centre or – yuck! – on a date or doing anything *normal* adults did.

However, pretty much the whole school had noticed, endlessly remarked upon and shrieked with evil laughter at the two idiots' positively skittish behaviour since Coach D. Hanson had arrived with such a bang on the sports scene. Both had stared, stunned, at his entrance into the first assembly of term and looked at each other as if they couldn't believe their eyes. Within two days, however, the three of them were completely inseparable. They appeared at every mealtime together, sat together in chapel and even gave each other freaking lifts into work on some kind of sick rota they obviously had going on. Wherever they went, you could hear the terrible snorting sounds of Strumpet and Gosh laughing at Dirk's stupid jokes.

Gosh was the cleverer of the two, but since Strimmer was an absolute bona fide card-carrying moron, that wasn't saying much. And – wouldn't you just know it – it had become increasingly obvious to all that Dirk was actually their male equivalent. He wore the same shockingly unfashionable sportswear, was never seen without a whistle round his neck and delighted in paying the same attention to the pettiest rules. The only difference between them, in fact, was the way he leered at the girls he taught. Annoying as the other two were, at least they didn't do that.

Standing purposefully slouched in front of these three fools, eyes lowered mutinously and awaiting their instructions, Jinx, Liberty and Chastity could hardly believe what a freaking chore this punishment was going to be. And in more ways than one, considering the taskmasters they had to put up with.

'So,' Dirk said to his colleagues, nodding his smarmy head at the sulky girls in front of them, 'to what do we owe *this* pleasure?'

'These three,' Gosh said with a delighted snarl at Jinx, who was her least favourite out of this very poor bunch, 'are going to be spending all their Tuesdays until the end of term cleaning out the sports centre, bagging and tagging all the equipment and basically doing whatever we tell them to.'

Strumpet and Gosh had hated Jinx ever since the summer term of the first year when she'd been instrumental in the freeing of a neighbouring farmer's flock of pygmy goats and the subsequent cancelling of a very important tennis match against Millfield. They hated Liberty because she couldn't care less about games of any kind. Also, since she was a favourite of Sister Minton's and thus able to throw medical sign-off notes around like confetti, there was nothing they could do to force her to attend games lessons when she seemed to get her period three times each month. And although Chastity was an excellent hockey player, captain of the tennis team and a brilliant swimmer, she was far too wealthy to be liked by this pair, who were extraordinarily jealous of some of the richer girls and made little attempt to hide it.

'Fucking hell,' muttered Chastity under her breath to Liberty. 'I'm not sure I can stand three weeks of this.'

'Shut up, Maxwell,' snapped Strumpet. 'We haven't finished with you yet, not by a long shot, and if I was you I'd keep quiet until we have.'

Chastity fixed Strumpet with a long glare, but by now the teacher was giggling like a cretin at something Dirk had whispered in her ear. The way these three carried on was frankly disgusting. Chastity wondered idly whether she should phone her mum and get her to complain. She decided, on balance and after remembering Mrs Bennett's furious expression on Sunday, against and resigned herself to whatever was coming next.

'Right then,' Strumpet intoned, delighted at having

these three exactly where she wanted them for once, 'we've come to a decision.'

'At last,' murmured Jinx to Liberty, earning herself a sharp look from Dirk.

'Yes,' continued Gosh – these two often spoke as if they were participating in a conversational relay race, the freaking idiots – 'you can all start upstairs in the gym. Normally you'll be separated, but some of the equipment up there is pretty heavy and you'll need to move it to clean it properly.'

'Don't worry. We've got special training for the inter-school badminton championship all afternoon on the court,' said Dirk, flashing an entirely inappropriate lewd wink at the girls, 'so we'll be able to keep a close eye on you.'

'There will be no talking, no laughing and absolutely *no* chewing gum, mobile phones or smoking this after-noon,' snapped Strumpet, who had caught the tail end of the wink and didn't like it at all.

'Go on then,' said Gosh. 'Up you go. We've been told to let you leave at half past five.'

Jinx, Liberty and Chastity looked at each other aghast. It was twenty past two now, so that meant over three hours' work in this stinking sweat factory. Troop-ing miserably up the stairs to the mezzanine level over the courts that housed the gym, listening to the backing track of the sports staff's uproarious laughter at their expense, the girls could hardly believe their bad luck and were beginning to feel very sorry for themselves indeed.

Two hours later, covered in dust and absolutely furious at being treated like slaves in this way, Chastity and Liberty were sitting on a pile of yoga mats talking to Jinx, who was hanging upside down from the monkey bars and very red in the face. Strumpet had checked on them ten minutes ago, so they felt pretty safe about taking this little break. Not, of course, that they really gave a shit whether they were caught slacking or not.

They could hear Dirk shouting instructions at a group of second years who were playing a very noisy game of badminton beneath them, so there was no need to lower their voices. In fact, messy and gross and covered in cobwebs as everything up here was, spending the afternoon with your two best friends in the whole world is really not such a bad deal. The girls had got on with the job while giggling non-stop about what dicks and pricks such a lot of people in the world were. The sports staff, lots of the other teachers and more than a few pupils were included in this list, and they'd actually cleaned most of the gym area already. The only things left to sort out were the mats — which Strumpet had infuriatingly insisted must each be cleaned individually and would be checked at the end of the day — and they were taking a much-deserved break before tackling them.

When they got going again, they split the pile into three and were busily wiping each one clean when Chastity let out a surprised yell. The other two looked up to see her waving a bunch of papers in their direction.

'What is it?' asked Jinx, leaving a grimy trail of black dust on her forehead as she wiped it with the back of one of her mucky hands.

'I don't know,' Chastity said, straightening up and unfolding one of the larger sheets before studying it intently. 'Hey,' she said, surprised. 'I think it's a plan of the school. How weird!'

'You're right, Chas,' said Jinx, walking across and peering over her shoulder. 'Look – this here is the main school building, those are the dining rooms and that's the sports hall. It looks like an architect's impression or something to me.'

'But what do all these squiggles mean?' asked Liberty, staring in confusion at the plan in front of them.

'I'm not *sure*,' replied Chastity, 'but I think it's Russian. Why would there be Russian writing all over architect's plans of the school?'

'Maybe,' said Jinx, who was more interested in clock-watching than she was in the plans, 'they're getting a Russian architect to redo the dining rooms or the sports hall or something. In fact,' she continued determinedly, intent on finishing the job bang on time so the evil sports staff wouldn't give them even more to do at next week's session, 'I bet it's this place and that's why they're making us sort it out like this.'

Chastity looked a bit doubtful. 'But why would they be left *here*, in the gym, shoved between a pile of yoga mats?'

'God! Who even cares?' Jinx said, walking back to her diminishing pile of dirty mats and pointing at them.

'These things won't have been used since last term. Everyone's so pathetically keen to join Dirk's classes now, no one bothers with yoga any more. Maybe there was a meeting in the sports hall and they just got misplaced and then buried under this lot. Whatever, guys, we've only got twenty-five minutes left until we're free to leave this dump and I for one can't freaking wait.'

Chastity put the plans in her book bag and the three of them finished the job in silence without discussing them again. At five twenty-nine exactly the three of them skipped down the stairs, flashed knowingly irritating grins at the sports staff and prepared to go back to Tanner. As Liberty was zipping up her green, fluffy-hooded parka jacket, the group of badminton-playing second years – headed by Betsy Johnson – trooped out through the double swing doors that led to the reception area of the sports hall, the staff office and the girls' suite of white-tiled changing rooms.

Katie Green was trailing miserably at the back of the group of second-year girls, unaware that the three lower sixths were standing almost in front of her nose. When she looked up and saw them at such close quarters, she flushed a deep, immediate red and started back in shock. The movement momentarily distracted Liberty from her zip. Unlike most of the others, Liberty did occasionally notice members of the lower school and she was immediately struck by how unhappy poor Katie seemed to be. Instinctively, before she turned round to dash after Jinx and Chastity, who had got bored of waiting for her, Liberty smiled extremely kindly at Katie.

Racing up the drive in a tangle of scarf, books and bag, Liberty instantly forgot this little scene. Indeed, throughout her whole life she would never once think of it again. Katie, conversely, had stopped where she stood, as if shot through the heart with a golden arrow. She stared after the older girl in a trance as the latter turned on her Ugg-booted heel and disappeared from sight.

It was only when Betsy Johnson, racing off to an extra English lesson intended to help her with her mild dyslexia, bumped into her as she went past that Katie managed to pull herself together and slump into the changing room. She could hardly believe it. Liberty Latiffe, one of the ultimate queens of the lower sixth, had smiled at her. Her . . . Katie Green. She thought about nothing else for the rest of that day and it was the first thing she thought of when she woke the next morning. She was still analysing it the following week. In fact, that very night she sat up until four o'clock in the morning writing, screwing up and rewriting sick little notes to Liberty. Fortunately for Liberty, she came to her senses eventually and the mispelt declarations of eternal love remained unsent and in the bin.

Jinx and the others had arrived home to find Daisy Finnegan sitting on the sofa, reading a chunky physics book.

'Hey, Dais,' they chorused, and sat down to tell her about their afternoon in the clink.

Things, Mr Morris thought as he smiled his way past them a few minutes later, followed by the ever-present but much-happier-looking Myrtle, had definitely changed in Tanner House this term.

For the next five days and nights it rained and rained and rained again. The girls were beginning to wonder darkly if it would ever stop. Their workload had been increasing steadily since January and they were feeling very bored and restless. This term had proved little more than one long fucking shower so far – thank God there wasn't much of it left to endure. Games were off, trips into town were off, smoking anywhere but the garage was off and it's fair to say a lot of tempers were off too.

Since anything involving fresh air was apparently on permanent hold, the sports hall had been in constant use for indoor netball, hockey, badminton and gymnastics. Knowing it would be beyond filthy when they next went in there to clean, Jinx, Liberty and Chastity glowered furiously every time they walked past the place on their way to and from Tanner.

Sitting in the library on Monday morning after a way more subdued than normal breaktime, Jinx was helping Liberty with a French translation they were due to hand in to Mr Christie that afternoon. When Liberty bent her dark head over her books to attempt at least some of it herself, Jinx looked out the rain-streaked window and let out a massive sigh. She couldn't help it; she hadn't heard a thing from Jamie since the party and was beginning to feel seriously down in the dumps.

'What's wrong, Jin?' asked Liberty, looking up and fixing Jinx with a worried glance. 'Have we done it wrong?'

'I'm not worried about our fucking French prep,' said Jinx, roughly pulling her curly blonde hair into a short ponytail and shaking her head. 'I'm just pissed off generally.'

Liberty knew Jinx was dying to hear from Jamie. Only a deaf, dumb and blind person could have missed the way her best friend leapt on her phone every time it bleeped with a new text message, followed by her invariably disappointed look when it proved – once again – not to be from him. She studied Jinx without saying anything but raised an eyebrow, silently encouraging her to share her feelings.

'OK,' admitted Jinx, who knew that Liberty knew what was wrong with her but hadn't felt inclined to discuss it until now. 'I want to know why the hell I haven't heard a word from Jamie. I mean,' she continued with a sigh, 'we had such a great time at the party until . . .'

'Chastity and Paul fucked it up!' finished Liberty, pushing her chair closer to Jinx's and wrapping her in a huge hug.

'Yeah,' muttered Jinx, 'but, you know, shit happens and people have to deal with it. George thought the whole thing was hilarious. Maybe he just doesn't fancy me. Maybe,' she added in extremely morose tones, 'he thinks I'm a bad kisser or something.'

'Liberty Latiffe!' Jo appeared from behind one of the

shelves in front of their desk, interrupting their little tête-à-tête, and stood there with her hands on her hips. 'I've been all over the school looking for you. I never imagined I'd find you in *here*.'

Jinx shook her head. She was pretty fed up with everyone assuming their group never did any bloody work. It was as good as slander and she'd had enough.

'Jo,' she began, intending to give the secretary a piece of her mind once and for all, 'we *are* in the lower sixth now, you know. We do have A levels next year and – contrary to popular opinion – we *do* intend to pass the things.'

'Whatever,' replied Jo, who wasn't really listening as she had a million things to do before lunch and talking to this lot certainly wasn't high on her list of priorities. 'Liberty, your father phoned an hour or so ago.'

Liberty blanched at this information. Jinx immediately forgot Jo, their work, Jamie and everything else as she registered the look of shock on her friend's face at this totally left-field information. She grabbed Liberty's hand and squeezed it tight as Jo leaned over and placed a telephone memorandum on the desk between them before stalking off to get on with her many chores.

Jinx and Liberty sat in stunned silence for a while, then Jinx said quietly, 'You haven't heard a thing from him since you left Riyadh, have you?'

'No,' Liberty muttered, picking up the piece of paper and studying it intently, 'I haven't.'

'So . . .' Jinx said, wanting to ask a hundred questions but also not wanting to freak Liberty out.

'So,' replied Liberty, folding the memo into a series of smaller squares, 'it doesn't say anything other than that he called and wants me to call him back when I can.'

'Are you going to?' Jinx enquired gently, slipping her free arm round Liberty's shoulders and pulling her close. 'Do you *want* to?'

'Yes, I'm going to, and yes, I want to, 'Liberty said determinedly. 'I've actually kind of been expecting him to get in touch. I know we had that massive scene at the end of last term and all, but he *is* my dad and I knew he'd want to know what I was up to at some point or other. Also,' she continued, smiling at Jinx, 'last time I spoke to Mum she told me he's still paying the fees.'

'Really?' said Jinx, surprised, for she'd never once thought about who was paying for what. 'You never said anything.'

'Yep!' Liberty nodded. 'Mum phoned to speak to Mrs Bennett about sorting it all out and Mrs B told her they'd been paid in full right through to the end of the upper sixth. Apparently he did it at the beginning of this term. And as soon as I heard that I knew he must have gotten over it. I don't know why I didn't tell you – I've been mulling it over in my own mind, I guess. The thing *is*,' she went on, sweeping her books into her bag, 'he's very stubborn.'

'And proud,' added Jinx, also gathering her things together.

'Yes,' Liberty replied. 'So I was thinking about writing him a letter or something, but I guess I don't have to now, do I? Let's go back to Tanner. Will you sit with me when I call him?'

'Of *course* I will,' answered Jinx.

Walking down the drive, heads lowered against the driving rain, which had succeeded in soaking them completely despite their parka jackets, oversized scarves and matching baker boy hats, the pair of them heard the trilling sound of a text message at the same time as Jinx felt a vibration against her thigh. She rummaged around in her deep coat pocket and grabbed her phone as they turned the corner to Tanner. She pulled her cap down low over her forehead to shield her face from the relentless rain as she opened her new text.

'It's him!' she screamed, punching the top of Liberty's arm, tossing her hat in the air and jumping up and down in delight. 'At fucking last!'

'What does it *say*?' Liberty yelled impatiently, stamping her foot and forgetting all about the conversation she was about to have with her father. 'Come on. Let's have it!'

'It says,' read Jinx from the phone's small screen, '"Hey there, hot chick, how's tricks?"'

Both of them shrieked at this point, gripped each other and started jumping up and down, regardless of the rapidly deepening puddle they were splashing all over themselves. Dirk, driving past in the opposite direction in his yellow Suzuki Swift – possibly the most cretinous car in existence, so very suitable for his purposes – shook his head and thought to himself that, fit as they undoubtedly were, these Stagmount girls were all stark raving mad. He put his foot down, intent on racing away from them as fast as possible. The girls glanced up but barely registered his passing.

'"If yr free next Saturday,"' Liberty took over the reading, '"bring yr friends and come to Get Down or Get Fucked at Skate Fest on the seafront. Love J x."'

'LOVE!' Jinx yelled. 'It says LOVE!'

'Yes,' giggled Liberty, 'so I see. But what the hell is Skate Fest?'

'I'm not sure,' said Jinx in her normal voice, 'but I've heard George talk about it. It must be one of those skateboard things all the surf dudes are into. It's a competition, I think, and there's a party for everyone in one of the seafront bars afterwards. In fact,' she went on, sounding more convinced as the memories filtered into her brain, 'I'm pretty certain George and Jamie went to it last year. Yes, and one of their friends – it was Jamie's housemate Daz – was showing off and tried to do a somersault or something off his board on the ramp and missed it and totally fucked his back up. And another one broke his leg and had to be taken off to hospital in an ambulance. And everyone got so drunk afterwards none of them remembered anything about it in the morning,' she finished with relish.

'Do you think George and Jamie will be in the competition?' Liberty asked, wide-eyed at the thought of all these injuries. 'It sounds really dangerous.'

'I don't think *they* will,' Jinx said, retrieving her hat

from the bush where it had landed when she threw it in the air earlier and shaking it violently to get rid of the water that had pooled inside it, 'but I bet some of their friends will. I guess they'll be watching it with us. Whatever, it's the last weekend of term and we've *so* got to go. God, I'm so excited! I thought I'd never hear from him again. I mean, I know about the three-day rule and everything, but it's been eight freaking days since the party.'

'I know,' Liberty said, beyond delighted that Jamie had finally seen fit to get in touch with her best friend, thrilled at the prospect of another big night out with no interruptions from Chastity and Paul this time and also secretly hoping that the dark-haired boy from the party would be there. 'I was a bit worried myself. And what a blast to go to this thing on our last Saturday of term!'

'Totally,' confirmed Jinx, smiling widely as she rammed her sopping hat back on head, blissfully unconcerned about the water now dripping down the back of her neck. She gripped Liberty's arm. 'Right, Latiffe. Let's get you back to Tanner and make this phone call.'

After shaking themselves like dogs in the reception area, splattering the notice board with drops of water, they dumped their bags in an untidy heap by the door and sauntered into the kitchen in search of sustenance.

Sitting back to front on Liberty's desk chair, Jinx blew on her mug of scalding-hot tea, nibbled on the corner of a Bourbon biscuit and looked out of the window.

Listening to her best friend's side of the conversation with her father, she shook her head and wondered for the thousandth time about Amir's sanity. Having dragged his daughter back to Saudi at the end of last term in a towering rage over some perceived transgression on her part, swearing she would never return to Stagmount again, here they were chatting away about Liberty's forthcoming exams and the terrible weather as if nothing had ever happened.

Her thoughts were interrupted when Liberty's voice suddenly took on a surprised, questioning tone. Jinx sat up and listened. She hoped Amir hadn't phoned to impart bad news of any kind.

'What do you mean you think it's Stagmount?' Liberty asked, frowning as she doodled on the cover of the notebook on her lap. 'Oh . . . Well,' she continued after a long pause during which Amir talked non-stop, 'I don't know anything about it, Dad.'

Liberty wiggled her fingers at Jinx to indicate that Amir was banging on about something or other at length and rolled her eyes. Jinx smiled. Even though she'd not heard a word about the fallout yet, at least they seemed to be getting on as well as they used to. She was sure Amir loved his daughter; it was just he didn't know how to show her he did – or not properly anyway. Designer clothes, flash handbags and bundles of cash were one thing, of course they were, but honesty, trust and respect were another entirely.

'OK, Dad,' said Liberty, winking at Jinx, 'thanks for calling. Yes, yes,' she said, nodding. 'I will. Love you too.

Bye, Dad. Bye!'

Liberty snapped her phone shut, uncrossed her legs and looked at Jinx. 'Well,' she said, 'that was weird. In more ways than one.'

'So what did he want?' asked Jinx, relieved to see Liberty looking so happy at having renewed communication with her father. 'Anything interesting?'

Liberty reached for her mug and sipped thoughtfully. 'He didn't say one single word about the row or me going to America or Mum or anything.' She laughed ruefully. 'But I didn't really expect he would. Why change the pattern of a lifetime?'

'Hmm,' Jinx murmured, not really knowing what to say about this at all.

'He asked me about my schoolwork and whether I had enough money. And then,' Liberty said, putting down her mug and frowning, 'he started banging on about some property plans he'd been sent by a business associate.'

'What do you mean?' Jinx asked, looking blank and wondering what the hell Amir had up his sleeve now.

'Well,' Liberty went on, 'he said he'd been sent the plans of some luxury new flats. He said the location was top secret but the developers were trying to ascertain interest or something, and he'd been approached.'

'So what?' a baffled Jinx replied, knowing that Amir never discussed any of his business ventures with his daughter. She'd once asked Liberty what her dad did and Liberty hadn't been able to tell her. 'What's it got to do with you?'

'He said he thought the plans looked like Stagmount,' Liberty answered. 'He said he recognised the formation of the main school houses and said the helipad is in exactly the same place as the one here.'

'I don't get it,' Jinx said, standing up and stretching. 'What's he saying?'

'Basically, he said he thought someone might be trying to buy Stagmount and turn it into a property development and,' Liberty went on, staring Jinx in the face, 'that since Mrs Bennett had visited him in Saudi in December he wondered if she had said anything about it.'

'Mrs Bennett went to Saudi!' Jinx asked incredulously, sitting down again. 'In December! *This* December!'

'Yep.' Liberty nodded. 'Apparently she was passing through on her way to a meeting about something and she came round to Dad's for coffee.'

'But –' Jinx interjected before Liberty cut her off, knowing what Jinx was thinking pretty much even before she did.

'When I was there,' Liberty said, 'exactly. He said they talked for two hours and she convinced him to send me to live with Mum. He also said he respected her as a sensible English woman and that I was lucky to have her as my headmistress.'

'Bloody hell,' Jinx gasped, truly shocked by all of this. 'I knew Mrs B was cool, but I never realised she was, like, the raddest dude alive. I can't believe she did all that. What a woman! What else did he say about it?'

'Well, he banged on about the plans,' Liberty continued, 'but then said he might well be wrong. I think he was looking for an excuse to get in touch and used them – it must be a coincidence.'

'Who knows,' said Jinx, still shocked by the revelations about their headmistress's intervention on Liberty's behalf, 'and who cares? I'm sure Stagmount can't be sold – the whole idea's ridiculous. It's a charitable trust as well as a listed building. I still can't believe Mrs Bennett went to Saudi and saved your ass and never said a word about it.'

'Me neither,' Liberty said, shaking her head and shuddering at what might have been if Mrs B hadn't acted. 'We owe her so much.'

'Yes,' agreed Jinx, 'we certainly do.'

After looking at their watches and realising they had only three minutes to make it back to the main school for lunch, they grabbed their bags and sprinted back up the drive. For once, the rain had stopped. They turned their faces to the weak March sun trying its best to shine through the clouds and laughed as the puddles splashed around their furiously racing feet. Weak with laughter and exertion, they skipped down the corridor undaunted by the prospect of a gross lunch and feeling happier than they had for ages.

By the time they hooked up with the others at their usual table, they were so intent on telling them about Mrs Bennett's visit to Saudi and Jamie's text that all thoughts of the plans Amir had mentioned had flown their minds entirely.

- ✳ -

Sitting in classroom 4B on Thursday morning, waiting for Mrs Carpenter and their daily tutor group session to commence, the lower sixth were positively delirious compared to how low they'd all been feeling a week ago. The weather must have something to do with it. While it had seemed floods of biblical proportions were scarily imminent for pretty much the whole freaking term, today had dawned cold but sunny and their moods had lightened as a consequence.

Chastity, Jinx and Liberty, in that order, were sitting in the very centre of the back row, with Liv next to Chastity and Charlie next to Liberty. The girls were whiling away their waiting time with good-humoured, idle gossip about dear old Mrs C. Fiona – who claimed she always sat at the front because of her terrible eyesight, though it was actually more to do with her terrible fear of missing something one of the teachers might say – was sitting on the side of Liberty's desk, swinging her legs and enjoying joining in the chatter until the teacher arrived. Even Daisy had thrown in a couple of remarks and not been shouted down. Their tutor had, they unanimously agreed, been in the very best of moods all that term.

'Hey,' Mimi Tate yelled over from where she sat at the end of the second row closest to the window, 'it's because she's in *lurve*.'

'Yeah,' said Chastity, looking round for Igor and not

spotting him anywhere, 'but where *is* the object of her affection?'

'Masha?' Jinx directed her comment at the three identical backs in front of them, knowing they'd all turn round when she said one of their names.

'Yes,' said Masha, who was wearing, if Jinx had only thought to look, the green diamond on her finger.

'Where's Igor?' Jinx asked, winking conspiratorially at them, for she liked these girls a lot.

'We don't know,' replied Irina with a shrug and an unconcerned glance at both her sisters. 'We haven't seen him yet this morning.'

'Some bodyguard,' muttered Liberty. 'My dad would have a fit if his security guys left him alone for even a second.'

'Oh, we don't care about that,' said Olga, flashing a blue glint around the room as she ran her right hand through her hair and the huge diamond on her finger caught the light. 'We don't need him anyway. We're going to tell our dad we don't need him next term.'

'Yes,' Masha added with a giggle, 'next term we won't need him at all. But he's here now, so it's a bit difficult for us to get rid of him with just a few days still to go.'

'What about him and Mrs C?' pressed Chastity. 'What do you think about that?'

'Oh,' Irina said, pausing to glance at her sisters, almost as if she wanted confirmation of something before continuing, 'we don't know what you're talking about.'

'Are you serious?' asked Liv, who found it very hard to believe all three of them had singularly failed to notice the budding romance as it occurred underneath their very noses. 'Come off it. We've been talking of nothing else for weeks. *You* guys can't have missed it, surely!'

Whatever the triplets' response might have been was lost to a gust of cold air as the door flew open. Mrs Carpenter strode in and headed straight for the chair behind her desk. The girls had always liked stylish, friendly Mrs C but were wary of igniting her legendarily schizophrenic temper. Fortunately, this term there had been a total sea change in both her moods and the way she interacted with the girls in her form. Sweetness and light were very much the order of the day and – strangely, considering the undiagnosed bipolar disorder the girls were utterly convinced she suffered from – she'd hardly been heard to raise her voice above polite conversational level once. She'd also not thrown a single lump of chalk at any of their heads. It was a frankly remarkable transformation and her form had finally begun to believe it might be permanent.

However, when she raised her head to look around the room the girls, by now arranged in neat rows in front of her, immediately realised all was not well in the mad, mad world of Mrs C. Dressed entirely in black, as usual, accessorised with chunky silver pieces of jewellery, the vibrant flash of block colour the tutor had, of late, been adding to her all-black repertoire on a daily basis was missing. Her red-rimmed, bloodshot eyes provided the only accent on today's outfit. Her swollen face, heaving shoulders and shuddering breaths indicated to all of them that Mrs C had rocked up to tutor group fresh from an absolutely mammoth crying fit.

The girls stared at her, beyond appalled. It was one thing to deal with *each other* having a personal crisis of some kind but quite another to be faced with a member of *staff* going through the same thing. And Mrs C was evidently in the midst of a really bad one. None of them knew quite what to do and they all felt more than a little uncomfortable. At that moment the silence in 4B was completely deafening.

Lulu Cooper was just rummaging around in the bottom of her bag for the packet of travel tissues she knew were in there somewhere, damn it, when the door began to creak open once more. The rest of the girls, who had been staring straight ahead, waiting for Mrs Carpenter to say something, anything, to break the silence, turned their heads to look at the doorway. Lulu, finally locating the pesky packet, jumped up to offer some much needed TLC to her tutor at the same time as Igor's tall, forbidding form was framed in the doorway. The expression on his face was so unlike anything the girls had ever seen before that little Lulu gasped and sat straight back down on her seat, all her kindly intentions immediately forgotten.

The tension in the room, alongside the sudden drop in temperature, somehow found its way through Mrs Carpenter's misery and the tutor raised her head to see what was causing it. When her anguished eyes landed on Igor they instantly welled up with fresh tears and a small moan escaped her lips. Igor's face appeared to have been moulded from the hardest granite. So fixed was the stern, forbidding and, above all, closed-off look on the bodyguard's face that some of the girls couldn't stop involuntary shivers from shuddering down their spines.

After what seemed like a lifetime of Mrs C and Igor staring at each other eye to miserable eye, the door slammed shut behind Igor. He strode across the room to his customary seat by the triplets, folded himself down into it, crossed his arms and stared pointedly out of the big window. The triplets appeared not to have noticed anything amiss whatsoever. Their blonde heads were bent together over a letter they'd received that morning and none of them so much as flickered an eyelash at the scene playing out in front of them. The rest of the girls had no idea what was going on, but a couple of things were abundantly clear. Mrs Carpenter, of whom they were very fond when she was nice, was absolutely devastated. And the cause of this devastation, obvious from the stricken glances she kept flicking his way while desperately trying to pull herself, was Igor.

'Girls,' Mrs C said in a voice hoarse from crying, a distant relation indeed to her usual booming tones, 'I . . .'

She then made the fatal mistake of looking over at Igor. The moment her eyes alighted on him it was game over as far as any chance of being able to hold it together went. The girls watched, alert to her every shaky move, as Mrs Carpenter grabbed her coat, bag and class register and dashed out of the room as fast as her legs would carry her. They continued to sit there in a state of shocked suspension for a few seconds. Then, all at once and seemingly out of nowhere, a buzz of chat enveloped classroom 4B. Chairs were scraped back and desks pushed aside as the girls gathered in small groups on the corridor side of the room, away from where Igor was sitting as if made of stone by the window. The triplets had still not looked up and were now, giggling occasionally, whispering softly to each other in Russian.

The bell sounded for the beginning of morning lessons and the girls watched, enthralled, as the triplets stood up as one and pushed their chairs underneath their desks. They smiled around the room as if nothing had happened, waved at Jinx and Liberty, who were closest to them, and walked out of the door. Igor followed close on their heels, his black coat flapping behind him like a crow's wings. Most of the rest followed suit, shooting meaningful glances at each other as they did so and raising their eyebrows in the direction of the dining rooms to indicate that today's morning break was going to be one hell of a gossip fest.

Since she'd finished this term's project the previous week, Jinx bade farewell to Chastity, Liberty, Liv and Charlie, who were heading off to double art, and agreed she'd see them at lunchtime. Left to her own devices in their form room, she took her time in packing up her bags and thought about what had just happened. God, but she felt sorry for Mrs C. Although, since Igor had looked so completely terrifying this morning, she had to admit she was hard pressed to see the attraction. Either way, thought Jinx as she turned left down the corridor, she'd never seen anyone as cut up as *that*. That was something else entirely.

Mincing along quite happily, studying the notice boards for anything new or interesting – not a chance – Jinx decided to pop into the ladies' loos on the off chance she might locate the trainers she'd misplaced the other day. As soon as she walked in, though, she regretted this decision. Sitting on the very end of one of the low slatted benches that hugged the walls around the small shower area was Mrs Carpenter. Her face was turned to the wall and she was hugging her knees, rocking slightly and moaning incoherently, while taking in great, shuddering breaths. She looked, frankly, like a mental patient and Jinx so did not want to be trapped in this confined space with her for any amount of time at all.

Needs must, however, for at that moment Mrs Carpenter looked up, wailed and held her arms out to Jinx, like one of those dolls that wets itself when you pull the string on its back. Oh, Christ, thought Jinx in a panic, the bloody woman obviously wants a hug. Yucksville! She managed to hold it together enough to smile weakly at her lachrymose form tutor before gingerly sitting down next to her, avoiding the outstretched arms at all costs. She patted Mrs C's knee while also desperately trying to avoid looking her in the face.

'The thing is, Jinx,' wailed Mrs Carpenter in a shaky, squeaky voice weakened by excessive recent emotion, 'I love him so much, b–b–b–but I just don't think I know enough about him.'

'Um . . .' Jinx really wasn't sure of the appropriate response to this and was busy thinking on her feet.

'An-an-and if you don't know someone properly, then can you truly love him?'

'Well –' Jinx was hating this more than she could ever have imagined possible.

'I mean,' Mrs C interjected, grabbing Jinx's hand and fixing her with a gimlet eye, 'I obviously KNOW him. But I don't *know* him. Do you understand me?'

Jinx's panicked prayers for intervention were answered from a most unlikely source. Scowling as she harangued some poor second year – about missing linen, of all the bloody things – Daisy Finnegan strolled round the corner of the washbasins and into view. She pulled up short when she saw her form tutor and Jinx sitting on the bench at the back like that. But since Daisy had witnessed the whole morning scene, she wasn't as shocked as she could have been. What's more, in her role as teacher's pet and chief suck-up, Daisy was a lot more used to 'crisis management' than Jinx and her crew.

'Betsy,' she snapped, turning round after winking surreptitiously at a delighted Jinx, 'none of your year seems to have the right number of towels. As head girl, it is one of your duties to make sure every pupil has the right equipment and I should not have to be checking up on you like this.'

'But,' Betsy said – staring mutinously at the lockers in front of her, she clearly didn't give two shits whether anyone had the right amount of towels or not – 'what am *I* supposed to do about it?'

'You,' Daisy said, twisting round again to block

Betsy's view of the shower area, 'are going to go back to your house, find the missing towels and bring them to me here.'

'But –' Betsy said again before Daisy cut her off.

'I'm not interested in buts,' snapped the older girl, causing a small wave of mirth to flow through Jinx's veins even in the midst of this undesirable scenario. 'I want you to go back to your house and scour the place. When you have done so, and not before you have found at *least* half of the missing amount, I want you to bring them back to me here and we will continue the inventory. Off you go!'

The second year threw a total death stare in Daisy's direction but raced off to do her bidding nonetheless. Daisy then waited until the door had closed behind her before moving over to sit on Mrs Carpenter's other side. Jinx was equally appalled as she was impressed when Daisy put an arm round Mrs C's shoulders and squeezed her tight, but since she'd rarely been so pleased to see anyone in her life she made a mental note to let it go.

The arm seemed to have a soothing effect on Mrs C, who dropped her head on to Daisy's shoulder. Her breathing certainly appeared a lot calmer than it had a few minutes earlier in Jinx's company anyway. Jinx and Daisy locked eyes over their teacher's bowed head and Jinx mouthed her extreme thanks for Daisy's excellent save. Daisy blushed slightly at yet more unexpected niceness from the unlikely Jinx Slater and shook her head to indicate it was nothing. They both raised their eyebrows at the same time, both smiling when it registered that for once they were on the same wavelength.

Mrs Carpenter chose that moment to wipe her eyes for the final time in their presence, stand up and nod her thanks at the pair who'd witnessed her breakdown. She didn't say a word, but smiled weakly as she gathered her things together and headed in the direction of the san. Mrs C was no stranger to Mister Sinton's lair and she knew the matron would give her a couple of strong sleeping pills and the loan of a private room for the rest of the day.

'Bloody hell!' said Jinx, staring at Daisy with uncharacteristic gratitude, 'am I glad you came in or what. I honestly don't know what I would have said to her if you hadn't turned up. She was practically babbling.'

'Poor thing,' Daisy replied, looking sideways at Jinx as she accepted the offer of half a piece of Juicy Fruit, 'what did she say? I've got the feeling something very weird is going on at this school.'

'Well,' said Jinx, chucking the gum wrapper at the bin and missing, 'she said a lot of stuff about knowing him, but not *knowing* him. I didn't understand a bloody word of it, Dais, I really didn't. And what do you mean about something weird going on? I mean, it's sad that they broke up and all, but I can't see it being anything more sinister than that. Can you *really*?'

'Yes, I can. Something's not right,' Daisy said, looking at Jinx and willing her to listen for once, 'and I'm not sure what it is, but it's definitely something and it's definitely not been right for a while now. And,' she continued, with a warning glance at Jinx not to interrupt her, 'I know you hate it when I say this, but I'm convinced it's something to do with the triplets and Igor.'

'What do you mean?' asked Jinx, who was suddenly exhausted and wanted nothing more than to be curled up in bed listening to the new mix Chastity had made her, drinking a Diet Coke, thinking about Jamie and maybe flicking through one of her old Malory Towers books.

'Have you noticed their rings?' Daisy responded, unable to believe any of the others had totally missed them.

'No,' said Jinx, who could distinctly feel a headache brewing behind her frontal lobes. 'What about them?'

Daisy, whose avaricious eye missed nothing, sighed deeply before continuing. 'The triplets all have matching diamond rings,' she said, speaking slowly to make sure Jinx was listening. 'One stone is blue, one is pink and one's green, but they're all set in exactly the same ornate gold base.'

'So?' Jinx was keen to get this chat over with and herself out of the loos as soon as possible. Someone must have left the heating on too high or something, because she was beginning to feel a bit queasy. 'What about it?'

'Igor,' Daisy said, her chest puffing up with delight at being the only one to have noticed, 'has exactly the same ring as they do. The only difference is the stone in his one is a regular white diamond. What kind of so-called bodyguard has exactly the same item of very expensive, unique jewellery as his clients? And,' she continued, pleased to see Jinx was concentrating at last, 'what kind of bodyguard is more often than not nowhere to be seen anywhere near his precious cargo? Lastly,' she said with an officious shake of her head, delighted at finally getting the chance to expound upon her theory, 'I saw him coming out of the bursar's office a few days ago. Whatever it was they'd been talking about was not to Igor's liking. Far from it. He was in a proper mood, Jinx – I heard him shouting in the office and he practically kicked the door when he came out. If he hadn't seen me waiting down the corridor, I think he would have done.'

'OK,' said Jinx, leaning forward, resting her elbows on her knees and cradling her head in her hands, 'so let's say you're right. Let's say there *is* something suspicious or sinister or whatever going on. Let's say the triplets, Igor and the bursar are all over it. But what the hell are *we* supposed to do about it?'

'I don't know yet,' muttered Daisy, 'but I do think we need to find out what's happening.'

'Join forces, you mean?' Jinx asked, not looking up but clutching her head tighter as she spoke.

'Yes,' agreed Daisy, smiling for the first time since she'd started talking. 'That's exactly what I mean. I think together we'll find out whatever it is a damn sight quicker than if I go it alone. Also you're much more friendly with the triplets than I am, so it'll be easier for you to hang around them and ask questions without looking suspicious.'

Jinx sighed but raised her head and looked Daisy in the eye. She held up her right hand and Daisy's left met it in a weak high five. They were now locked in together, for better or for worse, but at least Jinx was free to go back to Tanner and get into bed for a couple of hours.

Well, she would have been if Betsy Johnson hadn't chosen that moment to come crashing back in through the door of the loos, her face and most of her curly brown hair hidden behind a pile of towels she had clutched in a stack in front of her. In her surprise at seeing Jinx and Daisy in front of her, she stumbled and the stack went flying. As they settled around the place in messy heaps, a piece of paper dropped out from between two of the unattractive maroon ones. The three of them watched as it came to rest, front side up, on the white-tiled floor.

'Oh, my God,' Daisy gasped, leaping on it and glaring up at a flame-faced Betsy. 'It's my chemistry revision aid. What the hell is it doing here? Where,' she said furiously, taking a menacing step towards the second year in front of a completely confused Jinx, 'did you get it?'

'It's nothing to do with me,' snapped Betsy, beyond cross at the way these sixth formers thought they could boss everyone about all the time and get away with it. She had to bite her lip hard in order not to stamp her foot. 'You told me to gather up all the Steinem girls' towels and bring them down here and here they *are*, as requested. Whatever that piece of paper is, it must have been stuffed in between a couple and fallen out when I dropped them. Can I go now?'

'You just hold on,' Jinx interjected sharply, fixing Betsy with a look that told the junior this particular member of the lower sixth was not at all inclined to put up with any cheek from a member of the lower school, however disgruntled she might currently be feeling. 'Is that the thing you were looking for the night we came back in the police van and Mrs B opened her door and caught us all?'

'Yes,' said Daisy, throwing a by now terrified Betsy an even scarier look than Jinx just had and pointing at the offending items on the floor, 'it is. And I intend to find out exactly where it came from. Come on, Betsy, out with it. Now! Where did you get those maroon towels?'

'Katie Green's room,' said Betsy sulkily, staring at the floor and mentally cursing Katie Green to hell and back. 'She'd obviously washed them and shoved them in the back of her wardrobe instead of bringing them down here. She's very lazy, you know,' Betsy continued, throwing caution to the wind and deciding she couldn't be bothered to stand up for Katie, whom she didn't like much anyway, 'and weird. She's obsessed with you lot for a start.'

Jinx and Daisy both frowned at the obvious intended insult, but decided not to pass comment on it at this stage.

'Right,' said Jinx, standing up and looking down at Betsy, who was really quite short from this angle, 'we've heard all we need to from you. But before you go' – she took a step closer and narrowed her eyes as Betsy shrank back against the wall – 'there are a couple of things you *won't* be doing when you leave here. Number one, you will not mention a word to anyone – ANYONE –

about what you've seen in here. Number two, you will especially not be saying a word to Katie Green about any of this. And let's have number three for a bonus: if we find out you have said anything, your life will literally not be worth living.'

'*Capiche?*' Daisy added, thrilled with her new role as a *Sopranos*-style enforcer alongside Jinx. Truthfully, the head girl of the lower sixth couldn't remember the last time she'd had so much fun at her beloved Stagmount.

Betsy stared mutinously at the pair of them for a second before dropping her eyes in compliance and muttering her assent. No one said a word as she turned round and walked out, but as soon as she'd gone Jinx and Daisy stared at each other in amazement. What a fucking day.

'Let's go back to Tanner, Dais,' begged Jinx, who was concerned about what might happen next if they continued to lounge around in here and fearful for her sanity. 'Come on. We'll go and thrash the whole thing out if you like, but whatever we do we've got to get out of here.'

The two of them walked back to Tanner mostly in a stunned silence, each highly occupied with her own whirling thoughts. Since Daisy had a pressing English essay to write – although Jinx, who was in the same class, couldn't for the life of her think which one it might be – they separated once they walked through the front door, agreeing to hook up later on and discuss the whole shebang.

– * –

Jinx was sitting on her bed in between Liv and Chastity after dinner that evening. Charlie, whose cello practice sessions kept her over at the main school far later than the others, was sitting on a beanbag she'd brought with her and resting a plate containing four fish fingers alongside a handful of oven chips on her knees. Liberty was sitting on a pile of Jinx's clean bedsheets on the floor next to her and periodically grabbing a chip off the teetering plate. The five of them were arguing good-naturedly about who would go and get the two bottles of Merlot Chastity had stashed at the back of her jumper drawer when there was a timid tapping at Jinx's door.

'Come iiiiiin,' they chorused, looking up expectantly until the door opened and their faces registered shock at who stood before them.

'Hi, Dais,' Jinx said nonchalantly, standing up to greet her visitor and ignoring the shocked expressions of the others. 'Have a seat. I'd grab the desk chair if I was you. Hey, Lib, you're closest to the door – go and grab the wine!'

While they politely waited for Daisy to arrange herself behind Jinx's messy desk, the others exchanged querying glances as to the reason for the head girl's unusual presence at their soirée. When it became apparent Jinx was giving nothing away, they shrugged their shoulders and prepared to be entertained.

Daisy settled, Liberty returned and six glasses of wine

poured, a hush fell over the six girls in the small room as they each took their first sip.

'God,' giggled Daisy, who had also giggled nervously as she accepted her glass of red wine, 'I feel like I'm at some kind of initiation ceremony. Like I'm at a meeting of the inner elite or something! Do you call yourselves the IE for short?'

There was a brief embarrassed silence before Jinx spoke, keen to bring the discussion to order. 'Guys, we're here tonight because a few weird things happened today and, well, Daisy and I think we're on to something. Or rather, Daisy does, but I agree with her. Or something.' Jinx looked across the table at her old nemesis and smiled. 'Daisy, why don't you explain it? I think you'll do a better job than me. I'm not sure I quite understand most of it myself.'

'OK,' said Daisy, thrilled to be treated so respectfully by these girls for once and really rather enjoying drinking her wine in such a civilised manner, 'here goes. Basically, I think there's something fishy going on between Igor and the bursar.'

'No,' interrupted Jinx as she clocked the various sarcastic looks flying among the rest of the girls in the room. Since Daisy had saved her that morning, Jinx was determined that the head girl should be allowed to have her say. 'Let her finish.'

'Thanks, Jinx,' Daisy said, smiling shyly in gratitude. 'So, I've heard all of you guys talking about Mrs Bennett arguing with the bursar and I just think it's significant that Igor and he are looking pretty close all of a sudden. These are a couple of the things I've noticed,' she said, pulling a small notebook out of her cardigan pocket and flipping it open to a page closely covered with her small handwriting. 'The triplets and Igor all have matching rings. He's so *laissez-faire* about his so-called "shadowing" of them he's practically out of town. He broke up with Mrs Carpenter this morning and she has no idea why, except I saw him having a huge row with the bursar a few days ago and I just have a hunch it's all connected.'

'Oh, my God,' said Chastity, putting a hand over her mouth as something clicked in her mind. 'What about the plans we found in the gym? The plans of the school with *Russian* writing all over them?'

'What plans?' Daisy, Liv and Charlie asked in unison, not having been privy to the others' discovery during their punishment.

'Plans of the school,' said Jinx, staring at Daisy in amazement and wondering if maybe there was something in what she was saying after all. 'We found them stuffed between a couple of yoga mats when we were cleaning out the gym. I'd forgotten all about them. Go and grab them, Chas.'

Chastity jumped up and raced next door. Meanwhile, Jinx and Liberty quickly filled in the others on the background to how they'd discovered the plans. During this conversation Daisy went very still and thoughtful. She was obviously thinking deeply about something or other.

When Chastity returned, she spread the plans out

on the end of Jinx's bed. The girls were in total agreement that they were of the school. Charlie, whose father owned a very successful business building and running nursing homes, assured them that these were most definitely property-related. At that moment, Liberty's head shot up and she put a hand over her mouth in shock.

'Shit, guys,' she said, turning to Jinx and smacking her arm for emphasis, 'my *dad* said something to me about seeing a plan of what looked like Stagmount turned into luxury flats or something. He said he recognised the shape of the main school and the exact location of the helipad! I thought he was just making up some rubbish as an excuse to call me after such a long time.'

'I don't get it, though,' said Jinx, confused as hell and more than a little alarmed at how fast things seemed to be happening. She'd considered Daisy's theories little more than a series of coincidences and had only decided to humour her as payback for her help with Mrs C earlier. 'How does it all link up?'

'I think,' said Daisy, sitting up and looking round excitedly, 'we're all forgetting something very important. Maybe the most important thing yet, in fact.'

'What?' screamed Liv, who really could be very impatient and hated having important information withheld from her for any length of time. 'What is it we're all forgetting?'

'The day the fire alarm went off,' Daisy said triumphantly. 'Don't you remember Dirk coming from the sports hall?'

'Yes,' said Liv, who tended to grasp things quicker than the others. 'He said he heard *foreign voices* coming from the *gym*. Someone threw a Bloody Mary at him and he felt so threatened he honestly believed he'd been shot, so he ran all the way along to main school before collapsing at Mrs B's feet.'

'And,' Charlie added, bouncing up and down with excitement, 'the bursar didn't appear for ages, even though he's the one who's supposed to be in charge of all the fire regulation stuff.'

'And loads of us heard him and Mrs B having a massive row about it later on,' Liberty finished with relish.

'So what are the facts then?' asked Jinx, wanting to get this bundle of crazy information all neatly tied up in her head. 'What does all of this tell us?'

'Well,' said Daisy, who had been busily writing lists of everything they were saying on a fresh page of her notebook and connecting things with arrows back and forth, 'it reads like this to me. First, we have a meeting of what we can only assume is some kind of Russian business consortium in our gym on the day of the fire alarm some weeks ago. Second, we have Dirk disturbing this meeting and whoever was present at it subsequently seeing fit to get rid of him before, presumably, fleeing the scene, but mistakenly leaving some of their plans behind. Third, we have the bursar – alongside generally suspicious behaviour and an even more suspicious alliance with some Russian pupils' bodyguard – appearing late at the fire alarm roll call, as if he had rushed to the main school from somewhere a lot further away than his office. For our purposes here tonight, I think we must hypothesise that this place was indeed the gym. He did also, I clearly remember it, arrive *after* Dirk.'

'Don't forget the triplets and Igor having matching rings,' cut in Liv, who was quietly fuming at Daisy's casual takeover of her normal role as plan formulator and general brain behind the scams of the lower sixth.

'I won't,' Daisy replied tightly. 'After all, I was the one who thought of it first anyway.'

'OK, OK,' said Liv, 'keep your wig on. I was only *saying*. What do you suggest we do about all of this then, Ms Brainbox? How the hell are we supposed to find out whether the triplets' dad is involved with the bursar or whatever? I know we're clever and everything, but we're only schoolgirls and we've got seriously limited access to the kind of information we'll need to make this thing – whatever *it* is – stand up.'

'One of us,' Daisy said, shivering slightly as she thought of it, 'needs to speak to Igor. The thing is,' she continued, looking around and feeling exasperated by the blank stares that greeted this announcement, 'he's obviously in love with Mrs C. And she's clearly in love with him – we've never seen her look happier than she does this term, and I bet you it's mutual.'

'So?' muttered Liberty, concentrating hard on pulling apart one of her split ends.

'So,' Daisy said passionately, 'that's his Achilles heel. I also bet you he's involved in whatever it is that's going on and has suddenly got cold feet because of her, and somehow the bursar found out and forced him to dump her. I have never,' she went on, betraying a sensitivity no one would have thought existed inside that geeky, stuck-up, suck-up exterior, 'seen anyone quite so lovesick as he was this morning. Did you see his face?'

'So,' said Chastity thoughtfully, 'who's going to be the one to front him up?'

'Bagsy not me!' yelled Liberty, shaking her head from side to side so wildly half her ponytail came unstuck.

'Or me,' added Liv. 'I'm not doing it. No way!'

'I think,' said Daisy, looking as exasperated as she felt by now and keen to get back to her essay, 'Jinx should do it. Because,' she continued, holding up a hand to indicate they should let her finish and ignoring the expression of total horror that passed across Jinx's face when she heard her name, 'you were the one who comforted Mrs Carpenter in the loos this morning, so you can use that to start the conversation off. Also,' she added, fixing Jinx with a look not dissimilar to the one she'd given Betsy Johnson in the bathroom that morning, 'you've got two brothers, so I assume you know how to deal with men in moods.'

'Well,' said Jinx, 'yes, but . . .'

'And,' finished Daisy, standing up as if this was the end of the matter, 'you love the school and you'd do anything for Mrs Bennett. If anyone can find out what's going on, you can.'

'Hear, hear,' said Chastity. 'I think Fingers has got it bang on the nose.'

'Me too,' agreed Charlie. 'You're our man, Jinx!'

'You *are* good at stuff like this,' Liberty said, tapping

Jinx's knee. 'You know you are.'

'I'm NOT though,' yelled Jinx, feeling truly horrified at the task in front of her. 'I'm bloody crap at it. I couldn't think of a single comforting thing to say to Mrs C this morning – I just stared at her in mute horror until you came along, Dais. And as far as Igor goes, he and my brothers are, like, *exact* opposites. I can't do it.'

'You can,' said Liv. 'Come on, Jin. Think of what Mrs Bennett did for Liberty. This is nothing compared to what she did.'

'OK,' Jinx sighed. Really, when Liv put it like that she knew she didn't have any choice in the matter. However awkward, embarrassed and terrible this cringe-worthy scene was going to make her feel, she owed it to Mrs B to at least try and find out if anything was threatening the school. 'I'll do it tomorrow morning and I don't want to hear another word about it from any of you until afterwards. Hey,' she said to Daisy, suddenly remembering something and wanting to change the subject before they all started banging on and confusing her anyway, 'did you ever speak to that second year? The girl who stole your chemistry revision thing or whatever it was?'

'No,' replied Daisy, while all the others gaped at them in astonishment at these further revelations – since when had *these* two become so freaking friendly? – 'not yet. I'm going to tackle her about it tomorrow morning. I just can't see a second year banging on Mrs Bennett's door in the middle of the night to purposefully get us into trouble. The more I think about it, the more I think she must have just found the thing lying in the grounds somewhere and kept it. I'm going to speak to her after chapel, though, and tell her she should have given it straight back to me.'

'That other one this morning was bloody rude as well,' Jinx muttered, shaking her head in disgust at the wanton bad manners of the youth of today. 'She reminded me of my cousin Cassie – who I can't *stand* and who, my dear mother incidentally informed me last time we went home, might be coming to Stagmount next term.'

'Oh yes,' said Liberty with a giggle, 'she sounds awful!'

'She is. Anyway,' Jinx said, standing up and stretching her arms above her head as she yawned, 'I know Daisy's desperate to get back to her books and I've got to bank some serious Zs tonight so I'm on form for my torture session in the morning.'

Lying on her bed and staring at the ceiling after they'd all bundled out, Jinx was wondering how the hell she'd got herself sucked into the middle of yet another fine mess. This term, she thought with a scowl as she flicked her DAB radio on, was supposed to be nothing but fun – and a lot of it. Well, she had to admit, there *had* been some, but nowhere near enough of late and she really was not looking forward to buttonholing the scary Igor. That was an understatement. She was, in fact, beyond terrified about the impending encounter and decided she needed to work out exactly what she was going to say and how she was going to say it.

Since Jinx had a tried and tested theory that Diet Coke is the best thing in the world for sharpening one's brain power, she rummaged around in the bottom of her bag for a 50p piece and headed out of her room towards the vending machine just outside the ground-floor common room.

It was half past eleven and the house was in darkness. Jinx crept silently along the wall of her corridor with only the green glow of the emergency exit lights to help her on her way. She reached her destination without seeing a soul. The weather had been so bad of late and the nights so miserable that everyone had started going to bed way earlier than usual and it seemed the habit had stuck, for now anyway.

Jinx fed her coin into the slot and leaned slightly against the front of the machine to make sure the can fell properly from its slot. She was straightening up after collecting it from the tray below when she felt the air change around her. She had the distinct feeling someone was watching her and instinctively knew that whoever it was wasn't one of her friends. She gulped and turned around, telling herself to get a grip. Who the hell did she expect to be lurking by the Diet Coke machine in Tanner House anyway?

'Oh,' Jinx gasped, covering her hand with her mouth as her eyes lit on a shadowy figure behind her, 'it's you.'

Standing on the other side of the glass door that led into the common room was Igor. He was wearing a black shirt underneath a black jumper with black trousers and shoes, but the main thing Jinx noticed was the preponderance of silver jewellery about his person. In the greenish gleam of the emergency light the massive ring on his finger glimmered as he raked a hand through his jet-black hair. At his white throat a pair of chunky silver chains jangled together as he silently opened the door and motioned for Jinx to walk past him into the room beyond.

She did so without a word and went to stand next to one of the chairs at the table by the window, gripping her ice-cold can as if it was a weapon. As Jinx turned to face the bodyguard, a bank of dark cloud moved past the moon and Igor's face was lit with a ghostly pallor. Daisy, Jinx thought, was right. That something was seriously bothering Igor was evident from a single glance at the deep hollows underneath his sad eyes, the more-sunken-than-usual cheekbones, the not-so-designer stubble covering his jutting jaw and the deep lines recent pain had left etched across his forehead.

'Igor,' she said, putting her drink down on the table and moving towards him without a thought for her personal safety, 'you look terrible. Maybe if you tell me about it you'll feel better. What's *wrong*?'

'I can't discuss it, Jinx,' said Igor, clutching her icy hand in his own, so out of it he didn't even register the drop in temperature. 'I wish I could but I cannot.'

Jinx gritted her teeth. Not only was she now doing this for Mrs Bennett – as long as she lived, she'd never be able to pay her back for rescuing Liberty – but she also felt genuinely moved by Igor's plight, whatever it was.

'*I* think it's got something to do with Mrs Carpenter,' Jinx said, squeezing his hand and sitting down at the table without letting go, thereby forcing him to do the same. 'I had a very interesting talk with her this morning that you might be interested in hearing about.'

'Cathy?' asked Igor avidly, leaning forward. 'You spoke to Cathy about me today?'

'Yes,' Jinx said, looking away as she fought an urgent desire to laugh, 'I did speak to . . . um . . . Cathy and she said a lot of things I think you'll want to hear. But Igor' – she stared intently at him as she said this – 'I also think there are a few things you might want to tell me. Like what's going on with you and the bursar, for example. And why you and the triplets have matching diamond rings for another.'

'Ha!' Igor let out a short bark of amazed laughter. 'So you *have* noticed. I wondered whether someone would. With all due respect, Jinx, I didn't realise you were so on the ball. You're cleverer than I thought.'

'Well,' Jinx replied, having instantly decided it would be *far* too complicated to bring Fingers into the game at this late stage, 'I am, I'm afraid. Guilty as charged! So, come on then, what's going on with you and . . . um . . . Cathy?'

'Oh, Jinx,' Igor said, putting his head in his hands, 'I have never been so in love with a woman. This passion inside me is unlike anything I have ever known before.' He lifted his head and stared at her like a broken man.

'But there is nothing I can do. We are star-crossed lovers, the real deal. I can't see any way for us to be together that does not involve lying either to my family or to her. And true love such as ours should not be tainted by deception, deceit and disloyalty. I love her too much for that. If I can't be with her in the proper way, then I won't be with her at all.'

'I don't understand,' Jinx faltered. 'She said this morning that she loved you, and if you love *her* I can't see what the problem is. You're not,' she said quickly as an idea floated into her mind from a Jilly Cooper novel she'd been reading earlier, 'married already or anything, are you?'

'No,' Igor said crossly, fixing Jinx with a black look. 'Of course I do not already have a wife. Have you not listened to a word I have said? I am in love with Cathy! I want to marry Cathy! But,' he continued, pausing to bang his head on the table with what Jinx considered unnecessary force, 'I can't.'

'Why not?' Jinx pressed. Christ, this little chat had only been going on for ten minutes but she was already beginning to feel a tension headache starting up behind her eyes. 'I just don't get it. If you love her and want to marry her, then for God's sake tell her so. You'll be doing all of *us* a huge favour if nothing else, I promise you.'

'My father would –' Igor stopped suddenly and banged his head against the wooden table once more.

'What would he do?' asked Jinx. Exasperated beyond belief by all these dramatics, she just wanted to know what the hell was going on, once and for all. 'Come on, tell me. Mrs Carpenter, um, Cathy said she KNEW you, but she didn't *know* you. What did she mean?'

'Oh, Cathy,' Igor wailed, clutching his breast and staring at the moon, painful longing etched across his strong face, 'what have I done? What am I doing? What will I do?'

'Right,' said Jinx firmly, reaching for her drink, flipping back the ring pull and thinking this had gone quite far enough. It was time to regain some semblance of control over the situation. 'That's it. I've had enough. You've got one minute exactly and if you don't start speaking sense, then I'm afraid I can't help you any more.'

'OK, OK,' Igor said, looking impossibly hurt at the callous way he was being treated. 'Hold on. I was getting to it. So,' he continued, twisting himself around in his chair to stare moodily out towards the sea, 'you have already seen the rings. I suppose you have already worked out that Olga, Masha and Irina are my sisters. I am not their bodyguard any more than you are.'

'Of course,' Jinx nodded encouragingly, not giving away an inch of how completely blindsided she'd been by this information and pretending she'd known all along. 'That much was obvious.'

'My father has been planning this for ages, since at least the time he sent off for the Stagmount brochure four years ago and fell in love with the beautiful picture of the building on the front cover,' Igor said, still staring fixedly in the opposite direction from Jinx. 'He thought the girls could have a lovely time studying here and that, when they were finished with school, he could move in and buy the place. He had a vision of Stagmount as the most exclusive gated community in the world, an icon of modern property development and a sure-fire winner of the coveted design awards. He wants me to join the family business and thought sorting this out would be the perfect test. He decided I would be his man on the ground, so he arranged with the bursar that I could stay here with the girls under the guise of being their official bodyguard. Then he thought I could fix the sale for him and slip away at the end of term unnoticed.'

'But,' Jinx interjected, 'I don't understand how he imagined he could do that. How he thought it was even possible. Surely Stagmount is not for *sale*?'

'To my father,' Igor responded sadly, 'everything is for sale. Someone like him thinks he can get whatever he wants if he pays enough people off. Some things are just harder to organise than others, but nothing is impossible. That's the mentality, and normally, I must admit, it is true. But this case' – he shook his head – 'is proving very difficult indeed.'

'So the bursar . . .' Jinx said, trying hard to follow the incredible story she was hearing.

'The bursar is a very bad man indeed,' Igor said, looking at Jinx for the first time. 'He doesn't care about this school at all. Not like Cathy. She loves it here and, seeing it through her eyes, I have grown to love it too. The bursar is being paid a vast fixer's fee by my father to put pressure on members of the school board and the governors to find a way around things.'

'What about the triplets?' Jinx asked suddenly, leaning forward. 'What do they think about all this? They seem really happy here. Surely *they* don't want to see the place turned into a series of luxury flats, even if they are the most luxurious flats in the world?'

'My sisters,' Igor replied gravely, 'do not really understand what is going on. They pay no attention to the business, nor do I imagine they ever will. They think the whole thing is hilarious and have delighted in tormenting me ever since I arrived with them. It was they who told my father I had fallen in love with Cathy. They thought it was funny, but he then instructed the bursar to tell me to break up with her or be cut off and cast aside. I don't even want to be a property developer, but if Cathy had found out I was involved in this plot against Stagmount she would have hated me anyway. So what could I do, Jinx?'

'Well,' Jinx said, thinking that Igor really was a bit of an idiot, 'the way I see it, the whole thing is very simple.'

'It is?' he asked disbelievingly, before throwing his packet of cigarettes across the room in anger at her insouciance.

'Yes,' she said, standing up to make her point, for there was no way in the world she was going to be intimidated by him now. 'You just need to make some decisions and then stick with them. Here's what I think you should do. First, if you truly do love, you know,

Cathy, then you need to tell her so – the sooner the better I'd say. Second, you need to phone your father and tell him that you don't want to be a property developer. Third,' Jinx said, resting her hands on the back of the chair and leaning forward to press her point home, 'you need to start doing things for *yourself*. If you want to be a . . .'

'Poet,' Igor supplied sulkily. 'I mostly write poems about Siberia in the winter.'

'OK, so if you want to be a, um, poet,' Jinx continued, fighting a desperate urge to snort with laughter but beating it once again, 'then just *be* one. Write some poems, or, like, go to Siberia or whatever. And then tell your father you love Cathy. You can't predict his response,' Jinx carried on sagely, wondering where on earth all this stuff was coming from, 'but you can tell him the truth so all the facts are out there. Honesty *is* the best policy . . . um . . . in most cases. But moving on, what can your father do that's so bad? So he cuts you off – who cares! Write some decent poems and you won't need his money. And as far as *I'm* concerned,' she continued, looking warily at him for the first time since she'd entered the common room, 'I'm going to tell the truth too. Tomorrow morning I'm going to see Mrs Bennett and I'm going to tell her everything we've talked about here tonight. And I'm telling *you* that's what I'm going to do so you can speak to Cathy beforehand and sort everything out with her. OK?'

'It is more than OK,' Igor said, gripping Jinx's hand in his and holding it to his chest. 'I don't know how to thank you, Jinx, I really don't. Is there anything, anything at all, I can do for you?'

'Just be nice to Cathy,' Jinx said, a small giggle escaping her lips at this unlikely statement, 'and then she'll be nice to us. We love her too, when she's in a good mood.'

'I will be nice to Cathy for ever,' Igor said solemnly, 'I promise you that.'

'Good,' said Jinx, releasing herself from Igor's strong grip and making for the door. 'I'm beyond thrilled we had this little chat and I'm so pleased you've got everything sorted out. I can't wait to hear how Cathy takes the news, but right now I really must go to bed. Goodnight, Igor. God bless.'

'Goodnight, Jinx,' he replied, staring out of the window once more, an expression of dazed relief on his face this time. 'I will never forget this.'

A few minutes later a wide-eyed Jinx lay on her bed and marvelled at the sheer insanity of everything she'd just learned. She had never known Mrs Carpenter's name was Cathy. Cathy Carpenter, bloody hell. She could hardly have made it up. She could also hardly believe she had to go and inform Mrs Bennett of yet another dastardly plot so soon after last term's débâcle. She knew her friends would find it hard to believe, so she just hoped the headmistress would take this undoubtedly tall tale seriously. In spite of the jumbled thoughts running through her mind, Jinx took a rare Nytol and fell into a dreamless sleep five minutes after she switched her light off.

Sitting on a bench in the very same lock-up bike shed where she'd caught Mrs Gunn and the Dick doing unspeakable things to each other at the end of last term, Jinx took a deep drag on her Marlboro Light. She'd had a key to this place for as long as she could remember and she often shut herself away here for a bolstering cigarette before a tricky meeting or a nasty test. Running to Mrs B with shocking news at the end of term, she thought with a frown as she ground the fag end underneath her heel, was becoming just as much of a bloody tradition. And it wasn't one she liked much either.

She hadn't seen Liberty or Chastity or any of them when she'd emerged from her bedroom, but it was half past eight at the time and she presumed they'd all gone off to lessons or chapel happy in the assumption she was busy dealing with Igor. None of them knew she'd seen him the previous evening and she decided she preferred flying this mission solo. It meant she could take her time thinking about what to say to Mrs B without factoring anyone else's ideas into the equation. To be honest, though, she'd decided just to tell the truth and she intended to tell it in as clear, sane and unexcitable a way as possible.

At the same time that Jinx was standing next to Jo's desk outside Mrs Bennett's office, halfway down the main school corridor Daisy Finnegan was standing by the entrance to the chapel, waiting to buttonhole Katie Green and take her off for a little chat about things. Daisy craned her neck the better to peer over the top of the crowd at the stragglers crawling along behind, fast becoming frustrated by a sea of lower-school girls cracking gum and hitching up their skirts right in front of her when they were hardly out of the chapel door.

Jinx, meanwhile, was becoming frustrated by Jo's relentless questioning as to why exactly Jinx needed to see her boss, and Jo was becoming frustrated with the lack of information she was getting.

'I just need an appointment as soon as possible please,' Jinx said firmly, not wanting to go into things with anyone but Mrs Bennett, but also not wanting to cause offence since Jo liked to believe she knew everything going on at Stagmount at all times. 'It's, um, personal. Sorry.'

'Katie Green?' Daisy asked imperiously as she spied her quarry a metre or two in front of her, stunning both Katie and all the second years around her into a shocked silence. None of them could possibly imagine what a lower sixth would want with one of their humble lot. 'If I could just have a word,' she continued, gripping Katie's arm and ushering her towards the courtyard. 'This way.'

— ✳ —

'What on earth *is* it, Jinx?' Mrs Bennett pushed open her door and stuck her head through the gap. 'I can hear you haranguing poor Jo from all the way inside! Come in, come in. I've not got a huge amount of time but I can spare you ten minutes before my next meeting.'

Jinx smiled apologetically at Jo and dashed after her headmistress.

Mrs B's office was usually a peaceful place, but as Jinx seated herself in one of the red velvet hard-backed chairs opposite the vast mahogany desk she felt a lot less than calm. Mrs Bennett leaned her elbows on the desk and linked her fingers, her forearms making a pyramid shape in front of her. This was Jinx's cue to swallow, take a deep breath and start talking. And talk she did, without stopping for the next ten minutes. Mrs Bennett's spectacles slipped practically to her jaw, but she was too engrossed in what Jinx was telling her to even notice.

— ✳ —

'So the thing is,' Daisy said to a dazed Katie, sitting next to her on a garden bench by the koi carp pond in the cloisters, 'all you had to do was write me a note and put it in my pigeonhole and I wouldn't have had to go to all the trouble of making a new one. Do you understand that?'

'But . . .' It was slowly filtering into Katie's befuddled, panicky mind that Daisy was not accusing her of having had anything to do with knocking on Mrs Bennett's door that fateful night. Eventually, a good few minutes after most people would have cottoned on, it became clear that the older girl just assumed she had found the revision aid and pocketed it.

Katie had no idea, of course, that she was currently experiencing a classic 'fingering'. Daisy was adept at moving between anger and sorrow during an uncomfortable encounter, therefore negating the need to go into any situation with more of one than the other and confusing her opposing number, invariably to her own advantage.

While Katie's brain was straining to work out what the hell was going on, so was Mrs Bennett's. She stared at Jinx, marvelling at how on *earth* the girls had managed to find out all this information, wondering why the hell she herself had not heard even a whisper of anything and incredulous at the bursar's amazingly treacherous duplicity.

All finished now, Jinx regarded her headmistress somewhat warily across the gleaming expanse of desk. As she talked she had watched Mrs B's face register a huge variety of expressions and still had no idea what the end result would be. Initial shock had given way to bemused disbelief, which in turn – and as Jinx had expounded on Daisy's theories and what Igor had told her – gave way to a grudging acceptance. Now, however, was the turn of pure rage.

'Right,' Mrs Bennett said eventually, standing up and

pacing back and forth behind her desk. 'Right.'

Jinx didn't say a word. She felt beyond relieved just to have shared the information with her headmistress. Keeping things to oneself was a most tiresome business indeed, it really was. She hoped Mrs B believed her and would do something to sort the whole damn mess out.

Mrs Bennett stopped her pacing, pushed her glasses back up her nose and fixed Jinx with a very serious look indeed. 'Jinx Slater, I told you last term that you were a credit to this school and once again you have proved me absolutely correct. You might,' she continued in a much softer voice, smiling warmly at the squirming girl in front of her, 'just have saved the school from a fate worse than death.'

Jinx blushed and looked down at the toes of her silver Top Shop pumps. She absolutely adored Mrs Bennett, but she found all this gushing both unnatural and hard to deal with. Her blush swiftly became a magnificent magenta when Mrs B enveloped her in a huge hug and whispered, 'Thank you,' in her ear.

– * –

'So you see, Katie,' Daisy was saying to the second year, 'it's OK to be a geek. I mean, look at me. I've never been involved in the so-called "popular" crowd, but I'm still having the best time of my life at Stagmount. I've got plenty of friends who are just like me and I'm getting the best education in the world.'

'But . . .' Katie mumbled, still not quite able to believe Daisy Finnegan was giving her an unasked for pep talk like this and deeply wishing she was anywhere in the world but sitting here on this bench in the cloisters.

'No, don't interrupt,' Daisy cut across her imperiously, quite taken with her current agony-aunt pose. 'As I was saying, Katie, it's only natural to be fascinated with us older girls when you're in the second year. I can remember being quite obsessed with a girl called Annette Walker when I was your age. You can't let it take over your life, though, or the other people in your year might make fun of you.'

Daisy scowled as she remembered Jinx making her life an absolute misery by sending her a load of faked letters purporting to be from the aforementioned Ms Walker, a beautiful blonde American-cheerleader type of girl who'd been in the lower sixth when they first arrived. Daisy had made a right fool of herself when she'd lovingly, innocently replied to them on a despicable pink, heart-shaped notelet and the others had laughed long and hard at her about it for ages – oh, until the end of the bloody third year at least.

Katie herself was feeling so poleaxed, appalled and furiously embarrassed by the whole goddamned thing, so freaked out by Daisy's speech and so longing to get the hell out of there, that all her crushes on the older girls died an immediate, irreversible and largely painless death on that surprisingly sunny March morning. As long as she lived she never wanted to have a single thing to do with any of them. It would be an age before she could even see one of them passing in the corridor and not squirm involuntarily, remembering the hell of Daisy Finnegan telling her they were alike. Sparks practically flew out from under her Clarks brown lace-up shoes, such was her hurry to get off when Daisy indicated that their cosy chat was at an end.

As far as Jinx was concerned, she watched in awe as Mrs Bennett buzzed Jo and told her to get the bursar in to see her as soon as possible, *like yesterday* her steely tone implied, and wondered what would happen to the triplets.

'And let's not forget, Jinx,' Mrs Bennett said, looking up as if she'd read her pupil's mind, 'none of this has anything to do with the triplets. If their father wants them to continue their education at Stagmount – as I hope he will – then of course they must. I know I can count on you girls to keep this episode as quiet as possible and not treat them any differently because of it. Igor, of course, will have to leave, but I'm sure,' she went on, her eyes twinking – she'd found it very hard indeed not to laugh when Jinx was breathlessly recounting the love story of Cathy and Igor earlier – 'he will be absolutely fine.'

Finally released, Jinx smiled at Jo and began walking slowly, thoughtfully in the direction of the modern languages department, blissfully unaware of the nasty French vocabulary pop quiz that awaited her. Mr Christie had finally decided to toughen up and sort his act out. She was pondering Mrs B's promise to call a meeting of the school governors, investigate – and immediately get rid of – the bursar and wondering how

Igor's romance mission was going when she heard someone running up behind her and yelling her name.

'Hi, Dais,' she said, turning round to see Daisy, ginger hair flying behind her, pink with exertion and gaining on her fast. 'What's up?'

'Did you speak to Igor?' demanded Daisy as the pair fell into step and paused at the foot of the DOWN stairs. 'What happened?'

Jinx immediately recounted everything that had taken place the night before, naturally hamming up the bits about Cathy, and finished with leaving Mrs B's office a few minutes before. Daisy stared at her open-mouthed. She'd known something was up but, super-sleuth that she was, she could never have predicted all of *this*. Jinx held up her hand and the pair of them awkwardly high-fived before beginning the trudge to French. Daisy had never knowingly walked up the DOWN stairs before and the thrill it gave her caused her to throw caution to the wind and ask Jinx if she had anything planned for the weekend.

'Um,' Jinx muttered, thinking it was one thing to talk to Daisy on school property but quite another to take her out on the freaking town, 'we're going to, like, this skateboarding contest on the seafront on Saturday. Do you, um, want to come?'

'That's really kind of you, Jinx,' Daisy replied with a surprised smile. She could hardly believe that the great Jinx Slater had actually just invited her to a social event and for a moment she did consider accepting. After a second, however, she decided against. Calling a halt to hostilities was one thing. Spending their weekends together was another entirely. Daisy wasn't sure they'd quite reached that stage, or if indeed they ever would. It was best all round, she decided, to keep things on an even keel. 'I can't, I'm afraid,' she finished decisively, 'but thanks anyway.'

'S'all right,' Jinx said as they stood outside the classroom door, feeling relieved as hell that Daisy had declined and liking her all the more because of it, 'thanks to *you*. If you hadn't realised anything was up God knows what might have happened to Stagmount.'

The pair of them smiled sheepishly at each other for a second, locked in mutual understanding, before a totally new-look Mr Christie threw open his door and ushered them inside, loudly wondering what on earth had kept them so long. They took their seats amidst a chorus of winks, raised eyebrows and hissed questions. They gave nothing away, but smiled at each other once more before turning to their books.

Saturday morning dawned bright and sunny, although a biting wind blowing off the sea meant it was still business very much as usual as far as fluffy-hooded parkas, over-long scarves, mittens and the occasional beanie hat were concerned. The girls, milling about waiting for a *Days of Our Lives* rerun to start in their common room, had witnessed the bursar's quiet exit from Stagmount life yesterday lunchtime. He climbed into his Volvo Estate, put a cardboard box filled with the contents of his desk on the passenger seat, started the engine and quietly drove away, never to be seen again. Needless to say, nobody was there to wave him off.

Not a great deal had been seen of the triplets, but Liberty said they'd assured her they would meet up with the rest of them on the seafront later that day for the Skate Fest. The others were pleased – the triplets were a hell of a lot of fun and anyway, it wasn't *their* fault their dad was a grasping asshole who'd tried to turn the school into the world's most exclusive gated community, was it?

As far as Igor's conversation with Mrs C went, she had appeared at lunch on Thursday sporting a massive smile plastered across her face and an even bigger diamond ring on the fourth finger of her left hand. Mimi Tate had seen her skipping – yes, skipping – out of Mrs Bennett's office yesterday morning. None of them had seen her since, so they could only assume she and Igor were already en route to Gretna Green. Mimi also swore blind she'd been wearing a silver lamé skirt and a hot pink jumper. This, however, was simply way too hard to envision, a step too freaking far for sure.

Although none of them had noticed of course, Katie Green had become much more assertive after her little chat with Daisy. She'd discovered a couple of the girls in her own year were not as boring as she'd imagined and had even started a surprising alliance with Betsy Johnson. The pair of them bonded over a petition Betsy had started to extend their weekend curfew and they became thick as thieves as they planned to hand it to

Mrs Bennett at the end of term.

Liv and Charlie had been surprisingly enthusiastic about the Skate Fest, but were nowhere to be seen when the others were getting ready that morning. They'd already made a plan with Chastity, though, that they should all meet dead on two o'clock by the main ramp.

Wandering along the seafront in a throng of dudes and rudes, Jinx, Liberty and Chastity were in a state of high excitement as they pushed through the jostling crowds, keeping one eye on the huge set-up about a hundred metres ahead of them, just across from the volleyball court, and the other eye out for their friends and various love interests.

'Fucking hell!' Chastity gripped Jinx's arm as they passed one of the ubiquitous Redbull stands and pointed towards the top of the ramp. All the competitors were massed up there around a list, next to a man with a can of Red Stripe in one hand and a loudhailer in the other. 'Is that who I *think* it is?'

The three of them stopped dead, nearly causing a pile-up with the people behind them, and shaded their eyes from the weak sun as they peered over to where Chastity was pointing.

'Oh, my God,' Jinx exclaimed, covering her hand with her mouth. She'd suddenly turned rather pale. 'I think you're right.'

'What?' demanded Liberty, who couldn't see a freaking thing from this angle. 'Is it Jamie?'

'No,' Chastity replied, folding her arms and leaning back in amazement. 'It's Liv and Charlie. Look!'

The three of them, by now pushed to the side of the path by the insistent crowds coming in both directions, stood and stared at their friends in shock. Liv was wearing the baggiest jeans they'd ever seen, teamed with huge pink and grey Etnies trainers and a pale pink T-shirt with a white fairy on the front. Charlie was wearing what looked like green board shorts with equally huge trainers in bright white and a black T-shirt. Around her waist was looped a tough-looking chain belt, while her knees and elbows were covered with protective pads, just like those of all the boys hovering around them, and she was clutching a bright pink helmet with a black chin strap. Liv's short hair was gelled close to her head and Charlie's blonde hair was pulled back into a sporty-looking ponytail. They looked fresh-faced, cool as hell and ready for anything.

'Bloody hell!' Liberty whistled admiringly. 'I've never seen them wearing any of that skate shit before, but it really suits them. What are they *doing* up there though?'

'I don't know,' said Jinx, gripping Liberty with one hand and Chastity with the other as the crowd along the top of the ramp thinned out and it became apparent someone was about to throw themselves off the side of it into the bowl beneath, 'but I think we're about to find out.'

At that moment the man with the loudhailer pushed a button on the sound system next to him and Avril Lavigne's 'Sk8ter boi' blasted out into the sea air. They watched agog as Charlie turned to Liv, clasped her left hand to her chest and raised her right arm in a salute.

She then placed the tip of her board at the edge of the bowl, rocked back and forth, as if thinking about something very mundane, before shooting off at great speed into the centre of it. The crowd held its collective breath for a couple of agonised seconds until Charlie's jubilant face appeared above the parapet of the other side.

The girls gasped as she landed on the rim and jumped up, spinning her board beneath her feet to great applause from the male competitors, then launched herself off the side once again. She repeated this about five or six times, each one more impressive than the last, until she performed a perfect somersault to rapturous applause from the crowds of hot boys watching. Impressed hardly does justice to how Jinx, Liberty and Chastity were feeling as they finally reached the side of the bleachers and managed to get Liv's attention above the roar of whooping and cheering in Charlie's honour.

'I thought one of you dumb bitches would eventually put two and two together, but you're dumber than we thought,' Liv yelled rather impolitely over the heads of about fifteen people in between them.

'The bruises!' Jinx screamed, punching Chastity's arm in excitement as she realised they must have been training in secret all term. No wonder they'd hardly been around, and when they had they'd sported all those suspicious injuries . . . It was *such* a cool thing to do, the three on the sidelines couldn't help but feel slightly envious. What a freaking achievement.

Before they could scream and yell at each other any more, Charlie's round finished and it became obvious

Liv was next. Charlie barely had time to pull her helmet off and wave at her schoolfriends before she was surrounded by a crowd of skater boys, all of whom were clearly madly in love with her. They were showering her with more praise and attention than the others had ever seen at one time. This was a real master class in how to make guys dig your action going on right in front of their eyes.

The others looked on, laughing. The music was so loud they could hardly hear themselves think, but they caught occasional glimpses of Liv leaping into the air above the heads of Charlie and the myriad boys gathering round to pat her on the back, kiss her cheek and stuff their phone numbers into her deep pockets. Jinx, Liberty and Chastity were transfixed by the spectacle, madly impressed by and very proud of their friends.

Liberty suddenly spun around as the dark-haired boy from the party appeared from nowhere, tapped her on the arm, leaned forward and whispered something in her ear. Whatever it was, it was clearly to her liking, for she beamed and moved in close to hear the rest. His extremely tall, dark and very handsome friend stared at Chastity for a second, before instantly starting to chat her up. Jinx smiled at them both, moved away and turned round to scour the crowd, looking for Jamie. Her attention was diverted by a man clutching some delicious-looking sticky hot wings and she briefly wondered if she was hungry. She was aware of something going on behind his head, but it took her a second to realise what she was seeing.

There, to the side of the lowest tier of the silver bleachers, was Jamie. And he wasn't alone. Oh no, far from it. Attached to his face like a giant squid was a tall, leggy, triple-familiar blonde. Jinx turned round to check Liberty and Chastity were still occupied before moving to the side to get a closer look. Yes, there was no mistaking it. The pair of them were sucking each other's faces practically off down there and they didn't seem to care who saw them at it.

Jinx stood staring at them for a minute as so many things flashed through her mind. She wondered if she'd been an absolute idiot about the whole Jamie thing. The two parties where he'd dumped her as if she had a severe case of nits when George had turned up; the way he'd always involved her friends in things, especially the night Chastity and Paul broke up; how it had taken him eight days to contact her after she'd last been seen leaving his premises in the back of a police van.

Realising that Liberty and Chastity were engrossed in conversation and that Liv and Charlie were unlikely to emerge from the midst of their adoring throng at any time soon, Jinx got a grip on herself. She made the executive decision to remove herself from the scene ASAP, before Jamie looked up or she bumped into her brother – George was forever turning up where he wasn't wanted, it was one of his special skills.

Jinx turned and determinedly started walking up the steps to the main road opposite East Street. She was getting the hell out of here and she was getting out fast. The main thing bothering her was how foolish she felt.

Not to mention how embarrassed she'd be when her friends found out. She needed a coffee and she needed to have a think, away from the hustle and bustle and the suddenly too many dudes.

After a ten-minute, mostly uphill march, Jinx sat at one of the tables clustered together outside Caffè Nero in the town and disconsolately stirred two lumps of crystallised brown sugar into her soya latte. At the same time as contemplating the sad fact that dressing all in black like a suicidal French poet was never going to be a good look for her, even if she *had* just been kind of dumped in the most publicly humiliating fashion, she wondered why people never had sugar like this in their houses?

It was fair to say she was rallying admirably when she bent down and saw the cutest, tiniest Boxer puppy with the wrinkliest face and softest nose ever who was nudging her leg under the table. She pulled him on to her lap and searched for an identity tag. Bingo – there it was, attached to the circular join on his collar.

Jamie was the last thing on her mind as she held the pup close to her chest and reached for her phone. Punching out the digits, she wondered what kind of retard would let the cutest little dude in the world roam around the streets of Brighton on his own like this. She resolved to give the owner a piece of her mind as the ringing tone started. The voice that answered the phone, however, was beside itself with worry. Jinx found herself reassuring a woman who sounded about the same age as her mum that her puppy was fine. She told her where they were sitting and settled back to wait, delighted beyond reason to have this cutie for a few minutes.

She hardly noticed the man who appeared in front of her until he coughed and said her name.

'Yes?' said Jinx, looking up and blushing instantly at the vision of masculinity confronting her. Tall, bronzed, about her age and with shoulder-length, thick dark brown hair, this guy was seriously stacked and very good-looking. His green eyes bored into her own as he pulled up a chair and reached over to tenderly stroke the side of the squirming puppy's little nose.

'My mum said you were sitting here,' he said to her, laughing as the boxer caught his finger in its mouth and started nibbling furiously. 'I was furious with her for leaving the back door open, but I had no idea this one was clever enough to seek out such a gorgeous rescuer.'

Jinx blushed and reflected that, on balance, she really was over Jamie. He was so spring term. And since that was nearly over, it seemed fitting her crush should be too really.

'I don't suppose,' he said, leaning forward and smiling at her, 'you're doing anything on Tuesday, are you?'

Jinx smiled beatifically and mentally gave Irina, Masha and Olga the biggest high five. Thanks to them, kind of, Mrs Bennett had rescinded their Tuesday punishment cleaning and the girls had one free Tuesday afternoon left.

'Nothing,' she said, stroking the puppy's back as he fell asleep between her thighs and thinking how great her life was, 'and I'd love to.'